"Mark, look out!"

A porker dashed f
that could never have

Mark replied with
fury. He slid in the ~~m~~ ~~...~~ ~~p~~ ~~...~~ feet and
charged forward, screaming again as he stabbed
with his spear and felt it slip into the thick
hide. The porker shoved against him, and Mark
fell into the mud. He desperately held the spear,
but the beast walked steadily forward. The point
went through the hide on the back, and came out
again, the shaft sliding between skin and meat,
and the impaled animal advanced inexorably
up the shaft. The tusks neared his manhood.
Mark heard himself whimper in fear. "I can't
hold him!" he shouted. "Run!"

She didn't run. She got to her feet and shoved
her spear down the snarling throat, then thrust
forward, forcing the head toward the mud. Mark
scrambled to his feet. His hands slipped but he
held the spear and thrust it into the animal,
thrust again and again, stabbing in insane fury
and shouting, "Die, die, die!"

Praise for *The Mercenary*:

"A rousing adventure, yet with something to
say about the old-fashioned virtues—courage
and honor—in the far future."
—*Isaac Asimov's Science Fiction Magazine*

"*The Mercenary* is a parable for our times: the
dirt of politics, the evil of war, the loneliness
of command, and the rewards of comradeship
. . . even with my pacifist bent, I liked it."
—*Library Journal*

# JERRY POURNELLE

## A NOVEL OF FALKENBERG'S LEGION

# PRINCE OF MERCENARIES

BAEN BOOKS

PRINCE OF MERCENARIES

Copyright © 1989 by Jerry Pournelle

Portions of this novel have been published in substantially different form as follows: "His Truth Goes Marching On" appeared in *Combat SF,* © 1975. "Silent Leges" appeared in *New Voices in Science Fiction,* © 1977.

A Baen Books Original

Baen Publishing Enterprises
P.O. Box 1403
Riverdale, NY 10471

ISBN: 0-671-69811-7

Cover art by Keith Parkinson

First printing, March 1989
Second printing, November 1989
Third printing, March 1991

Printed in the United States of America

Distributed by Simon & Schuster
1230 Avenue of the Americas
New York, NY 10020

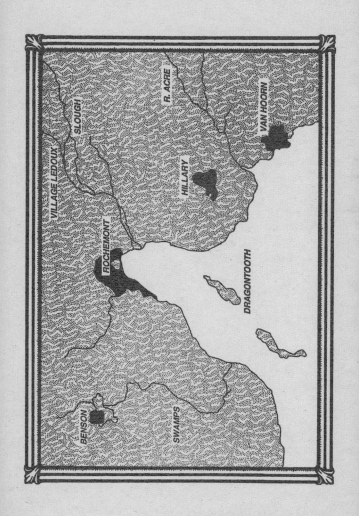

# I

Lysander peered down through orange clouds. The ground was invisible, but cloud wisps streaked past, and stress diamonds formed near the wingtips of the landing ship. It was eerily quiet in the passenger cabin. Lysander turned from the viewport to his companion, a young man about twenty and much like himself. "Mach 25, I'd guess," Lysander said, then caught himself. "Fast. Faster than sound, Harv. A lot faster."

Harv leaned across to try to look through the port. "I can't see the ground."

"We won't for a while. The book says most of Tanith has clouds all the time. And it's hot."

"Oh. I don't like hot much." Harv smiled briefly and leaned back in his seat.

The landing ship banked sharply, then banked again. Strange accelerations lifted the more than two hundred passengers from their seats, then slammed them down again. The ship turned, banked, turned again in the opposite direction. Lysander remembered the dry voice of his ground school instructor explaining that delta wing ships lose energy in turns. Lysander had certainly learned that on the flight

1

simulator and later in his practice re-entry landings. He glanced outside. The landing boat had a lot of energy to lose before it could settle on one of Tanith's protected bays.

A dozen turns later the ship slipped below the cloud cover, and he could see Tanith below.

It didn't look any different from the veedisk pictures. Green and yellow seas, with inlets jutting far into the bright green of the land areas. Land and sea were mixed together in a crazy quilt.

Harv leaned over to look out. "Looks—looks flat."

"It is flat. The whole planet."

"No mountains, Prince?"

"None. Like Earth during the Carboniferous. No mountains, no snow, no glaciers. That's why it's hot everywhere."

"Oh." Harv strained to see out the port. "Am I in your way?"

"No, it's all right." Lysander didn't really like having Harv lean over him like that, but he would never say so. Harv Middleton would be devastated by any criticism from his prince, Brotherhood or no.

The landing ship streaked over the swamps and lowlands, losing speed at each turn. Finally it banked over a series of hills that rose above an inlet of the sea. The hills were covered with low buildings set in a grid of broad, straight streets. The city was left behind as the ship went beyond and out over the green and yellow sea. Then it turned sharply.

"Taxpayers, we are on final approach to Lederle, the capital city of Tanith. Please keep your seat and shoulder belts securely fastened until we have docked at the landing port. Tovarisches . . ." The message was repeated in Russian, then in several other languages.

They came in over the water. The low ridges that

held Lederle and its suburbs rose on their left. The ship settled in closer, then touched down. Spray flew up by the port.

We're here, Lysander thought. Tanith. The CoDominium prison planet.

Heat lay over the dock area in moist waves, doubly unpleasant after the air conditioned landing ship. The Customs shed was corrugated iron, manned by three bored workers in grimy white canvas jackets, supervised by a clerk who wore a blue guayabera shirt with CoDominium badges sewed to the epaulettes. The clerk checked identifications carefully, making each passenger stare into a retinal pattern reader, but his subordinates were content with hasty X-ray scans of the baggage.

Makes sense, Lysander thought. What in the name of Dracon would anyone smuggle *into* Tanith?

The helicopter that waited beyond the Customs shed was an ancient Nissan with an unpleasant tick in the engine. It would hold twenty friendly people. Lysander shamelessly used his rank to get a seat up in the cockpit and left Harv in the rear to deal with the baggage. The pilot wasn't a lot older than Lysander. He eyed Lysander skeptically, then glanced at the passenger list. "Lysander Collins. They tell me you're to sit up here with me. You bribed someone. Who?"

Lysander shrugged. "Does it matter?"

"Not a lot, since it wasn't me. I'm Joe Arabis." He pulled down a folding seat. "Here, this is the flight inspector's seat." Arabis cocked his head to listen to the engine, then laughed. "Not that I ever saw an inspector. Oh, the heck with it, take the left-hand seat, there's no co-pilot this trip. So. Welcome to Tanith, mate."

"Thanks." Lysander sat and strapped himself in. "I've heard there are some big critters in the oceans. Big enough to give the landing ships problems?"

Arabis shrugged. "Well, they *say* the dam the CoDominium put in across the inlet keeps the nessies out. Me, I don't fly out there any more than I have to."

Lysander lifted an eyebrow.

"Yeah. Well, mate, if you ever pilot a chopper over the real oceans here, be damned sure you stay thirty meters up. Not twenty, thirty."

And I can believe as much of that as I want to, Lysander thought. Newcomers are always fair game. Of course sometimes the tallest tales are real. . . .

"Thanks." Lysander pointed to the stub-winged landing ship at the end of the wharf. "Are your nessies really big enough to be a problem for those?"

"That's sure one reason for the dam," Arabis said. "Other stuff, too. I wouldn't want to set one of those shuttles down anywhere but here. Christ, I wouldn't want to ride a Fleet Marine assault boat down to some random stretch of water on Tanith. Ah. There's our clearance."

Arabis gunned the engines and lifted off from the floating dock. In seconds they were a hundred meters about the city. They circled, then headed in a direct line. The diffuse light from the eternal cloud cover cast no real shadows, so that Lysander found it impossible to get his bearings. The compass showed they were flying northwest.

"Looks like rain." Lysander said.

Arabis glanced upward and shrugged. "It generally does look like rain." He laughed. "Naturally. It's generally going to rain. At least there's no storms coming."

"Get bad ones?"

"Lots of storms. Also hurricanes like you wouldn't believe, mate. You ever do any flying here, you damn well check with the weather people early and often. Tanith can brew up a storm in a couple of hours."

"You do have weather satellites?"

"Sure. And like most stuff on Tanith they work most of the time. The ground net works most of the time, too. And most of the time the convicts they've got watching the screens remember to tell somebody, and most of the time the CD clerks remember to broadcast a general alert, and—"

"I see." Lysander examined the city below. Most buildings here were low, one story, covered with white or pastel stucco and roofed with broad slabs of what seemed to be light-colored rock. The city was laid out in a standard grid, broad streets, some divided with strips planted in fantastic colors and shapes. Most of the buildings were very much alike. Off the major streets there were jumbles of what were no more than shacks built of some kind of wood and roofed with wilting green thatch. Far down past the landing area was what looked like a separate city dominated by a massive concrete building.

The neighborhoods became more colorful as they went north. Soon they were in an area where the buildings had two stories. Wide verandas circled them at the second floor level. "Rich people," Arabis shouted above the engine noise. "Like to get up out of the mud. Can't say I blame them."

They crossed a large park, and now the city was cut across with broad diagonal avenues converging toward a complex of taller buildings dominated by one at least six stories tall.

Government House Square, Lysander thought. Lederle was laid out much like the capital city of the

United States, where avenues too broad to be easily barricaded converged on the Capitol. Like Washington, Lederle was designed to let a small band of soldiers keep the mob at bay.

Tanith didn't have any magnificent public buildings to match Washington's. Government House shared the Square with a branch of Harrod's and a Hilton, none of them more than five stories high. At the far corner of the square was Lederle House, Tanith headquarters for the ethical drug company that sponsored the first colonies on Tanith, and easily the finest building Lysander had seen in the city. It had terraces and fountains, and a rooftop botanical garden that blazed with colors.

They landed in the center of the square. A handful of men in dirty white canvas coats came up to help with the baggage, but Harv waved them away when one reached for Lysander's trunk.

Lysander watched long enough to be sure that no one objected when Harv lifted a large footlocker on each shoulder and staggered across the square in Tanith's high gravity. Harv claimed the privilege of looking after his prince, but it wasn't worth making a scene over. They were already conspicuous enough. Not that his mission required much secrecy, but it was best not to attract attention.

The Hilton was no more than fifty meters away. The rain began before he got to the entrance.

The small lobby was up a flight of broad stairs from the street level. A ceiling fan turned endlessly above the registration counter. Opposite the registration desk was a wide door leading into a bar on a large screened and roofed porch. Half a dozen men and two women sat at tables in the bar room, but there was no one at the registration desk. Lysander tapped impatiently on the counter. Eventually a small Eurasian woman in a clean white canvass jacket came out from a back room. She wore a necklace of bright blue stones, and matching earrings.

"Yes, sir?" She was polite but seemed distracted.

"Lysander Collins and Harvey Middleton, of Sparta."

"Ah." She tapped keys on the console. "Yes, Your Highness. Two rooms. Right away, sir. We've put you in the Governor's Suite. I'm sure you'll find it satisfactory. Taxpayer Middleton's room is just across the hall. Your suite is fully furnished; I'm sure everything will be to your liking, but if there's anything else we can do, just call the desk."

"Thanks. Right now what I most want is a hot shower."

She nodded in sympathy. "Not much water on those liners, even in first class. That's one thing we have here. Plenty of water. Thumbprint here, please— thank you." She tapped the bell on the counter. "Joaquin will show you to your room."

Joaquin was short and stocky. His white canvass jacket had sweat stains under the arms.

"Uniform?" Harv asked.

"Sir?"

"White jackets. Uniforms?"

"Yes, sir. Trustees. Let me take your trunks—"

Harv looked at Lysander.

"It's OK, Harv."

Joaquin loaded the trunks onto a cart and led the way to the elevator. "The service elevator isn't working, sir. Please go up to the fifth floor, and I'll follow you."

"There's room." Lysander flattened himself against the elevator wall. It was crowded with the three of them and two footlockers.

The fifth-floor corridor was carpeted with some

bright synthetic. The walls held plastic decorative panels depicting strange animals in bas relief. One of the creatures looked very like a giant woodchuck with three short horns. "Wouldn't want to see him in the dark," Harv said.

The Governor's Suite was bright and airy, and the air conditioning had been turned on long enough to cool the room before they arrived. There were a dozen plastic pots of brilliantly flowered plants, and baskets of fruit, some familiar like oranges and kiwi, and others that Lysander didn't recognize. "Very nice," Lysander said. He handed Joaquin three five-credit bills. "Please see that the receptionist gets one of these."

"Yes, sir. May I help you unpack, sir?"

"Thank you. No, but you might see if Citizen Middleton needs anything."

"Citizen." The bellman frowned. "Yes, sir."

I'll need to watch that, Lysander thought. Citizen isn't a title of respect on Earth. Or here. He chuckled as he thought of the tests to pass and obligations to assume before one became a Citizen of Sparta. Different worlds, in every way.

When the bellman left, Lysander carefully bolted the door. It was the first time he had been alone in the weeks since they left Sparta, and he welcomed the feeling. He stretched elaborately, and sought out the shower.

The bathroom was large. The floor was tile inlaid in intricate designs. Most of the fittings were gold plated. Lysander felt like a Sybarite. *And I'm probably the only one on this planet who knows who the Sybarites were!* The room held both shower and a round tub already filled and liberally furnished with water jets. The water was cold, but there were instructions on heating it and starting the jets. The instructions were written in a dozen languages and five alphabets, and there were diagrams for anyone left out.

Lysander chose the circular shower. There were five shower heads around three quarters of a circle. Each had separate hot and cold controls. The control handles were shaped like sea creatures, the cold water tap like a fish, hot something like a dragon. Lysander frowned at them. "I'd hate to meet that—"

"Meet what, sir?"

He turned, startled. A girl, younger than himself but definitely a woman, stood naked at the shower entrance. Her dark red hair was beginning to curl from the steam of the hot water. Lysander dropped momentarily into fighting stance, then relaxed. "Who the devil are you?" he demanded.

"Ursula, sir. I'll be your hostess. I thought you might like to have me scrub your back."

"Hostess." He nodded to himself. He'd heard of such customs. "Thank you, I can shower by myself."

She smiled slightly. "As you wish. Would you like me to turn on the hot tub? Or do you care for a cold plunge? Afterward I can massage your back."

"That's a fairly tempting offer. Cold plunge and back rub."

She knelt to feel the water in the tub. "Cold enough, I think. I'll wait for you—"

"No, you needn't do that. I'll come out when I'm ready for a back rub."

She shrugged slightly and smiled again. He retreated into the shower compartment to sort out his thoughts.

Ursula. He like the name, and he liked her smile. It was clear that she was offering herself to him. That was exciting. He hadn't had much experience with women.

*Melissa will never know. And the Hilton won't have a diseased hostess.*

She was definitely available, even eager, but what were the conditions? What obligations would he have—

He chuckled mirthlesly. None, of course. The girl was clearly a whore.

Ugly word. He didn't like "prostitute" much more. Ursula looked altogether too young, and her eyes— were they really as green as they had seemed in this light? Whatever color, they didn't have the hardness he associated with the women of Minetown's dance halls.

He had tried to read up on Tanith customs, but the veedisks on the passenger liner only gave him standard tourist spiels. Visit exotic Tanith. Gorgeous flowers, bright plumaged birds, the thrill of hunting real dinosaurs. Not much about Tanith's principal industry, which was hardly surprising.

And almost nothing about local customs.

Ursula had put on a rose-colored short-skirted one-piece garment that tied in front. It reminded him of the stola worn by hetaera in classical Greece. *That's a custom we could have revived with some profit. Maybe it's not too late.* He glanced around, half expecting to see a white canvass jacket somewhere, but if she had any other clothes here they had been put away. She was seated on a big easy chair with her legs tucked appealingly under her, and was staring at the big room screen. Words flowed swiftly across the veedisk reader screen, and she leaned forward in total concentration. Lysander walked up quietly behind her.

*"The primary economic conflict, I think, is between people whose interests are with already well-established economic activities, and those whose interests are with the emergence of new economic activities. This is a conflict that can never be put to rest except by economic stagnation. For the new economic activities of today are the well-established economic activities of tomorrow which will be threatened in turn by further economic development. In this conflict, other things being equal, the well-established activities and those whose interests are attached to them must win. They are, by definition, the stronger. The only possible way to keep open the economic opportunities for new activities is for a 'third force' to protect their weak and still incipient interests. Only governments can play this economic role. And sometimes, for pitifully brief intervals, they do. . . ."*

He read the status line. Page 249, Jane Jacobs. *The Economy of Cities,* first publication New York, 1970. Volume: Grolier's Collection of Classics in Social Science, Catalog 236G-65t—

She looked up, startled, flinched away from him, and quickly switched the screen to bring a local news program. "I'm sorry—"

"Whatever for? You're further in that book than I am." He chuckled. "Actually, I haven't started, but it's on the list my tutor gave me. Were you reading my copy?"

"On, no, the whole Grolier's collection is in the Hilton's library." She stood, and the tunic draped itself in interesting ways. She had good legs, with well-articulated calves. Her finger and toe nails were carefully painted in a light pink that contrasted sharply with the startling green of her eyes. "Ready?" she asked.

*For what? Of course I'm ready, but—* "Uh—I have an appointment with the governor. I'd better get dressed."

"Oh. Well—"

"Will you be here when I get back?"

"I come with the suite. I'll be here if you want me, and if I'm not here call 787."

"Do you have a reader in your room?"

"Well, yes—it's not as big as yours."

"Then stay here. And I'll be looking forward to that back rub."

# II

"We have some time before our appointment with Governor Blaine," Lysander said. "Let's walk."

Harv nodded agreement. "Be good to stretch our legs, and the rain's stopped. Shouldn't go too far, Prince. Better early than late."

"Right." Not this early, Lysander thought. If he'd stayed in the suite he'd have had to do something about Ursula, and he wasn't ready to decide what that should be. "Were you alone in your room?"

"Sure, Prince."

Another data point. Maybe only the Governor's Suite come automatically—equipped. Guests in other rooms call the desk. I'll have to ask Ursula how many girls work for the hotel. Wonder if the Hilton heirs on Earth know what kind of services the Lederle Hilton provides? Or maybe the stories about Earth's decadence are true. . . .

He knew he wasn't ready for this mission, didn't know enough about Earth or Tanith or anywhere else, but that didn't really matter. There wasn't any-one else to do it. *If I just had a better idea of what I'm supposed to do!*

They walked past the Lederle Building. A riot of

color hung from the balcony. A woman in bright pink leaned over the veranda railing. Others moved behind her, obviously enjoying the fresh air after the tropical rain. The building had clearly been inspired by the legends of Babylon's Hanging Gardens. "Maybe not the only thing this place has in common with Babylon."

"Oh. OK," Harv said.

Irrationally he wished that Ursula were walking with him. She'd have understood. Harv was competent and reliable and one of the Brotherhood, but sometimes it was a little trying to spend so much time with a man who—didn't care much for intellectual matters.

Beyond the square were several blocks of the two-story homes with verandas. Generally the ground floor was windowless, with few doors, giving the houses a fortress-like appearance. Most were surrounded by gardens of the ubiquitous Tanith flowering shrubs. One had only Earth hibiscus. They looked dull and prosaic in this setting. A kilometer further north the houses changed to single-story dwellings of dull-colored stucco. A few people sat on porches or strolled through the streets, but nowhere near as many as there had been nearer Government Square.

They came to a broad concrete highway. There were few vehicles, but it was wider than anything yet built on Sparta. It reminded Lysander of the veedisk pictures of freeways that ran the whole length of the California coast on Earth. A monorail supported on massive concrete columns ran down the highway's center.

In contrast, a horse and wagon trotted down the empty street past them. The bearded driver was dressed in black and wore a black hat. He gave them a cheery wave as he rode past.

They went under the highway through a pedestrian tunnel that smelled sourly of urine. The tunnel was deserted, and so was the area beyond.

The stucco houses went one more block beyond the highway, then gave way to a tangle of wooden shacks. Nothing was neat or well kept here. Discarded furniture rotted at the street corner. Litter and garbage were scattered through gardens that looked more like untended jungle than anything planned or deliberate.

"It's like Minetown, only it's wet," Harv said.

"Sort of," Lysander agreed. Except that Minetown wasn't walking distance from Government House Square, and the government of Sparta would never have permitted any place *this* unsanitary to exist anywhere on the planet. "We'd better—"

Three young men were coming toward them, and when Lysander turned to go back toward the pedestrian tunnel he saw two more had moved in behind them. All five walked arrogantly toward him.

"Trouble, Prince," Harv said. He smiled.

Lysander examined them carefully for weapons. They weren't wearing jackets, white or otherwise, and their jeans and shirts were formfitted over their muscled chests and hips leaving no room to conceal anything. They carried nothing except a length of chain and a couple of knives. Lysander's Walther rested comfortable in its holster under his guayabera, but he didn't reach for it. "Maybe they just want the time of day."

"Sure, Prince." The five came closer.

"Prince," one of the men said. "What kind of prince?"

"Jimmy, maybe he is," one of the others whined. "Maybe we— "

"Fuck off, Mario. Hey, Prince, you got any money? We'd sure like five credits."

They were not much younger than Lysander and

Harv. Drop them outside the capital city of Sparta and you might not notice them, Lysander thought. They dress a bit sloppily, but there's little else different about them. "What will you do to earn the money?" Lysander asked.

Harv laughed.

One of the men giggled. Jimmy, their leader, said "Oh, well, like this is a bad place, you know? You're lost, right? And we can show you how to get out of here, you know? Ten credits. That's all we want. Ten."

"Thank you, but I know the way out," Lysander said.

"Have it your way—"

Harv had all the time in the world. He struck as the gang leader was still speaking. His upthrust palm took the leader under the nose and rocked him back on his heels as the stiffened fingers of the other hand stabbed at the boy's abdomen. Harv's foot darted out in a snap kick to the knee. Jimmy fell as if shot. Before he hit the ground, Harv was standing relaxed as if he had never moved.

"Jesus Christ!" One of the two who had come up behind reached toward Lysander. His hand drew back and dangled uselessly, and he stared in amazement at bright blood welling from elbow to wrist. Harv carefully shifted the knife to his left hand. He still hadn't said a word, but his grin was broad.

"Who the fuck *are* you?" The one the leader had called Mario backed away. "Who?" He looked at his companions. "Fellows, maybe—"

"Maybe you made a mistake," Lysander said. "Please leave us alone."

The third one thought he had studied martial arts. He kicked at Harv, then pivoted to swing a three foot length of chain. Lysander swayed back to let the chain miss. Harv moved just behind the chain until he was close to the boy. His right hand moved upward as his left foot landed on the youth's instep. The boy fell groaning.

"Please," Lysander said.

"Yeah, sure, man. Sure," Mario said. He helped the third boy to his feet.

Harv looked disappointed when they all turned and walked away, walking, carefully not running, but not looking back at their fallen leader.

Governor Carleton Blaine was just under forty standard years old. Lysander's uncle had said Blaine was crazy: with his family connections he had enough political clout to get nearly any post he wanted, and he'd chosen Tanith. Every previous governor of Tanith had found himself on the prison planet because he had *lost* a power struggle.

He came out to meet them in the anteroom. The reception area was paneled in some exotic wood that might have been imported from Earth, although Lysander was sure it hadn't been. Tanith didn't merit that kind of expense. When Lysander unobtrusively touched one wall, the panels left like wood, but the new plastics often did.

Blaine was noticeably taller than Lysander's 180 centimeters, and thinner. His sandy brown hair looked to have been combed with his fingers. He wore the CoDominium seal on the left pocket of his light blue guayabera shirt. His handshake was firm. "Glad to see you, Prince Lysander. Taxpayer Middleton."

"Thank you."

"It's Citizen," Harv said proudly.

"Oh. Er, Your Highness, we were told this is an unofficial visit."

"Yes. Quite."

Blaine nodded. "I also have a message from the Chairman of Lederle A.G. requesting us to cooperate with you. Of course we will. What can we do for you?" Blaine ushered them toward his office door.

"You might find someone to show Citizen Middleton around and perhaps buy him a drink."

Blaine raised one eyebrow, then turned to his receptionist. "Ann, ask Mr. Kim to come up and take Prince Lysander's friend to the club room. Thank you." He led the way into his private office.

The office was paneled in the same stuff as the reception room. The desk was much more spectacular, banded in exotic woods framing thin panels of highly polished stone. It dominated the room, and invited questions. "That's really handsome. I've never seen anything like it," Lysander said.

Blaine smiled broadly. "Thank you. All native materials. Snakewood, and Grey Howlite. Of course the electronic innards were made on Earth by Viasyn. It will take us a few years before we can make anything like that here. Drink?"

"Thank you."

"We have an excellent liqueur, rum based with flavoring from the Tanith Passion Fruit, but perhaps it's a bit early in the day for something so sweet. Tanith whiskey, perhaps?"

"Thank you." Lysander sipped gingerly at the dark whiskey. "That's quite good."

"Glad you like it. Bit like Scotch only more so. Some find it strong."

"Sparta's whiskey is descended from Irish," Lysander said. "We think it's better than Earth's best. We had a master distiller from Cork—"

"Much the same story here," Blaine said. "Whole family from near Inverary. Can't imagine what they did to annoy BuRelock, but up they came; Tanith's benefit and Earth's loss. One of my predecessors set them up in the distilling business. So. I trust your stay on Tanith has been pleasant?"

"It *began* pleasantly enough—may I ask you about local customs?"

"Please do."

"There was a girl in my suite—"

"Ah. Blonde or red hair?"

"Red."

"That would be Ursula Gordon. Bright girl. I believe you when you say things began pleasantly—"

"What the hell is she doing there?"

"I beg your pardon?"

"Isn't she a bit young for prostitution?"

Blaine looked embarrassed. "Actually, she had no choice in the matter."

"I thought not. We don't have slavery on Sparta."

"Ah. Yes, and we do on Tanith. Something I'm trying to change. Takes longer than you might think."

"Yes, we've had much the same experience, everything takes longer and costs more, but slavery! Can't you stop that?"

"It's not slavery. Not precisely. Indentured," Blaine said. "Children born to convicts are indentured to the owner of the mother's contract. The theory is that since the owner has been burdened with the child's upbringing and education, he's entitled to something out of the arrangement. The Hilton bought her contract when she was quite young, and paid for her education. Now they expect some return. It's a nasty practice, and I've put an end to it for the future. Unfortunately I can't do anything retroactively. Tried. CoDominium arbitrator held for the contracts." Blaine was talking very fast. He went to the bar and brought the bottle back. "Shoot you in the other hip?"

"Thank you—how long will she be indentured?"

"Until she turns nineteen. That's Earth years. Tanith years are longer. The days are a bit shorter, but we measure 365 Tanith days as an Earth year. Too much trouble to measure hours." Blaine tapped keys on a console by his desk. "She'd be free in 209 local days."

"What will she do then?" Lysander asked.

Blaine took a deep breath. "If she's lucky she'll keep that job with the Hilton."

"And that's the best she can do?"

"I suppose it depends on which friends she makes. Or has made. This is a hard world, Your Highness." The governor went back to his desk. "You said things *began* pleasantly. Any problems?"

"Actually, yes." Lysander told Blaine about the five young men who'd approached him. "They ran away. Their leader was lucky. Harv only broke his nose. Possibly his leg as well, but I don't think so. I wondered if I ought to report it, but I didn't see any police—"

Blaine's smile had vanished. "In theory, of course you should have reported it, but in practice no one ever does. I'd stay out of that section of the city in future—"

"We will."

"But you said you were still among the stucco houses. You hadn't actually crossed into the Wattletown area?"

"No."

"I see. Excuse me, please." Blaine touched buttons on his desk. "Ann, please ask the chief of police to send a squad into Wattletown and round up the usual suspects. They can pass the word that Jimmy and Mario have stirred the soup."

"No need for that," Lysander protested.

"But there is," Blaine said. "We can't police everything, but we certainly can't put up with attacks on tourists in parts of town where they should be safe," He sighed. "I've posted signs at the tunnels under the Bronson Highway but the people on the other side tear them down. Can't say I blame them. Wouldn't want to live in an abandoned area myself."

"We don't have abandoned areas on Sparta. Not yet."

"I take it your chap is quite an experienced bodyguard."

"He's not precisely a bodyguard. I doubt you have anything like the Phraetries on Tanith."

"Phraetries?"

"Brotherhoods. Every potential Citizen of Sparta is potentially assigned to one at birth. We try to mix the social classes and backgrounds. It's a bit hard to explain—we're all brothers in our Phraetrie. Harv is my traveling companion, and I pity anyone who tries to give me trouble, but he's my Brother, and a full Citizen, not my bodyguard. Incidentally, 'Citizen' is an honorific on Sparta. We don t have 'taxpayers.' "

"Oh. Quite. Now, Your Highness, what else can I do for you?"

"I need to see Colonel Falkenberg."

"Ah. Good man. Ordinarily it would be no trouble, but just now I have him out suppressing the last of the escapee pirate gangs. There's a bit of other work for him here as well."

"It's very important."

Blaine cocked his head to one side. "I make no doubt it's important. I've heard a story or two myself. Care to tell me anything?" When Lysander didn't answer, Blaine nodded. "Right. Look, I'll do what I can, but it will take a while. Meanwhile, we're having a small dinner party here next week, nothing fancy, informal in fact. Falkenberg is invited, should be there if he's not altogether tied up with the Free State mess. If you like you could bring Miss Gordon."

"That would be appropriate for a dinner at Government House?"

"Yes— Well, no, in fact. And I'd like to change that. You could help me. No one is going to be rude to *you*. Or your guest."

"My father told me not to interfere in foreign affairs."

"Good advice," Blaine said.

"But surely this can't do any harm. I'll be glad to come. With the young lady."

"Thank you. Your Highness, I'm convinced that the future of this planet lies with the convicts and involuntary colonists. Some of the original settlers, the planters and pharmaceutical processing officials, understand that. Many don't, and want to hang on to meaningless aristocratic privileges."

"We've had something of the same problem," Lysander said. "Of course it helps that we get—many of the convicts brought to Sparta have bribed their way there—"

"Giving you a slightly better grade of convict?" Blaine smiled. "Happens here, too, but of course on a lower scale. Still, anyone who can will pay to come here rather than be sent to Fulson's world. And once in a while we get a really bright one."

# III

# One Year Earlier . . .

The California sky was bright blue above eight thousand young bodies writhing to the maddening beat of an electronic bass. Some danced while others lay back on the grass and drank or smoked. None could ignore the music, although they were only barely aware of the nasal tenor whose voice was not strong enough to carry over the wild squeals of the theremin and the twang of a dozen steel-stringed guitars. Other musical groups waited their turn on the gray wooden platform erected among the twentieth-century Gothic buildings of Los Angeles University.

Some of the musicians were so anxious to begin that they pounded their instruments. This produced nothing audible because their amplifiers were turned off, but it allowed them to join in the frenzied spirit of the festival on the campus green.

The concert was a happy affair. Citizens from a nearby Welfare Island joined the students in the college park. Enterprising dealers hawked liquor and pot and borloi. Catering trucks brought food. The Daughters of Lilith played original works while Slime waited their turn, and after those would come even more famous groups. An air of peace and fellowship engulfed the crowd.

"Lumpen proletariat." The speaker was a young woman. She stood at a window in a classroom overlooking the common green and the mad scene below. "Lumpen," she said again.

"Aw, come off the bolshi talk. Communism's no answer. Look at the Sovworld—"

"Revolution betrayed! Betrayed!" the girl said. She faced her challenger. "There will be no peace and freedom until—"

"Can it." The meeting chairman banged his fist on the desk. "We've got work to do. This is no time for ideology."

"Without the proper revolutionary theory, nothing can be accomplished." This came from a bearded man in a leather jacket. He looked first at the chairman, then at the dozen others in the classroom. "First there must be a proper understanding of the problem. Then we can act!"

The chairman banged his fist again, but someone else spoke. "Deeds, not words. We came here to plan some action. What the hell's all the talking about? You goddamned theorists give me a pain in the ass! What we need is action. The Underground's done more for the Movement than you'll ever—"

"Balls." The man in the leather jacket snorted contempt. Then he stood. His voice projected well. "You act, all right. You shut down the L.A. transport system for three days. Real clever. And what did it accomplish? Made the taxpayers scared enough to fork over pay raises to the cops. You ended the goddamn pig strike, that's what you did!"

There was a general babble, and the Underground spokesman tried to answer, but the leather-jacketed man continued. "You started food riots in the Citizen areas. Big deal. It's results that count, and your result was the CoDominium Marines! You brought in the Marines, that's what you did!"

"Damned right! We exposed this regime for what it really is! The Revolution can't come until the people understand—"

"Revolution, my ass. Get it through your heads, technology's the only thing that's going to save us. Turn technology loose, free the scientists, and we'll be—"

He was shouted down by the others. There was more babble.

Mark Fuller sat at the student desk and drank it all in. The wild music outside. Talk of revolution. Plans for action, for making something happen, for making the Establishment notice them; it was all new, and he was here in this room, where the real power of the university lay. God, how I love it! he thought. I've never had any kind of power before. Not even over my own life. And now we can show them all!

He felt more alive than he ever had in all his twenty years. He looked at the girl next to him and smiled. She grinned and patted his thigh. Tension rose in his loins until it was almost unbearable. He remembered their yesterdays and imagined their tomorrows. The quiet world of taxpayer country where he had grown up seemed very far away.

The others continued their argument. Mark listened, but his thoughts kept straying to Shirley; to the warmth of her hand on his thigh, to the places where her sweater was stretched out of shape, to the remembered feel of her heels against his back and her cries of passion. He knew he ought to listen more carefully to the discussion. He didn't really belong in this room at all. If Shirley hadn't brought him, he'd never have known the meeting was happening.

But I'll earn a place here, he thought. In my own right. Power. That's what they have, and I'll learn how to be a part of it.

The jacketed technocracy man was speaking again. "You see too many devils," he said. "Get the CoDominium Intelligence people off the scientists' backs and it won't be twenty years before *all* of the earth's a paradise. All of it, not just taxpayer country."

"A polluted paradise! What do you want, to go back to the smog? Oil slicks, dead fish, animals exterminated, that's what—"

"Bullshit. Technology can get us *out* of—"

"That's what caused the problems in the first place!"

"Because we didn't get far enough! There hasn't been a new scientific idea since the goddamn space drive! You're so damned proud because there's no pollution. None here, anyway. But it's not because of conservation, it's because they ship people out to hellholes like Tanith, because of triage, because—"

"He's right, people starve while we—"

"Damn right! Free thoughts, freedom to think, to plan, to do research, to publish without censorship, that's what will liberate the world."

The arguments went on until the chairman tired of them. He banged his fist again. "We are here to *do* something," he said. "Not to settle the world's problems this afternoon. That was agreed."

The babble finally died away and the chairman spoke meaningfully. "This is our chance. A peaceful demonstration of power. Show what we think of their goddamn rules and their status cards. But we've got to be careful. It mustn't get out of hand."

Mark sprawled on the grass a dozen meters from the platform. He stretched luxuriantly in the California sun while Shirley stroked his back. Excitement

PRINCE OF MERCENARIES 27

poured in through all his senses. College had been like this in imagination. The boys at the expensive private schools where his father had sent him used to whisper about festivals, demonstrations, and confrontations, but it hadn't been real. Now it was. He'd hardly ever mingled with Citizens before, and now they were all around him. They wore Welfare-issue clothing and talked in strange dialects that Mark only half understood. Everyone, Citizens and students, writhed to the music that washed across them.

Mark's father had wanted to send him to a college in taxpayer country, but there hadn't been enough money. He might have won a scholarship, but he hadn't. Mark told himself it was deliberate. Competition was no way to live. His two best friends in high school had refused to compete in the rat race. Neither ended here, though; they'd had the money to get to Princeton and Yale.

More Citizens poured in. The festival was supposed to be open only to those with tickets, and Citizens weren't supposed to come onto the campus in the first place, but the student group had opened the gates and cut the fences. It had all been planned in the meeting. Now the gate-control shack was on fire, and everyone who lived nearby could get in.

Shirley was ecstatic. "Look at them!" she shouted. "This is the way it used to be! Citizens should be able to go wherever they want to. Equality forever!"

Mark smiled. It was all new to him. He hadn't thought much about the division between Citizen and taxpayer, and had accepted his privileges without noticing them. He had learned a lot from Shirley and his new friends, but there was so much more that he didn't know. I'll find out, though, he thought. We know what we're doing. We can make the world so much better—we can do anything! Time for the stupid old bastards to move over and let some fresh ideas in.

Shirley passed him a pipe of borloi. That was another new thing for him; it was a Citizen habit, something Mark's father despised. Mark couldn't understand why. He inhaled deeply and relished the wave of contentment it brought. Then he reached for Shirley and held her in his warm bath of concern and love, knowing she was as happy as he was.

She smiled gently at him, her hand resting on his thigh, and they writhed to the music, the beat thundering through them, faces glowing with anticipation of what would come, of what they would accomplish this day. The pipe came around again and Mark seized it eagerly.

"Pigs! The pigs are coming!" The cry went up from the fringes of the crowd.

Shirley turned to her followers. "Just stay here. Don't provoke the bastards. Make sure you don't do anything but sit tight."

There were murmurs of agreement. Mark felt excitement flash through him. This was it. And he was right there in front with the leaders; even if all his status did come from being Shirley's current boyfriend, he was one of the leaders, one of the people who made things happen. . . .

The police were trying to get through the crowd so they could stop the festival. The university president was with them, and he was shouting something Mark couldn't understand. Over at the edge of the common green there was a lot of smoke. Was a building on fire? That didn't make sense. There weren't supposed to be any fires, nothing was to be harmed; just ignore the cops and the university people, show how

Citizens and students could mingle in peace; show how stupid the damned rules were, and how needless—

There *was* a fire. Maybe more than one. Police and firemen tried to get through the crowd. Someone kicked a cop and the bluecoat went down. A dozen of his buddies waded into the group. Their sticks rose and fell.

The peaceful dream vanished. Mark stared in confusion. There was a man screaming somewhere, where was he? In the burning building? A group began chanting: "Equality now! Equality now!"

Another group was building a barricade across the green.

"They aren't supposed to do that!" Mark shouted. Shirley grinned at him. Her eyes shone with excitement. More police came, then more and a group headed toward Mark. They raised aluminum shields as rocks flew across the green. The police came closer. One of the cops raised his club.

He was going to hit Shirley! Mark grabbed at the nightstick and deflected it. Citizens and students clustered around. Some threw themselves at the cops. A big man, well-dressed, too old to be a student, kicked at the leading policeman. The cop went down.

Mark pulled Shirley away as a dozen black-jacketed Lampburners joined the melee. The Lampburners would deal with the cops, but Mark didn't want to watch. The boys in his school had talked contemptuously about pigs, but the only police Mark had ever met had been polite and deferential; this was ugly, and—

His head swam in confusion. One minute he'd been lying in Shirley's arms with music and fellowship and everything was wonderful. Now there were police, and groups shouting "Kill the pigs!" and fires burning. The Lampburners were swarming everywhere. They hadn't been at the meeting. Most claimed to be wanted by the police. But they'd had a representative at the planning session, they'd agreed this would be a peaceful demonstration—

A man jumped off the roof of the burning building. There was no one below to catch him, and he sprawled on the steps like a broken doll. Blood poured from his mouth, a bright-red splash against the pink marble steps. Another building shot flames skyward. More police arrived and set up electrified barriers around the crowd.

A civilian, his bright clothing a contrast with the dull police blue, got out of a cruiser and stood atop it as police held their shields in front of him. He began to shout through a bull horn:

"I read you the Act of 1998 as amended. Whenever there shall be an assembly likely to endanger public or private property or the lives of Citizens and taxpayers, the lawful magistrates shall command all persons assembled to disperse and shall warn them that failure to disperse shall be considered a declaration of rebellion. The magistrates shall give sufficient time . . ."

Mark knew the act. He'd heard it discussed in school. It was time to get away. The local mayor would soon have more than enough authority to deal with this mad scene. He could even call on the military, US or CoDominium. The barriers were up around two sides of the green, but the cops hadn't closed off all the buildings. There was a doorway ahead, and Mark pulled Shirley toward it. "Come on!"

Shirley wouldn't come. She stood defiant, grinning wildly, shaking her fist at the police, shouting curses at them. Then she turned to Mark. "If you're scared, just go on, baby. Bug off."

Someone handed a bottle around. Shirley drank and gave it to Mark. He raised it to his lips but didn't drink any. His head pounded and he was afraid. I should run, he thought. I should run like hell. The mayor's finished reading the act. . . .

"*Equality now! Equality now!*" The chant was contagious. Half the crowd was shouting.

The police waited impassively. An officer glanced at his watch from time to time. Then the officer nodded, and the police advanced. Four technicians took hoses from one of the cruises and directed streams of foam above the heads of the advancing blue line. The slimy liquid fell in a spray around Mark.

Mark fell. He tried to stand and couldn't. Everyone around him fell. Whatever the liquid touched became so slippery that no one could hold onto it. It didn't seem to affect the police.

Instant banana peel, Mark thought. He'd seen it used on tri-v. Everyone laughed when they saw it used on tri-v. Now it didn't seem so funny. A couple of attempts showed Mark that he couldn't get away; he could barely crawl. The police moved rapidly toward him. Rocks and bottles clanged against their shields.

The black-jacketed Lampburners took spray cans from their pockets. They sprayed their shoes and hands and then got up. They began to move away through the helpless crowd, away from the police, toward an empty building—

The police line reached the group around Mark. The cops fondled their nightsticks. They spoke in low tones, too low to be heard any distance away. "Stick time," one said. "Yeah, our turn," his partner answered.

"Does anyone here claim taxpayer status?" The cop eyed the group coldly. "Speak up."

"Yes. Here." One boy tried to get up. He fell again, but he held up his ID card. "Here." Mark reached for his own.

"Fink!" Shirley shouted. She threw something at the other boy. "Hypocrite! Pig! Fink!" Others were shouting as well. Mark saw Shirley's look of hatred and put his card back into his pocket. There'd be time later.

Two police grabbed him. One lifted his feet, the other lifted his shoulders. They carried him to the sidewalk. Then they lifted him waist high, and the one holding his shoulders let go. The last thing Mark heard as his head hit the pavement was mocking laughter of the cop.

The bailiff was grotesque, with mustaches like Wyatt Earp and an enormous paunch that hung over his equipment belt. In a bored voice he read, "Case 457-984. People against Mark Fuller. Rebellion, aggravated assault, resisting arrest."

The judge looked down from the bench. "How do you plead?"

"Guilty, Your Honor," Mark's lawyer said. His name was Zower, and he wasn't expensive. Mark's father couldn't afford an expensive lawyer.

But I didn't, Mark thought. I didn't. When he'd said that earlier, though, the attorney had been contemptuous. "Shut up or you'll make it worse," the lawyer had said. "I had trouble enough getting the conspiracy charges dropped. Just stand there looking innocent and don't say a goddamn thing."

The judge nodded. "Have you anything to say in mitigation?"

Zower put his hand on Mark's shoulder. "My client throws himself on the mercy of the court," he said. "Mark has never been in trouble before. He acted under the influence of evil companions and intoxicants. There was no real intent to commit crimes. Just very bad judgment."

The judge didn't look impressed. "What have the people to say about this?"

"Your Honor," the prosecutor began, "the people have had more than enough of these student riots. This was no high-jinks stunt by young taxpayers. This was a deliberate rebellion, planned in advance.

"We have recordings of this hoodlum striking a police officer. That officer subsequently suffered a severe beating with three fractures, a ruptured kidney, and other personal injuries. It is a wonder the officer is alive. We can also show that after the mayor's proclamations, the accused made no attempt to leave. If the defense disputed these facts . . ."

"No, no." Zower spoke hastily. "We stipulate, Your Honor." He muttered to himself, just loud enough that Mark could hear. "Can't let them run those pix. That'd get the judge *really* upset."

Zower stood. "Your Honor, we stipulate Mark's bad judgement, but remember, he was intoxicated. He did not actually strike the policeman, he merely gripped the officer's nightstick. Mark was with new friends, friends he didn't know very well. His father is a respected taxpayer, manager of General Foods in Santa Maria. Mark has never been arrested before. I'm sure he's learned a lesson from all this."

And where is Shirley? Mark wondered. Somehow her politician father had kept her from even being charged.

The judge was nodding. Zower smiled and whispered to Mark, "I stroked him pretty good in chambers. We'll get probation."

"Mister Fuller, what have you to say for yourself?" the judge demanded.

Mark stood eagerly. He wasn't sure what he was going to say. Plead? Beg for mercy? Tell him to stick it? Not that. Mark breathed hard. I'm scared, he thought. He walked nervously toward the bench.

The judge's face exploded in a cloud of red. There was wild laughter in the court. Another balloon of red ink sailed across the courtroom to burst on the high bench. Mark laughed hysterically, completely out of control, as the spectators shouted.

*"Equality now!"* Eight voices speaking in unison cut through the babble. *"Justice! Equality! Citizen judges, not taxpayers! Equality now! Equality now! Equality now! All power to the Liberation Party!"*

The last stung like a blow. The judge's face turned even redder. He stood in fury. The fat bailiff and his companions moved decisively through the crowd. Two of the demonstrators escaped, but the bailiff was much faster than his bulk made him look. After a time the court was silent.

The judge stood, ink dripping from his face and robes. He was not smiling. "This amused you?" he demanded.

"No," Mark said. "It was none of my doing."

"I do not believe the outlawed Liberation Party would trouble itself for anyone not one of their own. Mark Fuller, you have pleaded guilty to serious crimes. We would normally send a taxpayer's son to rehabilitation school, but you and your friends have demanded equality. Very well. You shall have it.

"Mark Fuller, I sentence you to three years at hard labor. Since you renounced your allegiance to the United States by participating in a deliberate act of rebellion, such participation stipulated by your attorney's admission that you made to move to depart after the reading of the act, you have no claim upon the United States. The United States therefore renounces you. It is hereby ordered that you be delivered to the CoDominium authorities to serve your sentence wherever they shall find convenient." The gavel fell to the bench. It didn't sound very loud at all.

# IV

The low gravity of Luna Base was better than the endless nightmare of the flight up. Mark had been trapped in a narrow compartment with berths so close together that the sagging bunk above his pressed against him at high acceleration. The ship had stunk with the putrid smell of vomit and stale wine.

Now he stood under the glaring lights in a bare concrete room. The concrete was the gray-green color of moon rock. They hadn't been given an outside view, and except for the low gravity he might have been in a basement on Earth. There were a thousand others standing with him under the glaring bright fluorescent lights. Most of them had the dull look of terror. A few glared defiantly, but they kept their opinions to themselves.

Gray-coveralled trustees with bell-mouthed sonic stunners patrolled the room. It wouldn't have been worthwhile trying to take one of the weapons from the trustees, though; at each entrance was a knot of CoDominium Marines in blue and scarlet. The Marines leaned idly on weapons which were not harmless at all.

"Segregate us," Mark's companion said. "Divide and rule."

Mark nodded. Bill Halpern was the only person Mark knew. Halpern had been the technocrat spokesman in the meeting on the campus.

"Divide and rule," Halpern said again. It was true enough. The prisoners had been sorted by sex, race and language, so that everyone around Mark was white male and either North American or from some other English-speaking place. "What the hell are we waiting for?" Halpern wondered. There was no possible answer, and they stood for what seemed like hours.

Then the door opened and a small group came in. Three CoDominium Navy petty officers, and a midshipman. The middle was no more than seventeen, younger than Mark. He used a bullhorn to speak to the assembled group. "Volunteers for the Navy?"

There were several shouts, and some of the prisoners stepped forward.

"Traitors," Halpern said.

Mark nodded agreement. Although he meant it in a different way from Halpern, Mark's father had always said the same thing. "Traitors!" he'd thundered. "Dupes of the goddamn Soviets. One of these days that Navy will take over this country and hand us to the Kremlin."

Mark's teachers at school had different ideas. The Navy wasn't needed at all. Nor was the CD. Men no longer made war, at least not on Earth. Colony squabbles were of no interest to the people on Earth anyway. Military services, they'd told him, were a wasteful joke.

His new friends at college said the purpose of the CoDominium was to keep the United States and the Soviet Union rich while suppressing everyone else.

Then they'd begun using the CD fleet and Marines to shore up their domestic governments. The whole CD was no more than a part of the machinery of oppression.

And yet—on tri-v the CD Navy was glamorous. It fought pirates (only Mark knew there were no real space pirates) and restored order in the colonies (only his college friends told him that wasn't restoring order, it was oppression of free people). The spacers wore uniforms and explored new planets.

The CD midshipman walked along the line of prisoners. Two older petty officers followed. They walked proudly—contemptuously, even. They saw the prisoners as another race, not as fellow humans at all.

A convict not far from Mark stepped out of line. "Mister Blaine," the man said. "Please, sir."

The midshipman stopped. "Yes?"

"Don't you know me, Mister Blaine? Able Spacer Johnson, sir. In Mister Leary's division in *Magog*."

The middie nodded with all the gravity of a seventeen-year-old who has important duties and knows it. "I recall you, Johnson."

"Let me back in, sir. Six years I served, never up for defaulters."

The midshipman fingered his clipboard console. "Drunk and disorderly, assault on a taxpayer, armed robbery. Mandatory transportation. I shouldn't wonder that you prefer the Navy, Johnson."

"Not like that at all, sir. I shouldn't ever have took my musterin'-out pay. Shouldn't have left the Fleet, sir. Couldn't find my place with civilians, sir. God knows I drank too much, but I was never drunk on duty, sir, you look up my records—"

"Kiss the middie's bum, you whining asshole," Halpern said.

One of the petty officers glanced up. "Silence in

the ranks." He put his hand on his nightstick and glared at Halpern.

The midshipman thought for a moment. "All right, Johnson. You'll come in as ordinary. Have to work for the stripe."

"Yes, sir, sure thing, sir." Johnson strode toward the area reserved for recruits. His manner changed with each step he took. He began in a cringing walk, but by the time he reached the end of the room, he had straightened and walked tall.

The midshipman went down the line. Twenty men volunteered, but he took only three.

An hour later a CoDominium Marine sergeant came looking for men. "No rebels and no degenerates!" he said. He took six young men sentenced for street rioting, arson, mayhem, resisting arrest, assault on police and numerous other crimes.

"Street gang," Halpern said. "Perfect for Marines."

Eventually they were herded back into a detention pen and left to themselves. "You really hate the CD, don't you?" Mark asked his companion.

"I hate what they do."

Mark nodded, but Halpern only sneered. "You don't know anything at all," Halpern said. "Oppression? Shooting rioters? Sure that's part of what the CD does, but it's not the worst part. Symptom, not cause. The case is their goddamn so-called intelligence service. Suppression of scientific research. Censorship of technical journals. They've even stopped the pretense of basic research. When was the last time a licensed physicist had a decent idea?"

Mark shrugged. He knew nothing about physics.

Halpern grinned. There was no warmth in the expression. His voice had a bitter edge. "Keeping the peace, they say. Only discourage new weapons, new military technology. Bullshit, they've stopped everything for fear somebody somewhere will come up with—"

"Shut the fuck up." The man was big, hairy like a bear, with a big paunch jutting out over the belt of his coveralls. "If I hear that goddamn whining once more, I'll stomp your goddamn head in."

"Hey, easy," Halpern said. "We're all in this together. We have to join against the class enemy—"

The big man's hand swung up without warning. He hit Halpern on the mouth. Halpern staggered and fell. His head struck the concrete floor. "Told you to shut up." He turned to Mark. "You got anything to say?"

Mark was terrified. I ought to do something, he thought. Say something. Anything. He tried to speak, but no words came out.

The bag man grinned at him, then deliberately kicked Halpern in the ribs. "Didn't think so. Hey, you're not bad-lookin', kid. Six months we'll be on that goddamn ship, with no women. Want to be my bunkmate? I'll take good care of you. See nobody hurts you. You'll like that."

"Leave the kid alone." Mark couldn't see who spoke. "I said let go of him."

"Who says so?" The hairy man shoved Mark against the wall and turned to the newcomer.

"I do." The newcomer didn't look like much, Mark thought. At least forty, and slim. Not thin though, Mark realized. The man stood with his hands thrust into the pockets of his coveralls. "Let him be, Karper."

Karper grinned and charged at the newcomer. As he rushed forward, his opponent pivoted and sent a kick to Karper's head. As Karper reeled back, two more kicks slammed his head against the wall. Then the newcomer moved forward and deliberately kneed Karper in the kidney. The big man went down and rolled beside Halpern.

"Come on, kid, it stinks over here." He grinned at Mark.

"But my buddy—"

"Forget him." The man pointed. Five trustees were coming into the pen. They lifted Halpern and Karper and carried them away. One of the trustees winked as they went past Mark and the other man. "See? Maybe you'll see your friend again, maybe not. They don't like troublemakers."

"Bill's not a troublemaker! That other man started it! It's not fair!"

"Kid, you better forget that word 'fair.' It could cause you no end of problems. Got any smokes?" He accepted Mark's cigarette with a glance at the label. "Thanks. Name?"

"Mark Fuller."

"Dugan. Call me Biff."

"Thanks, Biff. I guess I needed some help."

"That you did. Hell, it was fun. Karper was gettin' on my nerves, anyway. How old are you, kid?"

"Twenty." And what does he want? Lord God, is he looking for a bunkmate, too?

"You don't look twenty. Taxpayer, aren't you?"

"Yes—how did you know?"

"It shows. What's a taxpayer's kid doing here?"

Mark told him. "It wasn't fair," he finished.

"There's that word again. You were in college, eh? Can you read?"

"Well, sure, everyone can read."

Dugan laughed. "I can't. Not very well. And I bet you're the only one in this pen who ever read a whole book. Where'd you learn?"

"Well—in school. Maybe a little at home."

Dugan blew a careful smoke ring. It hung in the air between them. "Me, I never even saw a veedisk screen until they dragged me off to school, and no-body gave a shit whether we looked at 'em or not. Had to pick up some of it, but—look, maybe you know things I don't. Want to stick with me a while?"

Mark eyed him suspiciously. Dugan laughed. "Hell, I don't bugger kids. Not until I've been locked up a lot longer than this, anyway. Man needs a buddy, though, and you just lost yours."

"Yeah. Okay. Want another cigarette?"

"We better save 'em. We'll need all you got."

A petty officer opened the door to the pen. "Classification," he shouted. "Move out this door."

"Got to it pretty fast," Dugan said. "Come on." They followed the others out and through a long corridor until they reached another large room. There were tables at the end, and trustees sat at each table. Eventually Mark and Dugan got to one.

The trusty barely looked at them. When they gave their names, he punched them into a console on the table. The printer made tiny clicking noises and two sheets of paper fell out. "Any choice?" the trusty asked.

"What's open, shipmate?" Dugan asked.

"I'm no shipmate of yours," the trusty sneered. "Tanith, Sparta, and Fulson's World."

Dugan shuddered. "Well, we sure don't want Fulson's World." He reached into Mark's pocket and took out the pack of cigarettes, then laid them on the table. They vanished into the trusty's coveralls.

"Not Fulson's," the trusty said. "Now, I hear they're lettin' the convicts run loose on Sparta." He said nothing more but looked at them closely.

Mark remembered that Sparta was founded by a group of intellectuals. They were trying some kind of social experiment. Unlike Tanith with its CoDominium governor, Sparta was independent. They'd have a better chance there. "We'll take Sparta," Mark said.

"Sparta's pretty popular," the trusty said. He waited for a moment. "Well, too bad." He scrawled "Tanith" across their papers and handed them over. "Move along." A petty officer waved them through a door behind the table.

"But we wanted Sparta," Mark protested.

"Get your ass out of here," the CD petty officer said. "Move it." Then it was too late and they were through the door.

"Wish I'd had some credits," Dugan muttered. "We bought off Fulson's though. That's something."

"But—I have some money. I didn't know—"

Dugan gave him a curious look. "Kid, they didn't teach you much in that school of yours. Well, come on, we'll make out. But you better let me take care of that money."

CDSS *Vladivostok* hurtled toward the orbit of Jupiter. The converted assault troop carrier was crammed with thousands of men jammed into temporary berths welded into the troop bays. There were more men than bunks; many of the convicts had to trade off half the time.

Dugan took over a corner. Corners were desirable territory, and two men disputed his choice. After they were carried away, no one else thought it worth trying. Biff used Mark's money to finance a crap game in the area near their berths, and in a few days he had trebled their capital.

"Too bad," Dugan said. "If we'd had this much back on Luna, we'd be headed for Sparta. Anyway, we bought our way into this ship, and that's worth something." He grinned at Mark's lack of response. "Hey, kid, it could be worse. We could be with

BuRelock. You think this Navy ship's bad, try a BuRelock hellhole."

Mark wondered how Bureau of Relocation ships could be worse, but he didn't want to find out. The newscasters back on Earth had documentary specials about BuRelock. They all said that conditions were tought but bearable. They also told of the glory: mankind settling other worlds circling other stars. Mark felt none of the glory now.

Back home Zower would be making an appeal. Or at least he'd be billing Mark's father for one. And so what? Mark thought. Nothing would come of it. But something might! Jason Fuller had some political favors coming. He might pull a few strings. Mark could be headed back home within a year. . . .

He knew better, but he had no other hope. He lived in misery, brooding about the low spin gravity, starchy food, the constant stench of the other convicts; all that was bad, but the water was the worst thing. He knew it was recycled. Water on Earth was recycled, too, but there you didn't know that it had been used to bathe the foul sores of the man two bays to starboard.

Sometimes a convict would rush screaming through the compartment, smashing at bunks and flinging his fellow prisoners about like matchsticks, until a dozen men would beat him to the deck. Eventually the guards would take him away. None ever came back.

The ship reached the orbit of Jupiter and took on fuel from the scoopship tankers that waited for her. Then she moved to the featureless point in space that marked the Alderson jump tramline. Alarms rang; then everything blurred. They sat on their bunks in confusion, unable to move or even think. That lasted long after the instantaneous Jump. The ship had covered light-years in a single instant; now they had to cross another star's gravity well to reach the next Jump point.

Two weeks later a petty officer entered the compartment.

"Two men needed for cleanup in the crew area. Chance for Navy chow. Volunteers?"

"Sure," Dugan said. "My buddy and me. Anybody object?"

No one did. The petty officer grinned. "Looks like you're elected." He led them through corridors and passageways to the forward end of the ship, where they were put to scrubbing the bulkheads. A bored Marine watched idly.

"I thought you said never volunteer," Mark told Dugan.

"Good general rule. But what else we got to do? Gets us better chow. Always take a chance on something when it can't be no worse than what you've got."

The lunch was good and the work was not hard. Even the smell of disinfectant was a relief, and scrubbing off the bulkheads and decks got their hands clean for the first time since they'd been put aboard. In mid-afternoon a crewman came by. He stopped and stared at them for a moment.

"Dugan! Biff Dugan, by God!"

"Horrigan, you slut. When'd you join up?"

"Aw, you know how it is, Biff, they moved in on the racket and what could I do? I see they got you—"

"Clean got me. Sarah blew the whistle on me."

"Told you she wouldn't put up with you messing around. Who's your chum?"

"Name's Mark. He's learning. Hey, Goober, what can you do for me?"

"Funny you should ask. Maybe I got something. Want to enlist?"

"Hell, they don't want me. I tried back on Luna. Too old."

Horrigan nodded. "Yeah, but the Purser's gang needs men. Freakie killed twenty crewmen yesterday. Recruits. This geek opened an air lock and nobody stopped him. That's why you're out here swabbing. Look, Biff, we're headed for a long patrol after we drop you guys on Tanith. Maybe I can fix it."

"No harm in trying. Mark, you lost anything on Tanith?"

"No." But I don't want to join the CD Navy, either. Only why not? He tried to copy his friend's easy indifference. "Can't be worse than where we are."

"Right," Horrigan said. "We'll go see the Purser's middie. That okay, mate?" he asked the Marine.

The Marine shrugged. "Okay by me."

Horrigan led the way forward. Mark felt sick with excitement. Getting out of the prison compartment suddenly became the most important thing in his life.

Midshipman Greschin was not surprised to find two prisoners ready to join the Navy. He questioned them for a few minutes. Then he studied Dugan's records on the readout screen. "You have been in space before, but there is nothing on your record—"

"I never said I'd been out."

"No, but you have. Are you a deserter?"

"No," Dugan said.

Greschin shrugged. "If you are, we'll find out. If not, we don't care. We are short of hands, and I see no reason why you cannot be enlisted. I will call Lieutenant Breslov."

Breslov was fifteen years older than his midshipman. He looked over Dugan's print-out. Then he examined Mark's. "I can take Dugan," he said. "Not you, Fuller."

"But why?" Mark asked.

Breslov shrugged. "You are a rebel, and you have high intelligence. So it says here. There are officers who will take the risk of recruiting those like you, but I am not one of them. We cannot use you in this ship."

"Oh." Mark turned to go.

"Wait a minute, kid." Dugan looked at the officer. "Thanks, Lieutenant, but maybe I better stick with my buddy—"

"No, don't do that," Mark said. He felt a wave of gratitude toward the older man. Dugan's offer seemed the finest thing anyone had ever tried to do for him.

"Who'll look out for ya? You'll get your throat cut."

"Maybe not. I've learned a lot."

Breslov stood. "Your sentiment for your friends is admirable, but you are wasting my time. Are you enlisting?"

"He is," Mark said. "Thank you, Lieutenant." He followed the Marine guard back to the corridor and began washing the bulkhead, scrubbing savagely, trying to forget his misery and despair. It was all so unfair!

# V

Tanith was hot, steaming jungle under a perpetual orange and gray cloud cover. The gravity was too high and the humidity was almost unbearable. Mark had no chance to see the planet. The ship landed at night, and the convicts were marched between tall fences into a concrete building with no outside windows. It was sparsely furnished and clearly intended only for short-term occupancy.

The exercise yard was a square in the center of the massive building. It was a relief to have space to move around in after the crowded ship, but shortly after they were allowed in the yard a violent rainstorm drove them inside the prison building. Even with the storm the place was sweltering. Tanith's gravity seemed ready to crush him.

The next day he was herded through medical processing, immunization, identification, a meaningless classification interview, and both psychological and aptitude tests. They ran from one task to the next, then stood in long lines or simply waited around. On the fourth day he was taken from the detention pen to an empty adobe-walled room with rough wooden furniture. The guards left him there. The sensation of being alone was exhilarating.

He looked up warily when the door opened. "Biff!"

"Hi, kid. Got something for you." Dugan was dressed in the blue dungarees of the CD Navy. He glanced around guiltily. "You left this with me and I run it up a bit." He held out a fistful of CoDominium scrip. "Go on, take it, I can get more and you can't. Look we're pullin' out pretty soon, and . . ."

"It's all right," Mark said. But it wasn't all right. He hadn't known how much friendship meant to him until he'd been separated from Dugan; now, seeing him in the Navy uniform and knowing that Dugan was headed away from this horrible place, Mark hated his former friend. "I'll get along."

"Damned right you will! Stop sniffing about how unfair everything is and wait your chance. You'll get one. Look, you're a young kid and everything seems like it's forever, but—" Dugan fell silent and shook his head ruefully. "Not that you need fatherly advice from me. Or that it'd do any good. But things end, Mark. The day ends. So do weeks and months."

"Yeah. Sure." They said more meaningless things, and Dugan left. Now I'm completely alone, Mark thought. It was a crushing thought. Some of the speeches he'd heard in his few days in college kept rising up to haunt him. *"Die Gedanken, Sie sind frei."* Yeah. Sure. A man's thoughts were always free, and no one could enslave a free man, and the heaviest chains and darkest dungeons could never cage the spirit. Bullshit. I'm a slave. If I don't do what they tell me, they'll hurt me until I do. And I'm too damned scared of them. But something else he'd heard was more comforting. "Slaves have no rights, and thus have no obligations."

That, by God, fits. I don't owe anybody a thing. Nobody here, and none of those bastards on Earth. I

do what I have to do and I look out for number-one
and rape the rest of 'em.

There was no prison, or rather the entire planet
was a prison. As he'd suspected, the main CD penal
building was intended only for classification and assignment, a holding pen to keep prisoners until they
were sold off to wealthy planters. There were a lot of
rumors about the different places you might be sent
to: big company farms run like factories, where it
was said that few convicts ever lived to finish out
their terms; industrial plants near cities, which was
supposed to be soft duty because as soon as you got
trusty status, you could get passes into town; town
work, the best assignment of all; and the biggest
category, lonely plantations out in the sticks where
owners could do anything they wanted and generally
did.

The pen began to empty as the men were shipped
out. Then came Mark's turn. He was escorted into
an interview room and given a seat. It was the second time in months that he'd been alone and he
enjoyed the solitude. There were voices from the
next room.

"Why do you not keep him, *hein*?"

"Immature. No reason to be loyal to the CD."

"Or to me."

"Or to you. And too smart to be a dumb cop. You
might make a foreman out of him. The governor's
interested in this one, Ludwig. He keeps track of all
the high-IQ types. Look, you take this one, I owe
you. I'll see you get good hands."

"Okay. *Ja*. Just remember that when you get in
some with muscles and no brains, *hein*? Okay, we
look at your genius."

Who the hell were they talking about? Mark wondered. Me? Compared to most of the others in the ship, I guess you could call me a genius, but—

The door opened. Mark stood quickly. The guards liked you to do that.

"Fuller," the captain said. "This is Herr Ewigfeuer. You'll work for him. His place is a country club."

The planter was heavy-set, with thick jowls. He needed a shave, and his shorts and khaki shirt were stained with sweat. "So you are the new convict I take to my nice farm." He eyed Mark coldly. "He will do, he will do. Okay, we go now, *ja?*"

"Now?" Mark said.

"Now, *ja*, you think all day I have? I can stay in Whiskeytown while my foreman lets the hands eat everything and lay around not working? Give me the papers, Captain."

The captain took a sheaf of papers from a folder. He scrawled across the bottom, then handed Mark a pen. "Sign here."

Mark started to read the documents. The captain laughed. "Sign it, goddamnit. We don't have all day."

Mark shrugged and scribbled his name. The captain handed Ewigfeuer two copies and indicated a door. They went through the adobe corridors to a guardroom at the end. The planter handed the guards a copy of the document and the door was opened.

The heat outside struck Mark like a physical blow. It had been hot enough inside, but the thick earthen walls had protected him from the worst; now it was almost unbearable. There was no sun, but the clouds were bright enough to hurt his eyes. Ewigfeuer put on dark glasses. He let the way to a shop across from the prison and bought Mark a pair of dark glasses and a cap with a visor. "Put these on," he commanded. "You are no use if you are blind. Now come."

They walked through busy streets. The sky hung dull orange, an eternal sunset. Sweat sprang from Mark's brow and trickled down inside his coveralls. He wished he had shorts. Nearly everyone in town wore them.

They passed grimy shops and open stalls. There were sidewalk displays of goods for sale, nearly all crudely made or Navy surplus or black-marketed goods stolen from CD storerooms. Strange animals pulled carts through the streets and there were no automobiles at all.

A team of horses splashed mud on Ewigfeuer's legs. The fat planter shook his fist at the driver. The teamster ignored him.

"Have you owned horses?" Ewigfeuer demanded.

"No," Mark said. "I hadn't expected to see any here."

"Horses make more horses. Tractors do not," the planter said. "Also, with horses and jackasses you get mules. Better than tractors. Better than the damned stormand beasts. Stormands do not like men." He pointed to one of the unlikely animals. It looked like a cross between a mule and a moose, with wide, splayed feet and a sad look that turned vicious whenever anyone got near it. It was tied to a rail outside one of the shops.

There were more people than Mark had expected. They seemed to divide into three classes. There were those who tended the shops and stalls and who smiled unctuously when the planter passed. Most of those wore white canvass jackets. Then there were others, some with white canvass jackets and some without, who strode purposefully through the muddy streets; and finally there were those who wandered aimlessly or sat on the street corners staring vacantly.

"What are they waiting for?" Mark said. He hadn't meant to say it aloud, but Ewigfeuer heard him.

"They wait to die," the planter said. "*Ja*, they think something else will come to save them. They will find something to steal, maybe, so they live another week, another month, a year even; but they are waiting to die. And they are white men!" This seemed their ultimate crime to Ewigfeuer.

"You might expect this of the blacks," the planter said. "But no, the blacks work, or they go to the bush and live there—not like civilized men, perhaps, but they live. Not these. They wait to die. It was a cruel day when their sentences ended."

"Yeah, sure," Mark said, but he made sure the planter didn't hear him. There was another group sitting on benches near a small open square. They looked as if they had not moved since morning, since the day before, or ever; that when the orange sky fell dark, they would be there yet. Mark mopped his brow with his sleeve. Heat lay across Whiskeytown so that it was an effort to move, but the planter hustled him along the street, his short legs moving rapidly through the mud patches.

"And what happens if I just run?" Mark asked.

Ewigfeuer laughed. "Go ahead. You think they will not catch you? Where will you go? You have no papers. Perhaps you buy some if you have money. Perhaps what you buy is not good enough. And when they catch you, it is not to my nice farm they send you. It will be to some awful place. Run, I will not chase you. I am too old and too fat."

Mark shrugged and walked along with Ewigfeuer. He noticed that for all his careless manner, the fat man did not let Mark get behind him.

They rounded a corner and came to a large empty space. A helicopter stood at the near edge. There were others in the lot. A white jacketed man with a rifle sat under an umbrella watching them. Ewigfeuer threw the man some money and climbed into the nearest chopper.

He strapped himself in and waited for Mark to do the same. Then he used the radio.

"Weather service, Ewigfeuer 351." Ewigfeuer listened, nodded in satisfaction, and gunned the engines. The helicopter lifted them high above the city.

Whiskeytown was an ugly sprawl across a plateau. The broad streets of Tanith's capital lay on another low hill beyond it. Both hills rose directly out of the jungle. When they were higher, Mark could see that the plateau was part of a ridge on a peninsula; the sea around it was green with yellow streaks. The buildings on the other hill looked cleaner and better made than those in Whiskeytown. In the distance was a large square surrounded by buildings taller than the others.

"Government House," Ewigfeuer shouted above the engine roar. "Where the governor dreams up new ways to make it impossible for honest planters to make a profit."

Beyond the town were brown hills rising above ugly green jungles. Hours later there was no change— jungle to the right and the green and yellow sea to the left. Mark had seen no roads and only a few houses; all of those were in clusters, low adobe buildings atop low brown hills. "Is the whole planet jungle?" he asked.

"*Ja*, jungles, marshes, bad stuff. People can live in the hills. Below is green hell. Weem's beast, killer things like tortoises, crocodiles so big you don't believe them and they run faster than you. Nobody runs far in that."

A perfect prison, Mark thought. He stared out at the sea. There were boats out there. Ewigfeuer followed his gaze and laughed.

"Some damn fools try to make a few credits fishing. Maybe smart at that, they get killed fast, they don't wait for tax farmers to take everything they make. You heard of Loch Ness monster? On Tanith we got something makes Earth nessies look like an earthworm."

They flew over another cluster of adobe buildings. Ewigfeuer used the radio to talk to the people below. They spoke a language Mark didn't know. It didn't seem like German, but he wasn't sure. Then they crossed another seemingly endless stretch of jungle. Finally a new group of buildings was in sight ahead.

The plantation was no different from the others they had seen. There was a cluster of brown adobe buildings around one larger whitewashed wooden house at the very top of the hill. Cultivated fields lay around that on smaller hills. The fields blended into jungle at the edges. Men were working in the fields.

It would be easy to run away, Mark though. Too easy. It must be stupid to try, or there would be fences. Wait, he thought. Wait and learn. I owe nothing. To anyone. Wait for a chance—

—a chance for what? He pushed the thought away.

The foreman was tall and crudely handsome. He wore dirty white shorts and a sun helmet, and there was a pistol buckled on his belt.

"You look after this one, *ja*," Ewigfeuer said. "One of the governor's pets. They say he has brains enough to make supervisor. We will see. Mark Fuller, three years."

"Yes, sir. Come on, Mark Fuller, three years."

The foreman turned and walked away. After a moment Mark followed. They went past rammed earth buildings and across a sea of mud. The buildings had been sprayed with some kind of plastic and shone dully. "You'll need boots," the foreman said. "And a new outfit. I'm Curt Morgan. Get along with me and you'll be happy. Cross me and you're in trouble. Got that?"

"Yes, sir."

"You don't call me sir unless I tell you to. Right now you call me Curt. If you need help, ask me. Maybe I can give you good advice. If it don't cost me much, I will." They reached a rectangular one-story building like the others. "This'll be your bunkie."

The inside was a long room with places for thirty men. Each place had a bunk, a locker and an area two meters by three of clear space. After the ship, it seemed palatial. The inside walls were sprayed with the same plastic material as the outside; it kept insects from living in the dirt walls. Some of the men had cheap pictures hung above their bunks: pinups, mostly, but one had the Virgin of Guadalupe, and in one corner area there were charcoal sketches of men and women working, and an unfinished oil painting.

There were a dozen men in the room. Some were sprawled on their bunks. One was knitting something elaborate, and a small group at the end were playing cards. One of the card players, a small ferret-faced man, left the game.

"Your new man," Curt said. "Mark Fuller, three years. Fuller, this is your bunkie leader. His name is Lewis. Lew, get the kid bunked and out of those prison slops."

"Sure, Curt." Lewis eyed Mark carefully. "About the right size for Jose's old outfit. The gear's all clean."

"Want to do that?" Curt asked. "Save you some money."

Mark stared helplessly.

The two men laughed. "You better give him the word, Lew," Curt Morgan said. "Fuller, I'd take him up on the gear. Let me know what he charges you, right? He won't squeeze you too bad." There was laughter from the other men in the bunkie as the foreman left.

Lewis pointed out a bunk in the center. "Jose was there, kid. Left his whole outfit when he took the green way out. Give you the whole lot for, uh, fifty credits."

And now what? Mark wondered. Best not to show him I've got any money. "I don't have that much—"

"Hell, you sign a chit for it," Lewis said. "The old man pays a credit a day and found."

"Who do I get a chit from?"

"You get it from me." Lewis narrowed watery eyes. They looked enormous through his thick glasses. "You thinking about something, kid? You don't want to try it."

"I'm not trying anything. I just don't understand—"

"Sure. You just remember I'm in charge. Anybody skips out, I get their gear. Me. Nobody else. Jose had a good outfit, worth fifty credits easy—"

"Bullshit," one of the cardplayers said. "Not worth more'n thirty and you know it."

"Shut up. Sure, you could do better in Whiskeytown, but not here. Look, Morgan said take care of you. I'll sell you the gear for forty. Deal?"

"Sure."

Lewis gave him a broad smile. "You'll get by, kid. Here's your key." He handed Mark a magnokey and went back to the card game.

Mark wondered who had copies. It wasn't something you could duplicate without special equipment; the magnetic spots had to be in just the right places. Ewigfeuer would have one, of course. Who else? No use worrying about it.

He inspected his new possessions. Two pairs of shorts. Tee shirts, underwear, socks, all made of some synthetic. Comb, razor and blades. Soap. Used toothbrush. Mark scowled at it, then laughed to himself. No point in being squeamish.

Some of the clothes were dirty. Others seemed clean, but Mark decided he would have to wash them all. Not now, though. He tucked his money into the toe of a sock and threw the rest of his clothes on top of it, then locked the whole works into the locker. He wondered what he should do with the money; he had nearly three hundred credits, ten month's wages at a credit a day—enough to be killed for.

It bothered him all the way to the shower, but after that, the unlimited water, new bar of soap, and a good razor were such pleasures that he didn't think about anything else.

# VI

The borshite plant resembles an artichoke in appearance: tall, spiky leaves rising from a central crown, with one flowerbearing stalk jutting upward to a height of a meter and a half. It is propagated by bulbs; in spring the previous year's crop is dug up and the delicate bulbs carefully separated, then each replanted. Weeds grow in abundance and must be pulled out by hand. The jungle constantly grows inward to reclaim the high ground that men cultivate. Herbivores eat the crops unless the fields are patrolled.

Mark learned that and more within a week. The work was difficult and the weather was hot, but neither was unbearable. The rumors were true: compared to most places you could be sent, Ewigfeuer's plantation was a country club. Convicts schemed to get there. Ewigfeuer demanded hard work, but he was fair.

That made it all the more depressing for Mark. If this was the easy way to do time, what horrors waited if he made a mistake? Ewigfeuer held transfer as his ultimate threat, and Mark found himself looking for ways to keep his master pleased. He disgusted himself—but there was nothing else to do.

He had never been more alone. He had nothing in common with the other men. His jokes were never funny. He had no interest in their stories. He learned to play poker so well that he was resented when he played. They didn't want a tight player who could take their money. Once he was accused of cheating and although everyone knew he hadn't, he was beaten and his winnings taken. After that he avoided the games.

The work occupied only his hands, not his mind. There were no veedisk readers in the barracks. A few convicts had small radios but the only station they could tune in played nothing but sad country western music. Mark shuddered at the thought of getting to like it.

There was little to do but brood. I wanted power, he thought. We were playing at it. A game. But the police weren't playing, and now I've become a slave. When I get back, I'll know more of how this game is played. I'll show them.

But he knew he wouldn't, not really. He was learning nothing here.

Some of the convicts spent their entire days and nights stoned into tranquility. Borshite plants were the source of borloi, and half the Citizens of the United States depended on borloi to get through each day; the government supplied it to them, and any government that failed in the shipments would not last long. It worked as well on Tanith, and Herr Ewigfeuer was generous with both pipes and borloi. You could be stoned for half a credit a day. Mark tried that route, but he did not like what it did to him. They were stealing three years of his life, but he wouldn't cooperate and make it easier.

His college friends had talked a lot about the dignity of labor. Mark didn't find it dignified at all. Why

not get stoned and stay that way? What am I doing
that's important? Why not go out of being and get it
over? Let the routine wash over me, drown in it—

There were frequent fights. They had rules. If a
man got hurt so that he couldn't work, both he and
the man he fought with had to make up the lost work
time. It tended to keep the injuries down and dis-
couraged broken bones. Whenever there was a fight,
everyone turned out to watch.

It gave Mark time to himself. He didn't like being
alone, but he didn't like watching fights, especially
since he might be drawn into one himself—

The men shouted encouragement to the fighters.
Mark lay on his bunk. He had liquor but didn't want
to drink. He kept thinking about taking a drink, just
one, it will help me get to sleep—and you know
what you're doing to yourself—and why not?

The man was small and elderly. Mark knew he
lived in quarters near the big house. He came into
the bunkie and glanced around. The lights had not
been turned on, and he failed to see Mark. He
looked furtively about again, then stooped to try
locker lids, looking for one that was open. He reached
Mark's locker, opened it, and felt inside. His hand
found cigarettes and the bottle—

He felt or heard Mark and looked up. "Uh, good
evening."

"Good evening." The man seemed cool enough,
although he risked the usual punishments men mete
out to thieves in barracks.

"Are you bent on calling your mates?" The watery
eyes darted around looking for an escape. "I don't
seem to have any defense."

"If you did have one, what would it be?"

"When you are as old as I am and in for life, you

take what you can. I am an alcoholic, and I steal to buy drink."

"Why not smoke borloi?"

"It does little for me." The old man's hands were shaking. He looked lovingly at the bottle of gin that he'd taken from Mark's locker.

"Oh, hell, have a drink," Mark said.

"Thank you." He drank eagerly, in gulps.

Mark retrieved his bottle. "I don't see you in the fields."

"No. I work with the accounts. Herr Ewigfeuer has been kind enough to keep me, but not so kind as to pay enough to—"

"If you will keep the work records, you could sell favors."

"Certainly. For a time. Until I was caught. And then what? It is not much of a life that I have, but I want to keep it." He stood for a moment. "Surprising, isn't it? But I do."

"You talk rather strangely," Mark said.

"The stigmata of education. You see Richard Henry Tappinger, Ph.D., generally called Taps. Formerly holder of the Bates Chair of History and Sociology at Yale University."

"And why are you on Tanith?" Prisoners do not ask that question, but Mark could do as he liked. He held the man's life in his hands: a word, a call, and the others would amuse themselves with Tappinger. And why don't I call them? Mark shuddered at the notion, but it didn't quite leave his consciousness.

Tappinger didn't seem annoyed. "Liquor, young girls, their lovers, and an old fool are an explosive combination. You don't mind if I am more specific? I spend a good part of my life being ashamed of myself. Could I have another drink?"

"I suppose."

"You have the stigmata about you as well. You were a student?"

"Not for long."

"But worthy of education. And generous as well. Your name is Fuller. I have the records, and I recall your case."

The fight outside ground to a close, and the men came back into the barracks. Lewis was carrying an unconscious man to the showers. He handed him over to others when he saw Tappinger.

"You sneaky bastard, I told you what'd happen if I found you in my bunkie! What'd he steal, Fuller?"

"Nothing. I gave him a drink."

"Yeah? Well, keep him out of here. You want to talk to him, you do it outside."

"Right." Mark took his bottle and followed Tappinger out. It was hot inside and the men were talking about the fight. Mark followed Tappinger across the quad. They stayed away from the women's barracks. Mark had no friends in there and couldn't afford any other kind of visit—at least not very often, and he was always disturbed afterwards. None of the women seemed attractive or to care about themselves.

"So. The two outcasts gather together," Tappinger said. "Two pink monkeys among the browns."

"Maybe I should resent that."

"Why? Do you have much in common with them? Or do you resent the implication that you have more in common with me?"

"I don't know. I don't know anything. I'm just passing time. Waiting until this is over."

"And what will you do then?"

They found a place to sit. The local insects didn't bother them; the taste was wrong. There was a faint breeze from the west. The jungle noises came with it, snorts and grunts and weird calls.

"What can I do?" Mark asked. "Get back to Earth and—"

"You will never get back to Earth," Tappinger said. "Or if you do, you will be one of the first ever. Unless you have someone to buy your passage?"

"That's expensive."

"Precisely."

"But they're supposed to take us back!" Mark felt all his carefully built defenses begin to crumble. He lived for the end of the three years—and now—

"The regulations say so, and the convicts talk about going home, but it does not happen. Earth does not want rebels. It would disturb the comfortable life most have. No, you are unlikely to leave here, and if you do ship out, it will be to another colony. Unless you are very rich."

So I am here forever. "So what else is there? What do ex-cons do here?"

Tappinger shrugged. "Sign up as laborers. Start their own plantations. Go into government service. Start a small business. You see Tanith as a slave world, which it is, but it will not always be that. Some of you, people like you, will build it into something else, something better or worse, but certainly different."

"Yeah. Sure. The Junior Pioneers have arrived."

"What do you think happens to involuntary colonists?" Tappinger asked. "Or did you never think of them? Most people on Earth don't look very hard at the price of keeping their wealth and their clean air and clean oceans. But the only difference between you and someone shipped by BuRelock is that you came in a slightly more comfortable ship, and you will put in three years here before they turn you out to fend for yourself. Yes, I definitely suggest the government services for you. You could rise quite high."

"Work for those slaving bastards? I'd rather starve!"

"No, you wouldn't. Nor would many others. It is easier to say that than to do it."

Mark stared into the darkness.

"Why so grim? There are opportunities here. The new governor is trying to reform some of the abuses. Of course he is caught in the system just as we are. He must export his quota of borloi and miracle drugs, and pay the taxes demanded of him. He must keep up production. The Navy demands it."

"The Navy?"

Tappinger smiled in the dark. "You would be surprised at just how much of the CD Navy's operations are paid for by the profits from the Tanith drug trade."

"It doesn't surprise me at all. Thieves. Bastards. But it's stupid. A treadmill, with prisons to pay for themselves and the damned fleet—"

"Neither stupid nor new. The Soviets have done it for nearly two hundred years, with the proceeds of labor camps paying for the secret police. And our tax farming scheme is even older. It dates back to old Rome. Profits from other planets support BuRelock. Tanith supports the Navy."

"Damn the Navy."

"Ah, no, don't do that. Bless it instead. Without the CD Fleet, the Earth governments would be at each other's throats in a moment. They very nearly are now. And since they won't pay for the Navy, and the Navy is very much needed to keep peace on Earth, why, we must continue to work. See what a noble task we perform as we weed the borloi fields?"

Unbearably hot spring became intolerably hot summer, and the work decreased steadily. The borshite plants were nearly as high as a man's waist and were able to defend themselves against most weeds and predators. The fields needed watching but little else.

To compensate for the easier work, the weather was sticky hot, with warm fog rolling in from the coast. The skies turned from orange to dull gray. Twice the plantations and fields were lashed by hurricanes. The borshite plants lay flattened, but soon recovered; and after each hurricane came a few brief hours of clear skies when Mark could see the stars.

With summer came easy sex. Men and women could visit in the evenings, and with suitable financial arrangements with bunkie leaders, all night. The pressures of the barracks eased. Mark found the easier work more attractive than the women. When he couldn't stand it any longer, he'd pay for a few minutes of frantic relief, then try not to think about sex for as long as he could.

His duties were simple. Crownears, muskrat-sized animals that resembled large shrews, would eat unprotected borshite plants. They had to be driven away. They were stupid animals, and ravenous, but not very dangerous unless a swarm of them could catch a man mired down in the mud. A man with a spear could keep them out of the crops.

There were other animals to watch for. Weem's Beast, named for the first man to survive a meeting with one, was the worst. The crownears were its natural prey, but it would attack almost anything that moved. Weem's Beast looked like a mole but was over a meter long. Instead of a prehensile snout, it had a fully articulated grasping member with talons and pseudo-eyes. Man approached holes very carefully on Tanith; the Beast was fond of lying just below the surface and came out with astonishing speed.

It wouldn't usually leave the jungle to attack a man on high ground.

Mark patrolled the fields, and Curt Morgan made rounds on horseback. In the afternoons Morgan would sit with Mark and share his beer ration, and the cold beer and lack of work was almost enough to make life worth living again.

Sometimes there was a break in the weather, and a cooler breeze would blow across the fields. Mark sat with his back to a tree, enjoying the comparatively cool day, drinking his beer ration. Morgan sat next to him.

"Curt, what will you do when you finish your sentence?" Mark asked.

"Finished two years ago. Two Tanith, three Earth."

"Then why are you still here?"

Morgan shrugged. "What else do I know how to do? I'm saving some money; one day I'll have a place of my own." He shifted his position and fired his carbine toward the jungle. "I swear them things get more nerve every summer. This is all I know. I can't save enough to buy into the tax farm syndicate."

"Could you squeeze people that way?"

"If I had to. Them or me. Tax collectors get rich."

"Sure. Jesus, there's no goddamn hope for anything, is there? The whole deck's stacked." Mark finished his beer.

"Where isn't it?" Morgan demanded. "You think it's tough now, you ought to have been here before the new governor came. Place they stuck me—my sweet lord, they worked us! Charged for everything we ate or wore, and you open your mouth, it's another month on your sentence. Enough to drive a man into the green."

"Uh—Curt—are there—"

"Don't get ideas. I'd hate to take the dogs and

come find you. Find your corpse, more likely. Yeah, there's men out in the green. Live like rats. I'd rather be under sentence again than live like the Free Staters."

The thought excited Mark. A Free State! It would have to be like the places Shirley and her friends had talked about, with equality, and there'd be no tax farmers in a free society. He thought of the needs of free men. They would live hard and be poor because they were fugitives, but they would be free! He built the Free State in his imagination until it was more real than Ewigfeuer's plantation.

The next day the crownears were very active, and Curt Morgan brought another worker to Mark's field. They rode up together on the big Percheron horses brought as frozen embryos from Earth and repeatedly bred for even wider feet to keep them above the eternal mud. The newcomer was a girl. Mark had seen her before, but never met her.

"Brought you a treat," Curt said. "This is Juanita. Juanny, if this clown gives you trouble, I'll break him in half. Be back in an hour. Got your trumpet?"

Mark indicated the instrument.

"Keep it handy. Them things are restless out there. I think there's a croc around. And porkers. Keep your eyes open." Curt rode off toward the next field.

Mark stood in embarrassed silence. The girl was younger than Mark, and sweaty. Her hair hung down in loose blonde strings. Her eyes had dark circles under them, and her face was dirty. She was built more like a wiry boy than a girl. She was also the most beautiful girl he'd ever seen.

"Hi," Mark said. He cursed himself. Shyness went with civilization, not a prison!

"Hi yourself. You're in Lewis's bunkie."

"Yes. I haven't seen you before. Except at Mass."

Each month a priest of the Ecumenical Church came to the plantation. Mark had never attended services, but he'd watched idly from a distance.

"Usually work in the big house. Sure hot, isn't it?"

He agreed it was hot and was lost again. What should I say? "You're lovely" is obvious, even if I do think it's true. "Let's go talk to your bunkie leader" isn't too good an idea even if it's what I want to say. Besides, if she lives in the big house, she won't have one. "How long do you have?"

"Another two. Until I'm nineteen. They still run sentences on Earth time. I'm eleven, really." There was more silence. "You don't talk much, do you?"

"I don't know what to say. I'm sorry—"

"It's okay. Most of the men jabber away like porshons. Trying to talk me into something, you know?"

"Oh."

"Yeah. But I never have. I'm a member of the Church. Confirmed and everything." She looked at him and grinned impishly. "So that makes me a dumb hymn singer, and what's left to talk about?"

"I remember wishing I was you," Mark said. He laughed. "Not quite what I meant to say. I mean, I watched you at Masses. You looked happy. Like you had something to live for."

"Well, of course. We all have something to live for. Must have, people sure try hard to stay alive. When I get out of here, I'm going to ask the padre to let me help him. Be a nun, maybe."

"Don't you want to marry?"

"Who? A Con? That's what my mother did, and look. I got 'apprenticed' until I was nineteen Earth years old because I was born to convicts. No kids of mine'll have that happen to 'em!"

"You could marry a free man."

"They're all pretty old by the time they finish. And not worth much. To themselves or anybody else. You proposin' to me?"

He laughed and she laughed with him, and the afternoon was more pleasant than any he could remember since leaving Earth.

"I was lucky," she told him. "Old man Ewigfeuer traded for me. Place I was born on, the planter'd be selling tickets for me now." She stared at the dirt. "I've seen girls they did that with. They don't like themselves much after a while."

They heard the shrill trumpets in other fields. Mark scanned the jungle in front of him. Nothing moved. Juanita continued to talk. She asked him about Earth. "It's hard to think about that place," she said. "I hear people live all bunched up."

He told her about cities. "There are twenty million people in the city I come from." He told her of the concrete Welfare Islands at the edges of the cities.

She shuddered. "I'd rather live on Tanith than like that. It's a wonder all the people on Earth don't burn it down and live in the swamps."

Evening came sooner than he expected. After supper he fell into an introspective mood. He hadn't wanted a day to last for a long time. It's silly to think this way, he told himself.

But he was twenty years old, she was nearly seventeen, and there wasn't anyone else to think about. That night he dreamed about her.

He saw her often as the summer wore on. She had no education, and Mark began teaching her to read. He scratched letters in the ground and used some of his money to buy lurid adventure stories. He had no access to veedisk screens, and the only printed works available in the barracks were sex magazines and adventure novels printed on paper so cheap that it soon went limp in the damp Tanith heat.

Juanita learned quickly. She seemed to enjoy Mark's company and often arranged to be assigned to the same field that he was. They talked about everything: Earth, and how it wasn't covered with swamps. He told her of personal fliers in blue skies, and sailing on the Pacific, and the island coves he'd explored. She thought he was making most of it up.

Their only quarrels came when he complained of how unfair life was. She laughed at him. "I was born with a sentence," she told him. "You lived in a fine house and had your own 'copter and a boat, and you went to school. If I'm not whining, why should you, Mr. Taxpayer?"

He wanted to tell her she was unfair too, but stopped himself. Instead he told her of smog and polluted waters, and sprawling cities. "They've got the pollution licked, though," he said. "And the population's going down. What with the licensing, and BuRelock—"

She said nothing, and Mark couldn't finish the sentence. Juanita stared at the empty jungles. "Wish I could see a blue sky some day. I can't even imagine that, so you must be tellin' the truth."

He did not often see her in the evenings. She kept to herself or worked in the big house. Sometimes, though, she would walk with Curt Morgan or sit with him on the porch of the big house, and when she did, Mark would buy a bottle of gin and find Tappinger. It was no good being alone then.

The old man would deliver long lectures in a dry monotone that nearly put Mark to sleep, but then he'd ask questions that upset any view of the universe that Mark had ever had.

"You might make a passable sociologist some day," Tappinger said. "Ah, well, they say the best university is a log with a student at one end and a professor at the other. I doubt they had me in mind, but we have that, anyway."

"All I seem to learn is that things are rotten. Everything's set up wrong," Mark said.

Tappinger shook his head. "There has never been a society in which someone did not think there had to be a better deal—for himself. The trick is to see that those who want a better way enough to do something about it can either rise within the system or are rendered harmless by it. Which, of course, Earth does—warriors join the Navy. Malcontents are shipped to the colonies. The cycle is closed. Drugs for the Citizens, privileges for the taxpayers, peace for all thanks to the Fleet—and slavery for malcontents. Or death. The colonies use up people."

"I guess it's stable, then."

"Hardly. If Earth does not destroy herself—and from the rumors I hear, the nations are at each other's throats despite all the Navy can do—why, they have built a pressure cooker out here that will one day destroy the old home world. Look at what we have. Fortune hunters, adventurers, criminals, rebels—and all selected for survival abilities. The lid cannot stay on."

They saw Juanita and Curt Morgan walking around the big house, and Mark winced. Juanita had grown during the summer. Now, with her hair combed and in clean clothes, she was so lovely that it hurt to look at her. Taps smiled. "I see my star pupil has found another interest. Cheer up, lad, when you finish here, you will find employment. You can have your pick of convict girls. Rent them, or buy one outright."

"I hate slavery!"

Taps shrugged. "As you should. Although you might be surprised what men who say that will do when given the chance. But calm yourself, I meant buy a wife, not a whore."

"But damn it, you don't buy wives! Women aren't things!"

Tappinger smiled softly. "I tend to forget just what a blow it is to you young people. You expect everything to be as it was on Earth. Yet you are here because you were not satisfied with your world."

"It was rotten."

"Possibly. But you had to search for the rot. Here you cannot avoid it."

On such nights it took Mark a long time to get to sleep.

# VII

The harvest season was approaching. The borshite plants stood in full flower, dull-red splashes against brown hills and green jungles, and the field buzzed with insects. Nature had solved the problem of propagation without inbreeding on Tanith and fifty other worlds in the same way as on Earth.

The buzzing insects attracted insectivores, and predators chased those; close to harvest time there was little work, but the fields had to be watched constantly. Once again house and processing-shed workers joined the field hands, and Mark had many days with Juanita.

She was slowly driving him insane. He knew she couldn't be as naive as she pretended to be. She had to know how he felt and what he wanted to do, but she gave him no opportunities.

Sometimes he was sure she was teasing him. "Why don't you ever come to see me in the evenings?" she asked one day.

"You know why. Curt is always there."

"Well, sure, but he don't—doesn't own my contract. 'Course, if you're scared of him—"

"You're bloody right I'm scared of him. He could

74

fold me up for glue. Not to mention what happens when the foreman's mad at a con. Besides, I thought you liked him."

"Sure. So what?"

"He told me he was going to marry you one day."

"He tells everybody that. He never told me, though."

Mark noted glumly that she'd stopped talking about becoming a nun.

"Of course, Curt's the only man who even says he's going to—Mark, *look out!*"

Mark saw a blur at the edge of his vision and whirled with his spear. Something was charging toward him. "Get behind me and run!" he shouted. "Keep me in line with it and get out of here."

She moved behind him and he heard her trumpet blare, but she wasn't running. Mark had no more time to think about her. The animal was nearly a meter and a half long, built square on thick legs and splayed feet. The snout resembled an earth warthog's, with four upthrusting tusks, and it had a thin tail that lashed as it ran.

"Porker," Juanita said softly. She was just behind him. "Sometimes they'll charge a man. Like this. Don't get it excited, maybe it'll go away."

Mark was perfectly willing to let the thing alone. It looked as if it weighed as much as he did. Its broad feet and small claws gave it a better footing than hobnails would give a man. It circled them warily at a distance of three meters. Mark turned carefully to keep facing it. He held the spear aimed at its throat. "I told you to get out of here," Mark said.

"Sure. There's usually two of those things." She spoke very softly. "I'm scared to blow this trumpet again. Wish Curt would get here with his gun." As she spoke, they heard gunshots. They sounded very far away.

"Mark," Juanita whispered urgently. "There is another one. I'm getting back to back with you."

"All right." He didn't dare look away from the beast in front of him. What did it want? It moved slowly toward him, halting just beyond the thrusting range of the spear. Then it dashed forward, screaming a sound that could never have come from an Earthly pig.

Mark jabbed at it with his spear. It flinched from the point and ran past. Mark turned to follow it and saw the other beast advancing on Juanita. She had slipped in the mud and was down, trying frantically to get to her feet, and the porker was running toward her.

Mark gave an animal scream of pure fury. He slid in the mud but kept his feet and charged forward, screaming again as he stabbed with his spear and felt it slip into the thick hide. The porker shoved against him, and Mark fell into the mud. He desperately held the spear, but the beast walked steadily forward. The point went through the hide on the back, and came out again, the shaft sliding between skin and meat, and the impaled animal advancing inexorably up the shaft. The tusks neared his manhood. Mark heard himself whimpering in fear. "I can't hold him!" he shouted. "Run!"

She didn't run. She got to her feet and shoved her spear down the snarling throat, then thrust forward, forcing the head toward the mud. Mark scrambled to his feet. He looked wildly around for the other animal. It was nowhere in sight, but the pinned porker snarled horribly.

"Mark, honey, take that spear of yours out of him

while I hold him," Juanita shouted. "I can't hold long—quick, now."

Mark shook himself out of the trembling fear that paralyzed him. The tusks were moving wickedly. They were nowhere near him, but he could still feel them tearing at his groin.

"Please, honey," Juanita said.

He tugged at the spear, but it wouldn't come free, so he thrust it forward, then ran behind the animal to pull the spear through the loose skin on the porker's back. The shaft came through bloody. His hands slipped but he held the spear and thrust it into the animal, thrust again and again, stabbing in insane fury and shouting, "Die, die, die!"

Morgan didn't come for another half an hour. When he galloped up, they were standing with their arms around each other. Juanita moved slowly away from Mark when Morgan dismounted, but she looked possessively at him.

"That way now?" Morgan asked.

She didn't answer.

"There was a herd of those things in the next field over," Curt said. His voice was apologetic. "Killed three men and a woman. I came as quick as I could."

"Mark killed this one."

"She did. It would have had me—"

"Hold on," Curt said.

"It walked right up the spear," Mark said.

"I've seen 'em do that, all right." Morgan seemed to be choosing his words very carefully. "You two will have to stay on here for awhile. We've lost four hands, and—"

"We'll be all right," Juanita said.

"Yeah." Morgan went back to his mount. "Yeah, I guess you will." He rode off quickly.

Tradition gave Mark and Juanita the carcass, and they feasted with their friends that night. Afterwards Mark and Juanita walked away from the barracks area, and they were gone for a long time.

"Taps, what the hell am I going to do?" Mark demanded. They were outside, in the unexpected cool of a late summer evening. Mark had thought he would never be cool again; now it was almost harvest time. The fall and winter would be short, but Tanith was almost comfortable during those months.

"What is the problem?"

"She's pregnant."

"Hardly surprising. Nor the end of the world. There are many ways to—"

"No. She won't even talk about it. Says it's murder. It's that damned padre. Goddamn church, no wonder they bring that joker around. Makes the slaves contented."

"This is hardly the only activity of the church, but it does have that effect. Well, what is it to you? As you have often pointed out, you have no responsibilities. And certainly you have no legal obligations in this case."

"That's my kid! And she's my—I mean, damn it, I can't just—"

Tappinger smiled grimly. "I remind you that conscience and a sense of ethics are expensive luxuries. But if you are determined to burden yourself with them, let us review your alternatives.

"You can ask Ewigfeuer for permission to marry her. It is likely to be granted. The new governor has ended the mandatory so-called apprenticeship for children born to convicts after next year. Your sentence is not all that long. When it ends, you will be free—"

"To do what? I saw the time-expired men in Whiskeytown."

"There are jobs. There is a whole planetary economy to be built."

"Yeah. Sure. Sweat my balls off for some storekeeper. Or work like Curt Morgan, sweating cons."

Tappinger shrugged. "There are alternatives. Civil service. Or learn the business yourself and become a planter. There is always financing available for those who can produce."

"I'd still be a slaver. I want out of the system. Out of the whole damned thing!"

Tappinger sighed and lifted the bottle to drink. He paused to say, "There are many things we all want. So what?" Then he drained the pint.

"There's another way," Mark said. "A way out of all this."

Tappinger looked up quickly. "Don't even think it! Mark, the Free State you believe in is no more than a dream. The reality is much less, no more than a gang of lawless men who live like animals off what they can steal. Lawless. Men cannot live without laws."

I can damned well live without the kind of laws they have here, Mark thought. And of course they steal. Why shouldn't they? How else can they live?

"And it is unlikely to last in any event. The governor has brought in a regiment of mercenaries to deal with the Free State."

About what I'd expect, Mark thought. "Why not CD Marines?"

Tappinger shook his head. "A complex issue. The simplest answer is financial. There are not enough CD forces to keep the peace everywhere because the Grand Senate will not appropriate enough money."

"But you said Tanith drug profits go to the Navy—"

"In large part they do. And since that is a lot of money, do you not think others want some of it? The Grand Senate itself envies the Navy's share, for it is money the Senate doesn't control. The Senate sends the Navy anywhere but Tanith, so the planters are squeezed again, to pay for their protection."

And that's fine with me, Mark thought. "Mercenaries can't be much use. They'd rather lie around in barracks and collect their pay." His teachers had told him that.

"Have you ever known any?"

"No, of course not. Look, Taps, I'm tired. I think I better get to bed." He turned and left the old man. To hell with him, Mark thought. Old man, old woman, that's what he is. Not enough guts to get away from here and strike out on his own.

Well, that's fine for him. But I've got bigger things in mind.

The harvest began at the end of the hurricane season. The borshite pods formed and were cut, and the sticky sap collected. The sap was boiled, skimmed, boiled again until it was reduced to a tiny fraction of the bulky plants they had worked all summer to guard.

And Ewigfeuer collapsed on the steps of the big house. Morgan flew him to the Lederle hospital. Curt returned with a young man: Ewigfeuer's son, on leave from his administrative post in the city.

"That old bastard wants to see you outside," Lewis said.

Mark sighed. He was tired from a long day in the fields. He was also tired of Tappinger's eternal lectures on the horrors of the Free State. Still, the man was his only friend. Mark took his bottle and went outside.

Tappinger seized the bottle eagerly. He downed several swallows. His hands shook. "Come with me," he whispered.

Mark followed in confusion. Taps led the way to the shadows near the big house. Juanita was there.

"Mark, honey, I'm scared."

Tappinger took another drink. "The Ewigfeuer boy is trying to raise money," he said. "He storms through the house complaining of all the useless people his father keeps on, and shouts that his father is ruining himself. The hospital bills are very high, it seems. And this place is heavily in debt. He has been selling contracts. He sold hers. For nearly two thousand credits."

"Sold?" Mark said stupidly. "But she has less than two years to go!"

"Yes," Taps said. "There is only one way a planter could expect to make that much back from the purchase of a young and pretty girl."

"God damn them," Mark said. "All right. We've got to get out of here."

"No," Tappinger said. "I've told you why. No, I have a better way. I can forge the old man's signature to a permission form. You can marry Juanita. The forgery will be discovered, but by then—"

"No," Mark said. "Do you think I'll stay to be part of this system? A free society will need good people."

"Mark, please," Tappinger said. "Believe me, it is not what you think it is! How can you live in a place with no rules, you with your ideas of what is fair and what is—"

"Crap. From now on, I take care of myself. And my woman and my child. We're wasting time." He moved toward the stables. Juanita followed.

"Mark, you do not understand," Tappinger protested.

"Shut up. I have to find the guard."

"He's right behind you." Morgan's voice was low and grim. "Don't do anything funny, Mark."

"Where did you come from?"

"I've been watching you for ten minutes. Did you think you could get up to the big house without being seen? You damned fool. I ought to let you go into the green and get killed. But you can't go alone—no, you have to take Juanny with you. I thought you had more sense. We haven't used the whipping post here for a year, but a couple of dozen might wake you up to—" Morgan started to turn as something moved behind him. Then he crumpled. Juanita hit him again with a billet of wood. Morgan fell to the ground.

"I hope he'll be all right," Juanita said. "When he wakes up, Taps, please tell him why we had to run off."

"Yeah, take care of him," Mark said. He was busy stripping the weapons belt from Morgan. Mark noted the compass and grinned.

"You're a fool," Tappinger said. "Men like Curt Morgan take care of themselves. It's people like you that need help."

Tappinger was still talking, but Mark paid no attention. He broke the lock on the stable and then opened the storage room inside. He found canteens in the harness room. There was also a plastic can of kerosene. Mark and Juanita saddled two horses. They led them out to the edge of the compound. Tappinger stood by the broken stable door.

They looked back for a second, then waved and rode into the jungle. Before they were gone, Tappinger had finished the last of Mark's gin.

They fled southward. Every sound seemed to be Morgan and a chase party following with dogs. Then there were the nameless sounds of the jungle. The horses were as frightened as they were.

In the morning they found a small clump of brown grass, a minuscule clearing of high ground. They did not dare make a fire, and they had only some biscuit and grain to eat. A Weem's Beast charged out of a small clump of trees near the top of the clearing, and Mark shot it, wasting ammunition by firing again and again until he was certain that it was dead. They then were too afraid to stay and had to move on.

They kept moving southward. Mark had overheard convicts talking about the Free State. On an arm of the sea, south, in the jungle. It was all he had to direct him. A crocodile menaced them, but they rode past, Mark holding the pistol tightly, while the beast stared at them. It wasn't a real crocodile, of course; but it looked much like the Earthly variety. Parallel evolution, Mark thought. What shape would be better adapted to life in this jungle?

On the eighth day they came to a narrow inlet and followed it to the left, deeper into the jungle, the sea on their right and green hell to the left. It twisted its way along a forgotten river dried by geological shifts a long time before. Tiny streams had bored through the cliff faces on both sides, and plunged thirty meters across etched rock faces into the green froth at the bottom. They were the highest cliffs Mark had seen in his limited travels on Tanith.

At dark on the second day after they found the inlet Mark risked a fire. He shot a crownears and they roasted it. "The worst is over," Mark said. "We're free now. Free."

She crept into his arms. Her face was worried but contented, and it had lines that made her seem older than Mark. "You never asked me," she said.

He smiled. "Will you marry me?"

"Sure."

They laughed together. The jungle seemed very close and the horses were nickering in nervous fear. Mark built up the fire. "Free," he said. He held her tightly, and they were very happy.

# VIII

Lysander set down his fork and turned to his hostess. Ann Hollis Chang looked much more elegant here in the dining room of the governor's private apartments than she had when Lysander had seen her in the governor's office. Her silver grey hair was down in loose waves and held by a bright blue jeweled comb, and her gown was simply cut but clung in ways that flattered her somewhat bony figure. Still there was much of the senior bureaucrat about her. She was attentive to the guests at her end of the table, but she was also thoroughly aware of everything Governor Blaine said at the far end. She had mentioned earlier that her husband was a senior chemist with the Lederle company, and never came to government functions, official or not.

Lysander smiled. "Madame Chang, this roast is excellent."

"Thank you. But the real thanks should go to Mrs. Reilly."

"Oh?" He turned to his right. "Indeed?"

"Not really." Alma Reilly was a small woman, expensively dressed, but her hands were square and competent. Lysander guessed that she was in her mid-forties, a few years younger than her husband. The Reillys had been chemical engineers but were now planters. They held one of the largest and most productive stations. Alma Reilly's gown was sequined and she wore a large opal brooch, but her only ring was a plain gold band. "Actually, our foreman shot the porker three days ago, and we knew the dinner was coming up, and I knew the governor likes marinated porker so—" She laughed. "I know I talk too much."

"No, please go on," Lysander assured her. "Is there much wild game here?"

"More than we like," Alma said. "Henry—our son— had a fight with a Weem's beast last week and he's still in the hospital."

"Oh—"

"Nothing the regenners can't handle, but Henry's furious. He loves riding, and he won't be able to compete this year at all."

"I'm sorry to hear that. I take it you've had no trouble with the rebels, then?"

Alma Reilly glanced nervously up and down the table. "Trouble? We'd hardly have trouble with them, Your Highness. Most of them are our friends."

"Oh. But clearly you're not with them." He looked significantly at Colonel John Christian Falkenberg, who was seated near Governor Blaine at the head of the table.

"No, we've sent our crop in. Chris and I are agreed, Carleton Blaine is the best thing that has happened to Tanith since we got here. But it's not simple. Some of the reforms have been very hard on our friends." She looked across the table at Ursula Gordon. "Not that Governor Blaine wasn't right about many things, you understand. But it's very hard. There's precious little profit to be made on Tanith."

At the mention of profits, Dr. Phon Nol looked up from his plate and nodded. "Little enough before, and now we must make a further investment in— militia," he said. "More than worth the money once the escapees and pirates are killed, but I must say that Colonel Falkenberg's services are more expensive than I had hoped."

Captain Jesus Alana smiled thinly. "I appreciate your difficulties, Dr. Nol, but you of all people on Tanith must understand the economics. Without munitions we'd be useless, and we have to import most of our supplies and just about all our equipment."

"I understand, I sympathize," Nol said. "But permit me not to care much for the expenses."

Both Captains Alana, Jesus and Catherine, laughed at that. "Permit us to dislike them just as much," Catherine said. "I can't imagine the colonel is much happier than you." She looked at Ursula on her right. "That's a very nice gown. From Harrod's?"

"Actually, no. Ly—Prince Lysander bought it for me at a little shop in the garden district. He was looking for something made here."

"Ah, very astute," Dr. Nol said. "Tell me, Your Highness, did you know our governor before you came to Tanith?"

"Not at all. We'd heard about him of course. Seems very dedicated to his work."

"He is that," Hendrik ten Koop said from Alma Reilly's right. "Too dedicated for some."

White-jacketed servants cleared the table and brought an elaborate three-tiered compote of sherbets and ices. After desert they brought crystal decanters of a rose-colored liqueur. Governor Blaine stood to offer the first toast.

"To our guest, Prince Lysander of Sparta. May

there always be friendship between Tanith and Sparta."

That's a bold toast, Lysander thought. Considering that Sparta is sovereign and Tanith isn't. Not yet.

Lysander acknowledged the toast with a bow. "Our thanks. May we always be friends, and your enemies be ours." There was silence for a moment. Lysander looked across the table to smile reassurance at Ursula, then up toward the governor. Colonel Falkenberg caught his eye, and might have smiled. Lysander turned back to his left. "And if I may offer a toast to our charming hostess. Madame Chang."

Hendrik ten Koop laughed aloud. The portly Dutch planter had already drunk four glasses of port, but it hadn't seemed to affect him at all. "Good, good. May I second? To the real governor of Tanith."

"Why, thank you," Mrs. Chang said. "And in response —to the new order on Tanith." She looked significantly at Ursula Gordon. "But I can't quite let Mynheer ten Koop get away with that. To the best governor Tanith will ever have." She raised her glass toward Blaine.

Another moment of silence, even longer than the first. Then Falkenberg lifted his glass. "Well said," Captain Ian Frazer and both Captains Alana instantly lifted theirs. Dr. Nol smiled, a tiny smile at just the corners of his mouth. "If Colonel Falkenberg agrees, then it must be so."

Christopher Reilly was next. "Indeed. Thank you, Dr. Nol." He sipped at his liqueur.

"I see," Hendrik ten Koop said. "I see indeed." He drained his glass in one gulp.

The outside walls of Government House were bleak and fortified, with few windows. The building's roofed verandas all lined its inner walls, which enclosed a large courtyard dotted with fountain pools and crowned with a large illuminated aviary. Sprays of water traced sparkling paths through the multicolored spotlight beams, and the patter of the fountains was punctuated by the occasional cries of the birds.

There were ceiling fans out here as well as inside. Lysander watched a pair of brilliant blue-and-red hens strut in their cage, then turned to the others who had gathered around him at the veranda railing. "I'd thought Tanith was a young planet," Lysander said. "But surely birds are a late stage of evolution?"

"Quite late, Highness," Catherine Alana said. "Even though this planet looks like it's still in the Cretaceous, it's actually in an era beyond Earth's present period."

"Ah. I hadn't known that. And no intelligent life evolved. Not here, not anywhere—"

Ursula smiled. "Except on Earth, of course."

"Sometimes I wonder," Christopher Reilly said. He looked out over the fountains below. "If we're so intelligent, why do we act so stupid?"

"You're not being stupid," Captain Alana said. Her smile faded. "It's those others. They aren't going to win, so why are they making us fight? It will be expensive for everyone." She looked across the veranda where her husband stood with Colonel Falkenberg. "It could be very expensive."

"She ought to know," Beatrice Frazer said. "Catherine is the regiment's chief accountant."

"I see. Captain Alana is in uniform, but you're not, Madame Frazer," Lysander prompted.

"No, I'm a civilian." She laughed. "As much as we have civilians in Falkenberg's Legion. I teach in the regimental schools."

"Are there many women in your regiment?" Ursula asked.

"A fair number if you count the dependents," Beatrice said. "Most of the men are married, so there are nearly as many women as men. I expect Catherine could tell you exactly how many of us are in uniform. Actually, we don't make too strong a distinction between those in ranks and the dependents. We take care of our own."

"Do you fight?" Lysander asked Catherine Alana. He glanced at her holstered pistol.

"I presume you mean the women? Only if we have to. The regiment is organized so that it can take the field without us, and we manage the rear areas, so to speak. Sometimes things don't work the way they're planned." Captain Alana's blue eyes danced. "I should tell you? You've a whole planet to run. Or will have."

"It's not quite cut and dried," Lysander said. "Sparta has a dual monarchy, and the throne is elective in each royal house. Then there's the Senate, and the Council."

"How could they pass you over?" Catherine said.

"Well, it would be pretty stupid, wouldn't it?" Lysander grinned and turned so that he faced her, with his back to the others. "You seem to know everything, Captain. Tell me, please: What *is* all this about a revolt of the planters?"

"I expect you'll find out soon enough," Catherine said. "Very soon, in fact. Here's the governor, and if no one's already told you, he's revived the custom of inviting the menfolk into his office for after-dinner cigars."

Governor Blaine had brought Falkenberg down to join them. Like his officers, Falkenberg wore dress whites. Lysander smiled to himself. He'd already noticed that the colonel and his staff were the only guests wearing white upper garments.

"Your Highness, Colonel Falkenberg has asked me

to provide you transport to his regimental compound tomorrow," Blaine said. "Easy enough to do, if you like."

"Oh, please," Lysander said. "Good of you to invite me, Colonel."

"My pleasure. I'll ask the mess president to come up with something special for dinner. Lunch as well?"

"Certainly, if it's not an inconvenience."

"Not at all."

Blaine turned to Ursula. "Meanwhile, if the ladies would excuse us? Gentlemen, if you'd care to join me in my office, I can offer you genuine Havana cigars. Rolled on Tanith, of course, but the tobacco is imported from Cuba. It'll be another few years before we can grow our own."

"Not too long, I hope," Lysander said. "I confess I've never smoked a genuine Havana. Thank you." He looked to Ursula. "You'll excuse me?"

She glanced nervously around. Beatrice Frazer caught Falkenberg's eye, then smiled at Lysander. "Your Highness, with your permission we'll bore your young lady with tales of life in the regiment."

"Ah. Yes. Thank you." He squeezed Ursula's hand and turned to Blaine. "Governor, I would very much like a taste of your tobacco."

A detailed map swam up on the monitor screen. Blaine pointed at an inlet of the sea. The view zoomed in until Government House Square filled the screen, then zoomed back out to show an area of several hundred kilometers around the city. The screen held the display for a moment, then the view zoomed out once more.

"The last pirates are down here, between us and the southern province," Blaine said. "They call themselves the Free State."

Hendrik ten Koop drained his glass of port and poured another. "Free State. Yes, that's what they called themselves. Last month they killed five of my people and kidnapped three women on my south station. Then they burned what they could not carry away."

"Yes. Well, it shouldn't take Colonel Falkenberg long to root them out." Blaine zoomed the map to an area a few hundred kilometers west of Lederle. "It's the rebel planters who're likely to be more trouble to us all. Most of them are in this area here." He pointed.

"I would not go so far as to call them rebels," Dr. Nol said. He drew delicately on his cigar. "Excellent tobacco. Thank you. Governor, is it wise to think of our friends as rebels?"

"Perhaps not." Blaine looked thoughtful. "Think rebel and drive them to rebellion. Note taken. Still— what should we call them?"

"The opposition?" Christopher Reilly asked.

"Hardly a loyal opposition," Blaine said. "But very well. 'Opposition' it is."

"Your pardon, Governor," Lysander said. "If they're not rebels, what have they done that you're about to send some of the best troops in the galaxy against them?"

"Withheld their crops," Blaine said.

"They won't pay taxes," ten Koop said. "Often I wonder why I do not join them."

"For the same reason I don't," Reilly said. "The Navy will have our crops, or someone else will. Better we keep something than nothing."

"Will they kill all the geese?" ten Koop demanded.

"I expect that'd depend on the goose supply," Falkenberg said carefully. "Fifty geese laying silver eggs might be worth as much as one that lays gold, if the one that lays gold eats too much."

"Now, there's an unsettling notion for you," Christopher Reilly said. "Colonel, I'm very glad it's our side you're on."

"Oh, indeed. I am also," ten Koop said. He turned to Lysander. "I expect this is nothing new for a prince of Sparta. I understand you have rebels there also."

"Unfortunately, yes. I wish things were different."

"So," ten Koop said. "Tell us, Colonel, once you have killed the last of the pirates, what will you do about the—opposition?"

"Are you sure the Legion needs to do anything?" Falkenberg asked. Ten Kook opened his mouth to speak but Falkenberg went on. "They must know just how little military force they can field. No, this is a political problem, gentlemen. With any luck you'll find it has a political solution."

"I certainly hope so," Blaine said.

Ten Koop shut his mouth. "Yes, yes. Much better that way," he muttered.

Lysander couldn't be sure, but he thought one or two of the others gave the Dutch planter a sidelong look. He filed the impression and turned back to the maps on the monitor screen. "Just how much force does this opposition group command? I shouldn't think much compared to Falkenberg's Legion."

"Precisely," Christopher Reilly said. "I'm sure they'll see reason."

Falkenberg nodded. "That's as it may be. Meanwhile we have the pirates to deal with."


"Out of bed, sleepy bunnies."

Ursula moaned and pulled the bedclothes over her head. "Noooo . . . Five minutes more—"

"Not another second!" Lysander threw the covers

to the foot of the bed and got to his feet. He turned the air conditioner to full cold.

Ursula shivered visibly. "Not fair. I don't have to get up yet!"

"Yes you do. I told you, you're coming with me."

She sat up and tucked her knees under her chin. "Lysander, I wasn't invited."

"Not your worry. I want you with me. What's wrong now?"

"Take Harv."

"He wasn't invited either. One unexpected guest is enough."

She turned away from him.

"Ursula—"

"You'll lose me my job, and then where will I be?"

"Oh, come now—"

"You will. One word from Colonel Falkenberg to the governor, and I'll be doing tours of worker barracks at the plantations."

"That's a horrible thought!"

"It happens."

"Besides, Colonel Falkenberg wouldn't do that, and even if he did I can't think the governor would let that happen."

"Why not?"

"I just don't think so—after all, you were the star of his reconciliation dinner last night."

"That was a nice dinner." She stretched her arms toward him. "Don't we have a few more minutes?"

"No, Miss Minx. Now get your clothes. Traveling clothes."

The Legion's encampment covered the top of a low hill thirty kilometers from the capital city. It was laid out much like the classical Roman camp, except that it was much larger, with more space between tents and houses. There were other differences. Radar dishes pivoted ceaselessly at every corner of the encampment. The spaces between the rows of tents were dotted with low bunkers, personnel shelters, revetments for air defenses.

As the helicopter circled well away from the camp, the governor's pilot spoke carefully into his headset, and seemed relieved to be acknowledged. They flew straight in. As they got close Lysander saw three battle tanks and two infantry fighting vehicles. He knew there were many others, but they were nowhere in sight. At the landing area there were two helicopter gun ships and one small fixed-wing observation plane.

Soldiers in jungle camouflage moved between the orderly lines of tents. None of them seemed interested in the approaching helicopter.

A young officer greeted them at the landing pad. "I'm Lieutenant Bates, sir. Colonel Falkenberg is expecting you." He indicated a waiting jeep. "I hadn't been told the lady was coming. The ride may be a bit bumpy."

"I'll manage." Ursula smiled. "Thank you."

Muddy water stood in the unpaved tracks around the perimeter of the camp. Sentries saluted with a wave as they passed through the gates and splashed toward the headquarters area. As they entered Lysander heard trumpets sound. In seconds men rushed out of the tents, spread groundcloths, and began laying out equipment. Sergeants and centurions moved along the neat lines to inspect the gear.

"Moving out?" Lysander asked. "Or is this for me?"

"Don't know," Bates said.

Ursula stifled a giggle.

Headquarters was a low stucco building. Falkenberg

and Beatrice Frazer stood waiting on the porch. "Glad you could come," Falkenberg said.

"Thank you. I hope you won't mind if Miss Gordon has a look around—"

"Not at all." He nodded slightly at Ursula. "Pleased to have you, Miss Gordon. I've asked Mrs. Frazer to see that you're comfortable. You'll join us for lunch, of course."

"Thank you," Ursula said.

"Excellent. Now if you'll excuse us, the regiment is going into the field tomorrow, and I've a few matters to discuss with Prince Lysander."

The office was dominated by an elaborately carved wooden desk. Other wooden furniture matched it. The walls were decorated with photographs and banners.

"Well. You've come a long way, Your Highness." Falkenberg indicated a chair, and sat at his desk. "Drink?"

"No, thank you. Impressive show out there."

"It was meant to be. I take it you have bad news."

"Not entirely bad."

"Not entirely bad," Falkenberg said. "But not good either. You haven't come to take us to Sparta." He looked up with a slight smile. "Despite the show we put on for you."

"I truly wish I could, but we don't have the resources yet. We still want you. We certainly want your good will."

"Thank you," Falkenberg said. "I'm afraid good will doesn't buy many munitions."

"No, of course not."

"Rather sudden change of plans?" Falkenberg said.

"Well, yes, sir, I suppose so," Lysander said. *Damned sudden. One day Father was eager to get*

Falkenberg *to Sparta, and the next he was worried about money. The budget's tight, but not that tight. I really don't understand. I guess I don't have to.* "Colonel, I've brought a sight draft as a retainer against future need. Sort of an option on your services."

"Services when?"

Lysander glanced around the room. Falkenberg smiled thinly. "Your Highness, if this room's bugged, there's no place safe on the planet."

"I well believe it. Very well, I was told to be honest with you. We won't be ready to move for another four or five standard years. Admiral Lermontov agrees with that. Provided—" He let his voice trail off.

"Provided that things on Earth don't come apart on their own before then," Falkenberg said. "Yes. Now, how real is that Tanith-Sparta friendship Governor Blaine was hinting at?"

"I think very real. As real as my father and I can make it, in any event."

"I thought so. Good. But does your father control Spartan foreign policy?"

Lysander looked thoughtful. "Just how much do you know about our Constitution?"

"Assume nothing," Falkenberg said.

"Well, I won't do quite that," Lysander said. "Do you know my father?"

"Met him once. Long ago," Falkenberg said.

"Yes. Well, Sparta's government was designed by— well, by intellectuals. Intellectuals who were disgusted with what happened to the United States, where by the year 2000 both houses of the Congress for all practical purposes held office for life, and the only really elective office was held by a president who had to spend so much time learning how to get the job that he never learned how to do it."

"An interesting way of putting things."

Lysander grinned. "Actually I'm quoting my grand-father. Who was, of course, one of those disgusted intellectuals. Anyway, Sparta was designed differently. The dual monarchy controls foreign policy. The two kings are supposed to be a check on each other, but my father and his colleague are very much in agreement. If something happens to Father, it's nearly certain that I'll take his place. As the junior king, of course. Really, Colonel, I don't think you need to worry too much about changes in Spartan policy."

"Who controls the money? Your legislature?"

"We don't exactly have a legislature," Lysander said. "But yes, the Senate and Council control most of Sparta's budget. Not all of it, though. Control of some revenues is built into the Constitution. There are funds reserved for the monarchy, and others controlled by the Senate, and the Senate— well, it's pretty complicated. Some seats are elected in districts and some are virtually hereditary. Others are appointed by the unions and the trade associations. I'd hate to have to explain it."

"The bottom line, though, is that you can't get the money right now."

"The bottom line, Colonel, is that we don't *have* the money right now. But we're pretty sure we know where to get it."

Falkenberg sat impassively.

"If it's any consolation, Admiral Lermontov agrees with us," Lysander said. "I'm surprised he hasn't made you party to his views."

"He has," Falkenberg said.

"Ah. I see. Then you know his ultimate goal hasn't

changed." Lysander frowned. "One thing concerns me, Colonel. This—Blaine doesn't want to call it a rebellion, but we may as well. If they're holding back their crops, what does that do to Admiral Lermontov's budget?"

"It could be grim. Which is why Blaine can't let them get away with it."

"Yes. I thought as much. There's more at stake here than Blaine and his reforms. Just how much of the crop has been withheld?"

"At least a quarter. Maybe as much as a third."

Lysander whistled softly. "Colonel, that—that could mean—what? Half the Fleet's operations budget?"

"Not quite that. The Grand Senate still appropriates *something* for operations. But it would certainly wipe out Grand Admiral Lermontov's discretionary funds."

"I can't say I care for that. Still, Colonel, what can they *do* with their crop if they don't sell it to the government? Surely they won't carry out their threat to destroy it."

Falkenberg laughed. "With that much money at stake? Hardly. I'm afraid there are a lot of markets, Prince Lysander. Some will pay more than the government."

"But—"

"The most likely customer is a company owned by the Bronson family."

"Oh. I see. Grand Senator Bronson. With his protection—"

"Precisely. His faction doesn't control a majority in the Grand Senate, but he doesn't have to, does he? No one else has a majority either. Lots of horse trading, I'm told."

"Yes," Lysander looked at the far wall. It was covered with holographs. One showed the Legion in formal parade with battle banners and victory streamers. "Still, I gather you don't anticipate any trouble recovering the crops?"

"I always anticipate trouble, Your Highness."

"Colonel, let me be frank. You're very heavily involved in Admiral Lermontov's plan, but we are even more so. Anything that changes or delays it— well, we would have to take that very seriously back on Sparta." He spread his hands wide. "Of course I'm only a message carrier. I'm not empowered to negotiate."

Falkenberg raised an eyebrow. "Well, if you say so. But you do carry messages to high places. Your Highness, you have to appreciate my situation. I'm certain this mess with the opposition planters will be cleared up in weeks, months at most. It will have to be. After that the regiment won't be able to stay on Tanith very long. Certainly not five years. The economy won't support us, and besides, I can't condemn my people to five years in this place."

"What will you do?"

"We have offers. I'll have to take one of them."

"Preferably something that doesn't tie you down for too long—"

"Preferably," Falkenberg agreed. "But the Regimental Council makes that decision."

"Colonel, my father—all of us regret putting you in this situation."

"I'm sure you do," Falkenberg said. "How long will you be on Tanith?"

"It's not definite, but—let's say weeks. Months at most."

Falkenberg smiled and nodded "Right. I expect you'll want to see a bit of the country beyond the capital while you're here. I'll have Captain Rottermill draw up a travel guide if you like."

"Very kind of you. Should be helpful." Lysander frowned. "Colonel, what *is* your impression of Governor Blaine?"

Falkenberg chuckled. "At the risk of being offensive, he seems much like the people who established your government. Let's hope he learns as much from experience as your father and grandfather did."

"I see. Do you think he will?"

"He has held on quite well so far."

"Colonel, I have reasons for asking your opinion. I'm authorized to tell Governor Blaine certain things about Lermontov's plans, provided you agree."

Falkenberg touched a button on the side of his desk. "Whiskey and soda. Ice. Two glasses, please." He turned back to Lysander. "I repeat. He has managed quite well so far."

"With your Legion at his back. What happens when you leave?"

"That is the question, isn't it?" Falkenberg touched controls in a desk drawer. The gray of the desktop flashed into a brightly colored map of the region around Lederle. "The main opposition to Blaine's new policies is out here in the bush. Until recently they were unable to form any effective organization. Now they have done so. They've even hired a battalion of mercenaries. Light infantry, mostly."

"I hadn't heard that," Lysander said.

"Governor Blaine isn't particularly proud of having let things go that far."

There was a tap at the door. An orderly brought in a tray and set it down. "Anything else, sir?"

"Thank you. No." Falkenberg poured for both of them. "Cheers.'

"Cheers. Colonel, I notice that *you* haven't told the governor anything—or if you have, he's very discreet."

"He is discreet, but in fact I was waiting for your father's views. Incidentally, I'd be careful when and where you told him anything. This room is secure, but I wouldn't bet that the governor's office is. Or the study in his apartments, for that matter."

"Who?"

Falkenberg shrugged. "When was a politician's office ever secure? In this case it's even more likley to be leaky. You will remember Mynheer ten Koop?"

"Certainly."

"I don't recall it was mentioned at Blaine's dinner, but ten Koop's oldest daughter is married to one Hiram Girerd—who just happens to be one of the leaders of the planters' boycott. That's just one of the odd mixtures you can find at Government House."

"Hah. Then perhaps it would be best to wait until this boycott affair is settled before we come to any decisions about Tanith's role in—" He shrugged. "We've no name for Lermontov's grand scheme."

"Just as well."

"I suppose. In any event, Colonel, I can't think that even with their mercenary battalion the planters could muster much force against your Legion."

"Military, no. But they've hired Barton's Bastards, and Major Barton is no fool." Falkenberg chuckled. "If he were, I'd hardly say so. He was once a captain in the 42nd."

"Oh? Why did he leave?"

"His hitch ran out and he got a better offer," Falkenberg said. "After that we were allies for a while."

"I see." Classic situation? Lysander wondered. Two condottiere captains facing each other, neither willing to fight a battle because the losses would be too costly. A long confrontation but no fighting. Mercenary paradise. Surely not Falkenberg's game? "What will you do?"

"That rather depends on what the opposition intends, doesn't it?" Falkenberg studied the map table. "One thing is certain. They'll have to deliver that crop to someone, presumably a Bronson agent. Major Barton will see to that. It's the only way he can be paid, and he needs the money."

"So if you can intercept the delivery—"

"The conflict is ended, of course. Governor Blaine will have his taxes, the Navy will have its drugs, and Lermontov will have his secret funds." Falkenberg glanced at his watch and stood. "But first things first. This week we have to clean out that nest of pirates in the south."

"Of course. Colonel, I don't want to keep you from your work, but there is one thing. May—I would very much like to accompany your troops on this campaign."

Falkenberg considered it for a moment. "I think not this time. Ordinarily I wouldn't mind having a volunteer subaltern along, but this looks like a job for specialists. Hostage situations generally are."

"Another time, then?"

Falkenberg looked thoughtful again. "It makes sense. In fact, it's as good a way as any for you to get the intelligence your father will need. When we get back from this mission, you'll be welcome aboard."

# IX

Mark Fuller awoke with a knife at his throat. A big, ugly man, burned dark and with scars crisscrossing his bare chest, squatted in front of them. He eyed Mark and Juanita, then grinned. "What have we got ourselves?" he said. "A couple of runaways?"

"I got everything, Art," someone said from behind them.

"Yeah. Okay, mates, up and at 'em. Move out. I ain't got all day."

Mark helped Juanita to her feet. One arm was asleep from holding her. As Mark stood, the ugly man expertly took the gun from Mark's belt. "Who are you?" Mark asked.

"Call me Art. Sergeant to the Boss. Come on, let's go."

There were five others, all mounted. Art led the way through the jungle. When Mark tried to say something to Juanita, Art turned. "I'm going to tell you once. Shut up. Say another word to anybody but me, and I kill you. Say anything to me that I don't want to hear, and I'll cut you. Got that?"

"Yes, sir," Mark said.

Art laughed. "Now you've got the idea."

They rode on in silence.

The Free State was mostly caves in hillsides above the sea. It held over five hundred men and women. There were other encampments of escapees out in the jungles, Art said. "But we've got the biggest. Been pretty careful—when we raid the planters, we can usually make it look like one of the other outfits did it. Governor don't have much army anyway. They won't follow us here."

Mark started to say something about the mercenaries that the governor was hiring. Then he thought better of it.

The boss was a heavy man with long, colorless hair growing to below his shoulders. He had a handlebar mustache and staring blue eyes. He sat in the mouth of a cave on a big carved chair as if it were a throne, and he held a rifle across his knees. A big black man stood behind the chair, watching everyone, saying nothing.

"Escapees, eh?"

"Yes," Mark said.

"Yes, boss. Don't forget that."

"Yes, boss."

"What can you do? Can you fight?"

When Mark didn't answer, the Boss pointed to a smaller man in the crowd that had gathered around. "Take him, Choam."

The small man moved toward Mark. His foot lashed upward and hit Mark in the ribs. Then he moved closer. Mark tried to hit him, but he man dodged away and slapped Mark across the face. "Enough," the boss said. "You can't fight. What can you do?"

"I—"

"Yeah." He looked backward over his shoulder to the black man. "You want him, George?"

"No."

"Right. Art, you found him. He's yours. I'll take the girl."

"But you can't!" Mark shouted.

"No!" Juanita said.

The other men looked at the boss. They saw he was laughing. They all laughed. Art and the two others took Mark's arms and began to drag him away. Two more led Juanita into the cave behind the boss.

"But this isn't right!" Mark shouted.

There was more laughter. The boss stood. "Maybe I'll give her back when I'm through. Unless Art wants her. Art?"

"I got a woman."

"Yeah." The boss turned toward the cave. Then he turned back to Mark and the men holding him. "Leave the kid here, Art. I'd like to talk to him. Get the girl cleaned up," he shouted behind him. "The rest of you get out of here."

The others left, all but the black man who stood behind the boss's throne. The black man went a few meters away and sat under a rock ledge. It looked cool in there. He took out a pipe and began stuffing it.

"Come here, kid. What's your name?"

"Fuller," Mark said. "Mark Fuller."

"Come over here. Sit down." The boss indicated a flat rock bench just inside the cave mouth. The cave seemed to go in a long way; he could hear women talking. "Sit, I said. Tell me how you got here." The boss's tone was conversational, almost friendly.

"I was in a student riot." Mark strained to hear, but there were no more sounds from inside the cave.

"Student, eh. Relax, Fuller. Nobody's hurting your girlfriend. Your concern is touching. Don't see much of that out here. Tell me about your riot. Where was it?"

The boss was a good listener. When Mark fell silent, the man would ask questions—probing questions, as if he were interested in Mark's story. Sometimes he smiled.

Outside were work parties: wood details; a group incomprehensibly digging a ditch in the flinty ground out in front of the caves; women carrying water. None of them seemed interested in the boss's conversation. Instead, they seemed almost afraid to look into the cave—all but the black man, who sat in his cool niche and never seemed to look away.

Bit by bit Mark told of his arrest and sentence, and of Ewigfeuer's plantation. The boss nodded. "So you came looking for the Free States. And what did you expect to find?"

"Free men! Freedom, not—"

"Not despotism." There was something like kindness in the words. The boss chuckled. "You know, Fuller, it's remarkable how much your story is like mine. Except that I've always known how to fight. And how to make friends. Good friends." He tilted his head toward the black man. "George, here, for instance. Between us there's nothing we can't handle. You poor fool, what the hell did you think you'd do out here? What good are you? You can't fight, you whine about what's right and fair, and you don't know how to take care of yourself, and you come off into the bush to find us. You knew who we were."

"But—"

"And now you're all broken up about your woman. I'm not going to take anything she hasn't got plenty of. It doesn't get used up." He stood and shouted to one of the men in the yard. "Send Art over."

"So you're going to rape Juanita." Mark looked

around for a weapon, for anything. There was a rifle near the boss's chair. His eyes flickered toward it.

The boss laughed. "Try it. But you won't. Aw, hell, Fuller, you'll be all right. Maybe you'll even learn something. Now I've got a date."

"But—" If there was something I could say, Mark thought. "Why are you doing this?"

"Why not? Because I'll lose your valuable loyalty? Get something straight, Fuller. This is it. There's no place left to go. Live here and learn our ways, or go jump over the cliff there. Or take off into the green and see how far you get. You think you're pretty sharp. Maybe you are. We'll see. Maybe you'll learn to be some use to us. Maybe. Art, take the kid into your squad and see if he can fit in."

"Right, boss. Come on." Art took Mark's arm. "Look, if you're going try something, do it and get it over with. I don't want to watch you all the time."

Mark turned and followed the other man. Helpless. Damn fool, and helpless. He laughed.

"Yeah?" Art said. "What's funny?"

"The Free State. Freedom. Free men—"

"We're free," Art said. "More'n the losers in Whiskeytown. Maybe one day you will be. When we think we can trust you." He pointed to the cliff edge. The sea inlet was beyond it. "Anybody we can't trust goes over that. The fall don't always kill 'em, but I never saw anybody make it to shore."

Art found him a place in his cave. There were six other men and four women there. The others looked at Mark for a moment, then went back to whatever they had been doing. Mark sat staring at the cave floor and thought he heard, off toward the Boss's cave, a man laughing and a girl crying. For the first time since he was twelve, Mark tried to pray.

Pray for what? he asked himself. He didn't know. I hate them. All of them.

Just when, Mark Fuller, are you going to get some control over your life? But that doesn't just happen. I have to do it for myself. Somehow.

A week went past. It was a meaningless existence. He cooked for the squad, gathered wood and washed dishes, and listened to the sounds of the other men and their women at night. They never left him alone.

The crying from the boss's cave stopped, but he didn't see Juanita. When he gathered wood, there were sometimes women from the boss's area, and he overheard them talking about what a relief it was that Chambliss—that seemed to be the boss's name— had a new playmate. They did not seem at all jealous of the new arrival.

Play along with them, Mark thought. Play along until—until what? What can I do? Escape? Get back to the plantation? How? And what happens then? But I won't join them, I won't become a part of this! I won't!

After a week they took Mark on hunting parties. He was unarmed—his job was to carry the game. They had to walk several kilometers away from the caves. Chambliss didn't permit hunting near the encampment.

Mark was paired with Art. The older man was neither friendly nor unfriendly; he treated Mark as a useful tool, someone to carry and do work.

"Is this all there is?" Mark asked. "Hunting, sitting around the camp, eating and—"

"—a little screwing," Art said. "What the hell do you want us to do? Set up farms so the governor'll know where we are? We're doin' all right. Nobody tells us what to do."

"Except the boss."

"Yeah. Except the boss. But nobody hassles us. We can live for ourselves. Cheer up, kid, you'll feel better when you get your woman back. He'll get tired of her one of these days. Or maybe we'll get some more when we go raiding. Only thing is, you have to fight for a woman. You better do it better'n you did the other day."

"Doesn't she—don't the women have anything to say about who they pair up with?" Mark asked.

"Why should they?"

On the tenth day there was an alarm. Someone thought he heard a helicopter. The boss ordered night guards.

Mark was paired with a man named Cal. They sat among the rocks at the edge of the clearing. Cal had a rifle and a knife, but Mark was unarmed. The jungle was black dark, without even stars above.

Finally the smaller man took tobacco and paper from his pocket. "Smoke?"

"Thanks, I'd like one."

"Sure." He rolled two cigarettes. "Maybe you'll do, huh? Had my doubts about you when you first come. You know, it's a wonder the boss didn't have you tossed over the side, the way you yelled at him like that. No woman's worth that, you know."

"Yeah."

"She mean much to you?" Cal asked.

"Some," Mark swallowed hard. His mouth tasted bitter. " 'Course, they get the idea they own you, there's not much you can do."

Cal laughed. "Yeah. Had an old lady like that in Baltimore. Stabbed me one night for messing around with her sister. Where you from, kid?"

"Santa Maria. Part of San-San."

"I been there once. North San-San, not the part where you come from. Here." He handed Mark the cigarette and struck a match to light both.

They smoked in silence. It wasn't all tobacco, Mark found; there was a good shot of borloi in the cigarette. Mark avoided inhaling but spoke as if holding his breath. Cal sucked and packed.

"Good weed," Cal said. "You should have brought some when you ran off."

"Had to get out fast."

"Yeah." They listened to the sounds of the jungle. "Hell of a life," Cal said. "Wish I could get back to Earth. Some Welfare Island, anyplace where it's not so damned hot. I'd like to live in Alaska. You ever been there?"

"No. Isn't there—don't you have any plans? Some way to make things better?"

"Well, the boss talks about it, but nothing happens," Cal said. "Every now and then we go raid a place, get some new women. We got a still in not long ago, that's something."

Mark shuddered. "Cal?"

"Yah?"

"Got another cigarette?"

"You'll owe me for it."

"Sure."

"Okay." Cal took out paper and tobacco and rolled two more smokes. He handed one to Mark. "Been thinking. There ought to be something better'n this, but I sure don't see what it'll be." As Cal struck his match, Mark shut his eyes so he wouldn't be blinded. Then he lifted the rock he'd found in the darkness and brought it down hard onto Cal's head. The man slumped, but Mark hit him again. He felt something wet and sticky warming his fingers and shuddered.

Then he was sick, but he had to work fast. He took

Cal's rifle and knife and his matches. There wasn't anything else useful. Mark moved from the rocks onto the narrow strip of flinty ground. No one challenged him. He ran into the jungle with no idea of where to go.

He tried to think. Hiding out until morning wouldn't help. They'd find Cal and come looking. And Juanita was back there. Mark ran through the squishy mud. Tears came and he fought them back, but then he was sobbing. *Where am I going? Where? And why bother?*

He ran on until he felt something moving beside him. He drew in a breath to cry out, but a hand clamped over his mouth. Another grasped his wrist. He felt a knifepoint at his throat. "One sound and you're dead," a voice whispered. "Got that?"

Mark nodded.

"Right. Just keep remembering that. Okay, Ardway, let's go."

"Roger," a voice answered.

He was half-carried through the jungle from the camp. There were several men. He did not know how many. They moved silently. "Ready to walk?" someone asked.

"Yes," Mark whispered. "Who are—"

"Shut up. One more sound and we cut your kidneys out. You'll take a week dying. Now follow the man ahead of you."

Mark made more noise than all the others combined, although he tried to walk silently. They went a long way through knee-deep water and thick mud, then over harder ground. He thought they were going slightly uphill. Then he no longer felt the loom of the trees. They were in a clearing.

The night was pitch black. *How do they see?* Mark wondered. *And who are they?* He thought he could make out a darker shape ahead of him. It was more a feeling than anything else, but then he touched something soft. "Through that," one of his captors said.

It was a curtain. Another was brought down behind him as he went through, and still another was lifted ahead of him. Light blinded him. He stood blinking.

He was inside a tent. Half a dozen uniformed men stood around a map table. At the end of the tent opposite Mark was a tall, slender man. Mark could not guess how old he was, but there were thin streaks of gray in his hair. His jungle camouflage uniform was neatly pressed. He looked at Mark without expression. "Well, Sergeant Major?"

"Strange, Colonel. This man was sitting guard with another guy. Neither one of them knew what he was doing. We watched them a couple of hours. Then this one beats the other one's brains out with a rock and runs right into the jungle."

Mercenaries, Mark thought. They've come to—"I need help," Mark said. "They've got my—my wife in there."

"Your name?" the colonel asked.

"Mark Fuller."

The colonel looked to his right. Another officer had a small desk console. He punched Mark's name into it, and words flashed across the screen. The Colonel read for a moment. "Escaped convict. Juanita Corlee escaped with you. That is your wife?"

"Yes."

"And you had a falling-out with the Free Staters."

"No. It wasn't that way at all." Mark blurted out his story.

The colonel looked back to the readout screen. "And you are surprised." He nodded to himself. "I know the schools on Earth were of little use. It says here that you are an intelligent man, Fuller. So far you haven't shown many signs of it."

"No. Lord God, no. Who—who are you? Please."

"I am Colonel John Christian Falkenberg. This regiment has been retained by the Tanith governor to suppress these so-called Free States. You were captured by Sergeant Major Calvin, and these are my officers. Now, Fuller, what can you tell me about the camp layout? What weapons have they?"

"I don't know much," Mark said. "Sir." Now why did I say that?

"There are other women captives in that camp," Falkenberg said.

"Here," one of the other officers said. "Show us what you do know, Fuller. How good is this satellite photo map?"

"Christ, Rottermill," a third officer said. "Let the lad be for a moment."

"Major Savage, intelligence is my job."

"So is human compassion. Ian, do you think you can find this boy a drink?" Major Savage beckoned to Falkenberg and led him to the far corner of the tent. Another officer brought a nylon musette bag from under the table and took out a bottle. He handed the brandy to Mark.

Falkenberg listened to Savage. Then he nodded. "We can only try. Fuller, did you see any signs of power supplies in that camp?"

"No, sir. There was no electricity at all. Only flashlights."

"Any special armament?"

"Colonel, I only saw rifles and pistols, but I heard talk of machine guns. I don't know how many."

"I see. Still, it is unlikely that they have laser weapons. Rottermill, have any target seekers turned up missing from armories? What are the chances that they have air defense missiles?"

"Slim, Colonel. Practically none. None stolen I know of."

"Check that out, please. Jeremy, you may be right," Falkenberg said. "I believe we can use the helicopters as fighting vehicles."

There was a moment of silence; then the officer who'd given Mark the brandy said, "Colonel, that's damned risky. There's precious little armor on those things."

"Machines not much better than ours were major fighting vehicles less than a hundred years ago, Captain Frazer." Falkenberg studied the map. "You see, Fuller, we could have wiped out this lot any time. The hostages are our real problem. Because of them we have kept Aviation Company back and brought in our troops on foot. We've not been able to carry heavy equipment or even much personal body armor across these swamps."

No, I don't expect you would, Mark thought. He tried to imagine a large group traveling silently through the swamps. It seemed impossible. What had they done when animals attacked? Certainly no one in the Free State had heard any gunfire. Why would an armed man let himself be killed when he could shoot?

"I expect they will threaten their prisoners when they know we are here," Falkenberg said. "Of course we will negotiate as long as possible. How long do you think it will take for them to act when they know that we will not actually make any concessions?"

"I don't know," Mark said. It was something he could not have imagined two years before: men who'd kill and torture, sometimes for no reason at all. No. Not men. Beasts.

"Well, you've precipitated the action," Falkenberg

said. "They'll find your dead companion within hours. Captain Frazer."

"Sir."

"You have been studying this map. If you held this encampment, what defenses would you set up?"

"I'd dig in around this open area and hope someone was fool enough to come at us through it, Colonel."

"Yes. Sergeant Major."

"Sir!"

"Show me where they have placed their sentries." Falkenberg watched as Calvin sketched in outposts. Then he nodded. "It seems this Chambliss has some rudimentary military sense. Rings of sentries. In-depth defense. Can you infiltrate that, Sergeant Major?"

"Not likely, sir."

"Yes." Falkenberg stood for a moment. Then he turned to Captain Frazer. "Ian, you will take your scouts and half the infantry. Make preparations for an attack on the open area. We will code that Green A. This is not precisely a feint, Ian. It would be a good thing if you could punch through. However, I do not expect you to succeed, so conserve your men."

Frazer straightened to attention. "Sir."

"We won't abandon you, Ian. When the enemy is well committed there, we'll use the helicopters to take you out. Then we will move on both their flanks and roll them up." Falkenberg pointed to the map again. "This depression seems secure enough as a landing area. Code that Green A-one."

Major Jeremy Savage held a match over the bowl of his pipe and inhaled carefully. When he was satisfied with the light, he said, "Close timing needed, John Christian. Ian's in a spot of trouble if we lose the choppers."

"Have a better way, Jerry?" Falkenberg asked.

"No."

"Right. Fuller, can you navigate a helicopter?"

"Yes, sir. I can even fly one."

Falkenberg nodded again. "Yes. You are a taxpayer's son, aren't you? Fuller, you will go with Number 3 chopper. Captain Owensford."

"Sir."

"I want you to lead the rescue of the hostages. Sergeant Major, I want a squad of headquarters assault guards, full body armor, in Number 3. Fuller will guide the pilot as close as possible to the cave where the women are held. Captain Owensford will follow in Number 2 with another assault squad. Every effort will be made to secure the hostages alive."

"Yes, sir," Owensford said.

"Fuller, is this understood?"

"Yes, sir."

"Very good. You won't have time to go in with them. When the troops are off, those choppers must move out fast. We'll need them to rescue Ian's lot."

"Colonel?" Mark said.

"Yes?"

"Not all women are hostages. Some of them will fight, I think. I don't know how many. And not all the men are—not everybody wants to be in there. Some would run off if they could."

"And what do you expect me to do about it?"

"I don't know, sir."

"Neither do I, but Captain Owensford will be aware of the situation. Sergeant Major, we will move this command post in one hour. Until then, Fuller, I'll ask you to show Captain Rottermill everything you know about that camp."

It isn't going to work, Mark thought. I prayed for her to die. Only I don't know if she wants to die.

And now she will. He took another pull from the bottle and felt it taken from his hand.

"Later," Rottermill said. "For now, tell me what you know about this lot."

# X

"They've found that dead guard." The radio sergeant adjusted his earphones. "Seem pretty stirred up about it."

Falkenberg looked at his watch. There was a good hour before sunrise. "Took them long enough."

"Pity Fuller couldn't guide that chopper in the dark," Jeremy Savage said.

"Yes. Sergeant Major, ask Captain Frazer to ready his men, and have your trail ambush party alerted."

"Sir."

"I have a good feeling about this one, John Christian." Savage tapped his pipe against the heel of his boot. "A good feeling."

"Hope you're right, Jeremy. Fuller doesn't believe it will work."

"No, but he knows this is her best chance. He's steady enough now. Realistic assessment of probabilities. Holding up well, all things considered."

"For a married man." Married men make the kinds of promises no man can keep, Falkenberg thought. His lips twitched slightly at the memory, and for a moment Grace's smile loomed in the darkness of the jungle outside. "Sergeant Major, have the chopper teams get into their armor."

§§§

"Is it always like this?" Mark said. He sat in the left hand seat of the helicopter. Unlike fixed wing craft, the right hand seat is the command pilot's position in a helicopter.

Body armor and helmet were an unfamiliar weight, and he sweated inside the thick clothing. The phones in his helmet crackled with commands meant for others. Outside the helmet there were sounds of firing. Captain Frazer's assault had started a quarter of an hour before; now there was a faint reddish gray glow in the eastern skies over the jungle.

Lieutenant Bates grinned and wiggled the control stick. "Usually it's worse. We'll get her out, Fuller. You just put us next to the right cave."

"I'll do that, but it won't work."

"Sure it will."

"You don't need to cheer me up, Bates."

"I don't?" Bates grinned again. He was not much older than Mark. "Maybe I need cheering up. I'm always scared about now."

"Really? You don't look it."

"All we're expected to do. Not look it." He thumbed the mike button. "Chief, everything set back there?"

"Aye-aye, sir."

The chatter in Mark's helmet grew still. A voice said "Missiles away." Seconds later a new and sterner voice said *"All helicopters, start your engines. I say again, start engines."*

"That's us," Bates reached for the starting controls and the turbines whined. "Not very much light."

*"Helicopters, report when ready."*

"Ready aye-aye," Bates said.

"Aye-aye?" Mark asked.

"We're an old CD Marine regiment," Bates said.

"Lot of us, anyway. Stayed with the old man when the Senate disbanded his regiment."

"You don't look old enough."

"Me? Not hardly. This was Falkenberg's Mercenary Legion long before I came aboard."

"Why? Why join mercenaries?"

Bates shrugged. "I like being part of the regiment. The pay's good. What's the matter, don't you think the work's worth doing?"

*"Lift off. Begin helicopter assault."*

"Lift-off aye-aye." The turbine whine increased and the ship lifted in a rising, looping circle. Bates took the right hand position in the three-craft formation.

Mark could dimly see the green below, and the visibility increased every minute. Now he could make out the shapes of small clearings among the endless green marshes.

"You take her," Bates said. His hands hovered over the controls, ready to take his darling away from this stranger.

Mark grasped the unfamiliar stick. It was different from the family machine he'd learned on, but the principles were the same. The chopper was not much more than a big airborne truck, and he'd driven one of those on a vacation in the Yukon. The Canadian lakes seemed endlessly far away, in time as well as in space.

Flying came back easily. He remembered the wild stunts he'd tried when he was first licensed. Once a group from his school had gone on a picnic to San Miguel Island and Mark had landed in a cove, dropping onto a narrow, inaccessible beach between high cliffs during a windstorm. It had been stupid, but wildly exciting. After that, they always let him drive when they wanted to do something unusual. Good practice for this, he thought. And I'm scared stiff, and what do I do after this is over? Will Falkenberg turn me in? They'll sell me to a mining company. Or worse.

There were low hills ahead, dull brown in the early morning light. Men huddled in the rocky areas. Some lay sprawled, victims of the bomblets released by the first salvo of rockets. Gatlings in the compartment behind Mark crackled like frying bacon. The shots were impossibly close together, like a steady stream of noise. The helicopter raked the Free State. The small slugs sent chips flying from the rocks. The other choppers opened up, and six tracer streams twisted in crazy patterns intertwining like some courtship dance.

Men and women died on that flinty ground. They lay in broken heaps, red blood staining the dirt around them, exactly like a scene on tri-v. It's not fake, Mark thought. They won't get up when the cameras go away. Did they deserve this? Does anyone?

Then he was too busy piloting the helicopter to think about anything else. The area in front of the cave was small, very small—would the rotors clear it? A strong gust from the sea struck them and the chopper rocked dangerously.

"Watch her—" Whatever Bates had intended to say, he never finished it. He slumped forward over the stick, held just above it by his shoulder straps. Something wet and sticky splashed across Mark's left hand and arm. Brains. A large slug had come angling upward to hit Bates in the jaw, then ricochet around in his helmet. The young lieutenant had almost no face. Get her down, Mark chanted, easy baby, down you go, level now, here's another gust, easy baby. . . .

Men poured out of the descending chopper. Mark had time to be surprised: they jumped down and ran into the cave even as their friends fell around them.

Then something stabbed Mark's left arm, and he saw neat holes in the Plexiglas windscreen in front of him. The men went into the cave. They were faceless in their big helmets, identical robots moving forward or falling in heaps. . . .

Lord God, they're magnificent. I've got to get this thing down! Suddenly it was the most important thing in his life. Get down and get out, go into the cave with those men. Find Juanita, yes, of course, but go with them, do something for myself because I want to do it—

"*Bates, stop wasting time and get to green A-one urgent.*"

God damn it! Mark fumbled with the communications gear. "Bates is dead. This is Fuller. I'm putting the chopper down."

The voice in the phones changed. Someone else spoke. "Are the troops still aboard?"

"No. They're off."

"Then take that craft to Green A-one immediately."

"My—my wife's in there!"

The colonel's aware of that." Jeremy Savage's voice was calm. "That machine is required, and now."

"But—"

"Fuller, this regiment has risked a great deal of those hostages. The requirement is urgent. Or do you seriously suppose you would be much use inside?"

Oh, Christ! There was firing inside the cave, and someone was screaming. I want to kill him, Mark thought. Kill that blond-haired bastard. I want to watch him die. A babble filled the helmet phones. Crisp commands and reports were jumbled together as a background noise. Frazer's voice. "We're pinned. I'm sending them back to A-one as fast as I can."

There was more firing from inside the cave.

"Aye-aye," Mark said. He gunned the engine and

lifted out in a whirling loop to confuse the ground fire. Someone was still aboard; the Gatlings chattered and their bright streams raked the rocks around the open area below.

Where was Green A-one? Mark glanced at the screen in front of the control stick. There was gray and white matter, and bright red blood in a long smear across the glass surface. Mark had to lift Bates's head to get a bearing. More blood ran across his fingers, and something warm trickled down his left arm.

Then the area was ahead, a clear depression surrounded by hills and rocks. Men lay around the top of the bowl. A mortar team worked mechanically, dropping the shells down the tube, leaning back, lifting, dropping another. There were bright flashes everywhere. Mark dropped into the bowl and the flashes vanished. There were sounds; gunfire, and the whump! whump! of the mortar. A squad rushed over and began loading wounded men into the machine. Then the sergeant waved him off, and Mark raced for the rear area where the surgeon waited. Another helicopter passed, headed into the combat area.

The medics off-loaded the men.

"Stand by, Fuller, we'll get another pilot over there," Savage's calm voice said in the phones.

"No, I'll keep it. I know the way."

There was a pause. "Right. Get to it, then."

"Aye-aye, sir."

The entrance to the boss's cave was cool, and the surgeon had moved the field hospital there. A steady stream of men came out of the depths of the cave: prisoners carrying their own dead, and Falkenberg's men carrying their comrades. The Free State dead were piled in heaps near the cliff edge. When they were identified, they were tossed over the side. The regiment's dead were carried to a cleared area, where they lay covered. Armed soldiers guarded the corpses.

Do the dead give a damn? Mark wondered. Why should they? What's the point of all the ceremony over dead mercenaries? He looked back at the still figure on the bed. She seemed small and helpless, and her breath rasped in her throat. An IV unit dripped endlessly.

"She'll live."

Mark turned to see the regimental surgeon.

"We couldn't save the baby, but there's no reason she can't have more."

"What happened to her?" Mark demanded.

The surgeon shrugged. "Bullet in the lower abdomen. Ours, theirs, who knows? Jacketed slug, it didn't do a lot of damage. The colonel wants to see you, Fuller. And you can't do any good here." The surgeon took him by the elbow and ushered him out into the steaming daylight. "That way."

There were more work parties in the open space outside. Prisoners were still carrying away dead men. Insects buzzed around dark red stains on the flinty rocks. They look so dead, Mark thought. So damned dead. Somewhere a woman was crying.

Falkenberg sat with his officers under an open tent in the clearing. There was another man with them, a prisoner under guard. "So they took you alive," Mark said.

"I seem to have survived. They killed George." The boss's lips curled in a sneer. "And you helped them. Fine way to thank us for taking you in."

"Taking us in! You raped—"

"How do you know it was rape?" the boss demanded. "Not that you were any great help, were you? You're no damned good, Fuller. Your help didn't make a damned bit of difference. Has anything you ever did made any difference?"

"That will do, Chambliss," Falkenberg said.

"Sure. You're in charge now, Colonel. Well, you beat us, so you give the orders. We're pretty much alike, you and me."

"Possibly," Falkenberg said. "Corporal, take Chambliss to the guard area. And make certain he does not escape."

"Sir." The troopers gestured with their rifles. The boss walked ahead of them. He seemed to be leading them.

"What will happen to him?" Mark asked.

"We will turn him over to the governor. I expect he'll hang. The problem, Fuller, is what to do with you. You were of some help to us, and I don't like unpaid debts."

"What choices do I have?" Mark asked.

Falkenberg shrugged. "We could give you a mount and weapons. It is a long journey to the farmlands in the south, but once there, you could probably avoid recapture. Probably. If that is not attractive, we could put in a good word with the governor."

"Which would get me what?"

"At the least he would agree to forget about your escape and persuade your patron not to prosecute for theft of animals and weapons."

"But I'd be back under sentence. A slave again. What happens to Juanita?"

"The regiment will take care of her."

"What the hell does that mean?" Mark demanded.

Falkenberg's expression did not change. Mark could not tell what the colonel was thinking. "I mean, Fuller, that is unlikely that the troops would approve turning her over to the governor. She can stay with us until her apprenticeship has expired."

Emotions raged through him. Mark opened his mouth, then bit off the words. *So you're no better than the boss!*

"What Colonel Falkenberg means," Major Savage said, "is that she will be permitted to stay with us as long as she wishes. We don't lack for women, and there are other differences between us and your Free State. Colonel Falkenberg commands a regiment. He does not rule a mob."

"Sure. What if she wants to come with me?"

"Then we will see that she does. When she recovers," Savage said. "That will be her choice. Now what is it you want to do? We don't have all day."

What do I want to do? Lord God, I want to go home, but that's not possible. Dirt farmer, fugitive forever. Or slave for at least two more years. "You haven't given me a very pleasant set of alternatives."

"You had fewer when you came here," Savage said.

A party of prisoners was herded toward the tent. They stood looking nervously at the seated officers, while their guards stood at ease with their weapons. Mark licked his lips. "I heard you were enlisting some of the Free Staters."

Falkenberg nodded. "A few. Not many."

"Could you use a helicopter pilot?"

Major Savage chuckled. "Told you he'd ask, John Christian."

"He was steady enough this morning," Captain Frazer said. "And we do need pilots."

"Do you know what you're getting into?" Falkenberg asked. "Soldiers are not slaves, but they must obey orders. All of them."

"Slaves have to obey, too."

"It's five years," Major Savage said. "And we track down deserters."

"Yes, sir." Mark looked at each of the officers in turn. They sat impassively. They said nothing; they did not look at each other, but they belonged to each other. And to their men. Mark remembered the clubs that children in his neighborhood had formed. Belonging to them had been important, although he could never have said why.

"You see the regiment as merely another unpleasant alternative," Falkenberg said. "If it is never more than that, it will not be enough."

"He came for us, colonel," Frazer said. "He didn't have to."

"I take it you are sponsoring him."

"Yes, sir."

"Very well," Falkenberg said. "I doubt, Mister Fuller, if you realize just how you have been honored. Sergeant Major, is he acceptable to the men?"

"No objections, sir."

"Jeremy?"

"No objection, John Christian."

"Adjutant?"

"I've got his records, Colonel," Captain Fast indicated the console readout. "He'd make a terrible enlisted man."

"But not necessarily a terrible aviation officer?"

"No, sir. He scores out high enough. But I've got my doubts about his motivations."

"Yes. But we do not generally worry about men's motives. We only require that they act like soldiers. Are you objecting, Amos?"

"No, Colonel."

"Then that's that. Fuller, you will be on trial. It will not be the easiest experience of your life. Men earn their way into this regiment." He smiled suddenly. "The lot of a junior warrant officer is not always enviable."

"Yes, sir."

"You may go. There will be a formal swearing in when we return to our own camp. And doubtless Captain Fast will need information for his data base. Dismissed."

"Yes, sir." Mark left the command tent. The times are out of joint, he thought. Is that the right line? Whatever. Does anyone control his own life? I couldn't. The police, the Marines, the boss, now these mercenaries —they tell us all what to do. Who tells them?

Now I'm one of them. Mercenary soldier. It sounds ugly, but I don't have any choices at all. It's no career. Just a way out of slavery.

And yet—

He remembered the morning's combat and felt guilty at the memory. He had felt alive then. Men and women died all around him, but he'd felt more alive than he'd ever been.

He passed the graves. The honor guard stood at rigid attention, ignoring the buzzing insects, ignoring everything around them as they stood over the banner-draped figures laid out in neat rows. I'm one of them now, he thought, but whether he meant the guards or the corpses he couldn't say.

# XI

"Mr. President!"

"Mr. Vice!"

"I regret to report that, contrary to the rules of the mess, Captain Owensford brought his drink to his table. Sir!"

Captain Jesus Alana stood at the end of the head table and fixed Owensford with a chilly stare. "Captain Owensford!"

Owensford stood. "Mr. President."

"What have you to say in defense of your heinous crime?"

"It was a good drink, sir!"

"Unconscionable, Captain. You will report to the grog bucket."

"Sir!" Owensford marched to the end of the room.

"I presume you do this sort of thing on Sparta," Major Savage said.

"Perhaps we don't follow *all* of the old traditions," Lysander said. Then he grinned. "Actually, very little of this, but I may change that when I get back."

Owensford used fireman's tongs to remove a smoking flask from within a container marked with radiation trefoils. He carefully poured a metal cup full of the smoking brew, then put on welders' gloves and lifted the cup. "To our guest, to the mess president, and to the 42nd!" He drank, set the cup upside down on his head, and saluted.

"Mr. President!"

"Mr. Vice!"

"I regret to report that Captain Owensford neglected to salute the mess prior to imbibing. Sir!"

"Captain Owensford, what have you to say for yourself?"

"Previous drink was a *very* good drink, sir!"

"We'll excuse you. Once. Take your seat!"

"*Thank* you, sir!"

The ladies, except those in uniform, had long since retired from the dining hall. Catherine Alana had worn a civilian gown, and didn't return after escorting Ursula to her room in the regiment's guest quarters. *And I sleep alone tonight.* Lysander looked down to the far end of the table where Falkenberg sat impassively. *Interesting that he arranged our rooms that way. Or does he even know?*

Guests were excused from following the customs of the mess, but even without visiting the grog bucket Lysander had drunk more than he usually did. There had been cocktails before dinner, wine during dinner, port after dinner, and brandy after the port. Then Falkenberg had signaled, and the stewards brought whiskey, Scotch so smooth that it was more like brandy.

Now the colonel caught Alana's eye. The mess president nodded. "Pipe Major!"

"Sir!" A dozen pipers marched into the hall. Stewards brought more whiskey.

"Good God, Major," Lysander said. "Do you do this often?"

"Only when we've a good excuse."

And I expect you can always find one. "Of course, your victory last week needed celebrating."

"Right. We already did that, you know. You're the excuse tonight." Savage glanced at his watch. "Actually, I expect things will end soon enough. Staff meetings in the morning." He stood. "And on that score, if you'll excuse me, I have some preparations."

"I don't suppose you need help?"

Savage grinned. "It can be a bit much. Tell you what, I'll have a word with the mess president on my way out."

Ten minutes later the pipers paused for refreshments, and Captain Alana announced the formal end of the dining-out. Lysander got unsteadily to his feet.

Captain Owensford came over and spoke quietly. "Some of them will stay at it all night. Would you like a guide to your room?"

"Yes. Please!"

It was almost cool outside, and Lysander felt a little less drunk.

"Actually, the noise gets to me as much as the whisky," Owensford said. "I've never been crazy about pipers myself. Feeling all right now?"

"Not too bad—"

"I know a way to feel better."

"Yes?"

"We have a concoction. Vitamins. Tonic. Other stuff. Works every time. Would you care for some?"

"Captain, I would *kill* for a glass of that. Or two glasses. Please?"

Owensford grinned. "This way." He led Lysander to a small bar at the far end of the officers' mess, and ushered him to a table. "Billings, two Night Befores, please."

"Sir." The bartender was an old man, but he carried himself like a soldier. His left hand was a prosthetic adapted to bartending. He grinned and set two tall glasses on the table, went back, and brought a pitcher of water.

"You sip it," Owensford said. "Then down at least two glasses of water. Works like a charm."

Lysander sipped, and grimaced.

"I didn't say it *tasted* good," Owensford said. "Cheers." He sipped at his drink. "Understand you see the governor fairly often."

"Yes. Things heated up a bit while you were out in the field."

Owensford's eyes narrowed. "How so?"

"More plantation owners have joined the combine. Several dozen more. The boycott is working better than anyone expected."

"Damn. But I'm not surprised."

"Why not?"

"I've known Ace Barton for a while."

"Barton. The major in charge of the opposition's mercenaries."

"That's Ace."

"How did you get to know him?"

"Well—actually he was responsible for my being recruited into the Legion. It's a long story."

Lysander sipped at the drink and grimaced again. "I may be a while getting this down—"

Owensford leaned back and stared at the ceiling. "It was quite a long time ago, long enough that it's almost as if it happened to someone else. I was much younger then. . . ."

# XII

"As He died to make men holy, let us die to make men free. . . ."

The song echoed through the ship, along gray corridors stained with the greasy handprints of the thousands who had traveled in her before; through the stench of the thousands aboard, and the remembered smells of previous shiploads of convicts.

Peter Owensford looked up from the steel desk that hung from the wall of his tiny stateroom. The men weren't singing very well, but they sang from their hearts. There was a faint buzzing from a loose rivet vibrating to a strong bass voice. Owensford nodded to himself. The singer was Allan Roach, one-time professional wrestler, and Peter had marked him for promotion to noncom once they reached Santiago.

The trip from Earth to Thurstone takes three months in a Bureau of Relocation transport ship, and it had been wasted time for all of them. It was obvious to Peter that the CoDominium authorities aboard the ship knew that they were volunteers for the war. Why else would ninety-seven men voluntarily ship out for Santiago? It didn't matter, though. Political

Officer Stromand was afraid of a trap. Stromand was always suspecting traps.

In all the three months Peter Owensford had held only a dozen classes. He'd found an empty compartment near the garbage disposal and assembled the men there; but Stromand had caught them. There had been a scene, with Stromand insisting that Peter call him "Commissar" and the men address him as "Sir." Instead, Peter addressed him as "Mister" and the men made it come out like "Comics-star." Stromand had been livid, and he'd stopped Peter's classes.

Now Peter had ninety-six men who knew nothing of war. They were educated men. He had students, workers, idealists; but it might have been better if they'd all been zapouts with a long history of juvenile gangsterism.

He went back to his papers, jotting notes on what must be done when they landed. At least he'd have some time to train them before they got into combat.

He'd need it.

Thurstone is usually described as a hot, dry copy of Earth and Peter found no reason to dispute that. The CoDominium Island is legally part of Earth, but Thurstone is twenty parsecs away, and travelers go through customs. Peter's ragged group packed away whatever military equipment they had brought privately, and dressed in the knee breeches and tunics popular with businessmen in New York. Peter found himself just behind Allan Roach in the line to debark.

Allan was laughing.

"What's the joke?" Peter asked.

Roach turned and gestured at the men behind him. All ninety-six scattered through the first two hundred passengers leaving the BuRelock ship, and they were all dressed identically. "Humanity League decided to save money," Roach said. "What do you reckon the CD makes of our comic-opera army?"

Whatever the CoDominium inspectors thought, they did nothing, hardly glancing inside the baggage, and the volunteers were hustled out of the CD building to the docks. A small Russian in baggy pants sidled up to them.

"Freedom," he said. He had a thick accent.

"No passaran!" Commissar Stromand answered.

"I have tickets for you," the Russian said. "You will go on the boat." He pointed to an excursion ship with peeling paint and faded gilt handrails.

"Man, he looks like he's lettin' go his last credit," Allan Roach muttered to Owensford.

Peter nodded. "At that, I'd rather pay for the tickets than ride the boat. Must have been built when Thurstone was first settled."

Roach shrugged and lifted his bags. Then, as an afterthought, he lifted Peter's as well.

"You don't have to carry my goddamn baggage," Peter protested.

"That's why I'm doing it, Lieutenant. I wouldn't carry Stromand's." They went aboard the boat and stood at the rails to stare at Thurstone's bright skies. The volunteers were the only passengers, and the ship left the dock to lumber across shallow seas. It was less than fifty kilometers to the mainland, and before the men really believed they were out of space and onto a planet again, they were in Free Santiago.

They marched through the streets. People cheered, but a lot of volunteers had come through these streets and they didn't cheer very loud. Owensford's men were no good at marching and they had no weapons; so Stromand ordered them to sing war songs.

They didn't know very many songs, so they always
sang the Battle Hymn of the Republic. It said everything they were feeling, anyway.

The ragged group straggled to the local parish
church. Someone had broken the cross and spire off
the building, and turned the altar into a lecture
desk. It was nearly dark by the time Owensford's
troops were bedded down in the pews.

"Lieutenant?"

Allan Roach and another volunteer stood in front
of him. "Yes?"

"Some of the men don't like bein' in here, lieutenant. We got church members in the outfit."

"I see. What do you expect me to do about it?"
Peter asked. "This is where we were sent." *And why
didn't someone meet us instead of having a kid hand
me a note down at the docks? But it wouldn't do to
upset the men.*

"We could bed down outside," Roach suggested.

"Nonsense. Superstitious garbage." The strident,
bookish voice came from behind him, but Peter didn't
need to look around. "Free men have no need for
that kind of belief. Tell me who is disturbed."

Allan Roach set his lips tightly together.

"I insist," Stromand demanded. "Those men need
education, and I will provide it. We cannot have
superstition within our company."

"Superstition be damned," Peter said. "It's dark
and gloomy and uncomfortable in here. If the men
want to sleep outside, let them."

"No."

"I remind you that I am in command here." Pe-
ter's voice was rising despite his effort to control it.
He was twenty-three standard years old, while
Stromand was forty, and this was Peter's first com-

mand. He knew this was an important issue, and the men were all listening.

"I remind *you* that political education is totally up to me," Stromand said. "It is good indoctrination for the men to stay in here."

"Crap." Peter stood abruptly. "All right, everybody outside. Camp in the churchyard. Roach, set up a night guard around the camp."

"Yes, sir!" Allan Roach grinned.

Commissar Stromand watched his men melt away. A few minutes later he followed them outside.

They were awakened by an officer in synthileather trousers and tunic. He wore no badges of rank, but it was obvious to Peter that the man was a profressional soldier. Someday, Peter thought, I'll look like that. The thought was cheering.

"Who's in charge here?"

Stromand and Owensford answered simultaneously. The officer looked at them for a moment, then turned to Peter. "Name?"

"Lieutenant Peter Owensford."

"Lieutenant. And why might you be a lieutenant?"

"I'm a graduate of West Point, sir. And your rank?"

"Captain, sonny. Captain Anselm Barton, at your service, God help you. The lot of you have been posted to the Twelfth Brigade, second battalion, of which battlion I have the misfortune to be adjutant. Any more questions?" He glared at Peter and the commissar. Before either of them could answer there was a roar and the wind whipped red dust around them. A moment later a fleet of ground-effects trucks rounded the corner and stopped in front of the church.

"Okay," Barton shouted. "Into the trucks. You, too, Mister Comics-Star. Lieutenant, you ride in the cab with me. Come on, come on, we haven't all day. Can't you get them to hop it, Owensford?"

No two of the trucks were alike. One Mercedes stood out proudly from the lesser breeds, and Barton went to it. After a moment Stromand took the unoccupied seat in the cab of the second truck, an old Fiat. Despite the early hour, the sun was hot and bright, and it was good to get inside.

The Mercedes ran smoothly, but had to halt frequently while the drivers worked on the other trucks. The Fiat could only get ten centimeters above the road. Peter noted the ruts in the dirt track.

"Sure," Barton said. "We've got wheeled transport. Lots of it. Animal-drawn wagons too. Tracked railroads. How much do you know about this place?"

"Not very much," Peter admitted.

"At least you know that," Barton said. He gunned the engine to get the Mercedes over a deeply pitted section of the road and the convoy climbed up onto a ridge. Peter could look back and see the tiny port town, with its almost empty streets, and the blowing red dust.

"See that ridge over there?" Barton asked. He pointed to a thin blue line beyond the far lip of the saucer on the other side of the ridge. The air was so clear that Peter could see for sixty kilometers or more. Distances were hard to judge.

"Yes, sir."

"That's it. Dons territory beyond that line."

"We're not going straight there, are we? The men need training."

"You might as well be going to the lines, for all the training they'll get. They teach you anything at the Point?"

"I learned something, I think." Peter didn't know what to answer. The Point had been "humanized" and he knew he hadn't had the military instruction that graduates had once received. "What I was taught, and a lot from books."

"We'll see." Barton took a plastic toothpick out of one pocket and stuck it into his mouth. Later, Peter would learn that many men developed that habit. "No hay tobacco" was a common notice on stores in Santiago. The first time he saw it, Allan Roach said that if they made their tobacco out of hay he didn't want any. "Long out of the Point?" Barton asked.

"Class of '77."

"Just out. U.S. Army didn't want you?"

"That's pretty personal," Peter said. The toothpick danced across smiling lips. Peter stared out at the rivers of dust blowing around them. "There's a new rule now. You have to opt for CoDominium in your junior year. I did. But they didn't have any room for me in the CD service."

Barton grunted. "And the U.S. Army doesn't want any commie-coddling officers who'd take the CD over their own country."

"That's about it."

They drove on in silence. Barton hummed something under his breath, a tune that Peter thought he would recognize if only Barton would make it loud enough to hear. Then he caught a murmured refrain. "Let's hope he brings our godson up, to don the Armay blue . . ."

Barton looked around at his passenger and grinned. "How many lights in Cullem Hall, Mister Dumbjohn?"

"Three hundred and forty lights, sir," Peter answered automatically. He looked for the ring, but Barton wore none. "What was your class, sir?"

"Sixty-two. Okay, so the U.S. didn't want you, and the CD's disbanding regiments. There's other outfits. Falkenberg's recruiting. . . ."

"I'm not a mercenary," Peter said stiffly.

"Oh, Lord. So you're here to help the downtrodden masses throw off the yoke of oppression. I might have known."

"But of course I'm here to fight slavery! Everyone knows about Santiago."

"Everyone knows about other places, too." The toothpick danced again. "Okay, you're a liberator of suffering humanity. God knows, anything makes a man feel better out here is okay. But to help *me* feel better, remember that you're a professional officer."

"I won't forget." They drove over another ridge. The valley beyond was no different from the one behind them, and there was another ridge at its end.

"What do you think those people out there want?" Barton said.

"Freedom."

"Maybe to be left alone. Maybe they'd be happy if we all went away."

"They'd be slaves. Somebody's got to help them—" Peter caught himself. There was no point to this, and he was sure Barton was laughing at him.

Instead, the older man's expression softened from his usual sardonic grin to a wry smile. "Nothing to be ashamed of, Pete. Most of us read those books about knighthood. We wouldn't be in the services if we didn't have that streak in us. But remember, you get over most of that or you won't last."

"Maybe without something like that I wouldn't want to last."

"Suit yourself. Just don't let it break your heart."

"If you feel that way about everything, why are you here? Why aren't you in one of the mercenary outfits?"

"Commissars ask that kind of question," Barton said. He gunned the motor viciously and the Mercedes screamed forward.

It was late afternoon when they got to Tarazona. The town was an architectural hodgepodge, as if a dozen amateurs had designed it. The church, now a hospital, was Elizabeth III modern; the post office was American Gothic; and most of the houses were white stucco. The volunteers unloaded at a plasteel barracks that was a bad copy of the quad at West Point. It had sally ports, phony portcullis and all, and plastic medieval shields decorated the cornices.

Inside there was trash in the corridors and blood on the floors. Peter set the men to cleaning up.

"About that blood," Captain Barton said. "Your men seem interested."

"First blood some of 'em have seen," Peter told him. Barton was still watching him closely. "All right. For me, too."

Barton nodded. "Two stories about that blood. The Dons had a garrison here. They made a stand when the Revolutionaries took the town. Some say the Dons slaughtered their prisoners here. Others say when the Republic took the barracks, our troops slaughtered the garrison."

Peter looked across the dusty courtyard and beyond the hills where the fighting was. It seemed a long way off. There was no sound, and the afternoon sun was unbearably hot. "Which do you think is true?"

"Both." Barton turned away toward the town. Then he stopped for a moment. "I'll be in the bistro after dinner. Join me if you get a chance." He walked on, his feet kicking up little clouds of dust that blew across the road.

Peter stood a long time in the courtyard, staring across fields that stretched fifty kilometers to the hills. The soil was red, and a hot wind blew dust into every crevice and hollow. The country seemed far too barren to be a focal point in the struggle for freedom in the known galaxy.

Thurstone had been colonized early in the Co-Dominium period, but the planet was too poor to attract wealthy corporations. The third Thurstone expedition was financed by the Carlist branch of the Spanish monarchy, and eventually Carlos XII and a group of supporters—malcontents, like most voluntary colonists—founded Santiago.

Some of the Santiago colonists were protesting the Bourbon restoration in Spain. Others were unhappy with John XXVI's reunification of Christendom. Others still protested the cruel fates, unhappy love affairs, nagging wives, and impossible gambling debts. The Carlists got the smallest and poorest of Thurstone's three continents, but they did well enough with it.

For thirty years Santiago received only voluntary immigrants from Spanish Catholic cultures. The Carlists were careful who they let in, and there was plenty of good land for everyone. The Kingdom of St. James had little modern technology, and no one was very rich, but few were very poor either.

Eventually the Population Control Commission designated Thurstone as a recipient planet, and the Bureau of Relocation began moving people there. All three governments on Thurstone protested, but unlike Xanadu or Danube, Thurstone had never developed a navy; a single frigate from the CoDominium Fleet convinced them they had no choice.

BuRelock ships carried two million involuntary colonists to Thurstone. Convicts, welfare frauds, criminals, revolutionaries, rioters, street gangsters, men who'd offended a BuRelock clerk, men with the wrong color eyes, and those who were just plain unlucky; all of them bundled into unsanitary transport ships and hustled away from Earth. The other nations on Thurstone had friends in BuRelock and money to pay for favors; Santiago got the bulk of the new immigrants.

The Carlists tried. They provided transportation to unclaimed lands for all who wanted it and most who did not. The original Santiago settlers had fled from industry and had built very little; and now, suddenly, they were swamped with city dwellers from a different culture who had no thought of the land and less love for it.

In less than a decade the capital grew from a sleepy town to a sprawling heap of shacks. The Carlists demolished the worst of the shacks. Others appeared on the other side of town. New cities grew from small towns.

When industries appeared in the new cities, the original settlers revolted. They had fled from industrialized life, and wanted no more of it. A king was deposed and an infant prince placed on his father's throne. The Cortes took government into its own hands, and enslaved everyone who did not pay his own way.

It was not called slavery, but "indebtedness for welfare service"; but debts were inheritable and transferable. Debts could be bought and sold on speculation, and everyone had to work them off.

In a generation half the population was in debt. In another the slaves outnumbered the free men. Finally the slaves revolted, and overnight Santiago became a *cause celebre*.

In the CoDominium Grand Senate, the U.S., with a nudge from the other governments on Thurstone and the corporations who bought agricultural products from Santiago, supported the Carlists, but not strongly. The Soviet senators supported the Republic, but not strongly. The CD Navy was ordered to quarantine the war area.

The fleet had few ships to spare for that task. The Navy grounded all military air and spacecraft in Santiago, and prohibited the import of any kind of heavy weapons. Otherwise Santiago was left alone.

It was never difficult for the Humanity League to send volunteers to Santiago as long as they brought no weapons. Because the volunteers had no experience, the League also searched for trained officers to lead them.

The League rejected mercenaries, of course.

# XIII

Peter Owensford sat in the pleasant cool of the Santiago evening at a scarred table that might have been oak, but wasn't. Captain Ace Barton brought a pitcher of dark red wine and joined him.

"I thought they'd put me in the technical corps," Peter said.

"Speak Mandarin?" Peter looked up in surprise. Barton grinned. "The Republicans hired Xanadu techs. What with the quarantine we don't have much high tech equipment. Plenty of Chinese for what little we've got."

"So I'm infantry."

Barton shrugged. "You fight, Pete. Just like me. They'll give you a company. The ones you brought in, and maybe another hundred recruits. All yours. You'll get Stromand for political officer, too."

Peter grimaced. "What use is he?"

Barton made a show of looking around. "Careful." His grin stayed, but his voice was serious. "Political officers are a lot more popular with the high command than we are. Don't forget that."

"From what I've seen the high command isn't very competent. . . ."

"Jesus," Barton said. "Look, Pete, they can have you shot for talking like that. This isn't a merc outfit under the Mercenary Code, you know. This is a patriotic war, and you'd better not forget it."

Peter stared at the packed clay floor. He'd sat at this table every night for a week now, and he was beginning to understand Barton's cynicism. "There's not enough body armor for my men. The ones I've got. You say they'll give me more men?"

"New group coming in tomorrow. No officer with them. Sure, they'll put 'em with you. Where else? Troops have to be trained."

"Trained!" Peter snorted. "We have enough Nemourlon to make armor for about half the troops, but I'm the only one in the company who knows how to do it. We've got no weapons, no optics, no communications—"

"Yeah, things are tough all over," Barton poured another glass of wine. "What'd you expect in a non-industrial society quarantined by the CD?"

Peter slumped back into the hard wooden chair. "Yeah, I know. But—I can't even train them on what we do have. Whenever I get the men assembled, Stromand starts making speeches."

Barton smiled. "International Brigade Commander Cermak thinks the American troops have lousy morale. Obviously, the way to fix that is to make speeches."

"Their morale is lousy because they don't know how to fight."

"Another of Cermak's solutions to the morale problem is to shoot defeatists," Barton said softly. "I've warned you, kid."

"The only damn thing my men have learned in the last week is how to sing and which red-light houses are safe."

"More'n some do. Have another drink."

"Thanks." Peter nodded in resignation. "That's not bad wine."

"Right. Pretty good, but not good enough to export," Barton said. "Whole goddamn country's that way, you know. Pretty good, but not quite good enough."

The next day they gave Peter Owensford 107 new men fresh from Earth. A week later Peter found Ace Barton at his favorite table in the bistro.

Barton poured a glass of wine as Peter sat down. "You look like you need a drink. I thought you were ordered to stay on nights to train the troops."

Peter drank. "Same story, Ace. Speeches. More speeches. I walked out. It was obvious I wasn't going to have anything to do."

"Risky," Barton said. They sat in silence as Barton looked thoughtful. Finally he spoke. "Ever think you're not needed, Pete?"

"They act that way, but I'm still the only man in the company with any military training."

"So what? The Republic doesn't need your troops. Not the way you think. The main purpose of the volunteers is to see the right party stays in control."

Peter sat stiffly silent. He'd promised himself that he wouldn't react quickly to anything Barton said. "I can't believe that," he said finally. "The volunteers come from everywhere. They're not fighting to help any political party, they're here to set people free."

Barton said nothing. A red toothpick danced across his face, and a sly grin broke across his square features.

"See, you don't even believe it yourself," Peter said.

"Could be. Pete, you ever think how much money

they raise back in the States? Money from people who feel guilty about not volunteerin'?"

"No. There's no money here. You've seen that."

"There's money, but it goes to the techs," Barton said. "That at least makes sense. Xanadu isn't sending their sharp boys for nothing, and without them, what's the use of mudcrawlers like us?"

Peter leaned back. "Then we've got pretty good technical support. . . ."

"About as good as the Dons have. Which means neither side has a goddamn thing. Either group gets a real edge that way, the war's over, right? But nobody's going to get past the CD quarantine, so all the Dons and the Republicans can do is kill each other with rifles and knives and grenades. Not very damn many grenades, either."

"We don't even have rifles."

"You'll get them. Meantime, relax. You've told Brigade your men aren't ready to fight. You've asked for weapons and more Nemourlon. You've complained about Stromand. You've done it all. Now shut up before they shoot you for a defeatist. That's an order, Pete."

"Yes, sir."

The trucks came back to Tarazona a week later. They carried coffin-shaped boxes full of rifles and bayonets from New Aberdeen, Thurstone's largest city. The rifles were covered with grease, and there wasn't any solvent to clean them with. Most were copies of Remington 2045 model automatics, but there were some Krupps and Skodas. Most of the men didn't know which ammunition fit their rifles.

"Not bad gear." Barton turned one of the rifles over in his hands. "We've had worse."

"But I don't have much training in rifle tactics," Peter said.

Barton shrugged. "No power supplies, no maintenance ships. Damn few mortars and rockets. No fancy munitions. There's no base to support anything more complicated than chemical slug-throwers, Peter. Forget the rest of the crap you learned and remember that."

"Yes, sir."

Whistles blew, and someone shouted from the trucks. "Get your gear and get aboard!"

"What?" Owensford turned to Barton. "Get aboard for where?"

Barton shrugged. "I'd better get back to my area. Maybe they're moving the whole battalion up while we've got the trucks."

They were. Men who had armor put it on, and everyone dressed in combat synthileather. Most had helmets, ugly hemispheric models with a stiff spine over the most vulnerable areas. A few men had lost theirs, and they boarded the trucks without them.

The convoy rolled across the plains and into a greener farm area. After dark the air chilled fast under clear, cloudless skies. The drivers pushed on, driving too fast without lights. Peter sat in the back of the lead truck, his knees clamped tightly together, his teeth unconsciously beating out a rhythm he'd learned years before. No one talked.

At dawn they unloaded in another valley. Trampled crops lay all around them.

"Good land," Private Lunster said. He lifted a clod and crumbled it between his fingers. "Very good land."

Somehow that made Peter feel better. He formed the men into ranks and made sure each knew how to load his weapon. Then he had each of them fire at a crumbling adobe wall. He chose a large target that they couldn't miss. More trucks pulled in and unloaded heavy generators and antitank lasers. When Owensford's men tried to get close to the heavy weapons the gunners shouted them away. The gunners seemed familiar with their equipment, and that was encouraging.

Everyone spoke softly, and when anyone raised his voice it was like a shout. Stromand tried to get the men to sing, but they wouldn't.

"Not long now, eh?" Sergeant Roach said.

"I expect not," Peter told him, but he didn't know, and went off to find the commissary truck. He wanted to be sure the men got a good meal that evening.

Orders to move up came during the night. A guide whispered to Peter to follow him, and they moved out across the unfamiliar land. Somewhere out there were the Dons with their army of peasant conscripts and mercenaries and family retainers. Peter and his company hadn't gone fifty meters before they passed an old tree and someone whispered to them.

"Everything will be fine," Stromand's voice said from the shadows. "All of the enemy are politically immature. Their vaqueros will run away and their peasant conscripts will throw away their weapons. They have no reason to be loyal."

"Why the hell has the war gone on three years?" someone whispered behind Peter.

He waited until they were long past the tree. "Roach, that wasn't smart. Stromand will have you shot for defeatism."

"He'll play hell doing it, lieutenant. You, man, pick up your feet. Want to fall down that gully?"

"Quiet," the guide whispered urgently. They went on through the dark night, down a slope, then up

another, past men dug into the hillside. No one
spoke.

Peter found himself walking along the remains of a
railroad. Most of the ties were gone, and the rails
had been taken away. Eventually his guide halted.
"Dig in here," he whispered. "Long live freedom."

"No pasaran!" Stromand answered.

"Please be quiet," the guide urged. "We are within
earshot of the enemy."

"Ah," Stromand answered. The guide turned away
and the political officer began to follow him.

"Where are you going?" Corporal Grant asked in a
loud whisper.

"To report to Major Harris," Stromand answered.
"The battalion commander ought to know where we
are."

"So should we," a voice said.

"Who was that?" Stromand demanded. The only
answer was a juicy raspberry.

"That bastard's got no right," a voice said close to
Peter.

"Who's there?"

"Rotwasser, sir." Rotwasser was the company run-
ner. The job gave him the nominal rank of monitor
but he had no maniple to command. Instead he
carried complaints from the men to Owensford.

"I can spare the P.O. better than anyone else,"
Peter whispered. "I'll need you here, not back at
battalion. Now start digging us in."

It was cold on the hillside, but digging kept the
men warm. Dawn came slowly and brought no
warmth. Peter took out his light-amplifying binoculars and cautiously looked out ahead. The binoculars
had been a present from his mother, and were the
only good optical equipment in the company.

The countryside was cut into small, steep-sided

ridges and valleys. Allan Roach lay beside Owensford and whistled softly. "We take that ridge in front of us, there's another just like it after that. And another. Nobody's goin' to win this war that way. . . ."

Owensford nodded silently. There were trees in the valley below, oranges and dates imported from Earth mixed in with native fruit trees as if a giant had spilled seeds across the ground. The fire-gutted remains of a whitewashed adobe peasant house stood among the trees.

Zing! Something that might have been a hornet but wasn't buzzed angrily over Peter's head. There was a flat crack from across the valley, then more angry buzzes. Dust puffs sprouted from the earthworks.

"Down!" Peter ordered.

"What are they trying to do, kill us?" Allan Roach shouted. There was a chorus of laughs. "Sir, why didn't they use IR on us in the dark? We should have stood out in this cold—"

Peter shrugged. "Maybe they don't have any. We don't."

The men who'd skimped on their holes dug in deeper, throwing the dirt out onto the ramparts in front of them. They laughed as they worked. It was very poor technique, and Peter worried about artillery, but nothing happened. The enemy was about four hundred meters away, across the valley, stretched out along a ridge identical to the one Peter held. No infantry that ever lived could have taken either ridge by charging across the valley. Both sides were safe until something heavier was brought up.

One large-caliber gun was trained on their position. It fired on anything that moved. There was also a laser, with several mirrors that could be moved about between flashes. The laser itself was safe. So were the mirrors, because the monarchists never fired twice from the same position.

The men shot at the guns and at where they thought the mirror was anyway until Peter ordered them to stop wasting ammunition. It wasn't good for morale to lie there and not fight back, though.

"I bet I can locate that goddamn gun," Corporal Bassinger told Peter. "I got the best eyesight in the company."

Peter mentally called up Bassinger's records. Two ex-wives and an acknowledged child by each. Volunteered after being an insurance man in Brooklyn for years. "You can't spot that thing."

"Sure I can, Lieutenant. Loan me your glasses, I'll spot it sure."

"All right. Be careful. They're shooting at anything they can see."

"I'm careful."

"Let me see, man!" someone shouted. Three men clustered in the trench around Bassinger. "Let us look!" "Don't be a hog, we want to see too." "Comrade, let us look—"

"Get away from here," Bassinger shouted. "You heard the lieutenant, it's dangerous to look over the ramparts."

"What about you?"

"I'm an observer. Besides, I'm careful." He crawled into position and looked out through the little slot he'd cut away in the dirt in front of him. "See, it's safe enough. I think I see—"

Bassinger was thrown back into the trench. The shattered glass fell on top of him, and he had already ceased breathing by the time they heard the shot that hit him in the eye.

That day two men had toes shot off and had to be evacuated.

They lay on a hill for a week. Each night they lost a few more men to minor casualties that could not possibly have been inflicted by the enemy. Then Stromand had two men with foot injuries shot by a squad of military police from staff headquarters.

The injuries ceased, and the men lay sullenly in the trenches until the company was relieved.

They had two days in a small town near the front, then the officers were called to a meeting. The briefing officer had a thick accent, but it was German, not Spanish. The briefing was for the Americans and it was held in English.

"We vill have a full assault. All international volunteers vill move out at once. We vill use infiltration tactics."

"What does that mean?" Captain Barton demanded.

The staff officer looked pained. "Ven you break through their lines, go straight to their technical areas and disrupt them. Ven that is done, the war is over."

"Where are their technical corpsmen?"

"You vill be told after you have broken through their lines."

The rest of the briefing made no more sense to Peter. He walked out with Barton after they were dismissed. "Looked at your section of the line?" Barton asked.

"As much as I can," Peter answered. "Do you have a decent map?"

"No. Old CD orbital photographs, and some sketches. No better than what you have."

"What I did see looks bad," Peter said. "There's an olive grove, then a hollow I can't see into. Is there cover in there?"

"You better patrol and find out."

"You will ask the battalion commander for permission to conduct patrols," a stern voice said from behind them.

"You better watch that habit of walking up on people, Stromand," Barton said. "One of these days somebody's not going to realize it's you." He gave Peter a pained look. "Better ask."

Major Harris told Peter that Brigade had forbidden patrols. Surprise was needed, and patrols might alert the enemy of the coming attack.

As he walked back to his company area, Peter reflected that Harris had been an attorney for the Liberation Party before he volunteered to go to Santiago.

They were to move out the next morning. The night was long. The men cleaned their weapons and talked in whispers. Some drew meaningless diagrams in the mud of the dugouts. About halfway through the night forty new volunteers joined the company. They had no equipment other than rifles, and they had left the port city only two days before. Most came from Churchill, and because they spoke English and the trucks were coming to this section, they had been sent along.

Major Harris called the officers together at dawn. "The Xanadu techs have managed to acquire some rockets," he told them. "They'll drop them on the Dons before we move out. Owensford, you will move out last. You will shoot any man who hasn't gone before you do."

"That's my job," Stromand protested.

"I want you to lead," Harris said. "The bombardment will come at 0815 hours. Do you all have proper timepieces?"

"No, sir," Peter said. "I've only got a watch that counts Earth time. . . ."

"Hell," Harris muttered. "Okay, Thurstone's hours are 1.08 Earth hours long. You'll have to work it out from that. . . ." He looked confused.

"No problem," Peter assured him.

"Okay, back to your areas."

Zero hour went past with no signals. Another hour passed. Then a Republican brigade to the north began firing, and a few men left their dugouts and moved onto the valley floor.

A ripple of fire and flashing mirrors colored the ridge beyond as the enemy began firing. The Republican troops were cut down, and the few who were not hit scurried back into their shelters.

"Fire support!" Harris shouted. "Owensford's squawk box made unintelligible sounds, effectively jammed as were all electronics Peter had seen on Santiago, but he heard the order passed down the line. His company fired at the enemy, and the monarchists fired back.

Within minutes it was clear that the enemy dominated the valley. A few large rockets rose from behind the enemy lines and crashed randomly into the Republican positions. There were more flashes across the sky as the Xanadu technicians backtracked the enemy rockets and returned counterfire. Eventually the shooting stopped for lack of targets.

It was 1100 by Peter's watch when a series of explosions lit the lip of the monarchist ramparts. Another wave of rockets fell among the enemy, and the Republicans to the north began to charge forward.

"Ready to move out!" Peter shouted. He waited for orders.

There was nearly a minute of silence. No more rockets fell on the enemy. Then the ridge opposite rippled with fire again, and the Republicans began to go down or scramble back to their positions.

The alert tone sounded on Peter's squawk box and he lifted it to his ear. Amazingly, he could hear intelligible speech. Someone at headquarters was speaking to Major Harris.

"The Republicans have already advanced half a kilometer. They are being slaughtered because you have not moved your precious Americans in support."

"Bullshit!" Harris's voice had no tones in the tiny speaker. "The Republicans are already back in their dugouts. The attack has failed."

"It has not failed. You must show what high morale can do. Your men are all volunteers. Many Republicans are conscripts. Set an example for them."

"But I tell you the attack has failed."

"Major Harris, if your men have not moved out in five minutes I will send the military police to arrest you as a traitor."

The box went back to random squeals and growls; then the whistles blew and orders were passed down the line. "Move out."

Peter went from dugout to dugout. "Up and at them. Jarvis, if you don't get out of there I'll shoot you. You three, get going." He saw that Allan Roach was doing the same thing.

When they reached the end of the line, Roach grinned at Peter. "We're all that's left, now what?"

"Now we move out, too." They crawled forward, past the lip of the hollow that had sheltered them. Ten meters beyond that they saw Major Harris lying very still.

"Captain Barton's in command of the battalion," Peter said.

"Wonder if he knows it? I'll take the left side, sir, and keep 'em going, shall I?"

"Yes." Now he was more alone than ever. He went on through the olive groves, finding men and keeping them moving ahead of him. There was very little fire from the enemy. They advanced fifty meters, a hundred, and reached the slope down into the hollow beyond. It was an old vineyard. The stumps of the vines reached out of the ground like old women's hands.

They were well into the hollow when the Dons fired.

Four of the newcomers from Churchill were just ahead of Owensford. When the volley lashed their hollow they hit the dirt in perfect formation. Peter crawled forward to compliment them on how well they'd learned the training-book exercises. All four were dead.

He was thirty meters into the hollow. In front of him was a network of red stripes woven through the air a meter above the ground. He'd seen it at the Point: an interlocking network of crossfire guided by laser beams. Theoretically the Xanadu technicians should be able to locate the mirrors, or even the power plants, but the network hung there motionless.

Some of the men didn't know what it was and charged into it. After a while there was a little wall of dead men and boys at its edge. No one could advance. Snipers began to pick off any of the still figures that tried to move. Peter lay there, wondering if any of the other companies were making progress. Most of his men tried to find shelter behind the bodies of dead comrades. One by one his troops died as they lay there in the open, in the bright sunshine of a dying vineyard.

Late in the afternoon it began to rain: first a few drops, then harder, finally a storm that cut off all visibility. The men who could crawl made their way back to their dugouts. There were no orders for a retreat.

Peter found small groups of men and sent them out to bring back the wounded. It was hard to get men to go back into the hollow, even in the driving rainstorm, and he had to go with them or they would vanish in the mud and gloom. Eventually there were no more wounded to find.

The scene in the trenches was a shambled hell of bloody mud. Men fell into the dugouts and lay where they fell, too tired and scared to move. Some of the wounded died there in the mud, and others fell on top of them, trampling the bodies down and out of sight because no one had the strength to move them. For several hours Peter was the only officer in the battalion. The company was his, and the men were calling him "Captain."

In mid afternoon Stromand came into the trenches carrying a bundle.

Incredibly, Allan Roach was unhurt. The huge wrestler stood in Stromand's path. "What is that?" he demanded.

Roach didn't move. "While we were out there you were off printing leaflets?"

"I had orders," Stromand said. He backed nervously away from the big sergeant. His hand rested on a pistol butt.

"Roach," Peter said calmly. "Help me with the wounded, please."

Roach stood in indecision. Finally he turned to Peter. "Yes, sir."

At dawn Peter had eighty effectives to hold the lines. The Dons would have had no trouble taking his position, but they were strangely quiet. Peter went from dugout to dugout trying to get a count of his men. Two hundred wounded sent to rear areas.

He could count one-hundred-thirteen dead. That left ninety-four vanished. Died, deserted, ground into the mud; he didn't know.

There hadn't been any general attack. The international volunteer commander had thought that even without it, this would be a splendid opportunity to show what morale could do. It had done that, all right.

The Republican command was frantic. The war was stalemated, which meant the superior forces of the Dons were slowly grinding the Republicans down.

In desperation they sent a large group to the stable front in the south. The previous attack had been planned to the last detail; this one was to depend entirely on surprise. Peter's remnants were reinforced with pieces of other outfits and fresh volunteers, and sent against the enemy.

The objective was an agricultural center called Zaragoza, a small town set among olive groves and vineyards. Peter's column moved through the groves to the edge of town.

Surprise was complete, and the battle was short. A flurry of firing, quick advances, and the enemy retreated. Communications were sporadic, but it looked as if Peter's group had advanced farther than any other. They were the spearhead of freedom in the south.

They marched in to cheering crowds. His army looked like scarecrows, but women held their children up to see their liberators. It made it all worthwhile: the stupidity of the generals, the heat and mud and cold and dirt and lice—all of it forgotten in their victory.

More troops came in behind them, but Peter's company camped at the edge of their town. The next day the army would advance again; if the war could be made fluid, fought in quick battles of fast-moving men, it might yet be won. Certainly, Peter thought, certainly the people of Santiago were waiting for them. They'd have support from the population. How long could the Dons hold?

Just before dark they heard shots in the town.

He brought his duty squad on the run, dashing through the dusty streets, past the pockmarked adobe walls to the town square. The military police were there.

"Never saw such pretty soldiers," Allan Roach said. Peter nodded.

"Captain, where do you think they got those shiny boots? And the new rifles? Seems we never have good equipment for the troops, but the police always have more than enough. . . ."

A small group of bodies lay like broken dolls at the foot of the churchyard wall. The priest, the mayor, and three young men. "Monarchists. Carlists," someone whispered. Some of the townspeople spat on the bodies.

An old man was crouched beside one of the dead. He cradled the youthful head in his hands, and blood poured through his fingers. He looked at Peter with dull eyes. "Why are you here?" he asked. "Are there not richer worlds for you to conquer?"

Peter turned away without answering. He could think of nothing to say.

"Captain!"

Peter woke to Allan Roach's urgent whisper.

"Cap'n, there's something moving down by the stream. Not the Dons. Mister Stromand's with 'em, about five men. Officers, I think, from headquarters."

Peter sat upright. He hadn't seen Stromand since the disastrous attack three hundred kilometers to the north. The man wouldn't have lasted five minutes in combat among his former comrades. "Anyone else know?"

"Albers, nobody else. He called me."

"Let's go find out what they want. Quietly, Allan." They walked silently in the hot night. What were staff officers doing in his company area, near the vanguard of the advancing Republican forces? And why hadn't they called him?

They followed the small group down the nearly dry creek bed to the town wall. When their quarry halted, they stole closer until they could hear.

"About here," Stromand's bookish voice said. "This will be perfect."

"How long do we have?" Peter recognized the German accent of the staff officer who'd briefed them. The next voice was even more of a shock.

"Two hours. Enough time, but we must go quickly." It was Brigadier Cermak, second in command of the volunteer forces. "It is set?"

"Yes."

"Hold it." Peter stepped out from the shadows. He covered the small group with his rifle. Allan Roach moved quickly away from him so that he also threatened them. "Identify yourselves."

"You know who we are, Owensford," Stromand snapped.

"Yes. What are you doing here?"

"That is none of your business, Captain," Cermak answered. "I order you to return to your company area and say nothing about seeing us."

"In a minute. Major, if you continue moving your hand toward your pistol, Sergeant Roach will cut you in half. Allan, I'm going to have a look at what they were carrying. Cover me."

"Right."

"You can't!" The German staff officer moved toward Peter.

Owensford reacted automatically. His rifle swung in an uppercut that caught the German under the chin. The man fell with a strangled cry and lay still. Everyone stood frozen.

"Interestin', Captain," Allan Roach said. "I think they're more scared of bein' heard by our side than by the enemy."

Peter squatted over the device they'd set by the wall. "A bomb of some kind, from the timers—Jesus!"

"What is it, Cap'n?"

"A fission bomb," Peter said slowly. "They were going to leave a fission bomb here. To detonate in two hours, did you say?" he asked conversationally. His thoughts whirled, but he could find no explanation; and he was very surprised at how calm he felt. "Why?"

No one answered.

"Why blow up the only advancing force in the Republican army?" Peter asked wonderingly. "They can't be traitors. The Dons wouldn't have these on a platter—but—Stromand, is there a new CD warship in orbit here? New fleet forces to stop this war?"

More silence.

"What does it mean?" Allan Roach asked. His rifle was steady, and there was an edge to his voice. "Why use an atom bomb on their own men?"

"The ban," Peter said. "One thing the CD does enforce. No nukes." He was hardly aware that he spoke aloud. "The CD inspectors will see the spearhead of the Republican army destroyed by nukes, and think the Dons did it. They're the only ones who could benefit from it. So the CD cleans up the Carlists, and these bastards end up in charge when the fleet pulls out. That's it, isn't it? Cermak? Stromand?"

"Of course," Stromand said. "You fool, come with us, then. Leave the weapons in place. We're sorry we didn't think we could trust you with the plan, but it was just too important . . . it means winning the war."

"At what price?"

"A low price. A battalion of soldiers and one village. More are killed every week. A comparatively bloodless victory."

Allan Roach spat viciously. "If that's freedom, I don't want it. You ask any of them?" He waved toward the village.

Peter remembered the cheering crowds. He stooped down to the weapon and examined it closely. "Any secret to disarming this? If there is, you're standing as close to it as I am."

"Wait," Stromand shouted. "Don't touch it, leave it, come with us. You'll be promoted, you'll be a hero of the movement—"

"Disarm it or I'll have a try," Peter said. He retrieved his rifle and waited.

After a moment Stromand bent down to the bomb. It was no larger than a small suitcase. He took a key from his pocket and inserted it, then turned dials. "It is safe now."

"I'll have another look," Peter said. He bent over the weapon. Yes, a large iron bar had been moved through the center of the device, and the fissionables couldn't come together. As he examined it there was a flurry of activity behind him.

"Hold it!" Roach commanded. He raised his rifle, but Political Officer Stromand had already vanished into the darkness. "I'll go after him, Cap'n." They could hear thrashing among the olive trees nearby.

"No. You'd never catch him. Not without making a big stir. And if this story gets out, the whole Republican cause is finished."

"You are growing more intelligent," Cermak said. "Why not let us carry out our plan now?"

"I'll be damned," Peter said. "Get out of here, Cermak. Take your staff carrion with you. And if you send the military police after me or Sergeant Roach, you can be damned sure this story—and the bomb—will get to the CD inspectors. Don't think I can't arrange it."

Cermak shook his head. "You are making a mistake—"

"The mistake is lettin' you go," Roach said. "Why don't I shoot him? Or cut his throat?"

"There'd be no point in it," Peter said. "If Cermak doesn't stop him, Stromand will be back with the MPs. No, let them go."

# XIV

Peter's company advanced thirty kilometers in the next three days. They crossed the valley with its dry river of sand and moved swiftly into the low brush on the other side. They were halted at the top of the ridge.

Rockets and artillery fire exploded all around them. There was no one to fight, only unseen enemies on the next ridge, and the fire poured into their positions for three days.

The enemy fire held them while the glare and heat of Thurstone's sun punished them. Men became snowblind, and wherever they looked there was only one color: fiery yellow. When grass and trees caught fire they hardly noticed the difference.

When the water ran out they retreated. There was nothing else to do. They fled back across the valley, past the positions they'd won, halting to let other units pass while they held the road. On the seventh day after they'd left it, they were back on the road where they'd jumped off into the valley.

There was no organization. Peter was the only officer among 172 men of a battalion that had neither command nor staff; just 172 men too tired to care.

"We've the night, anyway," Roach said. He sat next to Peter and took out a cigarette. "Last tobacco in the battalion, Cap'n. Share?"

"No, thanks. Keep it all."

"One night to rest," Roach said again. "Seems like forever, a whole night without anybody shooting at us."

Fifteen minutes later Peter's radio squawked. He strained to hear the commands through the static and jamming. "Call the men together," Peter ordered when he'd heard it out.

"It's this way," he told them. "We still hold Zaragoza. There's a narrow corridor into the town, and unless somebody gets down there to hold it open, we'll lost the village. If that goes, our whole position in the valley's lost."

"Cap'n, you can't ask it!" The men were incredulous. "Go back down into there? You can't make us do that!"

"No. I can't make you. But remember Zaragoza? Remember how the people cheered us when we marched in? It's our town. Nobody else set those people free. We did. And there's nobody else who can go help keep them free, either. No other reinforcements. Will we let them down?"

"We can't," Allan Roach said. "It needs doing. I'll come with you, Cap'n."

One by one the others got to their feet. The ragged column marched down the side of the ridge, out of the cool heights where their water was assured, down into the valley of the river of sand.

By dawn they were half a kilometer from the town. Republican troops streamed down the road toward them. Others ran through the olive groves that lined both sides of the road.

"Tanks!" someone shouted. "Tanks coming!"

It was too late. The enemy armor had bypassed Zaragoza and was closing on them fast. The Dons' infantry came right behind the tanks. Peter swallowed the bitter taste in his mouth, and ordered his men to dig in among the olive trees. It would be their last battle.

An hour later they were surrounded. Two hours passed as they fought to hold the useless groves. The tanks had long since passed their position, but the enemy was still all around them. Then the shooting stopped, and silence lay over the grove.

Peter crawled around the perimeter of his command: a hundred meters, no more. He had fewer than fifty men.

Allan Roach lay in a shallow hole at one edge. He was partially covered by ripe olives shaken from the trees, and when Peter came close, the sergeant laughed. "Makes you feel like a salad," he said, brushing away more olives. "What do we do, Cap'n? Why do you think they quit shooting?"

"Wait and see."

It didn't take long. "Will you surrender?" a voice called.

"To whom?" Peter demanded.

"Captain Hans Ort, Second Friedland Armored Infantry."

"Mercenaries," Peter hissed. "How did they get here? The CD was supposed to have a quarantine. . . ."

"Your position is hopeless, and you are not helping your comrades by holding it," the voice shouted.

"We're keeping you from entering the town!" Peter shouted back.

"For a while. We can go in any time, from the other side. Will you surrender?"

Peter looked helplessly at Roach. He could hear

the silence among the men. They didn't say anything, and Peter was proud of them. But, he thought, I don't have any choice. "Yes," he shouted.

The Friedlanders wore dark green uniforms, and looked very military compared to Peter's scarecrows. "Mercenaries?" Captain Ort asked.

Peter opened his mouth to answer defiance. A voice interrupted him. "Of course they're mercenaries." Ace Barton limped up to them.

Ort looked at them suspiciously. "Very well. You wish to speak with them, Captain Barton?"

"Sure. I'll get some of 'em out of your hair," Barton said. He waited until the Friedlander was gone. "You almost blew it, Pete. If you'd said you were volunteers, Ort would have turned you over to the Dons. This way, he keeps you. And believe me, you'd rather be with him."

"What are you doing here?" Peter demanded.

"Captured up north," Barton said. "By these guys. There's a recruiter for Falkenberg's outfit back in the rear area. I signed up, and they've got me out looking for a few more good men. You want to join, you can. We'll be off this planet next week; and of course you won't be doing any fighting here."

"I told you, I'm not a mercenary—"

"What are you?" Barton asked. "What have you got to go back to? Best you can hope for here is to be interned. But you don't have to make up your mind just yet. Come on back to town." They walked through the olive groves toward the Zaragoza town wall. "You opted for CD service, didn't you." Barton said. It wasn't a question.

"Yes. Not to be one of Falkenberg's—"

"You think everything's going to be peaceful out here when the CoDominium fleet pulls out?"

"No. But I like to choose my wars."

"You want a cause. So did I, once. Now I'll settle for what I've got. Two things to remember, Pete. In an outfit like Falkenberg's, you don't choose your enemies, but you'll never have to break your word. And just what will you do for a living now?"

He had no answer to that. They walked on.

"Somebody's got to keep order out here," Barton said. "Think about it."

They had reached the town. The Friedland mercenaries hadn't entered it; now a column of monarchist soldiers approached. Their boots were dusty and their uniforms torn, so that they looked little different from the remnants of Peter's command.

As the monarchists reached the town gates, the village people ran out of their houses. They lined both sides of the streets. As the Carlists entered the public square, the cheering began.

§§§

Lysander drained his glass. The water pitcher was empty. "That's quite a story, captain. One thing—what did you do with that fission bomb?"

"Turned it over to Falkenberg."

"And he—?"

"Damned if I know."

"In any event Major Barton doesn't have it," Lysander said.

"Remember, that all happened twelve years ago. If Ace Barton thinks he needs a nuke, he'll have one."

"Twelve years, and you still think quite highly of him."

"Obviously. I'm not looking forward to this fight."

"Maybe there won't be one," Lysander said. "Colonel Falkenberg told Governor Blaine this was a political matter, and should be settled by political means."

"I hope he's right, but Ace won't give up easily."

"Of course there's one simple solution. . . ."

"Yes?"

"Just get control of the harvest they've been holding back."

"That would do it, all right." Owensford chuckled. "But Ace knows that as well as we do. He's been damned clever about hiding the stuff. Rottermill has his people sweating blood over the satellite photos, but so far they've got damn all."

"You can't bribe one of the planters?"

"It's been tried. They don't know either. Apparently Barton tells them the delivery point, and his troops take it from there."

Lysander's mental concentration wasn't helped by the residual effects of the evening's liquor. He frowned. "It has to be a pretty big place. Even if it's concentrated there has to be tons of the stuff. Not easy to hide."

"Maybe not. But they've done it."

Lysander closed the door and leaned against it. He didn't bother with the room lights. Gray dawn let him see well enough to move without bumping into the furniture, and despite Owensford's nostrum, bright light was more than he wanted to deal with. "Sleep," he muttered. He stripped off his tunic and trousers and threw them over a chair, then staggered to the bed.

There was someone in it. "Who the hell?"

"Umm? Lynn?"

"Ursula?"

"Oh my God, what time is it?"

"Quarter past five. What the hell are you doing here?"

"I didn't want to sleep alone. Why are you just standing there? It's cold in here."

"Not for long." He slid in beside her and settled himself against the curve of her body. A few moments later he gently but firmly folded her hands together in front of her. "Not now, Ursa. Please."

"Aww. Head hurt?"

"Not as much as it did."

"You should drink water—"

"Good God, darling, what do you think I've been doing?"

"You've been drinking *water* for four hours? Uh—Your Highness—"

He laughed, but that hurt his head. "Water. Vitamin gunk. Listening to Captain Owensford's story."

"Must have been quite a story!"

"It was. Also trying to figure out where those damned ranchers are hiding gallons and gallons of drugs. But we didn't get anywhere."

"Oh. All right. Good night."

"Ursa—what the hell will you do in the morning?"

"Have breakfast with you. Good night."


The Officers' Mess was empty. Lysander and Ursula chose a table in the corner, out of earshot of the steward, and set down their breakfast trays.

"Sorry about the selection," Lysander said, grimacing at his bowl of what looked like green oatmeal.

"This late, we're lucky to get anything at all. Anyway, you look a lot more chipper than you did half an hour ago."

"I'm going to take the formula for that vitamin gunk back to Sparta. We'll make it a government monopoly and after five years we'll be able to abolish taxes." He clinked his coffee mug against hers. "Now suppose you tell me what's been on *your* mind since we woke up."

She sipped her coffee. "Lynn—they'd have to move those drugs by helicopter, wouldn't they?"

"Uh?"

"The planters. The rebels."

"Oh. Yes, I suppose they would. Why have you been brooding about that?"

"Shouldn't I be interested? Or is this purely a man's problem?"

"Come on, Ursa. I don't deserve that."

She sighed. "No. I guess you don't."

"What is it, then? Do you have an idea?"

"Maybe. I don't know."

"Well, tell me."

"I—I'm ashamed to."

"What? This is me, remember?" He set down his coffee mug and put his arm around her shoulders. "Whatever it is—"

"Of course. Very well. It happened about six weeks before you came to Tanith. Before we met."

"Yes?"

"Remember I told you that some of us, some of the hotel girls, got sent on tours of the plantations?"

"Good God! You mean you—"

"No, not me. Not exactly. I was luckier. I was— don't look at me while I tell you this."

"Whatever this is, you'd better tell me. Now, what was it?"

"I was—it was a birthday party for a planter's son. His sixteenth birthday. I was—you've read Mead and Benedict, haven't you? This was, well, Coming of Age On Tanith." She laughed dryly.

"Ursa—" His arm tightened around her.

"Never mind that. That was—business. There was something else. It didn't mean anything to me at the time, but now—"

Lysander set down his spoon. "Tell me."

# XV

"Attention, please," Captain Fast said formally. Everyone stood as Falkenberg came in and took his place at the head of the long table.

"Mr. Mess President, is the Regimental Council assembled?"

"Yes, sir," Captain Alana said.

"Thank you. Sergeant Major, has the room been secured? Thank you. I declare this meeting opened. Be seated, please."

Falkenberg looked down the twin rows of familiar faces, senior officers in descending rank to his right, Sergeant Major Calvin at the far end with the senior NCO's. Beatrice Frazer and Laura Bryant were present as representatives for the civilian women. Faces came and went but the basic structure of the Regimental Council hadn't changed since the 42nd CoDominium Line Marines had been disbanded and had chosen to stay together as Falkenberg's Mercenary Legion.

"First item. Congratulations to you all on ending the Free State campaign with so few casualties. Well done. Of course, it was rather an expensive operation, which brings us to our second item. Treasurer's report." Papers rustled as they picked up their print-outs. "In the past month we have expended over seven hundred cluster bombs and forty thousand rounds of small-arms ammunition. We used thirty Bearpaw rockets and sixty mortar bombs in the Free State operation alone. All necessary, of course, but we have to replace them. Captain Alana has made substantial economies in routine operations, but I'm afraid that's not enough. Further cutbacks will be necessary. Comments?"

"We can hardly cut back on SAS operations against the rebel planters. Or the air support for them," Ian Frazer said.

"Of course not. I think I speak for us all on that? Thank you. Other suggestions?"

"Pay cuts, sir?" Sergeant Major Calvin asked.

"Possibly. Last resort, of course, but it may come to that."

"Not a good time for that, sir."

Falkenberg smiled grimly. "Sergeant Major, if any of the troops want to desert on Tanith, I wish them well. I expect we can find more recruits here if we have to."

"Sir."

"Next item," Falkenberg said. "We've received a sight draft for one point five million credits as a stand-by retainer from Sparta. It should clear the Tanith banks within the month. If the coming campaign doesn't get too expensive that will ease the economic situation a little."

"Stand-by," Major Savage said. "I gather we needn't rush packing up."

"That's right. The retainer gives them priority on our services for five years, but we'll have to find other work in the meantime."

There was a moment of silence. Beatrice Frazer

looked unhappy. "I must say we were all looking forward to permanent homes," she said.

"This doesn't rule out a permanent home for the regiment. It just means we may have to wait longer than we thought. First question: do we accept Sparta's retainer?"

"On what terms?" Centurion Bryant asked.

"First choice on our services, with the usual provisions for letting us finish any active job."

"We certainly can use the money," Catherine Alana said.

"As I see it, turning down this retainer would play hob with our long-term plans," Jeremy Savage said. "I move we allow the colonel full discretion in this matter."

"Second," Sergeant Major Calvin said.

"Discussion?" Falkenberg prompted.

"What's to discuss?" Ian Frazer said.

"Quite a lot, if we refuse this offer," Jeremy Savage said dryly. "Since we won't have the slightest idea where we're going."

"That's what I mean," Frazer said. "Question, Colonel. If we do take the retainer, what are our chances of salvaging the plan?"

"Good, I'd say."

"Thank you, sir."

"Further discussion?" Falkenberg nodded. "There being none, those in favor? Opposed? Thank you. Off the record, I'm going to quibble about the terms, but I'll accept the Spartan retainer.

"Next item. Captain Fast, what offers do we have?"

"There's a prisoners' rebellion on Fulson's World—"

Several officers laughed. Laura Bryant looked horrified. "That's worse than here!" she said.

Falkenberg nodded. "It happens that the offer from

Fulson's World is likely to be the most profitable, but I take it Laura speaks for us all?"

Everyone nodded vigorously.

"New Washington," Captain Fast said. "A dissident group wants help breaking loose from Franklin. The Franklin government has brought in Friedlanders and some other mercenary outfits, and has a pretty good army of its own."

"That one's dicey," Major Savage said. "Likely to take time. Good living on New Washington, though. Cool."

A senior battalion commander looked thoughtful. "What have these dissidents got in the way of an army?"

Falkenberg smiled thinly. "Lots of troops. Hardly an army."

Centurion Bryant frowned, then grinned. "Colonel— if they don't have an army, and we do, and we win—"

"The thought had crossed my mind," Falkenberg said. "We might well be the only organized militia on a wealthy—well, relatively wealthy—world."

"No drug trade," Beatrice Frazer said. "We might not be under so much pressure from the Grand Senate. Or Admiral Lermontov. I know you love him, Colonel, but some of us wouldn't mind being free of him."

There were murmurs of approval.

"It would be a while before we could bring in the families," Falkenberg said. "You'd have to make do here."

Beatrice shuddered slightly. "Better here than Fulson's World. Or rattling all around the galaxy."

"We're agreed, then," Falkenberg said. "We'll look further into the New Washington situation. In favor—"

There was a chorus of ayes.

"I see none opposed. Captain Fast."

"Colonel, there are situations in three other places, but no firm offers. Worth discussing now?"

"Get us more information on them first, I think," Falkenberg said. "We don't want to pin all our hopes on New Washington. All agree? Thank you. Next item. Mrs. Frazer."

"The school equipment is breaking down in the heat and wet," she said. "About half our veedisk readers are on the fritz, and we're only keeping the rest together by overworking the technicians. When you take the hardware into the field, everything comes apart."

"That sounds like the right place to put part of the Spartans' retainer," Falkenberg said. "Ladies and gentlemen? Discussion?"

"How much are we talking about?" Jesus Alana asked. "Oerlikon has a new smart rocket out. Coded laser target designators. Countermeasures aren't going to be cheap. And we might want some of the offensive munitions. They're damned expensive, but they could be the edge against that Friedland armor in New Washington. And we'll certainly need new chaff shells."

"It would be nice if the children could read," Captain Catherine Alana said. "Sixteen thousand credits would buy milspec readers for the school. Then we could stop worrying about them."

"They'd make a difference," Beatrice Frazer agreed. "Of course if it's a choice between making do and winning the next campaign there's no choice at all. Classes have been taught with paper and chalkboards, and even less."

"Sixteen thousand. It's not that much," Centurion Tamago said. "I move we appropriate it for the readers." He grinned. "With luck we'll get much more than that out of this operation against the planters."

Falkenberg frowned slightly. Loot was an unpleasant subject, and chancy as well. He never let it enter formal discussions. "Is there a second?"

"Second," Catherine Alana said.

"Ayes? Thank you. I believe I hear a majority. Does anyone wish no votes recorded? I hear none. Captain Alana, you will consult with Mrs. Frazer and order the necessary equipment, not to exceed sixteen thousand credits' worth. Next item?"

"Thank you, Amos." Falkenberg looked down the long table. "That concludes the agenda. Are there any other items to bring before the Council? There being none, do I hear a motion to adjourn? Thank you. Those in favor. Thank you. This meeting is adjourned." He stood and strode out of the meeting chamber.

"Attention," Amos Fast said. All stood until Falkenberg had left the room. The Adjutant looked at his watch. "There will be a staff meeting in ten minutes. Thank you. Dismissed."

The meeting dissolved in babble. "Jesus, Sergeant Major," Centurion Bryant said. "Fulson's World? We ain't *never* going to be that broke."

"I sure hope not, Alf."

Catherine Alana and Beatrice Frazer went out together, deep in a discussion of brand names and shipping schedules. Ian Frazer took Jesus Alana by the elbow. "Tell me more about this Oerlikon missile."

"Just saw the write-up in *Military Technology*," Alana said.

"Eh? Where—"

"I'll show you. Catherine brought it. She had lunch in the wardroom of that CD cruiser that came through here last week. Anyway, the missile looks like something new, not just a reshuffle of the same old stuff."

Orderlies came in to clear the table and bring fresh coffee cups.

§§§

"Ten-hut!" Sergeant Major Calvin said as Falkenberg entered and again took his place at the head of the table.

"At ease," he said automatically and sat. There were fewer people around the table. No enlisted personnel except Sergeant Major Calvin. The only woman was First Lieutenant Leigh Swensen, the senior photo interpreter and one of Rottermill's deputies.

Her fingers moved rapidly over the keyboard. The tabletop turned translucent and the crystals below its surface swarmed together to form the map of the areas held by the rebels.

"Jesus, there's a sight I'm sick of," someone muttered.

Major Savage smiled. "Tiresome, isn't it."

Swensen moved the joystick, and military unit symbols appeared on the map: dark and solid for enemy units located with certainty, fading to ghostly outlines for those whose positions were only guessed at. The outlined symbols far outnumbered the solid ones.

"I see Major Barton's lost none of his skills at camouflage," Falkenberg observed.

"Ian's lads are doing their best," Savage said.

A dozen small blue dots crawled across the map. "Captain Frazer's Special Air Services teams," Lieutenant Swensen said. As they watched, three of the dots were replaced by red splotches.

"Christ," Captain Fast muttered. "Battles. Isn't there a better way to locate Barton's gang?"

"Those weren't battles!" Frazer protested.

"Casualties, Captain?" Falkenberg prompted.

"Very light, sir. Three men killed. Seven wounded, all extracted by air. Hardly what anyone would call battles."

"Sorry, Ian," Fast said. He glanced at Falkenberg, then at Captain Rottermill. "Is it fair to say we don't know where most of Barton's troops are, and we've no idea at all where the planters are hiding the borloi?"

Rottermill nodded reluctantly. "You could put it that way. I don't like it, but it's fair."

"Also," Captain Fast continued, "we face unroaded terrain. Worse than unroaded. Swamp and jungle. The only possible transportation is by air, and the enemy has effective infantry carried anti-aircraft missiles. We can smuggle a few troops behind their lines, but effective strikes deep into their territory are impossible."

"Fair summary," Rottermill said. "You can add that their satellite observation security is excellent, and the governor's office leaks like a sieve."

"Suggestions?" Captain Fast asked.

Rottermill shrugged.

"Occupy their bloody plantations," one of the senior batallion commanders said. "Start with the close ones and roll them up. There aren't more than a couple of hundred—"

"Sure. And garrison them how?" Rottermill demanded. "Two maniples per farm? Why don't we just wrap up the troops with ribbons and tell Barton to come get them? Christ, Larry—"

"Burn the damn farms! I've got troops ready to do

that. The rebels can't stand that, they'll *make* Barton fight."

"I'm afraid we don't have proper transport to set up the necessary ambuscades," Falkenberg said. "And there are political considerations. I doubt Governor Blaine will let us kill his geese."

"Yeah. So what the hell can we do?"

"Let Ian's lads carry on scouting," Major Savage said.

"I could go out myself," Ian Frazer offered.

"No," Falkenberg said. "This is hardly our favorite kind of campaign, but it's going as well as we can expect. The—opposition—has to hand the merchandise over to Bronson's people. Or someone else, never mind who. All we need do is keep them from delivering it. Major Barton can't operate on credit and he won't fight on promises."

"If we can take the borloi, he won't fight at all," Captain Fast said.

"Yes, sir," Lieutenant Swensen said. "We're trying—"

"All my people are trying," Rottermill said.

"So are mine," Ian Frazer said.

§§§

Sergeant Taras Hamilton Miscowsky shut down the flame on the nearly buried mini-stove. "Tea time."

The other four members of his SAS team huddled under the basha formed by Miscowsky's poncho. Automatically they cradled the warm tea cups in their hands, even though the fine rain would limit IR scanning ranges to less than a hundred meters. Miscowsky looked at the tangle of vines, tree trunks, exotic flowers, and weirdly shaped leaves. He'd never heard of anything that could detect a hot teacup under this much jungle foliage, but good habits were always worth developing.

The jungle didn't look like anything that ever grew on Earth, but that didn't bother Miscowsky. He'd never been on Earth, and jungles there would have been just as strange as Tanith's. Miscowsky had been recruited from Haven, and his primary training was for mountain operations.

He'd had to learn fast. Everyone did. On Tanith you learned fast or you didn't live long. The insects didn't bother humans much, but there were plenty of big things that did. And fungus never much cared where it grew. He looked at his troops.

Two new faces. *I screwed the pooch this time*. Kauffman dead, Hwang off to the regenners and fucking just in time, new shave or not that goddamn Fuller can sure fly a chopper. High wind and rain pissing down, and Cloudwalker's chain saw dull as shit, that damn little patch we cleared was too small for the bird to land in . . . Howie lying there next to his leg. Son of a bitch that Fuller kid can fly! And he shouldn't have had to, 'cause I shouldn't have let the Bastards find us. Shit.

It wasn't Cloudwalker's turn to sit guard, but he liked doing it. He took his cup and moved out from under the basha, picking up his rifle and slinging it over his shoulder. As Cloudwalker padded down the trail Miscowksy surveyed the rest of the maniple. One of the new men was Andy Owassee. Miscowsky knew him; he'd been trying to get into the Special Air Service for years. The other—

Miscowsky raised his steel Sierra cup. As he drank he studied the new man's face. Buford Purdy. Mulatto, by the look of him. "Cap'n Frazer doesn't usually send recruits out with SAS patrols," Miscowsky said.

"Hell, Sarge, he *lives* out here," Owassee said. "Used to, anyway."

"Yeah, I heard that."

There was a long silence. Rain pattered down and dripped off the edges of the basha. Finally Purdy said, "I've got a lot to learn, don't I?"

"Looks that way," Miscowsky said, and set down his cup. "All right. Gimme your poncho." He folded the poncho twice and laid it flat on the ground. Tandon and Owassee moved closer. Miscowsky adjusted the controls on his helmet and the outlines of the area appeared, faint against the mottled green of the poncho. "OK. We're here." He ignored the red splotch that showed where Barton's Bastards had ambushed him. "Sat recon says there's a village over west of us. Twelve klicks. Standard procedure. We go set up to watch, be sure they're not working with Barton—"

"They not," Purdy said.

"Eh? How do you—"

"It's my Uncle Etienne's village," Purdy said.

"No shit?"

"No shit, Sarge."

"So where exactly do you come from, kid?"

"Village about ninety klicks south of here," Purdy said. "On a branch of the slough that goes through Etienne's village. Catfish don't like it this far downstream. Little nessies get them. We bring our catches down five, six times a year to trade for salt-water stuff."

"I will be dipped in shit. Okay, Purdy, what do they talk down in that village?"

"Cooney."

"What's that?"

Purdy cut loose with a string of musical but unintelligible words. He grinned. "It's more like Anglic than you think."

"Has to be more like it than I think," Corporal Tandon muttered.

"You really speak that stuff?" Miscowsky looked skeptical.

"Sure. Grew up with it."

"So how'd you learn real talk?" Tandon asked.

"From my mother. Most of us out here speak some Anglic." He coughed. "Spare some of that hot water, Sarge?"

"Sure." Miscowsky poured the last of the water from the tiny kettle and started dismantling the ministove. "Okay, trooper. Looks like we're in your territory. Lead off?"

"Sure, Sarge!" Purdy finished his tea while the others shouldered their packs and struck the basha. Then he moved noiselessly into the thick jungle. In seconds he had disappeared.

"Jesus Christ," Tandon said. "Sarge, that kid's all right."

"Yeah."

# XVI

Ann Chang stared out the window of her office at Government House, then back at her computer screen. The request was still there, and it was routine enough; but who the hell was Geoffrey Niles, and why was he asking permission to hunt a dinosaur? Actually, the why wasn't a problem; Governor Blaine's new regulations required his personal approval of every license to kill or capture one of the huge saurians that inhabited Tanith's northeastern island complex. Ann thought Blaine was carrying environmentalism a bit far, because all the reports showed there were plenty of dinosaurs; but it wasn't a burdensome regulation because there were so few would-be hunters these days.

But who was Geoffrey Niles? And where was he? A search through the Customs and Immigration files showed no sign that he had ever landed on Tanith.

She looked at the entry again. The Honorable Geoffrey Niles, Wimbledon, Surrey, United Kingdom, Earth; local address care of Amalgamated Foundries, Ltd. She didn't have to look that one up. AF was a conglomerate that dealt mostly in chemicals. Most of their operations were in Dagon; mining, and processing of Tanith fauna. If they still owned foundries, they didn't advertise it. Certainly there were none on Tanith.

Why would a Geoffrey Niles, who apparently had never landed on Tanith in the first place, give AF as an address? The computer wouldn't know, but it couldn't hurt to see what data they had. She keyed in the company name, waited for the screen to fill with the usual trivia, and typed in the code for details.

RESTRICTED DATA.

What the hell? She typed in her own access code.

RESTRICTED DATA.

That does it, she thought. She entered Carleton Blaine's override code.

AMALGAMATED FOUNDRIES, LTD. CHAIRMAN AND CHIEF EXECUTIVE OFFICER LORD HARVEY NILES, SURREY, UNITED KINGDOM, EARTH. WHOLLY OWNED SUBSIDIARY OF CONSOLIDATED EUGENICS, INC. OUTSTANDING SHARES ZERO. ESTIMATED WORTH: UNEVALUTED.

There followed several pages of listed assets. Warehouses, chemical processing plants. A drug store chain in North America. An item at the bottom of the third screenful caught her eye. Amalgamated Foundries, Ltd. owned three interstellar class merchant ships.

"Curiouser and curiouser," she muttered, and typed again.

DATA DETAILS CONSOLIDATED EUGENICS.

RESTRICTED DATA.

OVERRIDE BLAINE 124C41 + HUGO.

WHOLLY OWNED SUBSIDIARY OF BRONSON AND TYNDALL CONSTRUCTION ENTERPRISES, INC . . .

Fine, she thought. Which probably makes The Honorable Geoffrey Niles a twig on the old Bronson family tree. And still doesn't explain why he wants a dinosaur license. Why ask for one unless he's on

Tanith? Only he's not on Tanith. In orbit, maybe? But then he'd have turned up on the Customs list, and that showed no new traffic since last week's visit by the CoDominium warship.

Ann frowned and touched more keys.

AIR/SPACE TRAFFIC CONTROL.

ONLINE.

HOW MANY SHIPS IN ORBIT NOW?

ONE.

SHIP NAME.

FILE NOT FOUND.

OVERRIDE BLAINE 124C41 + HUGO.

FILE NOT FOUND.

That made no sense at all. Still frowning, she clicked back to the Amalgamated Foundries data window and called up more details. Of the company's three ships, two were noted as being on scheduled runs. The third was CDMS *Norton Star*.

Not likely. But—Ann touched buttons on the speakerphone. Government House had once had vidphones, but Tanith's climate had long since sent them to the scrap bin.

"Air/Space Commissioner's Office."

"Chief Administrator Chang here. Deputy Commissioner Paulik, please." A moment later she was put through to him. "Hello, Don. It's Ann. Quick question for you. The Governor has friends aboard the *Norton Star*. Everything all right up there?"

"Sure is." Her speakerphone deepened his familiar reedy voice. "Amalgamated chartered one of our landing boats to send up supplies just this morning. Rather a lot of stuff, actually. Looks like they're planning to be there a while."

"Ah. Thanks. Don, there's something screwy with my data system this morning. I can't seem to find their landing request."

"Oh? Hold on a moment. Yes, here it is. They've got a standby for a remote-area water landing. Location to be named later. Seems a bit unusual . . . Are you sure you don't have it, Ann? It looks like it was approved by your office."

"Oh, I'm sure it was," she said. *Just what is our fearless leader up to? And why didn't he tell me about it? I could have upset his plans—*"Just to help me sort this out, who does it say approved the request?"

"It says here that Everett did."

Everett. Everett Mardon. Her son-in-law. "Oh. Thanks."

"Look, Ann, there's nothing irregular about this, is there?"

"No, I'm sure it's all in order. Thanks, Don. Will we see you at the Lederle party next week?"

"Sure thing. Bye, Chief."

Her hand trembled slightly as she turned off the speakerphone.

"Good work, boss."

She turned, startled. "Everett—"

"Let's take a break, Ann. You look like you could use one."

"Everett, what the hell's going on?"

He came around her desk and put his hand on her shoulder. "Like I said. You need a break. Let's take a walk."

She waited until they were outside Government House and halfway across the square. "All right, Ev," she said. "What's this all about, and why would the governor tell you and not me?"

"Governor—oh. Ann, Governor Blaine doesn't know anything about this. He can't find out, either."

"What?" She stopped, then turned and started

back toward the building. Everett reached out and caught her by the sleeve.

"Really, Ann. Stop a minute and listen."

"No." She jerked her sleeve free and faced him. "Listen, Ev. Whatever you've done to my database access, you fix it, and now. Then I'll try to keep the governor from firing you."

"Not good enough."

Her eyes narrowed. "Everett, you may be able to treat my daughter like this—"

"The hell I can, and you know it! Now just for one lousy minute, will you *listen*?"

She took a deep breath. "All right. Alicia's sake. But this had better be good."

"Where do I start? Start at the beginning, go on to the end, then stop. That's what you told Philip—"

"And you needn't keep bringing Alicia and my grandson into this—"

"I'm not the one who brought up Alicia. Look, I'm trying to—" He stopped. "Sorry, Ann. I didn't mean to bite. Okay, let's start at the beginning. Where does the borloi go?"

"The borloi? What's that got to do with—"

"Just listen, would you, please?"

She raised one eyebrow at him. "Very well. Lederle AG buys the borloi."

"Right. Lederle. At least that's the theory. But we all know that most of it actually goes to the Navy. They sell it, and that gives them money over and above what they get from the Grand Senate. Lets them do whatever they want, no matter what the Senate says they should do. The fact is, every single person on Tanith is party to a conspiracy against the CoDominium Treaty."

"Well . . ." She reflected. "Yes, I suppose technically that's true, but—"

"But nothing! It's not just technically true. It *is* true. So far we've gotten away with it, but that can't last. Did you know that Grand Senator Bronson is starting an investigation? By the time he's done, your precious governor will be in jail. So will you, if we don't cooperate with Bronson's people."

"Cooperate." Her face turned stony. "How, cooperate?"

"You don't have to do anything. Not one thing. Just forget you ever heard about the *Norton Star*. How did you tumble to it, anyway? I installed a flag to alert me if you or Blaine asked for any space-traffic info, but it didn't tell me how you found out."

Ann glanced at him, and found she was smiling in spite of herself. "Geoffrey Niles asked for a dinosaur hunting permit."

"What!" Everett spluttered a guffaw. "That fathead! He would."

"But you're working for him—"

"Not for him. For his father. Lord Niles is one of Bronson's key people, and Captain Yoshino is plenty sharp—"

"Yoshino?"

"*Norton Star*'s skipper. Bronson brought him away from the Meiji navy. Geoff Niles is supposed to be Purser."

"I see now. I suppose they're planning to land a boat in the planters' territory and cart away the crop."

"But of course. What else?"

"When?"

"No idea."

"Soon?"

"What's soon? I don't really know, but I don't think it'll be tomorrow or anything near it."

"No, I suppose not. If Niles thinks he has time to

collect a dino—" She stopped and leaned against a tree. Everett looked quickly at her.

"Are you all right?"

"No. Yes, of course I'm all right. I just have to think. Everett, the governor trusts me."

"I know. And this is a lousy thing to do to him. But damn it, Ann, he's on the wrong side—"

"He's not! He's ending the slave trade, he's going to put up power satellites as soon as he gets the money, he's—"

"Sure, sure . . . All that's fine. But what about the other things he's doing? I know you weren't happy having that whore at your table in Government House last week."

"Well—maybe he is moving a little fast in some directions—"

"But that wasn't what I meant," Everett cut in. "Maybe I shouldn't have said the wrong side. Maybe I should have said the losing side. Because, Ann, everybody who fights Bronson loses. Always."

"Now that's not true. Governor Blaine's got the support of Grand Senator Grant—"

"It's true in the long run. Grant's losing support. Bronson's going to win this one, and where will that leave us? Look, it's not as though I'm asking you to *do* anything—"

"I don't know, Ev. I just don't know. I have to talk to Satay."

"I thought he was out of town."

"He'll be back at the end of the week."

"Good. I didn't know he cared about politics."

"He doesn't, but—I still think I ought to talk to him."

"All right. Talk to him. But promise me one thing, will you? Before you tell Blaine, will you come see me first?"

Ann took a deep breath. *Nothing makes sense anymore. Still, family has to count for something.* "All right, Ev. I will."

§§§

Ursula walked so slowly Lysander was afraid she might stop. He kept his arm around her waist as they entered Falkenberg's office.

"Good of you to see us, Colonel."

"Not at all, Your Highness." Falkenberg stood at his desk. "Miss Gordon. Please sit down. Would either of you care for a drink?"

"Thank you, no," Lysander said.

"Sherry?" Ursula said faintly.

"Of course." Falkenberg took a decanter and glasses from the credenza behind his desk. "Your Highness?"

"Well, since everyone else is. Thank you."

Falkenberg poured, then sat down facing them across his desk. "Cheers."

"Cheers," Lysander said automatically.

Ursula drained her glass. Lysander glanced at Falkenberg, then refilled her glass from the decanter.

"So," Falkenberg prompted.

"Colonel, Ursula has a story I think you should hear. It happens that six weeks ago she was an overnight guest at one of the Girerd family's establishments. The main one, I think, given the circumstances of her visit. Can you find it on your map there?"

"Should," Falkenberg said. He moved a stack of papers to the side table and pulled out the keyboard drawer. "Hmm. Girard. G-I-R-A-R-D-?"

"No, it ends in 'ERD,' " Ursula said.

"Ah. There are three villas. Let's see—" The map appeared and zoomed in.

"Not that one," Ursula said. "There was a sea inlet to the south."

"Was there? Ah. Here we are. 'Rochemont Manor.' Grand name for a drug farm on a prison planet." A satellite photograph replaced the map. "Nine hundred kilometers southwest of here."

"That's it, I'm sure it is," Ursula said.

"Good." Falkenberg's refilled her glass and waited.

"It was about four in the morning," Ursula said. "I was—the party was over, and it was hot, and I couldn't sleep. The room was on a balcony, and I thought I heard something. More like thunder than wind, but there wasn't any thunder. No wind either. I got up. I told myself it was to go look, but really I just wanted to walk around. While I was getting my robe I heard a helicopter land."

"At four A.M.," Lysander said.

Falkenberg nodded.

"When I got outside, I swear I heard some people talking down below somewhere, but I couldn't see anyone, and there wasn't any helicopter."

"And you should have seen it?" Falkenberg asked.

"Yes. The helipad was down the hill from the balcony."

"But they hadn't put her in a room facing it," Lysander said.

Falkenberg frowned.

"The veranda runs all the way around the house." Ursula pointed to the satellite photo. "See, there it is. The room was over here, and the helipad is down there. I don't know why I walked around to the north side. I suppose I was curious about the helicopter. It did seem a little unusual—"

Falkenberg waited, but she was staring at the map. "I see," he said. "You were in a room on the east side."

"Yes, I thought that was strange, because the best rooms are always on the north side. But that's where we were. And they would have given us—I mean—"

"It's all right, Ursa," Lysander said, and squeezed her hand.

"You were in an east room," Falkenberg repeated. "You heard sounds. As you got up, you heard a helicopter land. By the time you were above the helipad, there wasn't any helicopter. How long did it take you to get around to the north side?"

"Not very long at all. Well, a minute or two," Ursula said. "I had to find my robe. And the bedroom isn't really off the veranda. It has a little balcony of its own, with steps that go down to the veranda. It was still dark, and the veranda lights were out, so it took a little time getting down the steps. And I wasn't in any hurry. Really, Colonel—"

"So you walked around the veranda until you could see the helipad, but there was no helicopter. What happened then?"

"Not much at all. There was nothing there, so I walked back around to the balcony. My—Oskar was waiting for me there and we went back inside."

"I see. And you say the noise that woke you sounded like thunder?"

"Well, at first I thought it was thunder. But it wasn't anywhere near as loud, and it lasted a lot longer than thunder does."

"And there was no storm."

"None at all. The night was quite calm."

Falkenberg took out a pair of rimless spectacles and put them on. He leaned over the map for a minute. "This party. Who were the guests?"

"Uh, Colonel, is this relevant?" Lysander asked.

"I think so."

"It's all right," Ursula said. "It was—Oskar Girerd's

sixteenth birthday party. There were about a dozen planters and their sons. Most of the boys were about Oskar's age. But they all left about midnight."

"All? No overnight guests?"

"Well, let's see. There was quite a crowd at breakfast. Supervisors and overseers and—of course. Jonkheer van Hoorn and his son were still there."

"Supervisors and overseers," Falkenberg said. "Any military people?"

"I don't think so—well, there were the Girerds' own guards. At least that's who I thought they were."

"Uniforms?"

She shrugged. "Standard camouflage coveralls. Nothing I'd recognize."

"Think hard," Falkenberg said. "Badges? Patches?"

She shook her head. "None I remember."

"Did any of them wear earrings?"

"Why—well, yes, now that you mention it. Not exactly rings. Cuffs. Two of the security people—"

"Wore bulldog ear cuffs," Falkenberg said.

"How did you know that?" Lysander began. "Ah. Of course. Barton's Bulldogs—"

"Was once their official name," Falkenberg said. "May still be. What would you engrave on a 'bastard' earring?" He shook his head. "One or two things puzzle me. Miss Gordon, what was the weather like the day before this party?"

"Terrible. It was one of the last big storms of the harvest season, and it rained all week. We weren't sure I'd be able to get there."

Falkenberg typed rapidly. "And more bad weather was forecast."

"I don't know. I guess so—"

"I'm not guessing," Falkenberg said. He gestured toward the data screen. "So. They knew they had exactly one night of good weather for at least several days to come. Still, it seems exceedingly stupid of them to have run the operation with strangers on the premises. Just what were—just how did you come to be invited to that party, Miss Gordon?"

"Colonel, really, I don't think—"

"Your Highness, Miss Gordon, I am not asking out of idle curiosity."

"I was—invited—by Jonkheer van Hoorn."

"Directly?"

"No, sir." She set her lips. "They brought me for the night from the Hilton."

"I see. Could—would they do this without consulting the Girerd family?"

"It's not the way it's usually done, but it does happen." She glanced quickly at Lysander and went on. "This wasn't the first time."

"Thank you."

"Colonel—"

"I'm sorry, Your Highness. I had to establish whether the Girerds were incredibly stupid or had no choice in the matter. Miss Gordon, the one thing that surprises me is that you were allowed to leave that house alive."

"I—" She shivered. "I never thought of that."

"Doubtless there were reasons. You would have been missed by your employers and—"

"And others," Ursula finished for him.

"Yes. Well. You may have done us quite a service," Falkenberg said. He took off his spectacles and turned to Lysander. "Your Highness. Under the circumstances, I suggest that Miss Gordon remain a guest of the Regiment. She might not be safe at the Hilton."

"But I have to go back!" Ursula protested. "My contract—"

"I doubt you need concern yourself with your

contract any longer," Falkenberg said. "We'll buy what's left of it."

"But—I need the job. Not that it matters, I guess. The Hilton won't keep a girl who talks about her clients."

"I think you'll find no lack of alternatives," Falkenberg said. "If need be, we can discuss the matter with Governor Blaine." He stood. "Now, if you'll both excuse me—"

"Certainly, Colonel." Lysander stood. As he opened the door for Ursula he heard Falkenberg talking rapidly into the intercom.

# XVII

Corporal Tandon heard a faint chirp in his left ear. He touched the control in his breast pocket. "Sarge," he whispered into his throat mike. "Stand by. Message coming in."

Sergeant Miscowsky acknowledged with a tiny shrug. He didn't look around to where Tandon was standing behind him, but went on talking with the village headman. Etienne Ledoux was the blackest man Miscowsky had ever seen. Although clearly past his forties, he had slim hips and a solid barrel chest. He spoke excellent Anglic, sometimes breaking into the Cooney patois to shout something to a villager or make a point with Purdy, then switching back to Anglic without a pause. His voice was musical and surprisingly high. Tough-looking, though, Miscowsky thought. Could have been a good boxer.

"Yeah, we can leave some of the penicillin, no problem," Miscowsky said. "Fungus powder, too. We carry lots."

"So do Major Barton's men," Ledoux said. He set his tea cup down on the table between them and grinned broadly. "For my people's sake I am not sorry you both are trying to bribe us."

Miscowsky grinned back. "And I'm glad we've got your nephew with us."

"Buford was ambitious," Ledoux said. "Not that this place could do much to keep an ambitious boy." His grin faded as he surveyed the oblong clearing from the open thatched pavilion where they sat. Miscowsky followed his gaze. Thatch-and-wicker houses stood on two-meter stilts. A long house on a low platform occupied the side of the village square opposite them. There was a well in one corner of the square, and the brick-lined fire pit in the center was surrounded by benches and tables much like picnic tables.

"Looks pretty good to me," Miscowsky said. "I've seen pictures of jungle living on Earth. This doesn't seem so bad."

"If you like the jungle it is not bad at all," Ledoux said. He paused, and Miscowsky thought he seemed to come to a decision. "Sergeant, let me be frank with you. We cannot help you. Whatever your quarrel is with Major Barton, we want no part of it. We hold no title to this land. In truth, we own nothing. We survive because the planters don't think we're worth the trouble to evict us—"

"I know," Miscowsky said. "The Old Man—Cap'n Frazer—told us. Maybe he could talk to the governor about it."

Ledoux laughed. "You are kind, Sergeant. But I cannot quite believe your governor would make enemies for our sake."

"Maybe not." Miscowsky sipped tea. Behind him Corporal Tandon excused himself and went off to the privy behind the long house. "Cap'n Frazer says the governor's a pretty good guy, though. And the local planters here are already his enemies. They hired Barton."

Ledoux poured more tea and Miscowsky waited. They'd stressed patience in his training. You don't ask too many questions on a prison planet, and anyway Purdy had told him most of the story. Ledoux, and Purdy's father, and some others like them had led a band of time-expired convicts into the jungle, as far from the plantations as they could get and still be able to get back to a road if they had to. By now most of the villagers didn't need or want anything to do with roads or what was at the end of them; but they'd done too much work, clearing jungle and damming streams, to move on.

Nobody knew how many villages like this existed. Satellite photos said several hundred, but most of those were a lot smaller: two or three families, no more. Purdy said his uncle's compound was one of the largest, with almost two hundred people, counting the children.

"Heck, a few more years and you folks will outnumber the planters," Miscowksy said.

He missed Ledoux's reply. Tandon's voice spoke in his ear. "Sarge, we've got new orders. There's a plantation about fifty klicks southwest, on the sea. Cap'n wants us to haul ass down there. Top priority."

*Shit fire.* Miscowsky visualized the map. Cut straight across the jungle, just about due southwest. No trails mapped. Maybe they'd find one. Have to find something. He gave hand signals to the others. Leave the supplies and get moving, and hope Ledoux didn't think they were being impolite.

"Sure ain't much for a trail," Miscowsky muttered. "They want somebody up there in a hurry, they'd do better to drop a new team in closer."

"Cap'n Frazer said they couldn't do that," Tandon

said. "Regiment thinks they'll be watching that place real close."

"What's up there anyway?" Cloudwalker asked.

"I couldn't ask, could I? Only transmission we made was a click to acknowledge orders. One thing, we're supposed to report helicopter traffic, day or night. Break radio silence on that one."

"Won't the rebels be waiting for us?" Purdy asked. "I mean, if we can hear headquarters, they can too, right?"

Miscowsky waved to shush them while they went through a thicket. Then the underbrush thinned and it was safe to talk again. "Nope," Tandon said. "Look, what happens is they send up a chopper so it can see us. Not really see us, but we're in the line of sight, right? Then they aim a beam where they think we are. When I hear it, I click the set. That sends back a signal they can home in on. They narrow the beam down so it's no bigger'n ten meters when it gets to us. Anybody wants to listen to that, he's got to be between us and the chopper. Not much chance of that."

"Besides, it's all in code," Miscowsky said.

"Oh." Purdy peered ahead into the jungle and automatically veered around to the right. "Watch it up ahead. Something in the mud."

"Weems?" Cloudwalker asked.

"Maybe just a log," Purdy said. "Sure rather not find out, though."

Miscowsky shuddered and held his bayonetted rifle warily at chest level. "Tell you, kid, I'm getting right glad you're along."

They were quiet until they were past the small open mud flat. "If it works so well, how come we can't talk back to them the same way?" Purdy asked.

"We don't carry enough gear. Can't aim close

enough," Tandon said. "Sure, give me a stable platform and enough time to set things up, I can lock on
to the chopper, but it sure ain't any use trying from
the crapper in your uncle's village."

They slogged on, Purdy in the lead. Thick mud
dragged at their boots but the spiny underbrush slid
harmlessly off the nylon of their tunics. After an
hour, Purdy stopped and let Miscowsky catch up.

"Sarge, it's getting thicker. We won't make much
time."

"Shit fire. We're not making any time now."

"Going to be slower yet."

"Yeah, I can see that. Nothing we can do."

"Well, there's one thing, Sarge. There's water off
east of us. Don't remember just how far, but it can't
be more than about five klicks. Slough. It runs past
the village, and down to the sea. We could get over
there and use boats."

"Boats, huh? And where are these boats gonna
come from?"

"I can go back and borrow them while you cut
over to the water. Then I pole down and pick you
up."

"Shit, I don't know," Miscowsky said. "Tandon,
just how'd they say that part about the place being
watched?"

"Just like that, Sarge. Barton's guys'll probably be
watching the whole area around the plantation. Chopper patrols, too, maybe, but probably not."

"Purdy, how close does this stream—"

"Not a stream, Sarge. More like a slough—"

"Stream, slough, whatever. How close does it get
to the plantation?"

"Let's out into open water about six klicks southeast of there, but we don't want to follow it that far.
Gets too deep. But we can get out straight east of the

plantation and cut across. It'll be thick, thick as this, but we won't have more'n a klick of it."

"Kid's got a point, Sarge," Cloudwalker said. "No way we'll make more than twenty klicks a day in this stuff no matter how hard we try. Maybe not even that."

"That's right," Purdy said. "The boats would save a day, maybe two."

Miscowsky stared hard at Purdy. "Well . . . Okay. Cloudwalker, you go with him—"

"He'd just slow me down, Sarge," Purdy said.

"Yeah. So how'll you know where to meet us?"

"You cut straight across, due east," Purdy said. "You'll hit the slough by dark. You can't miss it, the water's over your waist. Camp there. I'll start at first light. Can't take me more than two hours. Watch for me."

"Okay, but don't start at first light. Give us a couple hours in case we don't get through this stuff as fast as you do. Got that?"

"Right, Sarge!"

Miscowsky and the others watched as Purdy disappeared back into the underbrush they'd just come through.

"Not too shabby," Owassee said.

"Yeah, the kid just might do. Okay, let's hump it."

§§§

Captain Rottermill's light pointer swept around the image projected on the situation room wall. "Good location, all right," he said. "Deep water to the south. Low hills on three sides. Thick jungle for a hundred kilometers in all directions. One narrow road runs northwest to hit the main road to Dagon.

Big plantation, six registered helicopters, lots of chopper traffic."

"Did you see anything new in the survsat photos?" Ian Frazer asked.

"Not a thing," Lieutenant Swensen answered.

"Nothing real," Rottermill said. "But I did some fooling around. Watch."

The map table projected the satellite photograph of Rochemont Manor, then dissolved into a computerized drawing of the building and the hill it stood on. An outline formed on the side of the hill next to the helipad, solidified, and opened.

"It's big enough," Rottermill said. "Not one shred of evidence, of course. If there's a door they were careful to use material that gives off the same IR signature as the rocks around it. There's probably not a straight line anywhere in it. Not easy, but not all that difficult either."

"Deep water," Falkenberg said. "How deep?"

"Twenty, thirty meters," Rottermill said. "Maybe more. Charts aren't that accurate for that region. Less than fifty meters, more than twenty."

"Enough," Falkenberg said quietly. He bent over to study the photograph. "These structures here. Docks?"

"Well, some kind of floating platform, sir," Lieutenant Swensen said. "It could be used as a pier. Colonel, do you think—"

"Exactly," Rottermill said.

"It certainly is odd," Falkenberg said. "Only fools regularly go out in deep water on Tanith. Could a landing ship actually operate in that water, Captain?"

"Tough question, sir," Rottermill said. "The inlet's long enough. Bit short for takeoff, maybe. It would depend on the landing ship."

"Could any of Tanith's landing craft operate there?"

"No way, Colonel. Those crates shouldn't be allowed out of a wading pool. You just might get one in but you'd sure never get it out again."

"But military craft could land and take off," Falkenberg said. "Especially if the takeoff load wasn't too heavy."

"Yes, sir. I thought of that, but there aren't any CD Marine landing boats on Tanith," Rottermill said. "I checked. None here to start with, and that cruiser took all hers with her when she left last week."

"You're certain of that?"

"Yes, sir."

"Good work. I doubt Captain Andreyev would be involved in a plot against the Fleet, but it's well to be sure. No other ships have arrived since the *Kuryev* left?"

"No, sir. At least the governor's office hasn't reported any, and they're supposed to advise us of all space traffic."

Falkenberg frowned. "The harvest season's nearly over and more than ninety percent of the crop is in. Tell me, Captain Rottermill, is Ace Barton a fool?"

"No, sir."

"Precisely. So just what does he expect to *do* with that—merchandise?"

"We've known all along there had to be a ship coming for it," Major Savage said.

"No question about it, Major," Rottermill said. "There's sure no other way to turn the drugs into cash." He slid the keyboard tray out of the side of the map table and began typing.

"She should be coming soon, too," Captain Fast said. "The longer they wait, the more things can go wrong for them. Such as an assault on Rochemont. Colonel, shall I order an alert?"

Falkenberg frowned. "Jeremy?"

"Stage One. Get ready to move," Major Savage said. "But don't go in there just yet. Whatever else Barton is planning, you may be sure he'll have air defenses ringing that plantation."

"Agreed," Falkenberg said. "Amos, if you please . . ."

"Yes, sir." Captain Fast typed rapidly at his computer console.

"Pity we don't have a Fleet Marine assault boat," Jeremy Savage said. "That would give Barton a surprise."

"Sir, could we borrow one from *Kuryev*?" Lieutenant Swensen asked.

Falkenberg chuckled. "Ingenious, Lieutenant, but I'm afraid we'd never get that much cooperation from Captain Andreyev. Besides, by now they'll be halfway to the Alderson point."

Rottermill looked up from his keyboard. "No incoming shipping scheduled for a month, Colonel."

"Not good." Falkenberg ran one hand through his thinning straw-colored hair. "Damn it, they must have plans for what to *do* with the blasted drugs once they've collected them—Captain Fast, would you please get the governor on the line. Use the scrambler."

"Sir."

"Ian, when do your lads reach the plantation?" Major Savage asked.

"Be surprised if they're anywhere near the place before Wednesday night."

"Four days," Rottermill said. "Sounds about right. It's thick out there."

"Governor Blaine's office, sir."

"Thank you. Falkenberg here. Good afternoon, Mrs. Chang. I really do need to speak to the governor. Yes, thank you, I'll wait—Ah. Good afternoon, Governor. Yes. Yes, possibly something significant. I'd rather not discuss it on the telephone. Perhaps you'd care to join us for dinner tonight?" He glanced at Captain Fast and got a nod. "The Mess would be honored— Well, yes, it may be important. I'd like to show you. Excellent. Eighteen thirty, then. One other matter, not your concern of course, but we need a complete schedule of all ships expected for the rest of the year. Well, as soon as possible— Yes, of course. Perhaps I should speak to her directly? Good. I'll wait." Falkenberg touched the mute switch on the telephone. "Should have asked Mrs. Chang when I had her on the line. I'll put this on the speaker."

Lieutenant Swensen opened her notebook and unclipped her pen.

"Yes, Colonel?" Ann Chang's amplified voice filled the room. "What can we do for you?"

"We need a full shipping schedule as soon as possible," Falkenberg said. "All space traffic from now through the end of the year."

"Of—of course, Colonel. But you know not all traffic is scheduled—"

"Yes, of course," Falkenberg said impatiently.

Captain Rottermill frowned and reached under the table for his briefcase.

"I'll send you a copy of everything we have at the moment. If you'll wait just a moment. It'll take a few minutes to search the files."

Rottermill set his briefcase on the table in front of him and lifted out a small plastic box. He pressed a switch on it and placed it facing Falkenberg's speaker-phone.

"We can wait," Falkenberg said. He glanced at Rottermill and raised one eyebrow. Rottermill nodded curtly.

"Colonel, the computers are doing odd things with

the data base," Ann Chang said. "Let—let me call you back, please."

Falkenberg glanced at Rottermill. The intelligence officer nodded again. "Very well," Falkenberg said. "We really do need that schedule. We'll wait for your call."

"Thank you, Colonel," Ann Chang said. "It'll be just a few minutes. I appreciate your patience—"

"Not at all. Goodbye." Falkenberg punched the off button, looked to make sure the connection was broken, and looked back to Rottermill. "Well?"

Rottermill turned the Voice Stress Analyzer so that Falkenberg could see the readout. A line of X's reached far into the red zone. "Colonel, she's scared stiff."

"What put you onto her?" Ian Frazer asked.

Rottermill shrugged. "Do enough interrogations and you get a feel for it. Mind you, this isn't certain. That damn scrambler could affect the patterns. But I'll bet dinner for a week that woman's hiding something. Three days' dinners it's something to do with shipping schedules."

Jeremy Savage laughed. "Rottermill, I doubt anyone will take your bets no matter how you dress them up. I certainly won't."

Rottermill made a wry face. "Colonel, if we could have the next call without the scrambler?"

"Of course."

Captain Fast scratched his head. "Colonel, if the Chief Administrator is in league with the rebels—"

"We don't know that," Rottermill said.

"But it's not unlikely?" Amos Fast asked.

"With Rottermill willing to bet?" Ian Frazer said. "Christ, do you think she's been feeding Barton satellite data? No wonder they keep finding my patrols!"

Captain Fast whistled softly. "Colonel, shouldn't

we send some of the Headquarters Squad to see she doesn't run away?"

"A bit hasty, perhaps," Major Savage said. "Still, if this proves out—"

"I'll ask the governor to bring her to dinner tonight," Falkenberg said.

# XVIII

Ann Chang sipped at an unremarkable port while the mess stewards silently cleared away. She half-listened as Falkenberg went through a meaningless ritual of thanking the Acting Mess President, as if Captain Fast weren't Falkenberg's adjutant and chief assistant. *Come to that, this whole dinner has been pretty unremarkable.* Nothing wrong with it, really: there'd been four courses and two kinds of game, and nothing was overcooked; but you could dine on the same fare in a dozen restaurants within two kilometers of Government House. Certainly the meal wasn't anything worth inviting the governor to—and there was even less about it to have made Carleton Blaine insist that she change her dinner plans and come with him. *Funny. I don't think I've ever heard him so insistent about anything. Odd.*

Not a lot of people here. Colonel Falkenberg and Major Savage—apparently neither of them married, was there something strange about that? Captain Frazer's wife seemed to be the official hostess. And of course Prince Lysander had brought that hotel girl. Captain Catherine Alana had come in late. Odd. Didn't I see her in town, outside Government House, just this afternoon?

A trivial dinner, and that didn't make sense. Why would Falkenberg invite the governor and his Chief Administrator to a very ordinary meal on such short notice? But Blaine had seemed pleased, even eager; almost as if he were anticipating something—She gasped involuntarily.

Could he know? No. Certainly not. He wasn't that good an actor. "The guilty flee where no man pursueth." Who said that? It certainly applies to me, Ann thought.

The toasts were over. All at once Falkenberg, the governor, and Captain Rottermill were standing at her chair.

"Excuse me for a few minutes, would you, Ann?" Blaine said. "The colonel has some news for me. Apparently it's sensitive enough that I mustn't share it with anyone, even you. Can't imagine what it might be, but there it is. We shouldn't be long. Perhaps you'll join Prince Lysander and his young lady for a while?"

"I'm sure I'll be fine," Ann said automatically.

"Of course you will," Blaine said. He walked away with Colonel Falkenberg.

Captain Rottermill stayed behind. "It's really not all that complicated, Mrs. Chang," he said. "Something to do with shipping schedules, I think."

"I—shipping schedules?"

"A minor discrepancy somewhere," Rottermill said. "Ah. Here's Prince Lysander. I'll leave you in his good hands." Rottermill bowed and followed Falkenberg and Blaine.

*What is this?* Ann looked around wildly. Nothing seemed to have changed. No one was watching her. But— *Something's wrong. Terribly wrong.* She fled to the women's room.

No one else was inside. She stayed there as long as

she thought she decently could. When she came out, Captain Alana was waiting for her. Captain Catherine Alana, and five soldiers in combat fatigues. Three were women. They all carried weapons and wore "MP" brassards.

"I'm sorry, Mrs. Chang," Catherine Alana said. She didn't seem at all like the young lady who'd been at the governor's dinner party only two weeks before. "I must ask you to come with us."

"What? But I'm supposed to be with Prince Lysander—"

"We'll explain to His Highness," Captain Alana said. "I'm sorry, but I really must insist." Catherine gestured, and her soldiers surrounded Ann Chang.

No one had touched her, or even been impolite, but Ann knew better than to resist. She nodded helplessly and followed her captor.

They took her to a bare, unadorned room. A folding plastic table and two folding chairs stood on the plastic floor. They ushered her inside and left her there alone.

*They can't do this!* Inside, she knew they could. There were special laws and regulations for officials of very high rank. Governor Blaine had plenty of authority to deal with suspected treason.

*Treason. But it wasn't. I'm no traitor—*

The door opened, and a young man about thirty years old came in. He wore sergeant's stripes on his undress khaki uniform. "Good evening," he said perfunctorily. "I am Special Investigator Andrew Bielskis. For the record, are you Ann Hollis Chang, Chief Administrator of Tanith?"

"Yes. Yes, I am. And by what right are you talking to me like this?"

"Just routine, Ma'am."

A sergeant. Not even an officer. Ann set her lips in

a thin line. "I see no reason why I should speak to you at all. Please inform Governor Blaine that I want to go home now."

"The governor's busy with the colonel, Ma'am." Sergeant Bielskis said. "Now, we understand you're saying there are no ships in orbit around Tanith at present. Is this correct?"

"I don't have to answer that!"

"No, Ma'am. We have the tapes of your conversation with Colonel Falkenberg this afternoon. I'll play them if you like."

"This is none of your business!" Ann shouted. "I want to see the governor!"

"I'm afraid it is my business, Ma'am," Sergeant Bielskis said. "Colonel Falkenberg's contract stipulates the neutralization and suppression of all organizations and persons dedicated to the overthrow of the lawful authorities of Tanith. Do you deny cooperating with the rebels?"

"What? But—"

The door opened and Captain Rottermill came in. His face was slightly red, as if he'd been running. "Sergeant Bielskis, what is this? Madame Chang, my apologies!"

*Thank God!* "No harm done, Captain. Thank you."

"Now, Bielskis, just what do you think you're doing?"

"Preliminary interrogation of detainee, sir," Bielskis said.

"Sergeant, for heaven's sake, this is the Chief Administrator of this planet!"

"Makes no difference, sir. We have solid evidence—"

"Evidence, Sergeant?"

"Yes, sir. At 1548 P.M., suspect having been instructed by the governor to inform this Regiment of all space traffic at present and for the future, personally stated to Colonel Falkenberg that there were no ships in orbit around Tanith and none expected. At approximately 0845 two days ago a Tanith landing ship under contract to Amalgamated Foundries, Inc. delivered supplies, liquid hydrogen, and liquid oxygen to CDMS *Norton Star*, which ship was then and is now in orbit around this planet. The landing ship requested and received clearance from the governor's office. Sir."

"Good Lord. But surely Mrs. Chang was not aware—"

"You can spare me the act, Captain," Ann said. "Although I must say you're very good at it. Tell me, Sergeant, what do you do when you're not intimidating middle-aged grandmothers?"

Bielskis shrugged. "Pull the wings off flies, Ma'am?"

Ann chuckled. "All right, Captain, what's going on here?"

"We've got you, you know," Rottermill said. "Voice Stress Analyzers this afternoon, and this room is equipped with a full battery of remote physiological sensors."

"Got me—"

"That may not be the best way to put it," Rottermill said. "If we were concerned with legalities, we'd have you. But of course that's not part of our job here. Sergeant, why don't you find us something to drink? Would you care for a brandy, Mrs. Chang?"

"Captain Rottermill, I would *love* a brandy."

"Good. Now let's get square with each other. So far the only people who know about this conversation are you, me, Sergeant Bielskis, and Captain Alana."

"Captain Catherine Alana?"

"Of course. She's a witness. Would you like her to join us?"

"Why not, if she's going to listen?"

"Very well. Now, as I say, this hasn't gone very far yet. There's no reason for it to reach the governor unless you want it to."

"Well—I'd really rather not disturb him," Ann said.

Rottermill smiled briefly. "Precisely. So why don't you just tell us all about it."

"All about what?" Ann said.

"Mrs. Chang, I can't turn you over to Sergeant Bielskis without the governor's consent, and I'd really hate to go ask him for that, but I will if I have to."

The door opened and Catherine Alana came in. She carried a tray with a brandy decanter and glasses.

"I used to think you were nice," Ann Chang said. "That was you I saw outside Government House today, wasn't it?"

"Oh, dear, you weren't supposed to recognize me," Catherine said.

"So you knew, even then," Ann mused. "All right, what do you want to know?"

"To start with, how long you've been cooperating with the rebels," Rottermill said.

Ann laughed. "That's easy. Since about three o'clock yesterday afternoon."

Rottermill was shocked.

*That got him!* "I do believe your boss is nonplussed," Ann said to Captain Alana. "But it's true. I'm afraid if you want to 'turn' me and use me as a double agent, it won't work. You see, I'm not a rebel."

Rottermill glanced down at his oversized wristwatch and frowned. "I believe you. So why were you withholding important information from the governor?"

"Yes, of course, that is the question. I'd really rather not say—"

"Mrs. Chang," Rottermill said. "We can find out. But if my OSI people start moving around Government House, we won't be able to keep anything a secret. Won't it be better for all of us if we keep it among ourselves?"

Ann sighed. "Oh, I suppose so. May I have that brandy now? Thank you. Well, it started with a request for a dinosaur permit. . . ."

§§§

Everett Mardon stared at the uniformed men on his doorstep. "Let me get this straight. Mrs. Chang wants me to come with you to Colonel Falkenberg's camp?"

"Yes, sir," the sergeant said. "Here's her note, and she sent this compact along. Said you'd recognize it. Said to tell you it's something to do with keeping a promise she recently made to you."

Alicia called from the other room. "Who is it, Ev?"

"Some people your mother sent," Everett said. "She wants to see me tonight."

"What? But we're playing bridge at the Hendersons'!"

The sergeant coughed. "I was told to keep this as informal as possible, sir."

"Meaning I don't really have a choice?" Everett demanded.

The soldier shrugged.

"I see. Alicia, you'll have to call Brenda and tell her we can't make it. I really do have to go."

"Good thinking," Sergeant Bielskis said.

Alicia Mardon tried to telephone Brenda Henderson but the phone was dead. A few minutes later a very helpful young technician arrived. It would take a while to get the phone working, he said; but he'd be sure to see the Hendersons got the message.

§§§

Half a dozen men were clustered around the map table in the regiment's conference room. When Lysander was ushered in, Governor Blaine raised a questioning eyebrow at Falkenberg.

"Prince Lysander located the enemy's headquarters," Falkenberg said.

Lysander opened his mouth to correct Falkenberg, then thought better of it.

"Did he? Congratulations, Your Highness." Blaine turned back to his inspection of the map table. "Rochemont. I knew the Girerds had a major hand in this mess, but I hadn't thought they'd get them this dirty." He shrugged. "So now we know where they're probably storing the borloi. But—as I understand it, Colonel, you haven't the ability simply to take the place by storm."

"That's about the size of it," Falkenberg said. "Not even if we commandeered every air-transport vehicle on the planet. Barton's got more than enough anti-air defenses to hold that place long enough to get the stuff out." Falkenberg smiled faintly. "Of course we could very likely manage to destroy it."

"Good Lord," Blaine said. "Colonel, please! Assure me that won't happen. It's all Bronson's people would need to put Grand Admiral Lermontov in a cleft stick. Not to mention the whole Grant faction in the Senate."

"We'll take every precaution, Governor," Falkenberg said. "So, I imagine, will Barton's Bulldogs."

"That's certain," Amos Fast said. "If that crop's lost, there's nothing to pay him with."

"It occurs to me," Major Savage said, "that Major Barton must have made contingency plans. Specifically, he must have a way to remove the merchandise on short notice."

"Well, now that his ship's here, he can just send for the landing boats, can't he?" Captain Fast said.

Governor Blaine frowned. "Ship? What—"

"CDMS *Norton Star*. An asset of Amalgamated Foundries, Inc."

"Here now? In orbit? Why the devil wasn't I told?" Blaine demanded.

"We'll get to that," Falkenberg said. "Amos, you've got a firm ID on the ship? Good. What do we have on her?"

"Unscheduled merchantman," Fast said. He tapped keys on the control console. "Carries her own landing boat. One moment, sir—there's more coming in. Ahah. She's commanded by one Captain Nakata, formerly of the Imperial Meiji fleet. Let's see what we have on him . . . Hmm. As of last spring there was a Lieutenant Commander Yoshino Nakata on the rolls. Four standard years' service as skipper of an assault carrier."

Major Savage whistled softly.

"Good Lord." Blaine stared at the map. "An assault carrier commander, an experienced one at that, skippering a tramp merchantman with her own landing ship. My God, Colonel! I've been at Rochemont. It's on an inlet, you know—the deep water runs almost all the way to the main compound. A landing ship could—"

"Exactly," Falkenberg said. "That's the assumption we're working on."

"Well, damn it, Colonel, what are you going to do about it?"

"That's what we're here to decide, sir," Falkenberg said.

"Governor," Captain Fast said, "The *Kuryev*'s still in the system. You could recall her—"

"To do what?" Blaine asked.

"Recover the cargo from Nakata," Fast said. "If *Kuryev* gets here before *Norton Star*'s boat takes the stuff off planet, there's no harm done—we just borrow *Kuryev*'s assault boats and go in ourselves."

"Captain, that's absurd," Blaine said. "First, I've no authority whatever to order a CD warship to board a CD merchantman—"

"Not even to seize contraband, sir?" Fast suggested.

"Borloi's not contraband, Captain. And you can be sure *Norton Star* will have a perfectly legal bill of sale for anything anyone might find on board," Blaine said. "I suppose I could claim we're sequestering goods against payment of taxes, but I don't for a minute think the CD Council would back me up. Sure, they might order Amalgamated Foundries to pay taxes and imposts, but I have no doubt the Council will turn the cargo right back over to them."

"Excuse me, Governor," Prince Lysander said. "I'm a little confused. Aren't the planters committing a crime—even an act of rebellion—by keeping back their crops?"

"Of course they are. But it's only a crime on Tanith," Blaine said. "The regulation that says all borloi has to be sold to the Lederle Trust is a perfectly legal Order in Council; but it's an internal matter, quite outside the jurisdiction of the CD. Surely the circumstances are similar on Sparta. The CoDominium isn't likely to enforce your domestic regulations."

"Yes, of course. But somehow I thought it might be different here, since this is a CD planet—"

"I take it then," Major Savage said carefully, "that

in this case possession is considerably more than nine points of the law."

"Which leaves us exactly where we started," Captain Fast growled. "We can't just take Rochemont because we don't have transport to get enough troops there fast enough. Meanwhile, any minute now they could just drop in and pick up the stuff."

"At least the governor can refuse to give them a landing permit," Lysander said.

"Not that it would do any good," Blaine said. "Tanith doesn't have planetary defenses or warships. If they want to land, there's nothing to stop them."

"Besides, they already have a landing permit," Captain Fast said.

"What! How—"

"Approved by your office, Governor," Fast replied.

"How the—Colonel—"

"Later, please, Governor. At the moment we seem to have ourselves a problem."

§§§

"Christ on a crutch," Sergeant Miscowsky muttered. He glared at his watch, then back at the tangle of vines and bright flowers hanging over the brackish water. "I think I just screwed the pooch again."

"Nah," Corporal Tandon said. "You told him to start late, so he did. He'll get here."

"Shit, how's he going to *find* us?" Miscowsky demanded. "There's ten channels to this fucking excuse for a river."

"He'll find us," Owassee said.

"If he can get the boats. I didn't get the idea that uncle of his was all set to help us."

"Hell, Sarge, you worry too much."

"I get paid to worry." Miscowsky looked again at his watch. "He gets here or not, we still have to report our position. Better get set up, Nick."

"Right." Tandon took gear out of his knapsack. He set the point of what looked like a large corkscrew against a goshee tree trunk and drove it in, turning the handles until it was seated solidly in the corky wood. When he had the horn-shaped antenna firmly in place, he unpacked the hand-cranked generator and plugged the radio set into it. "Okay, Owassee, you're junior man now."

"One bad thing about letting the kid go," Owassee muttered, but he took the generator and strapped it to a log, attached the handles, and gave it an experimental turn. "Ready when you are, C.B."

Miscowsky consulted his watch. "Not long now. Maybe ten minutes. Wish that kid—"

There was a low whistle from upstream.

"Goddam," Miscowsky muttered.

Another whistle, then what might have been an answering one.

"Sumbitch! That's Cloudwalker all right," Tandon said.

A minute later two flatbottomed skiffs came into sight. Jimmie Cloudwalker was perched in the bow of the first. Buford Purdy stood in the back with a long pole. The second skiff was poled by Etienne Ledoux. They piloted the boats to the bank and tied them to low branches of the overhanging trees.

"Good to see you," Miscowsky said, as his troops and Ledoux jumped onto solid ground. "Wondered if you might have trouble borrowing a boat."

"I am still not certain this is wise," Ledoux said. "You have told me the Girerds are already enemies of the governor."

"That's for sure," Miscowsky said.

"I have considered. They claim this land. It is no real use to them—few can live and work here—but still they claim it." Ledoux shrugged. "Eh, bien. I can take you within three kilometers of the Girerd hills. We will be there by midnight. Then I will take my boats and go. With God's help the Girerds will not know the—guests on their land gave you aid. But if you should find our assistance of value—perhaps you will remember us. No one cares to be a guest forever."

"We won't forget you."

"Time to check in, Sarge," Tandon said. He plugged his helmet set into the radio and began speaking in a low voice. After a few moments he made adjustments with the control wheels on the antenna, listened, and adjusted again. Then he smiled and motioned to Owassee to begin cranking.

"My nephew has explained why you are not likely to be overheard," Ledoux said. "I confess I am still concerned—"

"So are we," Miscowsky said. "We don't want trouble any more than you do."

Tandon continued to speak in a low voice. Suddenly he straightened. "Sarge! The colonel wants to talk to you."

# XIX

Lysander wondered if he would be allowed in the situation room, but when he went there after breakfast the sentries saluted and let him pass. Despite the best efforts of the stewards and the air conditioning system, the conference room stank. Fear and excitement blended with stale tobacco and spilled coffee.

The scene inside hadn't changed from the night before. Intelligence NCO's bent over the big map table. The Officer of the Day sat in a high chair at one end of the room. Senior officers came in, examined the maps and spoke to the sergeants, and went out shaking their heads.

One thing had changed: now the map table showed the actual location of Frazer's patrols in green. In most cases that was all there was, but some patrols had shadow locations shown in yellow. Lysander frowned at the display, then finally asked one of the plot sergeants.

"That's what we're telling Barton, sir." The sergeant grunted in disgust. " 'Cause of those traitors in the Governor's office, the rebels have been getting satellite reports all along. Mostly those'll just show big troop movements, they won't see the patrols, but once in a while they get lucky and see some of Captain Frazer's specials." The sergeant grinned. "Our turn now. Cap'n Alana fed in a program to jigger things so when the satellite does get a reading, the Government House computer reports the location a little off from where they really are. Can't hurt."

"No, I don't suppose it can. Thank you, Sergeant." Lysander leaned over the map and frowned. It couldn't be that simple. If they cut off all data, the rebels would get suspicious, but what if they sent patrols of their own to verify the satellite information? Rottermill must have thought all that out. Or Falkenberg himself.

Probably it didn't matter. Things would get settled soon or not at all. The basic situation was thoroughly simple: they knew where the borloi was kept. The problem was what to do about it. So far no one seemed to have thought of anything.

Someone's watch chirped the hour. In the next few minutes most of the senior staff came in to stare at the map table. The plot didn't tell them anything they hadn't known twelve hours earlier, but if anything was going to happen, they'd know it in the chart room before anyone else did.

"Do you all a world of good to go for a walk," Rottermill said.

"Sure would." Ian Frazer bent over the map table and eyed the distances between Rochemont and the nearest airfields.

"Report time," Rottermill said. "Swenson."

"Sir." Lieutenant Swensen adjusted her headset and nodded to the communications sergeants. It took nearly an hour for Frazer's SAS teams to make all their reports. As they did, Lieutenant Swensen fed their present and anticipated positions into the map computer. All twenty-three teams would converge on Rochemont, but not for several days.

There was a sudden hush as the projected position of Miscowsky's team appeared on the map.

"Get a confirmation on that," Captain Rottermill said automatically.

"Confirmed," Captain Frazer said. "Looks like the lads have found themselves river transport. Cooperation from the locals."

Captain Fast leaned down for another look. Then he straightened in decision. "Swensen, hang onto that contact." He touched buttons on the intercom. "Colonel, there's something here you ought to see."

Falkenberg was grinning when he came into the staff room. It was infectious. Soon everyone in the room was smiling.

"We've made several promises in the governor's name," Falkenberg said. "All worth it, I think. Headman Ledoux swears he can put twenty troopers and a fair amount of equipment in the Rochemont hills by dawn if we get them to the river early tonight. I've sent Miscowsky on ahead with Purdy as guide, so we'll have some forces on the spot no matter what happens. Of course they won't be able to do very much without reinforcements."

"I like it, John Christian," Major Savage said. "A good mortar team with complete surprise might just be able to take out a landing boat."

"I can see some problems," Captain Fast said carefully. He looked at Falkenberg. "With your permission, I'll reserve my comments for later, though."

"Looks better than anything else I've seen," Ian Frazer said. "Only problem is, I don't have twenty SAS troops left. In fact, I don't have any."

"Your regular scouts will do for this, Ian," Captain

Fast said. "It's not like they'd have to stay out there for weeks."

"Harv and I will go," Lysander said quietly.

Everyone turned to look at him. There was silence for a moment. "Well, Your Highness, it could get a bit—" Frazer cut himself off.

Lysander smiled, not unkindly. "Captain, I don't know what notion you have of how princes of Sparta are brought up, but you might reflect on the name we've given our planet. Harv Middleton has spent the last couple of weeks teaching unarmed combat to your special forces troops, right?"

"Yes—"

"And they've learned from him, haven't they. Well, not to boast, but I can take him three falls in four."

"I—see," Frazer said.

"So that's settled," Lysander said. He thought he saw Falkenberg grin momentarily.

"Ian, I expect you ought to round up the other volunteers," Major Savage said. "Mortars and recoilless teams particularly wanted."

"You know, this just ought to work," Rottermill said. He grinned. "Legal, too. Provided they've put the borloi aboard the boat before we fire on it."

"Hadn't occurred to me," Major Savage said. "But yes, that could be important."

Falkenberg nodded slowly. "It could be critical. You can be sure Bronson's agents will file piracy charges. Let's make that an order, Ian. No one fires on the landing boat until we're certain a significant portion of the borloi is on board. If nothing else we'll make the governor's job a lot easier."

"Maybe we better reserve that decision for headquarters," Amos Fast said.

"Bit tricky," Rottermill said. "The field commander might not be able to communicate with headquarters."

"No, leave the authority in the field," Falkenberg said. "Just be sure the order's understood."

"Sir, why are you so sure they'll bring in the landing ship?" Captain Jesus Alana asked. "Mightn't they just transfer that crop to someplace else?"

Falkenberg smiled thinly. "Now that the observation satellites really belong to us, I hope they do."

"They're waiting for the harvest to finish," Rottermill said. "I don't know how long that will be."

"I don't either," Falkenberg said. "Time to help them decide. As soon as Captain Frazer's battle group is in place, we'll start an all-out assault on Rochemont." He pointed to a small island some fifty kilometers due south of the plantation. "Dragontooth Island. Appropriate name. This will be our assault base. Amos, we'll need all the transport we can get. Everything the governor can commandeer. We can't risk civilian craft in combat, of course; we'll use them to ferry gasoline and supplies for this operation. Rottermill, get your people started finding beaches, clearings—anything we can use as staging areas to move Second and Aviation Batallions to the island. From there Second will be well within striking range of Rochemont. Wait for final orders, but plan on starting the ferry operations not long after first light tomorrow. When this is done we'll have Aviation Batallion poised to run right down their throats."

"That should do it nicely," Captain Rottermill said. "Barton won't be able to stand just sitting back and watching us get into striking distance. He'll have to make his move. What's nice is that our troops won't have to hide—"

"I think it would be wise if they tried," Falkenberg said. "Barton will certainly see what we're doing. He'll know we can't possibly have thought we could hide an operation this size. He also knows we'd try our best to hide it anyway unless it's a feint, so that's what we'll do now. Best security you can manage. Act like this is all we can do."

Major Savage nodded. "Which it very nearly is. If we hadn't known about the landing ship, we wouldn't have had much choice."

"The one thing we do hide, of course, is that the whole operation is aimed straight at Rochemont," Falkenberg said. "What I want Barton to believe is that we're trying to outmaneuver him by placing a sizable force behind his lines. Given that strategy, Rochemont is an obvious target, but there are others." He indicated ranches dotted along the bay. "We don't single out Rochemont."

Captain Fast nodded. "Yes, sir."

Falkenberg turned to Major Savage. "Jeremy, I want you to do a second operation for cover. Overland assault with swamp boogies in the southeastern sector. This one really is a feint. After the first few hours we don't mind if they know that, but at the start it has to look real. Just look real, mind you, we don't want casualties. Steady troops on this, you'll roll through some of the most productive land on Tanith, and I don't want needless damage. I'd prefer none at all."

"There shouldn't be much," Captain Fast said. "That part's all right, Barton will fall back to regroup. If it goes on very long there could be some hard fighting, but we'll control that."

"If it goes on very long, we'll all be broke," Captain Alana said.

"So will Barton," Major Savage said. "I'll try to be frugal, Jesus."

"All right, Amos," Falkenberg said. "You say this part's all right. You don't like the rest."

"No, sir, I don't. And I'm not dead sure why."

Falkenberg looked around the table. "Who else doesn't like it?"

"I don't, sir," Peter Owensford said. "The problem is that the whole thing hangs on Ace Barton's cooperation."

"I'm afraid that's true," Major Savage said. "But have we any choice? Everything else we've thought of is a sure loss. This operation has surprise, and that means it has a chance. Barton can't possibly know we've found out about his ship, and he certainly has no reason to believe we know about Rochemont."

"How about this?" Captain Owensford said. "We go in. Barton calls in a landing boat and starts loading it up. You can be damned sure he'll put every last one of his troops on alert. He knows we have SAS teams out in the bush."

The others nodded agreement.

"He gets the stuff aboard. Or he gets *something* aboard. No way for our people to tell what. Eventually there's enough that we get worried, and our mortar teams open up. Say they're lucky. They cripple the landing boat without sinking it—"

"That's not luck," Ian Frazer said. "Just good shooting."

"Okay, Ian, and I believe your scouts are up to that," Owensford said. "But Barton will be ready for them. He's got to be. First salvo, he'll have his counterbatteries working."

"Well, we know that," Frazer said. "So our lads shoot and duck fast. Won't be a picnic—"

"Picnic be damned," Owensford said. "The troops can take care of themselves. Most of them should survive. Their mortars won't. Now what happens when the second landing boat comes in?"

"Second boat," Ian Frazer said, nodding slowly.

"Is that what was bothering you, Amos?" Falkenberg asked.

"Yes, sir. Except I hadn't thought it through as well as Captain Owensford did. But he's got it. We won't have any way at all to knock out a second boat."

"We don't know there is a second boat," someone muttered.

"We sure as hell don't know there isn't one," Amos Fast said. "It's not usual for a tramp freighter, but *Norton Star*'s hardly an ordinary tramp."

The others watched as Ian Frazer bent over the map table. Finally he straightened. "It's close all right, but it's not hopeless. Stash some helicopters in Ledoux's village. When the first lander comes in, we send in the choppers. Time it right and one of them will be in position to knock out the second lander—"

"If it gets through. It certainly will never get out," Captain Alana said. "And it'll take every credit we have to replace Aviation Batallion."

"It's worse than that," Amos Fast said. "We can't just start shooting at the second lander. It won't have any borloi aboard."

"It will by the time a CD inspector sees it," Rottermill muttered.

"You know," Frazer said, "maybe it would make sense to reverse things. Try to knock out the *first* landing ship with the choppers, and leave the recoilless teams as a surprise for the second. We do have those Sea Skimmer missiles. Maybe it's time to use them."

"Makes sense," Rottermill said. "But—"

"But—" Captain Jesus Alana repeated firmly. "Do you know what those birds cost?"

"What the hell good are they if we never use

them?" Frazer demanded. "We've been saving them for the right mission. This is it."

"I agree. Hang the expense. Sometimes there's no choice," Peter Owensford said.

"Sometimes there isn't," Major Savage agreed. "Colonel, shall we send the Skimmers out to Dragontooth? Thank you. All right, Jesus, you've got the word."

"Yes, sir," Alana's voice held no enthusiasm.

"We may not need them," Savage said. "Let's not concede anything just yet. Especially since Barton knows we have those missiles. He just may have set up defenses. We'll know when Miscowsky's lads get in place."

"I've seen situations I like better," Owensford said. "But maybe this is the best we can do."

There was a long silence. "Anyone else have suggestions?" Falkenberg asked.

"Not just now," Savage said. He tamped tobacco into a large pipe. "Seems to me that Ian is on the right track. The mortar and recoilless teams will be our biggest surprise. We ought to save that surprise until it's needed most. What we need is a cheaper way to knock out the first assault boat."

"Of course there may not be a second one," Lysander said softly.

Falkenberg put on his spectacles and bent over the map table. "Amos, what time is our next contact with Miscowsky's group?"

"Well, they're supposed to stop and listen for messages every two hours—about forty minutes."

"Good. I want to talk to Etienne Ledoux."

"Got an idea, John Christian?"

"Just may, Jeremy. I just may. Meanwhile, someone find me the best expert on local conditions we have here at the base."

"Fuller, I'd think," Amos Fast said.

"Right. Fuller it is. Although if we have anyone who's lived near the coast—wasn't there a recruit from the jungle villages?"

"Purdy. Ledoux's nephew," Ian Savage said. "He's out with Miscowsky's team."

"Yes, of course. Anyone else like that? Anyway, send Fuller to my office, and then ask McClaren to pick three men and come see me about equipment."

"McClaren? Colonel, you're not going in there—" Ian Frazer was shocked.

"I think I will," Falkenberg said.

"But Colonel—"

Falkenberg's smile was cold. "Your concern is noted, Captain."

"Yes, sir."

"Mr. Prince, I'd be pleased if you would accompany me as my aide. And your *korpsbruder*, of course."

"Thank you, sir."

"Right. Amos, I'll be in my office in five minutes. Carry on." Falkenberg strode to the door.

"Christ, that's torn it," Ian Frazer muttered. He lifted his personal communicator card. "Centurion Yaguchi. Get my orderly. We'll be going into the field tonight."

"I doubt that, Ian," Major Savage said.

"Sir?"

"He isn't going to let you go out there."

"Damn it, Jeremy— Look, you talked me out of it before, but this time I'm going to do it, I swear, next Regimental Council I'm going to—"

"No you won't," Savage said. "You'd lose, and the colonel wouldn't accept that kind of restriction if you won the vote. Be logical, Ian. Everything's cut and dried now. We're needed here to handle the details. The key command decisions will be made out there."

Major Savage shrugged. "If the colonel weren't going, I would be. Rather nice of him to spare me that."

"Yeah. Look, you don't mind if I worry about him?"

"We can all do that. If you think you're upset, imagine what Sergeant Major is going to say. I doubt John Christian will be taking him, either." Savage nodded to Lysander. "Sorry you had to hear all this—"

"Glad I did, sir. Now if you'll excuse me, I've some arrangements I'd best see to."

"Carry on, Mr. Prince."

# XX

The Officers Open Mess was a blurr of activity. There weren't any customers, but the staff had folded up most of the tables and chairs, and stacked the rest of the chairs on the tables. Two privates were enthusiastically mopping the floor. Another was behind the bar packing the bottles into boxes.

"Chance of dinner?" Lysander asked the mess steward.

"Yes, sir, but there's not much choice. Catfish and sweet potatoes—"

"Hum." Ursula smiled thinly. "Tanith standard fare—"

Sergeant Albright looked pained. "Yes, Ma'am, not up to the standards of the Mess, but we've got an alert on, you see."

"It's also all we'll get," Lysander said. "Please, Sergeant, I'd love some catfish and sweet potatoes. With beer, please."

"Yes, sir. Alieri, set up a table for Mr. Prince. Excuse me, sir, I'm needed in the kitchen."

"We don't have to eat," Ursula said. "I'd rather—"

"Of course we have to eat," Lysander said. "Certainly I do." He worked to keep his voice calm, and hoped he'd succeeded. Conflicting emotions boiled within him. He was eager to get away from Ursula, to get on with the mission and show Falkenberg what he could do. Odd, he thought; he liked being with Ursula. He even wondered if he might be in love with her, and what kinds of problems that would make for him. Certainly he felt guilty for being ready to leave her to go with Falkenberg. Mostly, though, he was more afraid that he wouldn't meet Falkenberg's expectations than anything else. He wanted to please Falkenberg more than he'd ever wanted to please his own father, and he didn't really understand that. Deep under all his emotions was the elemental fear of death, or worse, dismemberment.

Meanwhile, Ursula was being very understanding about his volunteering to go with Falkenberg, and while Lysander appreciated that, it was getting a bit hard to take.

They sat and waited for drinks. "I've made some arrangements," he said. "If I don't come back. The Regiment will take care of you—"

"If they'll give me my contract, I can take care of myself," Ursula said. "You won't be back, will you?"

"Don't be silly. I'm the colonel's aide. I'll have the best bodyguards in the galaxy. And besides all that, there's Harv."

"Sure. When are you leaving Tanith?"

"I'm not sure."

They sat in awkward silence for a moment. Then she smiled and said, "It's all right. I'll miss you."

*I'll miss you,* he thought. He wanted to say something, but he couldn't. The silence stretched on.

He was relieved when Sergeant Albright came over to their table. "Excuse me, sir, we're short handed, and the tables are packed. Would you mind if Captain Svoboda and Mrs. Fuller joined you? Thank you, sir." Albright left without waiting for an answer. A moment later a lanky officer limped up to the table.

"I'm Anton Svoboda. Headquarters Commandant. Your Highness, we've been told you've no objection to our joining you—"

"No, of course not, sir." Lysander stood. "I expect things will go better if you call me Lysander." He touched the cornet's insignia on his collar. "They told me the rule was first names in the mess. And this is Ursula Gordon."

"Pleased to meet you. Ursula. Lysander. Right." Svoboda said. "Juanita Fuller, Prince Lysander Collins of Sparta, at present a volunteer cornet of the regiment. Which means that your husband is no longer the junior cornet. And Miss Ursula Gordon."

Captain Svoboda held out his arm to help Juanita sit, then sat down carefully. His left leg was encased in what looked like a large pillow. "Couple of crocks," he said. "Actually, they just let us both out of hospital this afternoon. Juanita's husband is in conference—"

"Ah," Lysander said. "Cornet Mark Fuller? I met him this afternoon in the Colonel's office. Apparently he's the colonel's pilot tonight."

"I hope they get done with him pretty soon," Juanita said.

"Yes, that can't be much fun, first day out of hospital and no one to welcome you home," Ursula said.

Juanita shook her head. "We don't have a home—"

"I'll take care of that," Svoboda said. "We'll find something. Although I'm not sure what I can do for right now." Svoboda shook his head. "Maybe you ought to stay in the hospital tonight."

"I'd sure rather not," Juanita said.

"What's the problem?" Lysander asked.

"Well, Cornet Fuller just joined the regiment," Svoboda said. "Hasn't been assigned quarters. He's been staying in the BOQ. Juanita was hit in the rescue operation, so she was sent directly to hospital when she got here, and no one thought to assign them married quarters. Usually it would be my job to take care of that sort of thing, but—" He pointed to his leg. "I haven't been at my desk since we rescued Mrs. Fuller." He shrugged. "Wouldn't be a problem if they hadn't let us out in the middle of a general alert. Which reminds me." Svoboda raised his voice slightly. "Albright."

"Sir!" The mess steward came over to the table.

"Sergeant, it looks like you're packing up to pull out."

"Yes, sir."

"May I see your orders?"

"They're in the kitchen, sir."

"Please bring them. Along with a bottle of wine. Anything that's open."

"Yes, sir."

They waited until Albright returned carrying a large jug of red wine. "Not officer quality, sir," Albright said apologetically.

"It will do," Svoboda said absently. "Pour me a glass, please." He took the message flimsy Albright handed him and read for a moment. "Bloody hell."

"Problem, sir?" Lysander asked.

"You could say that. Sergeant, you've been given the wrong orders. The regiment itself isn't moving out, just most of the batallions. Regimental headquarters will stay right here. You shouldn't be packing up."

"Cap'n, the orders say right there—"

"I see they do," Svoboda said. "But someone has punched in the wrong codes on the computer. I'll straighten it out, but meanwhile, you can stand down. You're not going anywhere." Svoboda looked down at his leg. "Neither one of us is."

"Yes, sir."

"So. I'll take care of this nonsense. You go find us something decent to drink. And see what you can scare up to make the catfish a bit more palatable."

Albright grinned. "Yes, sir. I think I can unpack something."

Svoboda reached beneath the table and lifted a portable computer console onto the place in front of him. "If you'll excuse me for just a moment," he said.

"Certainly," Lysander said. "But I confess some confusion—"

"Well," Svoboda said, "we have a data base of detailed order sets for nearly anything the Regiment might want to do. The colonel has ordered a general alert, and is shipping quite a lot of the regiment's strength out to—well, to various places. It sounds simple, but actually it's pretty complicated to move a batallion and all its gear and all the supplies it will need. There are thousands of items to worry about, stuff from batallion headquarters, stuff that has to be drawn from central supply—now suppose a batallion is to be reinforced with units that don't belong to it. More orders. Believe me, it can get sticky."

"Oh," Ursula said. "Yes, of course—"

"Computers handle most of it," Svoboda said. "We keep canned order sets for nearly every contingency. All it takes is calling out the proper ones. Only in this case, someone punched in the wrong code, so Sergeant Albright got the wrong orders." Svoboda bent over the bright blue screen, then typed quickly. "Hah. And here they were. Hmmm."

"Who did it?" Ursula asked.

"Little hard to tell," Svoboda said. He shrugged. "Won't take long to straighten out." He looked thoughtful, then shrugged again. "Can't think Barton will be foolish enough to attack this headquarters, but I expect I ought to buck this over to Rottermill, just in case it wasn't a mistake." He typed furiously for a moment.

"Attack?" Ursula asked. "How?"

"Bombs. Missiles," Svoboda said. "Not likely any would get through. We have a few nasty surprises for anyone who tries. Less likely that Barton would try it."

"Why wouldn't he?" Juanita asked.

"What would— Ah. Here's Sergeant Albright with something more fit to drink." Svoboda waited until the steward had poured a sparkling wine for everyone. "Cheers. As I was saying, what would it get Major Barton to attack regimental headquarters? Besides making everyone mad at him? It's not strictly in the Code, but the tradition is strong that you don't do that until you've warned the other chap."

"But we're about to—" Lysander caught himself. "Aren't we about to attack Barton's headquarters?"

"Certainly not," Svoboda said. "We don't make war on women and children. Barton's Bulldogs have their base near Dagon. We won't go near that. Why should we?"

"Wouldn't it help win this war?" Ursula asked.

"Not really," Svoboda said. "Oh, we'd get his computers, and a lot of his central stores, all right. As against that, we'd make this place a legitimate target. We'd have to detail more troops and equipment to defend our headquarters. Our troops in the field would have to worry about their families." The captain shrugged. "It's making war on civilians, and we just don't do that sort of thing. Not without good reason."

"It would be expensive, too," Ursula said.

Svoboda looked at her through drooping eyelids. "Aye. Should we not be concerned wi' expenses, lassie?"

"You'd do better to adopt a Latin accent," Lysander said.

"One mimics Captain Alana at considerable risk," Svoboda said. "The Mess President has ways of getting his own back."

"I suppose a mercenary regiment is in business to make money," Ursula said. "I guess I just never thought that through."

"Well, yes, we are," Svoboda said. "Which means we keep the costs down. That includes troops, of course. Good people are the most expensive item we have." His voice had a bantering tone, but there was an edge of menace in it as well.

"But your business is winning," Ursula said.

"Ursa—"

"Actually, she has a point," Svoboda said. "Our business is winning. But at what cost? Some games aren't worth the candle— Excuse me." Svoboda's computer console gave out several soft bleeps. Svoboda typed an acknowledgment, then frowned at the screen. "As I thought, we wont be moving the Mess—but it looks like we'll have to forego its pleasures, Mr. Prince. We're both wanted in conference." He gripped the edge of the table and stood carefully.

"When will you be back?" Ursula demanded.

Svoboda glanced at his watch. "Lysander may not be back at all this evening."

"But—"

"I'll try to get away for a minute," Lysander said.

"But—Mark—" Juanita protested.

"Ah. And Cornet Fuller is flying the colonel's helicopter. Not likely he'll have much time off for the next few days. I'll try to remind the colonel that your husband will need a few minutes before they take off—O Lor', we haven't found you a place to stay, either!"

"Would you like to stay with me?" Ursula asked. "There's plenty of room."

"Oh—well I wouldn't like—"

"No trouble at all," Ursula said. "His Highness has other interests—"

"Well, thank you."

The computer console beeped more insistently.

"That's all right, then?" Svoboda asked. "Good. I'd best be going. Juanita. Ursula. Pleased to have met you." He bowed slightly and limped toward the door.

Lysander stood. "I'll try to see they give your husband a moment." He looked to Ursula. "Where will you be?"

"Here for dinner, then your rooms," Ursula said. "And—be careful."

§§§

"I wish I could be calm like you," Juanita said. "But I'm scared. You do this much?"

Ursula laughed. "Send my man off to war? First time. You too?"

"Yes, we haven't been married long—actually, we was never married at all, not in a church. Mark's from Earth. Sent here as a rebel. I was born to convicts on a borshite plantation. You from Sparta too?"

Ursula chuckled. "No-oo, not quite. I was born with a contract too. Except I had the good fortune to be owned by the Hilton, and they sent me to a good school. As an investment." Ursula smiled musingly.

"You're luckier than me. At least the man you're sending off will come back to you. Mine won't."

"I don't understand—"

"I was contracted to a hotel. As a hostess. A hotel where Lysander, Prince of Sparta happened to stay."

"Oh. But—I think he likes you," Juanita said.

"He likes me all right. And so what? I doubt that a future king has any large place in his future for a hotel girl."

"Oh. But that's awful. You like him—"

"Is it that easy to see?"

"Yes. Ursula—what will you do?"

"I'll get by." Ursula laughed suddenly. "After all, I've been ruined."

"Ruined?"

"A poem I ran across in the hotel library," Ursula said. "Written a hundred years ago on Earth by Thomas Hardy. I liked it enough to memorize it."

"Oh. My mother used to read poems to me. Do you really remember it? Tell me."

"Well—all right. Two girls from the country meet—

*"Oh, 'Melia, my dear, this does everything crown!
Who could have supposed I should meet you in
Town?*

*And whence such fair garments, such prosperi-ty?"*

*"Oh, didn't you know I'd been ruined?" said she.*

*—"You left us in tatters, without shoes or socks,
Tired of digging potatoes, and spudding up docks;
And now you've gay bracelets and bright feathers
three!"*

*"Yes: That's how we dress when we're ruined," said she.*

*—"At home in the barton you said 'thee' and 'thou',*

*And 'thik oon' and 'theas oon' and 't'other'; but now*
*Your talking quite fits 'ee for high compa-ny!"*

"Some polish is gained with one's ruin," said she.

—"Your hands were like paws then, your face blue and bleak
*But now I'm bewitched by your delicate cheek,*
*And your little gloves fit as on any la-dy!"*

"We never do work when we're ruined," said she.

—"You used to call home-life a hag-ridden dream,
*And you'd sigh, and you'd sock; but at present you seem*

*To know not of megrims or melancho-ly!"*

"True. One's pretty lively when ruined," said she.

—"I wish I had feathers, a fine sweeping gown,
*And a delicate face, and could strut about Town!"*

"My dear—a raw country girl, such as you be,
*Cannot quite expect that. You ain't ruined," said she.*

"That's—" Juanita turned away with tears in her eyes.

"Hey, no need to get upset," Ursula said. "Don't cry over me! I'll get by—"

"Not you," Juanita said. "I suppose I should be thinking about you, but—that poem is about me, too. What'd it say, 'raw country girl'? That's me! I'm supposed to be an officer's wife, and I don't know anything. I could dream, about—about marrying a foreman, or maybe a planter; I know plantation life, but what am I goin' to do here? I can do farming, and take in washing. I did some house work in the big house. I don't know anything else. You're educated—"

"And ruined," Ursula said. "Don't forget that."

# XXI

Pipe Major Douglas raised his baton and brought it down sharply to cut the pipes off in mid skirl. Lysander, feeling bulky in combat leathers and Nemourlon armor, followed Falkenberg into the first of the four waiting helicopters. Harv Middleton climbed in behind them.

"Prince, I like those," Harv said. He gestured to indicate the pipers. "We ought to do that at home."

Lysander nodded thoughtfully. He had been surprised to find pipers at the airfield, and had been ready to laugh at the needless ceremony. Why should they pipe troops aboard helicopters? Then they began to play the stirring old marches that had sent men to a thousand battles, and he knew.

They did nothing like that on Sparta. Why not? Leonidas and his Three Hundred had marched to Thermopylae to the sound of flutes. Something to mention to the Council . . .

The helicopter was surprisingly quiet even without combat helmets. When Lysander and the others put their helmets on in obedience to Falkenberg's gesture, every bit of the helicopter motor noise was gone. Instinctively Lysander adjusted the gain on the helmet's pickup until he could dimly hear the chopper motors again.

The helicopter held ten men in addition to its own crew, two rows of five on each side of the ship. The deck between them was covered with their equipment. The helicopter's crew chief inspected the equipment lashings. "Looks good, Mr. Fuller."

Lysander strapped himself into his seat. Falkenberg sat to Lysander's right. Harv was to his left, with two Scouts beyond him. Andrew Mace, the senior Scout lieutenant, sat across from Falkenberg, with second Lieutenant Harry Janowitz next to him. Then came Corporal McClaren, who seemed to be Falkenberg's bodyguard, and two others of the Headquarters Guard. The guards were all big men, and looked strangely alike. Harv had said they were pretty good troops, which was a lot for Harv to concede to anyone but Spartans.

"All correct, chief?" the pilot called.

"All correct, sir." The crew chief took his seat forward of the passengers. "Let 'er rip."

The motor sounds rose in pitch and the helicopter lifted. Lysander was surprised at how quiet it was even in flight.

"It had better be quiet," he muttered. "And what in hell am I doing here?"

"Good question." Falkenberg's voice startled him. "Sir?"

"Your mike is on, Mister Prince."

Lysander looked around in dismay. No one was staring at him.

"You needn't be alarmed. You're switched to my frequency," Falkenberg said.

"Oh." Lysander touched a stud on the side of his helmet to activate the status displays. There were five communications channels, each with a diagram showing its connections. Channel One was a link directly to Falkenberg. Channel Two showed links to Falkenberg, Mace, and Janowitz. The other three had not been configured. "I'll turn it off, sir."

"No need," Falkenberg said. "It was a good question. What the devil *are* you doing here?"

"Sir?"

"Not that we're ungrateful, but this isn't your fight," Falkenberg said. "And you don't strike me as a glory hunter."

"No, sir. If you—I was told that if I got a chance to watch you in action, I should take it."

"Good enough."

"Sir—why are you here?"

"We're paid to be here, Mr. Prince."

"Yes, sir."

"You can hardly say that protecting the Grand Admiral's secret funds isn't my fight," Falkenberg said.

"No, sir, but on that scoring it's my fight too."

"So it is, Mr. Prince."

Lysander listened to the thrum of the helicopter motors.

"Very well, Mr. Prince. You asked a question. Verbal games aside, you asked why we were here."

"Yes, sir."

"I may have an answer."

"I'd like to hear it."

There was another long silence. "I don't generally care much for preachers," Falkenberg said. "But I don't often get an opportunity to preach to a future king.

"We are here, Mr. Prince, because it is our job to be here. Have you ever read a book called *La Peste*?"

"*The Plague*. Albert Camus," Lysander said. "No sir. It's on the reading list my tutor prepared."

"Along with a hundred other books you don't particularly want to read, I make no doubt," Falkenberg said. "Read that one. You won't enjoy it, but you'll be glad for having read it."

"Yes, sir."

"Camus tells us that life consists of doing one's job. As I get older, I find that more and more profound. Mr. Prince, I have tried to live up to that notion. I believe that the sum total of your life is what you have accomplished. Some of us don't get to accomplish much."

"Sir? Some may not, but you have. You've changed the history of whole planets!"

"True enough. Whether for better or worse, whether anything I've done has any significance for the future, is another matter, and doesn't depend on me. Everything I've done could be made irrelevant by events I can't control. I like to think I have done what I could with the opportunities I had, but I do not delude myself. I have never had any great weight in the cosmic balance."

"Who does?"

"You may have. Statesmen and kings sometimes have. I once thought I might. That was easy to think as a boy in Rome, tramping the Via Flaminia and looking down the Tarpian Rock on the Capitolean. The ruins of glory. Do you know that for over two thousand years the Romans kept a female wolf in a cage on the Capitolean? During the Republic, in the Civil Wars, in the great days of the Empire. During the dark ages after the fall, during the Renaissance, the Papal States, the Risorgimento. Mussolini. But after the Second World War they couldn't do it any more. They couldn't protect the wolf from vandals. Modern vandals. I don't know what the original Vandals did."

Falkenberg laughed. "Enough of that. I've had no great weight in the cosmic balance because for better or worse, Mr. Prince, I chose the profession of arms."

"Surely you're not saying that violence never settled anything?"

"Hardly. But soldiers do not often get to choose what issues their actions settle. I suppose it's irrelevant in my case. I said I chose the profession of arms, but in fact it chose me."

"A good profession, sir."

Lysander felt Falkenberg's shrug. "Perhaps. Certainly a much misunderstood profession. In my case, as I was not born an American taxpayer or a Soviet Party Member, there was no chance I would rise high enough in the CoDominium service to have any great influence. Of course, we soldiers seldom have as much influence as we like to believe. It is true that what we do is necessary and often can be decisive, but we are not often asked to make the crucial decisions. War and peace. We don't make wars, and we seldom control the peace."

"Is peace the goal?" Lysander asked.

"What is peace?" Falkenberg asked. "On historical grounds I could argue that it is no more than an ideal whose existence we deduce from the fact that there have been intervals between wars. Not very many such intervals, or very long ones, either. But let's assume we know what peace is, and that we want it. At what price? Patrick Henry demanded liberty or death. Others say nothing is worth dying for. Again those are issues soldiers are seldom asked to deal with."

"Then what do we—"

"If you think of war and oppression and violence as a plague like the Red Death, then soldiers are the sanitation crew. We bury the dead. We sterilize regions, and try to keep the plague from spreading. Sometimes we spread plague, even when we try not to. Sometimes, not often, we are allowed to eliminate the causes of the plague. We are seldom asked to treat the victims, although good soldiers often do. The politicians are the physicians and surgeons, the ones who are supposed to find a cure."

"They never have—"

"They never have. There may not be one, which makes the sanitation crew even more necessary. You were born a politician, Mr. Prince. If you live, remember the sanitation crew. You need us. Interestingly, we need you as well. We need to believe that there are physicians and surgeons."

"It's a fascinating analogy, sir, but haven't you carried it too far? You say you have no weight, but you've certainly influenced events."

"And will again," Falkenberg said. "Sometimes we find the scales are balanced. Each pan holds enormous weight, far more than anything we control— but at times like that, a small weight can tip the balance. It's that way now."

The helicopter banked sharply. Lysander caught a glimpse of lights far below. The pilot's voice came through the intercom. "Coming down now. It'll be rough when we get to the deck. Be sure you're fastened in."

Lysander inspected his straps. Then he turned to Falkenberg. "Yes, sir. How do you know which side to choose?" Lysander demanded.

"The key question. I can tell you what I do. Which side will leave the human race with the greatest potential?" Falkenberg asked. "Find that out and the answer is clear enough. Mr. Prince, every man is born with a potential. Life consists of using that potential as well as possible. To hurt as few people as possible—but understand that to do nothing may be far worse than any harm you can possibly do."

"The greatest happiness for the greatest number?"

"No. That goal is often used to justify doing people good whether they like it or not. No, Mr. Prince, it's not that simple. You have to ask people what they want. You have to ask the experts what humanity needs. And you must listen to the answers. But having done all that you still must make your own decisions.

"You can't just count noses. You have to weigh them, but you can't just weigh opinions either. Numbers do count," Falkenberg laughed suddenly. "We're flying over a jungle toward a battle. If we're lucky we'll rescue a huge supply of drugs. Drugs that will keep Earth's hordes docile for a while longer. They may well think they are happy. Is that good? Or would Earth be a better place if we destroyed the crop? And that's only one question, because there is more at stake than borloi. Our job, Mr. Prince, is to give Admiral Lermontov his secret funds—and hope that he does more good than harm, more good than the borloi does harm. Will he?"

"We can't know," Lysander said. "My father supports Lermontov. I don't think he likes him."

"He doesn't have to. So, Mr. Prince, what do you fight for?"

"Freedom, Colonel. The rights of free men."

"And what are those? Where do they come from?"

"Sir?"

"Consider, Mr. Prince. The soldiers of the 42nd are under rigid discipline. Most would say they are not free—yet we are under no government. We may be the most free people in the galaxy. Of course, that kind of freedom has a damned high cost."

"Yes, sir, we're finding that out on Sparta."

Falkenberg chuckled. "I expect you are, Mr. Prince. I expect you are." He was silent for a moment. "Mr. Prince, would you like to know the most significant event in the history of freedom?"

"The American revolution?"

"A defensible choice, a close second even, but not mine. I would choose the moment when the Roman plebians required the patricians to write down the twelve tables of the law and put them where everyone could see them—and thereby proclaimed the law supreme over the politicians. The rule of law is the essence of freedom."

"I'll think about that, sir."

Lysander felt Colonel Falkenberg's shrug. "Please do. My apologies, Mr. Prince. When I have a politician for a captive audience it's tempting to lecture, but I suspect a young man brought up on a planet settled by professors of political science has heard enough of this to last a lifetime."

Not from you. Lysander wanted to ask Falkenberg to go on, but the colonel had already changed channels on his helmet radio.

"Gentlemen," Falkenberg said. "You were all introduced, so we can dispense with that." The two lieutenants across the aisle nodded agreement. "It's school time." The helicopter maneuvered violently. "We're close to the jungle top now, so we won't distract Cornet Fuller from his piloting. That leaves the four of us. Lieutenant Mace, I believe you are senior. Please explain to Mr. Prince."

"Yes, sir." Mace looked at Lysander. "The Colonel means that it's time for what he calls his school for captains. Since there aren't any captains aboard I guess we'll have to do. The colonel states a problem, then we say what we'd do about the situation, then we all discuss it. Ready? Good. Colonel—"

"Gentlemen, we have a decision to make," Falkenberg said. He pointed to the heavy gear lashed to the deck of the helicopter.

"Our objective is to get ourselves and that equipment from the Ledoux village to a point close to Rochemont. We can presume that we will reach Village Ledoux undetected. From there we load onto small boats. Propulsion will be provided by the villagers, with paddles and poles. They are experts and have made this journey many times. The boats are wooden, not large. As I understand it, each can carry two men and their personal gear, or an equivalent amount of equipment. There are some twenty boats, enough to carry all of us as well as our heavy equipment in one trip. Naturally we'll space the boats out somewhat. Clear so far? Good. The problem is, how do we load the boats, and in what order do we send them?

"Mr. Prince, as junior man you're first. What's in the first boat we send down river?"

"Two Scouts, sir?"

"Don't *ask*," Lieutenant Mace said.

"Scouts," Falkenberg said. "And in the second?"

"I guess I want to think about it," Lysander said.

"Lieutenant Janowitz has recently been promoted from cornet to second lieutenant," Falkenberg said. "Congratulations. What's in the first boat, Mr. Janowitz?"

"Two Scouts," Janowitz said. He sounded older than Lysander, and quite positive. "Officers in the second. We send the boats in waves, with the personnel first, then the heavy equipment following, the colonel and his guard in the last boat."

"I see. Why?" Falkenberg asked.

"Radar, Colonel. They may not be able to see into

the jungle, but if they can, there's less chance of being spotted—"

"Yes. Lieutenant Mace? Do you agree?"

"I don't know, Colonel. I see Harry's point. The heavy stuff will show up on radar better than troops. A lot better, so there's more chance some scope dope will see the blips. Easier to sneak the men through. Less chance of alerting Barton's people. But—"

"You have reservations," Falkenberg said. "Noted. Mr. Prince?"

"I have some reservations too, now that I think about it," Lysander said. "If the troops are spotted, if they even raise suspicions, then the heavy weapons are much more likely to be spotted."

"They may think they're Ledoux's people," Janowitz said. "Probably will."

"It's possible," Mace said. "Especially if all they see is people. Suppose they don't believe it's natives?"

"Calculated risk," Lieutenant Janowitz said. "The probabilities favor sending the troops first."

"Sure of that?" Falkenberg asked. "Mr. Mace?"

"It's the other way," Mace said. "We send the heavy stuff first, because if it gets through, then the troops will, and if Barton's people are alerted we'll never get the weapons through."

"And?" Falkenberg prompted.

"Well—I don't know, sir."

"Mr. Prince?"

"We can't do the mission without the heavy guns?"

"Precisely," Falkenberg said. "Our whole mission depends on getting our heavy equipment into place. If we fail in that, we're not likely to accomplish much. Well done, gentlemen. Now I have an entirely different problem for your consideration. . . ."

The clearing was small, and utterly dark except for tiny pencil beams of red light from the crews' flashlights. Four helicopters had come here. Two, refueled by the others, would go on. The other two would keep just enough fuel to get back to the last staging point.

Cornet Fuller squatted on the ground and used his helmet to project a map. "Fuel's going to be close," he said.

Falkenberg pointed to Village Ledoux. "Once we're there, what will be your operating radius?"

"Maybe a hundred klicks," Fuller said. "Depends on the winds for the rest of the way."

"That should be enough," Falkenberg said. "One way or another, you won't need more." He got up and strolled to the edge of the clearing.

"Now why does the way he says that scare hell out of me?" Fuller asked.

Lysander chuckled. "You too? Good."

"I never got a chance to thank you for putting Juanita up."

"It was Ursula's notion," Lysander said.

"Yeah. Thanks anyway. And for talking the colonel into giving me five minutes with her." Fuller wiped his forehead. "Sure hot."

"It is that."

"What's it like on Sparta?" Fuller asked.

"Well, it's much cooler—"

"Yeah. I heard that. I meant for convicts."

"We don't have contract labor like Tanith," Lysander said. "New chums from Earth can choose their employment."

"You just turn convicts loose?"

"Well, not precisely, but anyone willing to work won't find the restrictions onerous. The CoDominium doesn't like our giving citizenship to anyone still under formal sentence, but that doesn't come up often anyway. Not many try to become citizens."

"Uh? People want to be citizens?"

"Some do," Lysander said.

"Oh. Perks? Welfare?"

"Not precisely. Everyone on Sparta has political rights, but citizens have more. More obligations, too, of course."

"Oh. Sort of like taxpayers."

"No, not quite—"

The crew chief materialized next to them. "Fuel's aboard, Mr. Fuller."

"Thanks, Chief. Load 'em up." Fuller chuckled in the dark. "If I'd been a little smarter, I'd have got to Sparta. Had a chance, but I didn't know what to do. Maybe it's just as well."

# XXII

The school was over, and there was no more conversation with Falkenberg. The helicopter flew low over the jungle, sometimes maneuvering between the trees. Tanith's small moon came up, but was no more than a blur above the clouds. Sometimes when the helicopter banked sharply Lysander could see the jungle below, but as no more than a darkness even blacker than the clouds above.

After one violent maneuver, Lysander felt Harv's nudge. He gestured toward his helmet. Lysander set one of the channels to Harv's headset frequency.

"How does he see?" Harv said.

"Radar, I suppose," Lysander said, but he wondered, since radar might be detected from a distance. "IR? I don't know, but I'm glad I'm not flying it."

"He's pretty good," Harv conceded.

"Yes." I suppose he is, Lysander thought, and wondered what would have happened if Fuller had bribed his way to Sparta. Where would he have gone? His natural talents as a pilot might have brought him to an airline, or a wealthy mine owner in need of a chauffeur. He'd never have had a chance to become a Spartan officer.

The helicopter flew on, and despite its violent maneuverings, Lysander fell asleep.

Village Ledoux seemed crowded. The villagers had already prepared shelters for the helicopters. As soon as the passengers were out of the planes, a hundred men grabbed each one and carried it under a thatch-roofed structure. Mats were unrolled to form walls, and the helicopter vanished.

In moments the equipment was unloaded, and they followed the villagers into the dense jungle. Lysander felt rather than saw the thick growth around him. Then he was at the water's edge. A score of small flat-bottomed boats were pulled up against the shore.

Falkenberg's NCOs gestured. The recoilless rifle was loaded into the first boat. After a moment, Lieutenant Mace climbed in with it and lay flat on the bottom of the boat. A tall, dark civilian gestured, and the boatman poled the boat away from the shore. In seconds it vanished into the underbrush.

The next boat held lumpy gear, including what Lysander thought was a sea sled. It was sent into the night. Boat after boat was loaded and sent off. Mortars and mortar bombs. Communications gear. Radar antennae. Everything went swiftly and soon the equipment was gone. Then came the soldiers. Then it was Lysander's turn. He and Harv lay flat in the boat, and waited.

The boatman's pole had a sort of paddle blade so that it could be used as a scull as well as to pole the boat. There was so little light that Lysander couldn't see the boatman's face.

He knew it would be a long way, and tried to sleep, but despite his training he couldn't. Thoughts came and went. Pictures of himself killed, or wounded.

Harv falling. Falkenberg lying bleeding on the ground. What if I'm left in charge? Lysander wondered. No chance of that, or was there?

Ursula. What would happen to her? He thought of Melissa back on Sparta. Everyone assumed they'd marry. So had he. Now he wasn't so sure. Melissa was his friend, he could talk to her. They'd been a lot of places together, and twice they'd made love. The first time for both of them. He liked her a lot. She was easy to be with, and of course she was a full citizen. She'd be a good mother, and a good partner in government. That's not love, he thought. And so what? What is love? Am I in love with Ursula? I want her. I want to be with her.

What would Melissa think if he brought Ursula to Sparta? Would she understand? No. Neither would his father. No, it was ridiculous. There was no place for Ursula in the palace.

And why not? Kings in history books had mistresses. But the kings of Sparta weren't real kings, not like the old kings of France. There wasn't any Divine Right in the Spartan constitution. The kings of Sparta didn't have to grub for office by kissing babies, but they were supposed to be better trained, and better qualified than anyone else. Or at least as well qualified. They were also supposed to have children, legitimate children, children who would inherit positions of leadership. That way Sparta's leaders would have a long view of things, look to the next generation and not just the next election.

And we're supposed to be moral, whatever that means. Set an example for the people. Keeping a mistress isn't much of an example. The Council would find out, and there'd be hell to pay. And even if the Council would accept Ursula, Melissa never would.

So? Give up Melissa. Marry Ursula. He chuckled

aloud, and felt a quick pressure from Harv's foot to remind him to be quiet.

It really was impossible. The Council would want genetic tables and family history, information Ursula probably didn't have, and they wouldn't be likely to approve if she did have it. Suppose they liked her ancestry? She'd still have to qualify for citizenship. Even as bright as she is, starting at her age it could take years. If she'd do it at all. No. Ursula won't be going back to Sparta with me.

He didn't like that thought.

Change the subject.

He could hear the water streaming past beneath the hull of the pirogue. It was pitch dark in the jungle. Dark in here, but we're not invisible. Not to radar. Is someone looking at us right now? Falkenberg must have detection equipment. What if he does? What can we do? If they find us, they can take us. We don't have enough people or ammunition to hold out very long.

This isn't getting me anywhere. What is? Why am I here? Life consists of doing one's job. Is this my job? What is? The thoughts whirled through his head until he forced them away.

"Prince." Harv's voice was low and urgent. "We're here."

It was still dark, but there was faint grey light in the clouds above. Lysander climbed out of the boat. His left leg was asleep, and he rubbed it gently.

As soon as he was off the boat, the boatman backed it away from the shore, turned, and poled upstream. In moments the boat had vanished.

"This way," someone whispered. A shadowy figure led the way. Their footsteps squished in soft mud. Once Lysander's boot went in above the ankle, and there was a loud sucking noise when he pulled it out. There still wasn't enough light to see anything, only faint grey directly above the jungle canopy. Harv followed silently.

Lysander thought they'd walked half a kilometer when his guide stopped.

"Over here, sir. Under the tarp," the trooper whispered.

Lysander knelt to feel the edge of a tarp directly in front of him. He crawled under. It was stifling hot under there. When he was all the way under he felt the ground sloping down slightly. The tiny glow of a map projector was blinding.

Falkenberg, Lieutenant Mace, and a sergeant lay under the tarp, all facing a central area where the sergeant had projected a chart.

"Sergeant Miscowsky, my aide, Cornet Prince," Falkenberg said. His voice was low but unstrained. "Mr. Prince, you will study this chart. Sergeant—"

"Sir." Miscowsky reached out into the holographic image. "This is the coast. We're back inland, here. The stream we came in on is behind us. It runs south some more before it turns west into the bay." He touched his helmet and the view changed. "OK, this is us again, coast there. The jungle ends about a klick to the west here. Then there's just over three klicks of cleared hills, farmlands mostly, and Rochemont Manor. That sits on what passes for a big hill here, sort of a low mound. We were able to pick up lots of details on that area. Antenna farms here, and here. Some sheds here, I think they have heavy mortars under them but I can't be sure. They went to a lot of effort to hide everything from the satellites."

"How about the antennas?" Mace asked.

"Got a break on those, sir," Miscowsky said. "Least-wise this set of 'em. About two hours ago, after the satellite was past maybe twenty minutes, they peeled back the roof of this shed here. This thing that looks like a grape arbor is a frame the roof slides onto. Inside are search and surveillance antennas, no question about it, they showed up good in passive IR, and they put out a strong K-band search pattern too. Good thing we was dug in good." Miscowsky touched his helmet and the projected scene changed to a dark outline. "I got a good camera set up at the edge of the jungle, but there's not enough light to see anything yet."

"We have about an hour before Captain Fast starts Operation Hijack," Falkenberg said. "Call it another ten minutes after that for Barton to find out we're on the move. You'll want to get your observations fast, because after that we'll want to be dug in good. We don't want them to suspect we're here. Without surprise we might as well not be."

"Yes, sir," Mace said. "Shouldn't be a problem. Miscowsky, tell us what you've done for emergency shelters."

"Sir. We can't dig in without them seeing us, but I figure it's going to get thick when they do find out we're here. Seemed to me we'll need some shelter, so I rigged primacord around trees, here, and here. Soon as it's sure they know we're here, we'll drop those trees in a box pattern. Got a couple of shells dug in just in the center of the box, they'll help make it deeper. Not what I like, but it ought to make a storm cellar. I've got another crew doing the same thing over here." He pointed again, and a second area turned red in the hologram.

"Good work," Mace said. "Be sure all troops are warned."

Lysander studied the red areas in the projection. "I'll tell Middleton," he said.

"Right," Falkenberg said. "Pity we don't know what they're using to protect their guns. Sergeant, when they opened that antenna shed, did you get any estimate on what it's made of?"

"IR signature says wood, Colonel. Maybe there's something under it, but I don't think it's armor."

"Right. Probably nothing but wood. Mr. Mace, what's your opinion? Can we take those antennas out in the first salvo?"

"Yes, sir, I think we can."

"Of course we don't know where they keep their spares," Falkenberg said. "Even so, they'll be blind for a while. Mr. Mace, it's your tactical command, but my recommendation is to give target priority to the antennas. Hit them, then the CP if we can find it. Then go for the guns when they start shooting at us."

"Yes, sir."

"That's assuming you don't have a higher priority target," Falkenberg said. He leaned closer to the holographic projection. "Show me the docking area. Thank you. What is this structure?"

"Pretty big for a boat house," Mace said.

"Not likely a boat house, not on Tanith, sir," Miscowsky said. "Colonel, I never noticed until we got here and took a good look, but they've got solar screens all over that place, more than a farm that size would have. Lots of juice. I think they're making hydrogen and LOX, and where else would they store it but near the docks?"

"Hmm. As far as we can tell, *Norton Star* carries Talin class landers," Falkenberg said. "Just barely have the legs to make orbit from a sea launch. They'll need all the fuel they can get—all right, Miscowsky, I'll buy that, you've located the fuel facility." Falkenberg studied the hologram again. "And these will be barns?"

"Yes, sir. These two are cattle barns. This one's for horses. The ones set up above are farm worker barracks."

"The horses have better facilities. All right." Falkenberg studied the holographic display another few moments, then looked up. "Mr. Prince, you and Mace look as if you're melting. Come to that, I find it pretty warm myself. All right, everyone take ten minutes to cool off. Get outside and loosen up your equipment. Ventilate properly. Then I'll want you again. Under here, I'm afraid. We've gone to this much trouble to keep Barton's troops from knowing about us, no point in taking chances now. Ten minutes, gentlemen. Meanwhile, Sergeant, I have a task for your SAS team."

The sky was dull grey. There still wasn't enough light to see objects, but when he knelt Lysander could just tell where the lumpy tarp was, and he thought he could see someone approaching from the other side. He winced at the thought of the stifling heat, then crawled under. Mace and Janowitz were already there. A moment later Falkenberg joined them.

"Gentlemen. No doubt you're wondering what I'm doing here when I could be back at headquarters." He waited a moment, and when there was no answer, Falkenberg chuckled. "Only you're too polite to say so. To begin, Lieutenant Mace, I did not come here because of any lack of confidence in your ability to control the situation."

"Thank you, sir." Mace's voice was flat.

"In fact, there's not a lot for you to control," Falkenberg said. "We've laid our plans. The headquarters staff can carry out their end. You and Janowitz are more than competent to bring off your part. It's a good plan, and we have sufficient forces. With no more than ordinary luck we'll accomplish the objective. Cripple the landing ship and take Rochemont."

"Yes, sir." Mace said.

Falkenberg touched his helmet and the holographic image of the Rochemont area sprang up between them. "Unfortunately, given the enemy's position here, doing that is likely to be expensive, in lives and money. Anyone disagree?"

Lysander frowned at the projected map. "No, sir. And there's a chance it won't work at all. Or that they'll destroy the borloi."

"Exactly. So," Falkenberg said. "We have the best plan we can think of, but it's hardly an elegant solution to our problem. I've come to see if we can pass a miracle."

"Sir?"

"No battle plan survives contact with the enemy," Falkenberg said. "That's the elder Moltke, but the principle had been known for a long time when he said it."

"Wasn't Cannae according to plan?" Lysander asked.

"Yes, Mr. Prince. Of course Cannae required the Romans' cooperation. Commanders have been trying to duplicate Hannibal's success ever since. Most haven't done so, because the enemy generally won't be as obliging as Gaius Terentius Varro was. Certainly Major Barton won't be. On the other hand, Hannibal was in Italy in the first place because the Romans believed it impossible to cross the Alps with an army. Surprise can do a very great deal."

"Yes sir?"

"Let's look at the situation. First, the objective. What is our objective, Mr. Mace?"

"Sir? Ah. To capture the borloi."

"Correct," Falkenberg said. "Not to capture Rochemont, but to get possession of several tons of borshite juice. What's the first requirement for that, Mr. Janowitz?"

"Well, to keep them from moving it somewhere else while we get enough troops in place to take Rochemont," Lieutenant Janowitz said. "Which is where we come in."

"Right. That's the plan. Of course, it's the expensive way. Is there another?"

The officers peered at the maps and photographs. "I sure don't see how we can get the stuff without taking Rochemont," Lieutenant Mace said.

"Yet we think they are going to pack it into a landing boat," Falkenberg said. "If we could take that boat after they've loaded it—"

"Yes, sir, we've all been thinking of that all the way here, but there's no way," Lieutenant Mace said. "Colonel, the minute that landing boat comes in, they won't try to hide anything. They'll have those radars sweeping every inch of ground around Rochemont. They probably already have trip wires. Mine fields too."

"Besides," Lieutenant Janowitz said. "Even if we could take the landing boat, what would we do with it?"

"One thing at a time," Falkenberg said. "If you had that boat, Mr. Prince, what would you do with it?"

"Fly it to the capital," Lysander said.

"Fly? And who'd do that?" Mace demanded.

"I could."

"Precisely," Falkenberg said. "As it happens, Mr. Prince has had quite extensive training. He is one of the three qualified landing boat pilots in the Regiment."

"Sir? I'm hardly qualified. I've done the training, yes, sir—"

"Three flights, I believe? Takeoff, atmosphere flying, and landing from orbit. You're the best qualified pilot we have, actually."

"Well, if you say so, sir. Uh—Colonel, who are the other two?"

"Captain Svoboda. And me."

"Colonel—" Lieutenant Mace drew in his breath. "Colonel, just what do you have in mind?"

"About what you think, Mr. Mace. A miracle. A small change in Major Barton's plans."

Lysander looked at the projected charts of Rochemont's defenses. "With respect, Colonel, it would take a miracle. Granted I—we could fly that boat out of here, how do we capture it? We can't even get to it."

"That's certainly what Barton thinks," Falkenberg said. "Just as the Romans believed Hannibal couldn't get to them from North Africa."

"Colonel, the Alps is one thing, that field's another. They're bound to have radars sweeping that whole area right now."

"They do," Miscowsky said. "Random intervals, but often enough to keep anyone from getting across those fields. Even my squad couldn't make it."

"Precisely," Falkenberg said. "They're watching the fields. Makes them feel safe. But I doubt they have sonars—"

"Sonar?" Miscowsky said. "Colonel, you ain't thinking of swimming over there? Colonel, everybody knows you don't swim on Tanith! You'd be breakfast for a nessie before you got halfway!"

"Everyone agrees? You can't get past the nessies?" Falkenberg asked. "Good. I'm sure Barton believes it as well."

"Believes it because it's true, Colonel," Miscowsky said. "I don't know much about this crazy planet, but I know that! Sir, it ain't a matter of guts, or firepower. It wouldn't be easy to fight off a nessie, but maybe you could do that, only Barton's people would sure as hell know you did it! And the damn nessie might win the fight anyway."

"My analysis precisely, Sergeant," Falkenberg said. "I came to that conclusion before we left headquarters." He reached into his battle armor and produced a tape cassette. "We can't fight nessies, but perhaps we can avoid them. I had an advantage over you, Sergeant. Being at headquarters I could do some research. More precisely, find out who has already done the research. I called in Mrs. Chang and asked who knew the most about nessies. It turns out there is one team that does nothing but study them."

Falkenberg slapped the tape against his palm. "I got the reports and read them, then I had Mrs. Chang download this from the governor's data banks. It's a tape of nessie calls."

Lysander frowned. "Sir?"

"Feeding calls, mostly. As it happens, there were two deep diving sea sleds in the regimental quartermaster stores. When we loaded the choppers I brought them, and two scuba outfits," Falkenberg said. "Now suppose that we put this tape into an amplifier on a sea sled. I also have tapes of the sounds of crippled prey. Calls and swimming sounds. Put those in the sled, too. Now suppose we send that sea sled on autopilot out into the bay. Make part of that sled's load a dead porker. A bleeding dead porker. When it gets out a way, turn on the tapes."

Lysander nodded to himself. "And while the nessies are following that, we take the other sled over to the dock area. It might work, but won't the landing boat cause problems? How do nessies react to something like that? Will they even hear the tapes?"

"I don't know, Mr. Prince," Falkenberg said. "I don't propose to wait that long. My notion was to get over there while it's still dark. There seem to be ample places to hide."

"A porker isn't all that big," Lieutenant Mace said. "What happens when the nessies finish yours off?"

"Minigrenades," Falkenberg said. "Several of them in the porker, and more outside on the sled. They may not kill any nessies, but they'll wound a couple."

"And nessies are cannibals," Mace said. "Feeding frenzy. You sure don't want to be near that—"

"And won't be," Falkenberg said. "That will happen a couple of klicks out in the bay. We'll be much nearer the shore."

"We," Lysander said.

"I had presumed you'd volunteer," Falkenberg said. "If not, it's no discredit. The notion of swimming out among those creatures isn't exactly pleasant. McClaren will volunteer."

"Oh, I'm going, Colonel. That's not the problem."

"What is?"

"Harv will have to come."

"We only have two sets of scuba gear."

"That's enough. Colonel, you're needed here."

"That's for sure," Lieutenant Mace said.

"Mr. Prince—"

"Colonel, for God's sake! We're talking about swimming three klicks, then hiding out to wait for the landing boat. After that we have to take the boat. With all respect, Colonel, that's stuff Harv and I can do a lot better than you."

"Mr. Prince—"

"Colonel, you're twice my age. More. How long has it been since you took out a sentry? I'd never have thought this up, but Harv and I can sure do it better than you can."

"He's right, Colonel," Miscowsky said. "Only, about this Harv, maybe I ought to go instead—"

Falkenberg laughed softly. "Leave it, Sergeant. Mr. Prince, your point is made. Good luck."

# XXIII

Lysander stood waist deep in the soupy warm water. Here at one of the slough outlets the surf was mild, but he could hear crashing waves out beyond the stream mouth. There was just enough grey light to see the small whitecaps three meters away. When he put his head beneath the surface he had to strain to see the luminous dial of the compass even when he held it close to his face.

The water was warm, but cooler than the jungle had been. It felt good, but he couldn't forget that this wasn't the friendly Aegean on Sparta. This was Tanith, home to nessies. They'd already chased some small eel-like carnivores away.

"Good sign," Private Purdy said. "If there's little ones, the big ones aren't around. Take 'em a while to chew through Nemourlon, too. Take little ones a while, anyway."

They loaded the other sled and sent it on its way. Falkenberg's listening gear told them when the amplifiers began playing the taped nessie calls, and shortly after they heard large creatures moving. Certainly some of them had been attracted to the sled. Some. But had all? It only took one—

"One way to find out," Lysander muttered to himself. He splashed ashore to the stream edge. "Guess I'm off," he said softly.

He felt Falkenberg's hand on his shoulder. "Break a leg," Falkenberg said.

"Sir?"

"Good luck, Mr. Prince."

"Sir," Lysander hesitated. The colonel's hand was still on his shoulder. Lysander stood another moment, then sat in the warm water to put on his flippers. Harv followed close behind when Lysander dove forward into the chop. The second sea sled was waiting on the bottom.

Lysander guided the electric sled under the surf at the stream outlet, then out. When he estimated that he was thirty meters offshore, he turned west to parallel the shoreline. Tension on the tow line told him that Harv was right behind him. No need to worry about Harv. There never was.

Something large loomed ahead and he felt a moment of panic. Nothing happened. A log? Seacow? Whatever it was didn't follow him. He guided the sea sled downward until the gauge showed twenty meters. It was pitch black, murky water and no light above, so that he could barely see the dials.

Lysander concentrated on the compass and the water speed gauge. It was difficult holding a steady course and speed with no visibility, but that was the only way to verify the position he got from the tiny inertial navigation system built into the sled. The system gave him the direction and distance of the Rochemont docking area. It seemed to be working fine.

Sparta had introduced dolphins and orcas into the planet's seas. Both were domesticated, nearly tame, accustomed to swimming with humans. They liked being with people, swimming with them, towing them, and they were more than a match for the native Spartan sea life. Lysander wished he had orcas with him now. Lots of them for preference. A school of killer whales might be able to fend off nessies, at least for a little while. . . .

The seconds ticked away. Somewhere off to his left the other sled would be slowing. The nessies would begin to feed. He listened for the mini grenades, even though he knew they'd be too far away to detect. If the trick didn't work—

Lysander fingered the high pressure lance. In theory you stabbed something—it was designed for sharks—with the long hollow needle, and that would release carbon dioxide under high pressure, rupturing the innards of whatever you'd stabbed. In theory it would be instantly fatal, and the victim, inflated, would float to the surface. An ugly death from an ugly weapon. Lysander hoped he'd never have to test it. There was also the question of whether the needle would penetrate a nessie's armored hide—and what would happen if you killed a nessie and the others went into a frenzy.

After twenty minutes on course, Lysander tugged the tow line. Harv swam up beside him and took control of the sea sled. Lysander checked his tether line and let it reel out as he swam upward toward the surface.

The wind was onshore and there were whitecaps in the bay, nothing for a landing boat to worry about but quite enough chop to make it impossible to see the shoreline in the dim grey light. Instead he looked behind him. After a while there was a tiny blink from the shore as Sergeant Miscowsky briefly clicked a hooded flash. Lysander waited, and when it flashed again he was ready to take a bearing.

There wasn't any navigation satellite system on Tanith. Governor Blaine wanted to install one, but the CD wouldn't finance it. Sparta's system wasn't complete, but it was good enough to locate your position to a few meters, much better than he could do taking visual bearings in choppy seas. Here he had no choice.

The bearing was one more check on the sled's navigator. More importantly, the flash told him that the listening gear hadn't picked up any nessies near the shore, and none following him. Not yet . . .

After he had taken the bearing on Miscowsky's light he couldn't keep himself from staring off southward toward the place the other sled had gone. He couldn't see anything. A wave broke over his head.

*Enough.* He thumbed his buoyancy valve to let out air, and sank slowly toward the sled.

Concentrate, he thought. Stick to your job. The sled and its tapes and dead porker would attract all the nessies or it wouldn't. Worrying about it couldn't change that. He ignored the tight knot in his gut, and tried not to remember vivid images of nessies tearing at each other.

Once he was below the surface he used the helmet display to get his position from the inertial system. It agreed with his visual bearings. When he was sure, he pulled himself to the sled and tapped Harv. Middleton dropped back to let Lysander take the controls.

He held his course. More images of nessies came unwanted. He tried to dismiss them, and when that didn't work he began to recite slowly to himself. Leonidas. Megistias. Dieneces. Alpheus. Maro. Eurytus. Demaratus the lesser. Denoates. Three hundred names, the heroes of Thermopylae.

He was well into the second hundred when it was

time to change course and angle in toward the Rochemont dock area.

§§§

"Major Barton!" Ace Barton woke to find his orderly calling from the bedroom door. "Major!"

"Yeah, Carruthers?"

"Cap'n Honistu said you're needed in the staff room, sir. Looks like Falkenberg's making his move."

"Oh shit. Right. I'll be right there. Have coffee ready." There was bright light outside. The bedside clock showed an hour after sunrise. Not enough sleep, he thought.

When he stood his head pounded. *Shouldn't drink so damned much.* He found vitamins and headache powder and swallowed them, poured a second glass of water and drank that. *I don't even like to drink. Rather drink than talk to those rancher types.*

He dressed quickly. By the time he was done his head felt better.

The staff room had formerly been the Rochemont study, and was the kind of room that Barton would have wanted if he had been a wealthy rancher, although most of the books were ones he wouldn't be interested in reading. He wondered what it had cost to have leather-bound volumes brought from wherever they had been made. Earth? Someday he'd have the servants unlock one of the glass-fronted book cases and see just where those had been printed. They didn't look as if they'd ever been opened.

Anton Girerd stood at the foot of the big conference and map table. He always seemed to be there. Barton wondered when the rancher leader ever slept. He was certainly conscientious enough. Or just worried. Chandos Wichasta, Senator Bronson's representative, sat quietly in a far corner of the room. He acknowledged Barton with a raised eyebrow.

Captain Honistu looked up from the map table. "They're moving, Major."

Barton went to his place at the center of the table. His coffee mug was already there, and he drank a heavy swallow. *Someday Carruthers is going to slip up and I'll scald myself.* "Tell me about it, Wally."

"Two fronts. One's obvious, they're moving in force along the southeastern front. Almost no casualties. As you ordered, we're firing off our long-range weapons and getting the hell out. We've knocked out half a dozen of their swamp boogies, but we'll lose four ranches in the next hour."

"And another fifty in a week, and so what?" Barton mused. "They could have had those anytime they really wanted. OK, try to make them pay *something* for the land, but it ain't worth many casualties. Christian Johnny knows that, it won't be worth many to him, either. So what's he covering up?"

"Not exactly sure," Honistu said. "Reports are still coming in. Looks big enough, Major. Aircraft commandeered. Commercial, even ranchers' private planes. It looks like they're after every airplane on the planet. And some of their air assault troops have been consolidating ranch lands, bringing in engineers."

"Where?"

"Here's the places we know about." Blue lights came on across the map display. "And probables." More lights, in light blue.

"Moving southwest," Barton said.

"Yes, sir. We don't *know* anything, but the pattern makes me think they're after something in this area. Rochemont, even."

"Makes more sense than his other operation. Think they're on to us, Wally?"

"No data."

"What does our man in the governor's office say?"

"He can't be reached, sir."

"Can't be reached." Barton drank another heavy swallow of coffee. "As of when?"

"This morning, I guess. He went home at the usual time last night."

"What happens when you call his home?"

Anton Girerd said, "A stranger answers. A woman who claims to be Alicia Chang Mardon's visiting cousin. But Alicia has no cousin."

"Sure of that?"

"We are quite aware of our relatives, Major."

"I expect you are. Sorry."

"He's not the only one," Honistu said. "We can't reach any of our people in the governor's office."

"None. I see. OK. We're sure none of them knew about this place?"

"We told none of them," Girerd said. His voice was filled with disdain.

"And none of my troops who know ever talked to them," Barton said. "All right, Falkenberg's closed out our sources. We knew it would happen some day. Now he's on the move, possibly directed at Rochemont, possibly just getting a staging base in the southern area. Sure would be bad luck if he wanted Rochemont as a staging base."

"Wouldn't make a bad one," Honistu said.

"Yeah." Barton let the toothpick dance across his mouth again. "Especially if they look at the fuel facilities here. Mr. Girerd, Mardon may not have known about Rochemont, but he did know about *Norton Star*."

"Yes."

"Should we be worried?"

Girerd shrugged. "I have been considering that. I don't know, because I can't guess what pressures Falkenberg might put on him."

"Me either. So. We assume Falkenberg has learned we have a ship in orbit. What will he do?"

"As long as he doesn't know where it lands, nothing," Captain Honistu said. "There are no space defense forces on Tanith, and that CD warship is a long way off."

"Yeah. OK, Captain, what have you done about all this?"

"Put our people on full alert with orders to maintain security from satellite and air surveillance. Upped the frequency of our surveillance sweeps. Alerted *Norton Star* to stand by," Honistu said. "And sent for you."

"Right." Barton studied the situation map for another minute. Then he turned to Anton Girerd. "Sir, I recommend that we bring in the landing ship and get the stuff out of here."

Girerd sighed. "I thought you would decide that." He sighed again. "A few more days. Van Hoorn has had an excellent year. A few more days—but of course you are correct, Major. Better this much than nothing. I will notify Jonkheer Van Hoorn to make the best arrangement he can with the governor."

"You'll do nothing of the kind." Chandos Wichasta spoke quietly, his voice barely carrying through the library. "He must take his chances like everyone else."

"Now wait—" Girerd protested.

"Wait for what?" Wichasta asked. He got up from his place at the far corner of the room and came over to the big staff table. His voice remained low and persuasive. "All this is a strain, and I am sorry, but surely it is clear to you? The more of the crop the governor takes in, the lower the price we will get for what you have gathered. While it would be better if Jongkheer Van Hoorn's crops were added to our collection, we gain nearly as much if they are merely destroyed. If this disturbs you, pay the Jonkheer from your increased profits."

"What will you contribute?" Girerd demanded.

Wichasta looked thoughtful. "We will pay twenty-five percent of the value of Van Hoorn's crop if none of it reaches Falkenberg and Blaine. We will accept any reasonable estimate of its value."

"Not enough."

Wichasta shrugged. "It is all I have authority to give. Perhaps I can persuade my principals to pay more, but I would not be honest with you if I promised they would. They are hard men. I suggest that if you wish Van Hoorn to receive further compensation, you must provide it yourself. Major Barton, I take it you are requesting that we send down the landing boat?"

"Yes, sir."

"I shall arrange it. Immediately?"

"As soon as convenient," Barton said.

"Very well. I will call *Norton Star*." Wichasta left the room.

"Arrogant bastard," Girerd said.

"Yes, sir," Barton said. *Bronson's people usually are. And from here on you'll spend a lot of your life in debt to people like Wichasta.* "OK, Wally, satellite surveillance security can go hang. Full alert for everyone. Deploy air defenses. Full radar search. Get ready to transfer the borloi, and have the fuel people stand by. I want that damn thing in and out fast."

Sergeant Manuel Fuentes was taking a leak against the side of the horse barn when Private Hapworth found him.

"Corporal Hardy says tell you two things, Sarge. Full alert and stand by. Just got the word," Hapworth said.

"Another damn drill. Shit."

"No drill, Sarge. Leastwise the comm room people sure don't act like it's a drill. Falkenberg's on the move. The major's bringing in that landing boat."

"Oh, ho. Be glad of that. This duty's soft enough, but I'm gettin' tired of it. Time we was out of here," Fuentes said. "What's the other thing?"

"Sarge?"

"You said there was two things Hardy wanted you to tell me."

"Oh. Yeah, I did. Other thing is, the nessies are freaking out."

"Eh?"

"Whole shit pot of them, less than a mile off shore. Eatin' something. Eatin' each other, too."

Sergeant Fuentes shuddered. "Saw that once. They got a seacow, and by the time they were finished with it one of the nessies was wounded, and—" He shuddered again. Corporal Hardy knew about Fuentes's interest in nessies. When they'd first landed on Tanith, Fuentes took a dip in the ocean. Then the officers told them about nessies. Thinking about that incident still gave him the willies, but it had also given him a fanatical interest in the big sea carnivores. He wanted to go see what they were doing.

*And Hardy wants my job.* "Nessies will wait," he said. "We better go check on the fuel supply." He was halfway to the fuel shed when the alarms began to sound.

§§§

Sergeant Miscowsky lay in the goopy mud at the edge of the jungle and cursed whatever tiny thing had got inside his pants leg. He hoped it wasn't one of the thin red worms that passed for leeches on Tanith, but he was afraid it was. As long as it didn't climb up to his crotch— He ignored the crawly feeling and carefully panned his binoculars across the Rochemont scene for the tenth time in as many minutes. There was just enough light to see, and the sky was brightening by the minute. Miscowsky scanned slowly, from the docking area on his left to the big house in the center, then across fields and barns—

He'd just focused on a barn when its roof opened down the middle and the two halves dropped to the sides. A radar dish popped up and began to rotate.

*Holy shit.* He thumbed a button on the small console on his left sleeve. "Get the colonel. They're doing something," he said.

Even at lowest power a radio signal might be detected. Miscowsky was linked to the central communications computer through an optical fibre phone line, as thin and flexible as a thread. The fibre optic system was totally undetectable. It was also incomplete, since not everyone was wired into it. Miscowsky panned his binoculars across Rochemont again. There was more activity.

"Falkenberg."

"Colonel, they've opened the roofs on most of their buildings," Miscowsky said. "Antennas everywhere, sweeping everything. They don't care if somebody detects them. Field strength here's pretty amazing."

"Will they spot you?"

"Not me, Colonel."

"Sorry I asked. Do you think they've spotted Mr. Prince?"

"Colonel, I can't tell. All I know is all of a sudden they popped the roofs, and they're sweeping like hell."

"Right. How many observers do we have, and can you pipe any of it back here?"

"Five lookouts, and yes, sir, the cameras ought to be picking stuff up now."

"Thanks. I'll have a look, but keep talking."

"Yes, sir. OK, they're opening the rest of the sheds. I see guns. Couple on the roof of the manor house. More in the sheds. AA and dual purpose stuff mostly. Christ, Colonel, they've got damn near everything Barton owns here! There goes a Leopard. Nasty little bugger." The Leopard was a self-propelled twin rapid-fire gun system mounted on a tank chassis. Used in connection with long-range smart missiles, it was highly effective against helicopters. It could also deliver high volume direct fire against ground targets. "They're moving it this way. Still coming. My guess is they'll put it on the rise about a klick west of here."

"Right. Make sure the computer knows where it is."

"Aye aye, sir. There goes another Leopard, and a couple of missile launchers. I sure wouldn't want to try getting in here with a chopper. Colonel—hah. One whole goddam side of Rochemont hill is opening up! Chopper coming out. Two of them. Two choppers revving up."

"Command override, command override." Lieutenant Mace's voice broke into Miscowsky's helmet phones. "All personnel, secure against aerial observation. Choppers on the rise. I say again, all personnel, take cover, conceal from aerial observation. Choppers coming. Do not fire. I say again, do not fire."

Miscowsky touched the ACKNOWLEDGE button. The computer would collect the responses and tell Mace who hadn't answered.

"Anything else?" Falkenberg asked.

"Well, yes, sir, there's just a lot of activity. People milling around. Last time I looked, the dock area was empty, but there's lots of people there now. Bunch more going into the hill. Looks like a truck coming out of there— Must be a big cave. Truck coming out, heading for the dock area. Bunch of guys hanging on the running boards. Not Barton people, not most of 'em anyway. Different cammies, like what the ranchers wear."

"Any sign of Mr. Prince?"

"No, sir, none at all. Barton's troops still don't act like they've seen anybody, though."

"Carry on, Sergeant."

Miscowsky nestled closer to the squishy ground and adjusted his binoculars. They were definitely moving stuff from the house down to the dock area. Lots of stuff. "Has to be the drugs," he reported to Lieutenant Mace at communications central. "What else could it be?"

"No attempt at concealment?" Lieutenant Mace asked.

"No, sir, none at all. Like they don't care who sees—Holy shit."

They all heard it. A double sonic boom that crackled across the jungle. Then the roar of a hypersonic jet overhead.

"I think we can guess why they don't care who sees them," Mace said. "Command override, command override. Landing ship approaching. Full alert, I say again full alert. Battle plan Alfa, battle plan Alfa."

§§§

It was still grey dark when Lysander and Harv came ashore. They took off their flippers and moved silently toward the building Miscowsky had identified as a fueling station. Part of the building was an open-roofed area. Two tractors and a large harrow were parked there. They slipped into the shed area and toward the door to the building itself.

"Those tractors run on hydrogen," Harv whispered.

Lysander nodded. It made sense. It was easier to make hydrogen from seawater than to ship other kinds of fuel on a primitive world. It also made for less trouble with the various ecology groups. And if you could make liquid hydrogen, you could certainly make LOX. "Tanks are probably underground."

The main entrance to the building was a double door wide enough for vehicles. The long corridor beyond was dimly lit with overhead bulbs. There were a number of doors off the corridor.

They could hear soft voices inside, voices too low to be understood. This went on for a few minutes. Lysander looked around the shed area for a place to hide. Nothing looked very promising. The area was too open. He had decided they'd have to risk going inside when the nearest door off the long interior corridor opened.

A man and a woman came out. They leaned on each other and were obviously drunk. The man wore the faded camouflage uniforms favored by the Tanith rancher militia. The woman wore grey coveralls opened to the waist. They giggled as they walked past Lysander and Harv.

"Of course I love you," the man said. "Couple more years, I'll have enough saved, we can buy out—" He looked around furtively. "Best be quiet." They went out of the shed and toward the worker barracks.

Lysander waved Harv forward and pointed to the door the two had come out. The lock was a simple one that took Harv only seconds to open.

The room inside was filled with crates of spare parts for tractors and farm machinery. Lysander locked the door behind him, then risked using a flash held hooded in his fingers. He found a narrow passage through the crates. It led to a small compartment not high enough to stand in. There was a mattress and several empty beer and whiskey bulbs. A heavy air of sweat filled the compartment.

Harv wrinkled his nose in disgust.

"Yeah, but it looks OK for us." Lysander looked around the small area again. "Looks fine. Now we wait."

Their compartment was against the east wall of the shed. Lysander used his knife to make a tiny peephole in the corrugated sheet plastic wall. When there was enough light outside he could see part of the docking area. Perfect, he thought. We've been lucky.

Luck counts, Falkenberg once told him. But it's no use at all if you don't know enough to take advantage of good luck.

They waited. Harv dozed like a cat, his eyes opening whenever Lysander shifted weight or anyone moved outside. After a while Lysander let himself drift to the edge of sleep.

They heard the alarms first, then voices.

"Get them lines laid out, Hapworth," someone shouted. "Hardy, get the wrenches. Come on, come on, we ain't got all damn day!"

Sonic booms shook them, then there was the roar of the landing ship.

# XXIV

Ace Barton listened to staff reports as long as he could stand it, then left Captain Guilford in charge and took Honistu out to find some fresh air on Rochemont's wide veranda. The breeze off the sea felt heavy, laden with moisture, but it was better than the atmosphere in the staff room.

Honistu pointed out to sea. Barton scanned the area with his binoculars. About two kilometers out, the whitecaps were tinged with scarlet, and the water roiled with dark shapes. "Worst I ever saw them things," Honistu said.

Barton nodded. "Maybe so." There had been feeding frenzies before. Once the batallion cook had stimulated a frenzy by dumping garbage off the pier. The nessies had come for the garbage, and one rose out of the sea and grabbed the cook's assistant. Troops came running up to help, but it was too late to save the recruit. One of the man's messmates shot the nessie, and half a dozen other nessies attacked the wounded one. The resulting frenzy almost destroyed the docks.

After that they were more careful where they threw the garbage. . . .

There was a sharp double sonic boom.

"Right on time," Honistu said.

Barton's binoculars gave him an excellent view of the stubby-winged craft as it settled in on the choppy water. It skirted the crimson waves where the nessies were fighting and sped across to the dock area at too high a speed, turning just in time. It had come full speed close enough to the pier to make Barton wince.

"Hotshot," he muttered. Most landing boat pilots were.

"Worried about nessies. I would be too," Honistu said.

The Tallin class was the smallest of the CD's assault/pickup boats. It looked fairly large, but most of its bulk was tankage and engines behind a small cabin and cargo area. The Tallin class was designed to carry a marine assault section, two metric tonnes, to orbit, or bring twice that mass from orbit to ground. Its mission was to land troops in unexpected places.

*And that we've done*, Ace Barton thought.

Crewmen appeared at the aft hatches and caught lines thrown from the docks. The landing boat was winched in until it lay against the pier. The broad landing hatch opened.

"What the hell?" Barton said. A light armored vehicle rolled out. It was followed by a dozen armed men in dark cammies. "Command override," Barton shouted. "Cover the dock area."

Alarms hooted.

"Major, Guilford here."

"Yeah."

"Mr. Wichasta says that's ours. A present from Senator Bronson."

"Tell the son of a bitch—Captain, put me through to him."

"This is Chandos Wichasta."

"Mr. Wichasta, you damned near started a battle."

"I deeply regret any difficulties we may have caused," Wichasta said. "I did not know they were coming. I have the captain of *Norton Star* on line now. He says they were conducting an exercise, and could not unload the assault boat and still land during this orbit."

"And didn't have any way to tell us."

"I know nothing of that."

"Yeah. And I can believe as much of that as I want to. All right, Mr. Wichasta, but those troops are under my command. Mine, not yours."

"Of course."

"Guilford, get me the officer in charge of that assault team."

"Roger." There was a pause. "Lieutenant Commander Geoffrey Niles here."

"Niles, what the hell do you think you're doing here?"

"Sir, I'm sure Captain Nakata has explained. We were conducting an exercise."

"Yeah. OK, Niles, I want your people off that boat. All of them, except the pilot and crew. That damned thing's going to be overloaded as it is."

"But of course, sir."

"Good. Second, I want them out of the way. Take your vehicle up to the field on the east side of the house, and keep them there. *All* of them. Guilford, notify security we've got strangers among us." He thumbed off the mike. "Wally, that's all we bloody need."

"Watchdogs," Honistu said. "Looks like Bronson doesn't trust us."

"Yeah. And I don't trust him, either." He thumbed his mike again. "Get me Anderson on a secure circuit."

"Captain Anderson here."

"Barton. Bobby, I want you to have a Leopard where it can cover Bronson's people."

"Sir?"

"You heard me. He don't trust us, I guess, but come to that I don't trust him."

"Yes, sir. Anything else?"

"No. Just be sure to do that."

"Yes, sir. Anderson out."

"Want me to assign someone in addition?" Honistu said.

"Oh, Bobby's all right," Barton said. "Maybe you ought to, though. OK, let's get that damn ship loaded and out of here."

Honistu gave orders. As soon as Bronson's troops were clear, the waiting trucks drove out onto the docks.

Barton's crew helped the ranch hands pull fuel lines out and connect them up to the landing craft. Rancher militia began unloading the trucks and carrying crates aboard.

"Well, Wally, this is what it was all for," Barton said.

"Yeah. And none too soon, Major."

"Come on, it was soft duty."

"Sure, but— Hell, Major, you must have felt it. Wondering what Falkenberg was going to do. Not that there was much he *could* do, but it doesn't stop the troops from worrying. He's pulled rabbits out of empty hats before."

"Yeah," Barton said. "But it does look like we've stymied him this time." He touched buttons on his sleeve console. "Patch me to the pilot of that landing boat."

"Aye aye," the comm sergeant said.

"Commander Perkins here."

'Major Barton. Have a good trip?"

"Yes, sir, uneventful. Understand we surprised you with the troops aboard. Sorry about that."

"Yeah, sure. When will you be ready to take off?"

"Assuming fuel and cargo are aboard, the next launch window for rendezvous with *Norton Star* will open at 0930," Perkins said.

"Seventy minutes. OK, you'll make that," Barton said. He touched more buttons on his sleeve console. "Sergeant major, move it out," he said. "You got fifty minutes to refuel and get that cargo aboard. Hop it."

He turned his binoculars on the Bronson group and watched as they went up the hill. Then he took a toothpick from his pocket and chewed thoughtfully.

"Nagging doubts, Wally. I keep thinking Falkenberg has an ace up his sleeve." He lifted his binoculars and swept them across the jungle edge. "But what the hell, he doesn't know everything."

§§§

Lysander could just see the assault boat through his peephole. It was the center of a flurry of activity. First the assault crew came ashore, weapons ready, and for a moment it looked like there might be a fight right there on the pier. Then they went northwards out of sight.

A crew snaked fuel lines out. A minute after they were connected up, they glistened with condensing frost. The fuel and oxygen lines crossed the road to the pier, and the ranch hands had put up a steel crossover to allow trucks to drive over them without pinching them off. Now a mixed crew of ranch hands and Barton Bulldogs was unloading crates from the trucks and carrying them aboard the landing craft. There were ranch hands in soiled coveralls; rancher militia in their jungle stripes; Barton Bulldogs in darker cammies; and in addition, there were darker blue coveralls which Lysander thought must be the landing ship crew. They were all mixed together. Can't possibly know each other, he thought. And there were the troops from the assault boat itself.

"Harv. Get the insignia off our cammies," he whispered. "May give us an edge." Falkenberg's legion wore a tiger-stripe camouflage uniform that wasn't like either Barton's or the rancher militia. With all those others mixed in, each group might think he belonged to some other. It was worth a try.

"We got a jackpot," he whispered, and gestured for Harv to come look through the peephole. "Get the layout. When the time comes, we walk out there like we've got jobs to do. When we get into the ship, you handle the doors. Get the hatches closed and the lines cast off. I'll get it off the water."

"Right." Harv grinned. "Be something to tell the phratrie."

"May be." *Of course I'll also have to explain to Mother what the hell I was doing here.*

He let Harv study the situation outside while he tuned one channel of his receiver to Falkenberg's communications frequency, and slaved the other to his pocket computer. Then he called up a program to listen for and analyze electronic signals.

There were a *lot* of them. Apparently Barton wasn't worried about electronic security any longer. There was energy in all the radar frequencies, and widely across the communications bands. The communications signals were not strong and couldn't have been intercepted from very far away, but most of them were in plain English.

"—fifty minutes, you bastards! Move goddamit, that bird flies on schedule!" someone shouted.

Lysander tuned across the bands, and heard "Not now. Wait an hour and you got all the people you need, but let it wait."

Fifty minutes. Wait an hour. It was an easy inference that the landing ship would fly then. Lysander frowned in concentration on *Norton Star*'s ephemeris, then nodded in satisfaction. It would be about fifty minutes before the ship was in the proper position for orbital rendezvous with a minimum-energy landing boat. They'd fly then, about 0930.

He tapped Harv on the shoulder and took over the peephole. Should have made two, he thought. Too late now.

Another truck rolled down to the dock.

Lysander tuned his transmitter to the frequency Falkenberg's troops would be monitoring. He hesitated a moment, then keyed the microphone. "Yeah, this is Lion. We'll be ready for liftoff in fifty minutes." He cut off the transmitter and listened. There was a faint click. Lysander winked, and Harv grinned wolfishly.

§§§

"That was him, all right," Corporal Tandon said. "Right on our frequency. I didn't acknowledge except to key in a click, sir."

"Good," Falkenberg said. "That's enough to let him know we heard him. Any sign they know about him, or us?"

"Not one damn thing, Colonel," Tandon said. "They're chattering away like nobody's listening. Sir, Mr. Prince is a little off on the launch time; I've heard a dozen people say it geos up at oh-nine-thirty, and that squares with the ephemeris. Fifty minutes from his message is 0920."

"I see. I think you underestimate him, Corporal. Lieutenant Mace."

"Sir."

"I want you to be ready to start your bombardment at 0915. Tandon, five minutes before that you will use the code we worked out to alert Mr. Prince. Be prepared to notify Lieutenant Mace to change that schedule if Mr. Prince requests it."

"Aye aye, sir."

Falkenberg studied the time readout on his sleeve console. "And now we wait. Lieutenant Mace, I think we should discuss your target priorities."

§§§

At precisely 0910 Lysander heard Corporal Tandon's voice in his earpiece. "Oh, hell, Lion, hold your horses, we'll have the stuff on the way in five minutes flat."

And what will Barton's communications monitors make of that? Lysander wondered. Assuming they heard it at all. He gestured to Harv and led the way through the passage between the packing crates. They unlocked the door and stepped into the corridor. There were two people there, one close, the other an armed Bulldog near the main door.

"What the hell are you doing in there?" the closest man demanded.

Lysander thought he recognized him as the man who'd come out of the store room earlier that morning. It hardly mattered. Lysander gestured toward the further man. Harv moved ten feet in a single flowing motion. As he did, Lysander spun the rancher around and brought his hand down in a sharp blow to the base of the skull. The man dropped. When

Lysander looked up. Harv was dragging the soldier toward the store room.

They pushed both men inside. The rancher was still breathing. Harv thought the soldier was dead but he didn't really want to know. He locked the door. "Let's go."

There was no one in the tractor shed. They walked through that and toward the dock, striding briskly as if they had an errand there. No one stopped them.

The fuel lines were still rigged. There was no way to tell how much hydrogen and LOX had been pumped into the ship. Probably not enough to make orbit. What would happen if they took off with the fuel lines still in place? Presumably there were automatic shutoffs, but were there? Lysander tried to remember if they'd told him in training, and decided they'd never mentioned it. Why should they?

Just before they reached the pier there were sounds of mortar fire from the jungle edge. Several of Barton's people froze in their tracks. Someone shouted, "Incoming!" Several of Barton's troops hit the dirt.

There was a series of explosions up the hill near the house. Then the rattle of small arms fire, and more mortars fired. Several rounds hit the house itself. Part of the veranda was blown away, and the roof was on fire. A nearby shed was also burning. At the dock area people began to run, toward the ship or away from it, while others lay on the ground, or stared, or ran in circles.

There were more explosions from up the hill. The Leopard swivelled its guns to aim at the jungle edge and began to fire. Trees fell at the jungle's edge.

Lysander and Harv reached the dock and broke into a run toward the landing ship. A crewman was just beginning to close the hatch. Lysander leaped

across the loading gangplank and pushed past the man,
leaving him to Harv. Inside were narrow passageways.

"Who the hell are you?" someone called.

"Get the damn crates lashed in!" Lysander shouted.
"Secure for immediate takeoff!"

"Holy shit!" the crewman shouted. "Sir, goddamit—"

"Hop to it! We'll be under fire in a second,"
Lysander said. He rushed forward to the pilot compartment. There was no one in the right hand seat.

The pilot turned with a frown. "What's going on?"

"Immediate takeoff," Lysander said.

"We're not fueled for takeoff, you idiot!"

"We'll be blown away if we don't get off now. I
mean *now*."

"Off and go wh—uff."

Lysander unclipped the lap belt and heaved the
pilot over into the copilot's seat. As he was securing
the man's pistol, a crewman put his head into the
compartment. Lysander kicked him and pushed him
out, then slammed the cockpit door and locked it.
He climbed into the left hand seat and inspected the
control panel.

§§§

Ace Barton took a final look at the map table and
turned to Anton Girerd. He grinned widely. "All
done here. We can watch the takeoff from the veranda. Wally—"

He was interrupted by mortar fire. There was the
sound of crashing glass. The house shook, then shook
again. The door to the next room smashed open.
Another explosion shook them and his staff dived
under the heavy table. A third explosion nearby
knocked him off his feet.

"Fire! Fire!" one of the servants shouted.

Barton got to his feet. Something was burning in the next room, and he gestured toward the fire in annoyance. "Carruthers! Deal with that!" He punched in code on his sleeve console. "Comm room, report!"

There was nothing but static. Barton switched to speakers so that Honistu could hear, and methodically punched in codes for emergency communication channels. "Comm Central, report!"

*Surprise.* Barton recalled Falkenberg's dry voice in the officers mess. "Surprise is an event that takes place in the mind of an opposing commander." *You son of a bitch.*

"Comm Central, Centurion Martino here, sir." The Centurion spoke slowly and carefully as he'd been trained to do. "We are under heavy mortar and recoilless fire from a battery in the jungle approximately four klicks to the east. There was no warning. The first salvo took out the power plant and damn near every antenna we have. I've got damage control and power crews out now. I have no estimate of the time required to restore power. Captain Anderson is switching control of his units to auxilliary antennas."

Barton heard the sharp crump! of his own mortar units. "What's he shooting at?"

"Stand by one," Martino said. There was a long silence. "Counterbattery. Captain Anderson got some backtrack info with the secondary antennas. Is your plot table powered?"

Barton looked the question at Honistu. "Yes."

"Stand by, Major, I'll try to feed a report to the plot table now—plot responds. Successful feed."

Lights blinked on the liquid crystal map table. Bright orange bordered in blue for his disabled units. Antennas and power plants, and now guns. Too many. More orange blotches on the house itself. Barton could hear frantic sounds from the next room, but he ignored them. The air smelled of smoke, but less now than before.

Red squares for suspected enemy installations. Four guns for sure, all in the jungle. The squares were large, indicating uncertainty in locating them. "There'll be spotters," Barton said. "Have the Leopards chew up the jungle edge. Mortar fire on the probable enemy locations. And have the choppers stand by for target information."

Choppers. How had Falkenberg got troops into that jungle? They sure didn't walk. "They may have some new kind of stealthy chopper," Barton said. "Watch out for it. All AA units stand by."

"Yes, sir."

So what the hell did Falkenberg intend? "Martino, have they hit the landing ship?"

"Stand by one, sir." Another silence. "No, sir, they haven't been shooting at it."

Haven't been shooting at it. Barton's head hurt. He put his hands to the back of his neck and willed himself to relax. Slow. Send the pain away. Ignore the ringing. Forget the smoke. Forget everything, relax, concentrate. Surprise is an event that takes place in the mind of an enemy commander. Me.

They haven't been shooting at the landing ship. Why haven't they been shooting at it? Why didn't they disable it first thing? "Patch me through to the assault boat pilot."

"Stand by."

It seemed like an eternity.

"I'm still trying, but there's no answer, Major."

"No answer. No communications, or no answer?"

"Don't know, sir. Tried four channels."

"Keep trying. Sound a full security alert in the dock area. Then get somebody down there on line."

"Aye aye, sir."

"Wally, there's something damned wrong out there," Barton said. "Get your butt down to that ship and see what it is. Stay with Martino on Red Four. Martino, reserve Channel Red Four. You, me, and Captain Honistu."

"Aye, aye, sir."

"Major?" Honistu asked.

"Damn it, get down there! Secure that ship! I won't be happy until you're sitting in the pilot compartment. Take whatever troops you need."

"Right. I'm on my way."

Barton thumbed his mike again. "Get me Anderson."

"Aye aye, sir."

Another long wait. *That son of a bitch. Power plants, antennas, comm shack, damn near got me. Two salvoes and we're damn near out of business. That son of a bitch. He's out there—*

"Captain Anderson."

"Bobby, aim something at that assault boat. Do that now, then stand by to disable it on my command."

"Disable? With the fuel lines pumping? Not bloody likely, Major. We can blow it to hell, but I don't know how to disable it."

"Holy shit. Stand by anyway. Martino! Keep track of Captain Honistu's group. I want security forces in that boat *now!*"

"Major, you must not, you must not destroy—" Anton Girerd's hands fluttered frantically. "Major—"

"On the contrary," Chandos Wichasta said. "You must arrange to destroy it before Governor Blaine can capture it."

"He cannot capture—"

"Anton, of course he can," Wichasta said. "Clearly their objective is to disable the landing ship. Major Barton has told us of the buildup on Dragontooth Island. Once that is complete we can't hold Rochemont.

It is obvious they know this is the central storage place. If they did not know before, the landing ship told them that. I wonder if—but no, they had soldiers in the jungle. They must have come before the landing ship. Or did they?"

"They did," Barton said. "They're good, but they're not that good. Bobby, you sure you can't disable that assault boat without blowing it up?"

"Wouldn't want the responsibility, sir. Not till they get the fuel lines disconnected and capped. I've got artillery, not magic."

"Bring in another assault boat!" Girerd shouted.

"Right. Mr Wichasta, do you have communications with *Norton Star*?"

"I will see."

"Please do. So. Martino, where the hell's the pilot of that boat?"

"Still no answer, Major."

"God damn it—"

"Captain Anderson," Wichasta said. "This is Chandos Wichasta. I speak for Senator Bronson. Captain, that landing boat must not be recovered by Governor Blaine. If there is any chance of that boat falling into the hands of the governor, destroy it."

"No!" Anton Girerd screamed.

"Captain, I am authorized to offer you wealth beyond your wildest dreams," Wichasta said. "Major Barton, we will pay your expenses and fees in full, with a bonus, provided that the borloi does not come into Governor Blaine's possession. An extra bonus for delivering the crop to us, but we will pay even if it is destroyed."

"Major." Centurion Martino's voice took on the deadly calm note professional soldiers use when things get serious. "The landing boat has started its engines. I still have no contact with the pilot."

"Wally!"

"All true," Honistu said. His voice sounded strained. "I'm running like hell—"

"Captain Anderson," Wichasta shouted. "Destroy that ship now!" Then he turned away and spoke into his microphone. Barton heard nothing of what he said.

Ace Barton touched buttons on his sleeve console. "Martino, keep this secure. Bobby, belay that instruction."

Anderson's voice was in his earpiece. "Ace, how much is wealth beyond our wildest dreams? Enough to get out of this racket?"

"What do you care? Belay that order!"

"Honistu here. Bronson's tank is firing at the landing boat."

# XXV

Lysander examined the landing ship's control panel. All the test circuits glowed green except fuel line security. *Nothing I can do about that. No point in communications security, either.* "Harv."

"Right here, Prince."

"Mooring lines."

"Done, Prince. You all right up there?"

"Fine here. Watch my back." He thumbed the ship intercom button. "*Hear this. Secure for immediate liftoff. Hear this. Secure for immediate suborbital flight.*" He punched in the code for Falkenberg's alert frequency. "Schoolmaster, this is Lion. I've got her. Attempting to move now."

Then he said a silent prayer and hit the startup sequencer.

Displays flashed.

FUEL LINES NOT SECURE.

Lysander punched in OVERRIDE. IMMEDIATE STARTUP.

OVERRIDE. IMMEDIATE STARTUP. CONFIRM?

CONFIRM.

There was a loud whine of pumps, then the roar of the engines. Lysander steered to port, away from the dock. The ship began to move.

A geyser erupted in front of him. Someone was firing at him. Falkenberg?

"Schoolmaster, this is Lion. I say again, I have control. Attempting takeoff." Steer at the splashes, he thought. And hit the throttles. Accelerate. Moving target. Damned *big* moving target . . .

The pilot struggled into wakefulness. "What the hell are you doing?" he shouted.

"Getting us out of here! They're shooting at us."

"I'll be damned if—"

"Look, I haven't time to discuss this. If you touch the controls, I'll shoot you, provided that we live through it, which we probably won't. They're shelling us."

"Close the refueling valves, you moron! Christ, where did you learn to fly?"

"On Sparta. But I don't know how to do that."

"I'll get it—"

"Right. Be careful." Another geyser rose just to starboard. "If we slow down they'll hit us."

"Christ, I didn't contract to get killed." The pilot threw two switches. Red lights changed to green.

"Thanks," Lysander said.

"Jesus! Look, you'll never make it, there's not enough fuel—"

"I'm not trying for orbit. Just up and back down again."

"Down where?"

"Lederle for preference. Otherwise, anywhere I can set down."

"Did you ever fly one of these boats?"

"Landed once," Lysander said.

"Jesus Christ," the pilot said.

§§§

There was a scream of rage. Ace Barton turned to see Anton Girerd struggling with Chandos Wichasta. "He's ordered that tank to fire on the landing ship!" Girerd shouted. "We're ruined! Major, you must stop him!"

"Do not be a fool," Wichasta said. "Senator Bronson will pay your expenses. These wretches can pay nothing. As Girerd says, they are ruined."

"Yeah, you're right about that," Barton said. "All the same, I give the orders here. Corporal, see that Mr. Wichasta doesn't talk to anyone until I say he can."

"Sir." Barton's orderly moved up behind Wichasta.

"Get me Anderson," Barton said. "Bobby, concentrate on the enemy artillery. Ignore that landing boat."

"Sure you know what you're doing, Ace?"

"I think so. No time for discussion. Carry out your orders."

"He's talking real money, Major. And who's going to pay our fees if we lose the crop?"

"Captain Anderson, you have your orders."

There was a long pause. "All right. There goes wealth beyond my wildest dreams."

*There goes a life of looking over your shoulder.* "Channel Red Four. Wally!"

"Yeah."

"Tell whoever you put to covering Bronson's tank to take it out. *Now.*"

"Aye aye. Leopard Three, this is Honistu. Command override. Sergeant Billings, Fire Mission Dead Muskrat. Execute. I say again, command override, execute Dead Muskrat."

"You are a fool," Wichasta said.

"Yeah," Barton said. "I expect I am. But I do know who hired me."

§§§

"Corpsman!" someone shouted. "The lieutenant's down!"

"Coming."

Alf Tandon hunkered down as low as possible. The Leopard was chewing up the edge of the jungle, and if you stuck your head up you'd get it blown off. Then abruptly the firing stopped. Tandon waited. Still nothing. He lifted his head warily, then took a chance and used his binoculars. "Holy shit. Sarge!"

Nothing. The fibre optic lines were down. Maybe the computer was gone too. Lieutenant is down. Can't reach Miscowsky. Who's in charge? Maybe it's me. Hell with it. They sure as shit know we're here. He thumbed the radio switch. "Sarge, this is Alf."

§§§

The damned thing definitely was a leechworm, and it was crawling up his right leg toward his crotch, but right now the other leg was Miscowsky's biggest problem. His left thigh hurt like hell above the knee, and he couldn't feel a thing below that. His trouser leg was soaked with blood, and the last mortar round had been close enough to rattle his teeth. Stuff was whizzing overhead and all around so he didn't dare sit up to look at how bad he was hit. *It don't seem too much for the regenners. Not yet. If I just don't fucking run out of blood—*

"Sarge, this is Alf."

It was an effort, but Miscowsky punched buttons on the big radio box that lay next to him. *Fuckers are probably homing in on the set. My turn in the fucking barrel.* "Go ahead, Alf."

"Lieutenant's down. Corpsmen on the way."

"Roger that." *And not much I can do about it.*

"The Leopard's changed targets. It's shooting hell out of the light tank they brought in on the landing boat."

"Repeat that."

"The Leopard is firing at the troops brought in on the assault carrier. It has disabled the light tank."

"I'll be damned. OK, keep watching. Out."

Miscowsky felt himself getting weaker. There was enough of a lull in the firing that he could sit up and look at his leg— *In a damn minute.* He thumbed the mike switch on his helmet. "Command information. Lieutenant Mace is down. Orders. All units report status." He listened, then changed frequencies. "Colonel, Lieutenant Mace is out of action. You're in tactical charge, only there ain't much here. No more than ten effectives including wounded, and no working guns."

"I heard the reports."

"Any orders, sir?"

"I relieve you. Have you heard from Mr. Prince?"

"Nothing you didn't hear, sir."

"We'll have to hang on until we do hear from him. Are you hit?"

"Yes, sir."

"Take care of yourself, Sergeant. I'll mind the store."

"Aye aye, Colonel." *Hang on. Rather run for it. Only where the hell can we run? With this leg I ain't running anyway.* He wriggled painfully across the jungle floor, dragging the radio, his wounded leg dragging uselessly behind him, until there was a thick tree trunk between him and the jungle edge. Then he sat up with his back to the tree.

His left leg was broken and there were jagged holes in his Nemourlon armor. A thin shiny sliver stuck out halfway down his shin. The upper part of his leg hurt like hell, but the numbness in the lower half worried him more. *Tourniquet time. I can get that on, but . . .* "Medic. Any medic. This is Miscowsky. I'm hit. Need help."

"Kamaria here. I can get over there after I finish with the lieutenant. Five minutes. Can you hang on that long?"

"I'll have to." He tuned back to the general command frequency.

"That Leopard's finished with the tank," Tandon reported. "Guns swiveling. Looks like he's got us in mind."

*Oh, shit. Nothing we can hit him with, either.*

"Can you see the landing boat?" Falkenberg asked.

"Not without sticking my head out of the bush!"

"Is there anyone in position to report on the landing boat?" Falkenberg asked.

"Colonel, I can look."

*Jesus, Colonel, for God's sake don't make Alf stick his head up there. Oh, God, Damn, It.*

"Thank you, Coroporal, but hold off a moment," Falkenberg said.

The Leopard began firing again. Miscowsky wriggled down to get as close to the ground as he could. *Kamaria won't get to me through that. Better tell him not to try.*

The shellfire moved closer. Miscowsky didn't think his tree would last much longer. Then there was a roar louder than the cannon fire. A long sustained roar.

"That's the engines," Falkenberg said. "Tandon, keep your head down. Wait."

The roar got louder, then held steady.

"Schoolmaster, the Lion is aloft. Schoolmaster, this is Lion, the Lion is aloft."

"Colonel," Miscowsky shouted. "Goddamn, sir, he did it!"

"Right. Now can you get me Major Barton?"

"Sir? Well, I can try—I can use full power and try to cut in on a frequency I've heard him on."

"Do it, and patch me in."

"Aye, aye, sir. Stand by—" Miscowsky tuned his set and turned the dial to full power. "Done. Go ahead, Colonel."

"Major Barton, this is John Christian Falkenberg."

There was a long pause. "This is Barton."

"We surrender," Falkenberg said.

"Surrender. You've just won the damn war and you surrender. All right, Colonel, I accept. Wally, you heard him. All units cease fire."

"Yes, sir."

"Thank you," Falkenberg said. "We have wounded."

"So do we," Barton said.

# XXVI

"Bloody hell," Mark Fuller said. He sat at a small table under the canopy of leaves and vines that concealed his helicopter and sipped tea. He'd been there for hours, far too long, the ship ready to go at a second's notice. Now they heard the distant sound of artillery. "Bloody hell."

Crew Chief Hal Jordan nodded in sympathy. "The waitin's always hardest. But I wouldn't be too anxious for orders, was I you. Goin' after Barton'll be a little different from storming them pirates that had your lady."

"I know, Chief. It doesn't make waiting any easier." He glanced at his sleeve console. The time was 0935. "Listen to that. Something sure as hell is going on."

"Yeah," Jordan agreed. "Only from the sound of it they're not likely to have time to tell us about it."

"But maybe they'll want us. Better be sure we're ready."

"Mr. Fuller, if I get the damn thing any more ready, she'll fly off by herself! Relax, sir."

One of the villagers brought more tea. What they called tea here, anyway. Some kind of orange fla-

311

vored grass. It didn't taste bad, just very different. Mark sipped and tried to look patient. There was a loud roar, loud enough to drown out the gunfire.

"Holy shit!" Jordan said. "Landing ship taking off!" Something large flashed overhead, low above the village clearing. "Look at it go!"

"I never saw one take off before," Mark said.

"Yeah, mostly I was *in* the damn things when they went up. There she goes—ain't going to make orbit, that's for damn sure! Hope the poor bastards know what they're doing."

The landing ship vanished. Mark sipped tea and waited. "Guns are quiet," he said.

"Yeah," Jordan said. "Too damn quiet."

There was a chirp from the helicopter radio. Mark stood quickly, but restrained himself. Let Jordan answer it.

"It's someone claims to be the colonel," Jordan said. "He's sending authentication codes— It checks out, sir. He want us to answer."

"Crap doodle. The radio silence orders are damned clear."

"Yes, sir, I know, but I'm pretty sure it's the colonel," Jordan said. "Sounds like him, and the authentication codes check. And they knew what frequency to call on, and who to ask for."

"What the hell should I do?"

"They pay you to decide, Mr. Fuller. Not me."

"I keep forgetting that. All right. Acknowledge," Fuller said.

"Yes, sir." Jordan spoke briefly, then handed the phones and mike out.

"Cornet Fuller here, sir," Mark said.

"Falkenberg. Stand by to check authentication." He read a string of numbers, which Fuller punched into his console.

"Yes, sir. Authentication acknowledged. Standing by."

"Orders, Mister Fuller. Hostilities are ended. You may defend yourself if fired upon, but you are to take no aggressive action unless directly ordered by Regiment. Is this understood?"

"Yes, sir. Did we win?"

"We can discuss that later. I am a prisoner of war."

"Sir?"

"I have surrendered this small command, and this will be my last transmission to you. You will make contact with regimental headquarters for further orders."

"Yes, sir—Colonel—"

"That's all Mr. Fuller. Out."

"Oh, boy," Mark said.

"Problems, Mr. Fuller?" Jordan asked.

"You might say that. We've surrendered. Or Falkenberg has."

"Sir?"

Mark explained. "He said we could defend ourselves, so I guess he didn't surrender us. Only now what do I do?"

"Well, sir, we've already broken radio security by answering that transmission. Maybe we ought to try to get headquarters?"

Mark thought that over and nodded. "Right. See if you can raise them."

It took well over an hour. Finally Mark was speaking with Captain Frazer.

"Yes, we heard that the Colonel surrendered his force," Frazer said. "Understand that our transmissions to you are not secure, but yours to us should be all right. What is your situation?"

"Well, I've got fuel for maybe a hundred klicks if

I'm careful. The other chopper's bone dry, and the crew went down the river with Colonel Falkenberg so there's nobody to fly it. Sergeant Jordan and I are the only ones here."

"Right. Well, just sit put, Mark. We'll send someone in for you when we get the chance."

"Yes, sir, but— I know the colonel said hostilities were over, but shouldn't we be doing something?"

"It's all right, lad," Frazer said. "We've won. Didn't the colonel tell you?"

"No, sir."

"Oh. Of course he wouldn't. It's a bit complex. Prince Lysander hijacked their landing boat. They'd loaded the drugs into it. Mr. Prince brought over ninety percent of the holdout crops into Lederle harbor twenty minutes ago. Some of the ranchers are still trying to continue the revolt, but they don't have much to bargain with. They can't pay Barton, either. Stay alert and stay sober, there may be someone out there who didn't get the word, but this campaign's over."

"I see. Thank you sir. Could someone tell Mrs. Fuller I'm all right?"

"Of course. Right away. Fuller, it may be a couple of days before we get you out. When I've got transport we'll get some fuel and crew in there. Tell Mr. Ledoux the governor won't forget him. Otherwise, relax."

"But what happens to the colonel?"

"I wouldn't worry about it," Frazer said. "It's likely to cost us a bit, that's all. Relax, lad."

§§§

Everyone stood when Lysander came into the staff room. Major Savage nodded approval. "Well done, Mr. Prince."

"Thank you, sir."

"Sorry to hear about your corps brother."

"Surgeon says he'll be all right," Lysander said. "He won't like the inactivity, but a good rest won't hurt him. The colonel's all right, then?"

"So they tell me," Savage said. "We're expecting Barton's people to call with their terms. Shouldn't be too severe, they've little enough to bargain with, thanks to you." He shrugged. "Of course none of us will be sorry to see all our people back where they belong. For one thing, we've much better hospital facilities than Barton has."

The atmosphere was jovial, more like a luncheon in the Officers' Mess than duty in the staff room. Everyone was friendly.

Lysander studied the map table. The familiar lines were all changed. Instead of neat areas held by ranchers and other places held by Falkenberg's Legion or Governor Blaine's militia, there were mixed splotches, mutually penetrating lines, scattered bases and staging areas. One long pseudopod stretched out toward Rochemont. Another slashed into the former rebel territory in the southeast. As he watched one large block went from hostile orange to secure blue.

"Bit of a mess, actually," Major Savage said. "But that won't last. Ah. Is that our call, Amos?"

"Yes." Amos Fast frowned. "It's to Barton, it's a rancher. Anton Girerd. Wants to talk to you and no one else."

Savage shrugged. "No reason not to. Put him on the speaker phone. Mynheer Girerd? Jeremy Savage here. What can we do for you?"

"You can give our property back," Girerd said. His voice was very tense. Everyone in the staff room fell silent.

"I beg your pardon?"

"Our crop," Girerd said. "The harvest. Give it back."

"I'm afraid I don't quite follow. We don't have your crop. That was turned over to the governor."

"I don't care what you did with it. You took it from us, and you can take it back from Governor Blaine. I'm telling you, if you want to see Colonel Falkenberg and those others again, get our crops back to us!"

"Come now, we can't do that," Savage said. "We're prepared to pay a reasonable ransom for the colonel, of course. And if you haven't heard, the governor's offering amnesty on very reasonable terms."

"No terms," Girerd said. "No negotiations. The crop. All of it."

"I think you'd better put Major Barton on."

"Barton's got nothing to do with this," Girerd said. "Damn you people! It's all a game to you. Nothing but a lousy stinking game! Well, it's no game to us. It's our lives, and our fortunes, and our honor."

"Honor from a dope peddler," Captain Rottermill said *sotto voce*.

Savage held up a hand for silence. "Do I understand that you've taken Colonel Falkenberg from Major Barton's custody?"

"Damn right we have."

"And where is Major Barton now?"

"In hell for all I know!"

Jeremy Savage touched the button to cut off the mike on the phone. His voice was low and clear, almost pleasant. "Amos, perhaps we'd better resume operations against Dragontooth. And please see what else you can muster to the southern area. We may need to assault Rochemont after all."

"Yes, sir." Amos Fast began typing furiously on his keyboard.

Savage activated the phone again. "Be reasonable, Mr. Girerd—"

"No. No, I will not be reasonable," Girerd said. "I have been ruined by being reasonable."

"You are hardly ruined. The governor's terms are quite generous."

"It's ruin."

"I assure you that's not the case," Savage said. "A number of your friends have already accepted. I do think you should reconsider while you have a choice."

"No. You've finished me, and I won't go alone."

"What possible good could it do you to harm your prisoners?" Savage asked.

"None. But I'll get the satisfaction. You get my property back, or your colonel's dead."

"It might take some time."

"It better not take long. After 1700 today I will start executing prisoners. One per hour. Beginning with the youngest. Your colonel can watch them die. Goodbye."

There was a moment of silence.

"Well, that's torn it," Major Savage said. "You are all familiar with the colonel's standing orders on negotiating with terrorists."

"How serious are they?" Captain Fast asked. "Anyone know this Girerd?"

"Governor's office will know him," Rottermill said.

"Ursula has met him," Lysander said. "Major— Major, we have to *do* something!"

"Yes, of course we must. Ian, if you'd be kind enough to get those choppers in Ledoux's village ready? They'll need fuel, a pilot, guns and gun crews. Perhaps you could pick up any of your SAS troops who might be along the way there?"

"Right away, sir. I'll be going myself, of course." Captain Frazer lifted his phone and spoke urgently.

"Captain Rottermill, I would very much like to know what has become of Major Barton."

"Yes, sir."

"Mr. Prince, we'll speak to the governor's office, but if you would be kind enough to bring your friend here, it might be helpful to speak with someone who knows Mynheer Girerd."

"I don't know that she actually *knows* him—"

"I really would appreciate it, Mr. Prince."

Savage hadn't changed his tone, and his smile was pleasant, but Lysander felt a moment of fear. "Yes, sir. I'll get her."

"Thank you. Now, if you please. Captain Fast, perhaps it would be well to tell sergeant major about this latest development."

"Yes, sir."

Lysander felt relieved to get out of the staff room.

"You could have come to see me first."

"Ursula, be reasonable. They brought me here by helicopter. I had to go to the hospital with Harv, and then I had to report! This is the first chance I've had."

"I suppose. You don't act very glad to see me." She grinned. "Here you come back a genuine hero, and I'd already planned to give you a hero's welcome just for getting back alive."

'I'm looking forward to it. A lot. But just now— Ursa, the colonel's in trouble."

"What do you mean?"

"Girerd's threatening to kill him if we don't recapture their crop from the governor and turn it over to them."

"That's crazy. Falkenberg's soldiers won't do that. If they did, and the colonel got out of it alive, he'd have them shot! Even I know that!"

"Yes. And I'm scared." He took her arm and led her to the staff room.

"Miss Gordon," Major Savage said. "Kind of you to come. I was wondering if you could help with a problem that seems to have developed."

"If I can—"

"I'm told you know Anton Girerd."

"Not really," Ursula said. "I did get to know his son Oskar—briefly but quite well—but I don't really know Mynheer Girerd."

"Still, you've met him. I'd be grateful for an opinion. Is he likely to carry out his threat?"

"Yes."

"You sound quite positive. Why?"

"Things Oskar told me. Sometimes he was afraid of his father."

"Sometimes?"

"When his father had been drinking. I imagine he has been now. He drinks under stress."

"I see. So we dare not assume he is bluffing. Well, it won't be the first time alcoholism proved fatal. Thank you. Captain Rottermill, I'd appreciate that report. You may go, Miss Gordon."

"May I see Ursula to her rooms?"

"Certainly, Mr. Prince, but I would appreciate it if you'd come right back."

"Yes, sir."

Ursula shuddered when they were outside. "I won't try to keep you," she said.

"Thanks. You felt it too?"

"He's so calm and careful and polite, and I don't think I've ever been quite so frightened of anyone in my life," she said. "And he isn't even mad at *me*." They walked in silence for a moment. "I suppose you have to go with them?" Ursula asked.

"If they'll let me."

"Why?"

"Why? Because—damn it, it's obvious."

"No. No, Lysander, it's not obvious that you should risk getting yourself killed in order to rescue a man who has already manipulated you into doing his work for him."

"What? But he didn't do that—"

She laughed. "Didn't he? Think about it. Not much happens around him that he hasn't planned."

"Ursula, he was ready to do it himself. Without me."

"Sure."

"Well, he was."

She smiled and shook her head. "Lynn, Lynn my darling, you really don't understand him, do you? I wasn't even there, and I know what happened. He was ready to go himself. Of course he was. Him and one of his Headquarters Company guards. Be only too glad to, and of course he understood. No discredit for not volunteering, none at all. Only he didn't have to go himself because you were right there to talk him out of it. Isn't that what happened?"

"Well—"

"See? But no, you don't see. Forget that. But whatever happened doesn't obligate you to go get killed for him now."

"I won't get killed."

"Oh probably you won't, they won't even let you get close to the action now, but that isn't the point."

"What is the point?"

"One you'll never understand. When are you going back to Sparta?"

"What? I don't know. It will be a while. Have to wait for Harv to get out of the regeneration stimulators—"

"But not long after that."

"I don't know. I suppose not, father will be anxious for my report, Ursa, we have to discuss this
. . ."

"I wish I could go with you."

"Ursula—"

"I know. You wish it too, but it won't happen."
She smiled thinly. "It's all right. It would never
work. It's all wishes. Serves us both right for forgetting the rules. Goodbye, Lysander."

"We'll talk about this—I won't be long—"

"No. No, my dear it's hard enough this way." She
stood on tiptoe to kiss him, very lightly and very
quickly. "I won't be here when you get back."

"Where will you go?"

"I'll find something. I own my contract, you know.
Colonel Falkenberg saw to that. Maybe I'll look up
Oskar Girerd. He really was sweet, and even with
his father acting like an idiot, he's likely to keep
some of his wealth—"

"Ursula, stop, please stop—"

"I'm sorry. Maybe it wasn't funny. Maybe I wasn't
trying to be funny."

"How can you be so—so damned calm about it?"

"Probably caught it from Major Savage." They had
reached the door to her room. Not his. She went
inside, making it clear she didn't want him to follow.
She was already closing the door when she looked up
at him and said, "I do love you, you know. Goodbye,
my dear."

§§§

"I've got Barton," Rottermill said.

Major Savage gestured to indicate the speaker
phone. "Good afternoon, Major. Jeremy Savage here."

"Good afternoon."

"Sorry to trouble you, but I doubt I must explain why I have called," Savage said.

"No, of course not."

"Will you need our help?"

"No. We're going in now. Sorry to have been so long. They surprised us, and it took this long to get the forces together."

"Yes, of course," Major Savage said. "Still, I hope you won't be long about it."

"No, Major Savage, I won't be long about it. You'll hear from me in an hour. Barton out."

"Will someone please explain what's happening?" Lysander asked.

"What's to explain?" Captain Fast asked. "Ace Barton's meeting his obligations."

"He's going to rescue the colonel?"

"Certainly. Who else should?"

"Well—us."

"Oh, sure, we'd give it a try," Amos Fast said. "We're moving in backup units. But our motives wouldn't be quite the same as Barton's, would they?"

"So we're not going to rescue the colonel?"

"If we must, we will," Major Savage said. "As Amos says, we continue to make preparations. But I can't think it will be necessary. Barton's lot are thoroughly competent."

"But—they may kill Colonel Falkenberg."

Jeremy Savage's smile didn't change. "That really would be a mistake, you know. Hard to believe they'd be that stupid."

"But they might try! Major, our people are more competent than Barton's! We have to go in there!"

"I do think that's needlessly hard on Ace Barton," Savage said. "Let's give him a chance, shall we?"

"I don't think I'll ever understand you people," Lysander said.

"Politicians seldom do," Major Savage said.

§§§

The helicopter turned a tight spiral around Roche-mont before landing on the helipad outside.

The roof of the eastern wing had collapsed, and all the glass was broken out. Smoke blackened the walls outside two rooms. The rest of the house seemed repairable.

Ace Barton got out of the helicopter and strode toward the front door. Now's the time he shoots me, Barton thought. I'm getting too damned old for this.

He was nearly to the door when it opened. Anton Girerd came out. He had a small automatic pistol in his hand, but he held it barrel down. "What the devil do you want?"

"You know what I want," Barton said.

"No. I meant what I told that Savage—"

"I'm sure you did," Barton said. "But do the rest of your people understand what you've got them into?"

Barton waved to indicate the fleet of helicopters coming in around the house. "First there's my troops. You know what they can do. Let me show you." Barton waved in a complex gesture.

One of the helicopters circled the horse barn. A stream of fire poured from the gunship's door. Horses screamed in agony as tracers riddled the barn, then set it on fire. One of the horse herders staggered out of the barn door. He was covered in blood.

Barton waved again A dozen cattle burst from another barn. A helicopter circled and came in be-hind them, sending them in wild flight out into grain fields. The chopper's gatling opened fire. Tracers chewed the ground just behind the cattle, and the beasts ran faster in blind panic. The tracers moved slowly into the herd. Blood and meat and smoke mingled on the trampled grain.

Girerd screamed and aimed his pistol at Barton. "Stop! Stop it!"

Barton gestured again and the choppers ceased firing. "Okay. But my troops aren't your real problem. I'm a sweetheart compared to what you get if you shoot me. First off, my troops will be pissed. Maybe you can take them all out before they level this place. I doubt it, but suppose you can? After us, you damned fool, there's the whole Forty-second! Man, you've got yourself on the shit list of the toughest bastards in the galaxy! Don't you know what they're doing? They're not getting ready to negotiate. They don't negotiate with people like you. They're getting ready to come here and sterilize this place."

"They can't do that, I've got their colonel—"

Barton laughed. "Girerd, don't you think Falkenberg thought this might happen someday? His troops have standing orders. They won't negotiate." He spoke louder, so that everyone nearby could hear. "They'll never negotiate. They'll just see that nothing survives here. Nothing. Not you, not your animals, not your troops. Not even women and kids. Nobody and nothing. Then they'll burn everything. It's their colonel! They'll sow the ground with salt, Girerd. Hell, that's exactly what they'll do. Girerd, you're in trouble, and so is everyone here. You're all fucking *dead*." Ace kept his face turned toward Girerd, but he let his eyes look to the side. Several Girerd ranch hands were slinking away.

"You're just trying to frighten me—"

"Trying? I sure as hell hope I've done better than try! I hope I've scared the shit out of you." He waved again. One of the helicopters darted down.

"Wait, wait, don't!" someone screamed.

"But—they wouldn't—my children? My wife?" Girerd demanded.

"Every man, woman, and child," Barton said. "What the hell did you expect?" He waved again. The chopper opened up on the chicken house. In moments the ground outside it was strewn with flaming, squawking chickens. The building spewed out black smoke.

Girerd raised the pistol again.

"For God's sake, man, the next time you raise that damned piece, you're going to eat it, use it or not. I'm getting damned tired of this." Barton raised his hand again. The choppers circled closer.

"Mynheer," one of the ranch hands shouted. "Mynheer, please, Mynheer—"

Girerd looked at the pistol and shook his head. "I don't know what I expected. A miracle, perhaps," Girerd said.

"Not my department," Barton said.

"But what can I do?"

"You were talking pretty rough when you threw me out of here," Barton said. "Have you actually killed anyone?"

"No."

"Any of them die?"

"Two, but they were not expected to live."

"Yeah, those. No one else?"

"No."

"You're a lucky man," Barton said. He turned and waved to his helicopters. They rose slightly but continued to circle. He touched his sleeve console. "Wally, bring in the rest of the troops."

Girerd examined the pistol as if he'd never seen it before.

"Use it or give up," Barton said.

Girerd looked at the pistol, then tossed it under-handed down the stairs.

Barton winced as it hit the dirt. *Be a hell of a thing to be shot by accident just now.* "All right." He went up the stairs and took Girerd by the arm to lead him into the house. "Now you're getting smart."

"No. I am a fool." He led the way into the big study. Falkenberg and three of his men sat there. There were also four ranchers in militia uniform standing stiffly against the far wall. One of the doors lay twisted off its hinges, and seven Barton Bulldogs in full armor menaced the ranchers.

"Mynheer," one of the ranchers said. "While the guns fired outside they came—" The man simpered in terror. "Mynheer, we heard these men say— Mynheer, we have families."

Girerd shuddered. "I see. Major Barton rules here, as elsewhere. Odd. I thought he worked for me."

"I did," Barton said.

"And do again," Falkenberg said. "Mynheer, he's done you better service than you know."

"Colonel—"

"All correct, Major."

"Thank you, sir." Barton saluted.

"Rules, Codes. What good are they?" Girerd demanded.

Barton and Falkenberg exchanged glances. Then they both looked at Anton Girerd. Their eyes were filled with pity.

# XXVII

Waves of sound from the open door of the Officer's Mess battered Lysander with enough force to make him take a step backward. Skirl of pipes and stamp of marching feet. Songs of glory, songs of betrayal. "McPherson's time will nay be long, on yonder gallows tree . . ."

"Welcome aboard, Mr. Prince. They've saved a place for you."

Lysander didn't recognize the mess steward, but it hardly mattered. He breasted the waves of sound to get inside. The large room was crowded. Men in the blue and gold of Falkenberg's Legion mingled with the green of Tanith's militia. There was also a scattering of officers in blue and tan with silver bulldog badges.

Lysander let the corporal lead him to a table for four near the wall. Falkenberg sat alone at the far side. To his right was a man who wore oak leaves on the shoulder boards of his blue and tan uniform. Governor Blaine sat on Falkenberg's left.

Captain Jesus Alana got up from the next table and came over to clap Lysander on the back. "Good to have you," Alana shouted over the din.

"Welcome aboard," Falkenberg said. "We've saved you a place. You've already met Governor Blaine."

"Your Highness," Governor Blaine said.

"Your Highness, may I present Major Anselm Barton. Prince Lysander of Sparta."

Barton stood to shake hands. "An honor. One I would prefer under different circumstances, I think."

Lysander took the seat opposite Falkenberg. A steward brought him a glass of Tanith whiskey.

"Heard about what you did at Rochemont, Major Barton," Governor Blaine said. It was hard to hear him over the din from the party. "Good work, that. Must have been a bit tricky facing Girerd like that."

"Not as dangerous as it looked," Barton said. "I doubt that pistol of his would penetrate Nemourlon."

"Yes, well, good work anyway. Of course you do know Girerd has a trophy case of medals for his shooting."

And Barton wasn't wearing a face mask. On the other hand, how many Bulldog marksmen had Girerd in their sights? Wheels within wheels. But you couldn't fault Barton's success just because he took precautions.

"Is that what that tin in the study was about? Hmm. Well, I did need him alive. He's stupid, but killing him wouldn't make it easier to get the others to call off the revolt."

"Indeed. Most helpful, the way you managed things. Still, it is a bit odd you'd be concerned about our problems," Blaine said.

"Odd? No, sir," Barton said. "Seemed clear enough to me. Girerd's people can't pay me, and Bronson sure won't." He shrugged. "You and Falkenberg are the only ones on the planet who might hire me. Making your life difficult can't help me at all."

"Ah," Blaine said. He sipped at his whiskey.

"What will happen to Girerd?" Lysander asked.

"Oh, he's earned a stiff lesson," Blaine said. "But after all, I did proclaim a partial amnesty. No criminal penalties for the rebels, but some stiff civil fines. I'll use the money for a better satellite system, that kind of thing. I expect we ought to let the amnesty cover Girerd. Assuming it's all right with Colonel Falkenberg."

"I won't object," Falkenberg said. "I expect his lesson will be stiff enough. Among other things, he owes Major Barton quite a lot."

Barton looked glum, "I wish he had it to pay. Or someone did. We could use the money."

"You could have gone with Bronson," Falkenberg said.

"So I could," Barton said. "And from what I hear is happening in the Grand Senate, I might have been joining the winning side." He shrugged. "Never quite seemed to get around to it."

Falkenberg nodded. "You're available, then."

Barton chuckled. "Colonel, I doubt you've ever seen anyone as available as me."

"What makes you believe Bronson's faction is going to win?" Governor Blaine asked.

"Well, that investigation—"

"Will be quashed," Blaine said. "Bronson doesn't have the votes. If this borloi maneuver had worked it might have been a different story."

"Well, well," Barton said. "So nobody has a majority. Puts things back to what they were a year ago. Except that Falkenberg and I have both of us done ourselves out of a job. Governor, I may as well ask for the record. Are any of my people going to be charged? For that matter, am I under arrest?"

"I think that's what we're here to discuss. You certainly could be charged," Blaine said. "Arson, murder, aiding and abetting rebellion . . ."

"All done strictly in accord with the Laws of War," Barton said.

"Yes, certainly," Blaine said. "That's the only reason we have anything to discuss. Still, there is some question about the legitimacy of the group that hired you. Bona fide political group or criminal gang?"

"I guess it all depends on whether you want to put my arse in a sling."

"Actually," Blaine said, "I don't have much choice in the matter. If I charge you, I have to rule they're criminals, and that makes hash out of my political settlement."

"That's about how I read it, too," Barton said. "So?"

"So I would greatly prefer not to do that," Blaine said. "On the other hand, you have enemies. Some of the loyal ranchers were hit pretty hard. Many would be happy to see you hanged."

"I can live with their wanting it. Not so keen to see them get their wish."

"Indeed. It would be easier if you were no longer here. Remove the reminder, so to speak."

Barton shrugged. "Sure. How do we arrange that?"

"There might be a way," Falkenberg said.

'Ha. You have an offer?"

"I may have."

"Ah. But you're not quite prepared to make it?"

"We'll see. Time for another duty." Falkenberg caught the Mess President's eye, then stood. The pipers and singers fell quiet, and the babble in the room faded out. "Mr. President," Falkenberg said.

"Colonel!"

"A toast and a welcome. To Cornet Prince, once and future Prince of Sparta. He has earned the thanks of the Regiment."

Everyone stood. "Mr. Prince," Captain Alana said. The others echoed, "Mr. Prince."

Not quite everyone, Lysander saw. Barton stood when the others did, but he didn't say anything or raise his drink. *Can't really blame him.*

He saw a flash of green three tables away, and recognized the gown he'd bought in the local shop. *Of course she wore it. What else would she have?*

Ursula stood next to Captain Peter Owensford. Her eyes met Lysander's briefly as she raised her glass. Then she looked away, toward her escort.

He didn't have time to think about that. The toast was done. *My turn now. What do I say?* He waited until the others were seated, and stood. "Mr. President?"

"Mr. Prince."

"My thanks to the Regiment. A toast: May we be comrades in arms again."

"Hear, hear," someone shouted. Falkenberg nodded approval.

Ursula was leaning toward Captain Owensford. Whatever she said made him laugh. Then Mark and Juanita Fuller came over to sit beside her. They all seemed very happy.

There were more toasts, then Governor Blaine stood. "I can do no better than echo Prince Lysander," he said. "To Sparta and Tanith and Falkenberg's Legion, and a time when we will be comrades again. A time more likely now."

A few more minutes, then the pipers resumed. Someone started a song. *"The Knight came back from the quest, muddied and sore he came. Bat-*

*tered of shield and crest, bannerless, bruised and lame . . ."*

"Governor, Major, if you'll excuse me? Thank you. Mr. Prince, if you'd care to join me?" Falkenberg stood and gestured toward the door. "Perhaps we have a few items worth discussion."

"Thank you, sir, I'd love to." Lysander followed Falkenberg out. As he reached the door he heard Ursula's laugh.

The song continued. *"Fighting we take no shame, better is man for a fall. Merrily borne, the bugle-horn answered the warder's call.*

*"Here is my lance to mend, Haro! Here is my horse to be shot! Aye, they were strong, and the fight was long, but I paid as good as I got! Haro! I paid as good as I got!"*

Falkenberg's rooms were in a severely square detached building of sheet plastic that stood centered at the north end of the open area used as the regimental parade ground. They were met at the door by Corporal McClaren, who wore a very functional pistol over undress blues. Two more Headquarters Company troops were at the end of the hall.

The small study in Falkenberg's quarters had the look of a monk's cell. *Spartan,* Lysander thought. *Actually, we go in for more decoration than this. He lives as the old Spartans must have.*

There was one book case, of a wood native to Tanith. The desk was bare except for a screen set at a comfortable angle for reading. The keyboard was evidently concealed in a drawer. Lysander had once looked into the Regiment's electronic library, and had been amazed: tens of thousands of volumes, histories and world literature, atlantes, art, and technology, philosophy and cook books and travelogues, all available in an instant. *As long as the computers work he doesn't need real books. So why does he have any at all?* Lysander edged closer to the book case. The books were a jumbled collection, anthropology and military history mixed with biographies and novels. Most were cheaply bound, and they all looked as if Falkenberg had had them for a long time.

Falkenberg touched a hidden button. Music began, soft enough not to disturb conversation, loud enough to hear. Lysander frowned.

"Sir Hamilton Hardy," Falkenberg said. "It's called 'With The Wild Geese.' "

The room's big central table was functional duraplast, with a top of clear Plexiglas over the liquid crystal display. Snifters and a decanter of brandy were already in place on the table. Corporal McClaren waited until Lysander and the Colonel were inside, then went out, closing the door behind him.

"Welcome," Falkenberg said perfunctorily. "I won't keep you long."

As long as you like, Lysander thought. I doubt I'll ever get used to that kind of party. Too much noise. He tried not to think of Ursula's hand laid lightly on Captain Owensford's arm. What was he to her? New lover? A date for the evening? Both? He squirmed as pictures came uninvited.

They sat and Falkenberg waved to indicate the brandy. "Help yourself."

"I think I've had enough," Lysander said.

"Perhaps. You don't mind if I do? Thank you. You'll be leaving soon."

"I thought so. Now I'm not so sure. And you?"

"New Washington."

"That's a long way out from earth. What's there?"

Falkenberg looked thoughtful. "What are your plans, Mr. Prince? I suppose I'd best return to using your proper title."

"What's proper? I've earned being Cornet Prince. I think I'd rather be Mr. Prince than Prince Lysander."

"Certain of that?"

"No. Not certain."

"You have no real choice, you know."

"Sir?"

Falkenberg chuckled. "The stakes are too high, Your Highness. I won't say it never happened that someone as prominent as you joined the Legion, but in your case it won't work. If you choose to remain Cornet Prince, your orders will be to return to Sparta and become King. We need friends there."

"We?"

"That's the second time you've asked for information I can't give to Cornet Prince."

"But Prince Lysander—"

"Is an ally. Potentially a great deal more."

*More. What's more than an ally?* "What makes you think Prince Lysander can keep secrets?"

"We have our ways."

"I guess you do. All those friendly people buying me drinks and asking me questions—"

"That was part of it. Mostly, there comes a point when you have to trust someone, because if you don't, you can't accomplish the mission."

"Like sending the heavy weapons first?"

"Something like that. So. Who are you, Lysander Collins?"

"Colonel— Oh, damn it, Colonel, what will happen to her?"

"Her choice. She has choices now. You've given her that," Falkenberg said. "The governor has offered to hire her. I doubt she'll take that offer, because we'll make her a better one. The Regiment can always use toughminded bright people. Captain Alana has a post for her. Or—well, there are entirely too many bachelors and widowers among my officers. Women with the temperament for a soldier's life aren't easily found."

*Who gets her? You? She's too damned young for you. Or—*

"None of which answers the question I asked you."

"No, sir."

"Odd," Falkenberg mused. "A couple of hundred years ago it was a standard situation. Prince or Princess involved with commoner, conflict of love and duty. Lots of stories about that. None now, of course. How could there be? Not many people with a sense of duty."

*Not a lot of love, either. What's more rare, love or duty?* "Damn it all, Colonel. Mr. Fuller has his Juanita to take care of him. Someone—else—gets Ursula. I have Harv. It's not fair!"

"I can also point out that Mr. Cornet Prince would never have met her."

"Whereas Prince Lysander of Sparta could take her to dinner in the Governor's Palace. You would remind me of that, you son of a bitch."

Falkenberg's smile was thin but triumphant. "Your Highness, when junior officers get to feeling sorry for themselves, we tell them to shut up and soldier. In your case—"

"Shut up and princify. Especially if I'm going to talk to you like that. Hardly appropriate for Cornet Prince. Yes, sir. Bloody hell." Lysander smiled wistfully. "I don't suppose anything has to be fair. At least you're not telling me to count my blessings."

There was a long pause. Finally Lysander reached

up and took off the shoulder boards from his blues. "Colonel Falkenberg, I believe you were going to tell me something about New Washington."

It was well past midnight, and the sounds of the party were fading away. Lysander stared at the sketches and maps on Falkenberg's table screen. "God knows it's ambitious enough. There's a lot that can go wrong."

"Of course. There always is, when the stakes are high enough."

*And these can't get a lot higher.* "Let me be blunt about this. I've known something about Lermontov's plan for a year, but this is a lot more. You, the Blaine family, and half the senior officers of the Fleet are part of a conspiracy led by Grand Admiral Lermontov. You want Sparta to join that conspiracy."

"It's what I *want.* I do realize that you haven't the authority to commit your government."

"I can't even commit my *father* to this!"

"Your Highness, he joined us years ago."

"Oh, I'll be damned—yes, of course that would explain a lot of things I didn't understand. Colonel, this is going to take getting used to."

"You'll have time. While you're digesting that, get used to this: the only person who outranks your father in this—conspiracy—is Lermontov himself."

"What? But—Colonel, what are you saying?"

"Your Highness, the CoDominium is finished. Dr. Whitlock and Vice Admiral Harris of Fleet Intelligence don't give it ten years."

"Yes, of course, Sparta sees it coming too."

"Without the CoDominium there won't be any order at all. Not even the laws of war. Your Highness, I don't know what will—what can replace the

CoDominium. I just know something has to, and it will end a secure base."

"Ten years," Lysander mused.

"Maybe longer. The Grand Admiral believes we can hold on for twenty, and we might get a miracle after that." Falkenberg shook his head. "I think it will take a miracle just to keep things together for twenty years, and I don't believe in miracles."

"But you're going to New Washington anyway."

"I've told Lermontov about my doubts. Perhaps you can guess what he said."

"Shut up and soldier."

"Precisely," Falkenberg shrugged. "Actually, it makes sense. If things don't come apart too soon, we can keep the balance of power. If it all collapses, New Washington is a potentially valuable addition to the Alliance."

"But we need your troops as cadre for the new Spartan army. You're going to New Washington! How—?"

"You'll get your cadres. I'm merging Barton's troops into the 42nd. That frees up men to send home with you. Not as many as we'd like, but enough. We all make sacrifices, Mr. Prince. Pardon me. Your Highness."

"Who will you send?"

"I haven't thought about it."

"Owensford?"

"A good candidate, actually. Good teacher." Falkenberg stood. "And now, Your Highness, it's probably time I make a quick appearance at the party, then get some sleep. Major Barton and I have a number of details to iron out in the morning."

"Yes, sir. Thank you for your confidence."

Falkenberg's look said nothing. Or everything. "Just don't forget the sanitation workers," he said. "Goodbye, Mr. Prince."

The night outside was cool. Lysander left Falkenberg's quarters and went to the Officer's Mess. He stood outside the door. Inside he heard laughter. After a long while he turned and went to his empty room.